THE INNOCENCE OF PASSION

Roarke studied her for a long moment, seeing only pride in her uplifted face as she waited for him to speak. She was so serene, so beautiful . . . as though nothing could touch her.

"A stable boy?" he mocked, repeating the vicious rumor. But she did not try to give him a denial or an excuse. Bending over from a waist Roarke knew his hands could span, she picked up the rose she had dropped and examined its bruised petals.

"It's sad, is it not, to see something innocent injured for an evil purpose," she said. Then she smiled bitterly. "A stable boy? Aye, 'tis said of me."

She looked away, her profile delicate in the moonlight, her throat a slim column of alabaster. Roarke's hand moved to trace the fragile line of her jaw. A deep, hard ache gripped him in a desire to hold her, to love her with his flesh, his soul. His fingers sank into her silken hair and he drew her to him. His mouth touched hers in a kiss as soft as the brush of a butterfly wing. Releasing her lips, he held her close.

"Is it your intent, too, to take me by force, O'Conner?" Caitrin asked.

In answer, his mouth took hers again, this time in a searing kiss. He heard her unconscious moan, a plea to be released . . . or taken?

HEARTFIRE ROMANCES

SWEET TEXAS NIGHTS (2610, $3.75)
by Vivian Vaughan

Meg Britton grew up on the railroads, working proudly at her father's side. Nothing was going to stop them from setting the rails clear to Silver Creek, Texas—certainly not some crazy prospector. As Meg set out to confront the old coot, she planned her strategy with cool precision. But soon she was speechless with shock. For instead of a harmless geezer, she found a boldly handsome stranger whose determination matched her own.

CAPTIVE DESIRE (2612, $3.75)
by Jane Archer

Victoria Malone fancied herself a great adventuress, but being kidnapped was too much excitement for even Victoria! Especially when her arrogant kidnapper thought she was part of Red Duke's outlaw gang. Trying to convince the overbearing, handsome stranger that she had been an innocent bystander when the stagecoach was robbed, proved futile. But when he thought he could maker her confess by crushing her to his warm, broad chest, by caressing her with his strong, capable hands, Victoria was willing to admit to anything. . . .

LAWLESS ECSTASY (2613, $3.75)
by Susan Sackett

Abra Beaumont could spot a thief a mile away. After all, her father was once one of the best. But he'd been on the right side of the law for years now, and she wasn't about to let a man like Dash Thorne lead him astray with some wild plan for stealing the Tear of Allah, the world's most fabulous ruby. Dash was just the sort of man she most distrusted—sophisticated, handsome, and altogether too sure of his considerable charm. Abra shivered at the devilish gleam in his blue eyes and swore he would need more than smooth kisses and skilled caresses to rob her of her virtue . . . and much more than sweet promises to steal her heart!

Available wherever paperbacks are sold, or order direct from the Publisher. Send cover price plus 50¢ per copy for mailing and handling to Zebra Books, Dept. 3674, 475 Park Avenue South, New York, N.Y. 10016. Residents of New York and Tennessee must include sales tax. DO NOT SEND CASH. For a free Zebra/ Pinnacle catalog please write to the above address.

KATE O'DONNELL
Frontier Enchantress

ZEBRA BOOKS
KENSINGTON PUBLISHING CORP.

For my sons, Gregory and Gary,
In spite of you . . .

ZEBRA BOOKS

are published by

Kensington Publishing Corp.
475 Park Avenue South
New York, NY 10016

Copyright © 1992 by Kate O'Donnell

First printing: February, 1992

Printed in the United States of America

Prologue

Drawing in a deep breath, the boy studied the stone wall of the manor. Under the fragrance of earth, of autumn, of the wind from the North Sea, of peat smoke, was the tart odor of apples.

Saliva welled in his mouth and his stomach rumbled. He could almost feel the taut skin of an apple break under his teeth, the juice running down his throat and out the corners of his mouth. The memory of windfall apples, of bruised apples sliced with the old knife worn thin in its middle by the use of generations, fried with cabbage and served beside a mealy potato bursting with white steam, taunted him.

Slowly, feet dragging, the boy began to walk along the wall. There was, he knew, a poorly set stone that offered a perilous foothold to one rash enough to brave the forbidden grounds and Lord Cartland. His thin, patched shirt, folded over, gave protection enough from the jagged glass at the top of the wall, though he cut his hand in his eager anticipation.

Sucking at the wound, he sat at the top for a moment and gazed out at the endless orchard. The boughs of the trees, creaking with their fruit, arched over wide paths narrowing to tunneled vaults of green. Down one long aisle he caught a glimpse of a girlchild in a green habit on a chestnut pony. Then she was gone and he forgot her. It was to the earth he looked, to the grass almost invisible beneath its carpet of discarded bounty. Fear and long tradition insisted that he take only those unwanted by the lord of the manor . . . the bruised, the wormy, the wind-fallen.

Turning, he lowered himself feet first, his fingers clinging to the rough stones of the wall. He dropped onto apples that rolled beneath his feet and he fell, the apples bruising him.

Lying there, he struggled to regain his breath. The odor of apples was heavy with each gasp, apples crushed, pungent, and sharp, musky and wooly-rotten to the nose. He rose slowly, breath back, fear gone, driven from him by hunger for the richness around him. No longer was he to be satisfied by the single apple he munched as he walked, its juices filling his mouth, its flesh bursting under his teeth. With no thought to the glass barring his return over the wall, he tied his shirtsleeves to form a crude sack and began to fill it with only the ripest, the least marred of the fruit from the ground.

He didn't hear the huge hounds loping through the aisles of trees, the fruit rolling away under each long stride. Only when they reached him, when they were near enough to leap, slamming him flat with the force, did they give voice to their capture.

The ropes cut his skinny wrists, rubbing skin from bone too near the surface, turning his fingers numb. Rough wood scraped his face, raising tiny bubbles of blood from his chin as he pressed his mouth against the whipping block to smother the screams sure to come. And he waited, his eyes on his discarded shirt, the fruit pouring from it, a mocking cornucopia. Dimly, through his fearful anticipation, he heard the ring of horses' hooves on the stones of the courtyard and a girlchild's soft question.

"Is he to be whipped?"

He lifted his head and saw her, the daughter of the manor. She sat her pony with an ease taught through the endless patience of others. The soft fabric of her riding habit, the butter-yellow leather of the gloves petting her mount's neck, had been earned by the labor of those deemed beneath her, and the reins of his bondage seemed to be clasped in her small, pampered hands. The boy knew it was the alarm she had raised of an intruder in the orchard that had brought him to the block. Then his eyes moved to her guardian.

He stood arrogantly, legs apart and firmly planted on the land he held for his niece. The face, narrow as a hatchet blade, its skin tight over bone, contained an avarice no amount of feeding could fatten. His thin mouth was as rigid and cold as a trap.

"He is," he answered his niece. "And, Caitrin, I would have you gone from here."

The girl did not move, her eyes turning dark and concerned as they focused on the figure on the whipping block.

"But he is no more than a boy!" she pleaded, her words stripping from him his newly acquired manhood, leaving him naked, defenseless.

"He is thirteen, and old enough to use as an example to all who would think to follow him."

"But what did he do?"

Cartland negligently waved his riding crop toward the crushed and fragrant fruit, then slapped it against his polished, gleaming boot. The gesture conveyed impatience and scorn. Caitrin stared at the torn, patched shirt, at the fruit spilling from it.

"He stole apples?" she asked, incredulous, turning her imploring gaze back to her uncle. "My stepfather, and my father, too," she said, "used to turn the people into the orchard for a day . . . would let them take away all the windfall apples they could carry in shirts tied as this one is, before the hogs were turned in."

The lord's fleshless lips pressed tight in anger. He owed no explanations to a child of eight years. Nor was she capable of understanding the economic considerations making pigs more valuable than an Irish croppie.

"You will leave," he repeated.

Caitrin's chin lifted then, blinking back tears, and she caught her lower lip between her teeth. Her eyes held the boy's, telling him of her pity, of her impotence, before her riding crop touched her pony's flank and she was gone, this daughter of the Fitz-Geralds.

He stared after her, hating her with an enmity that swelled up from his loins, choking him. Her people had enslaved his for generation after generation, forcing them to bow in labor over land once their own. With their sweat and very blood they enriched the earth now held in thrall by those called lord and master, by men who had once named no man superior.

And, with the land, the English oppressor had taken the rights and privileges of all freeborn men. No longer could a true Irishman own land, lease land, inherit land, yet it was the land once his people's that housed the daughter of the house in splendor, paid for the gloves on her slim hands, the bottle-green riding habit she wore, her riding crop. They paid for her pony, while no Roman Catholic could own such a steed, not by law. No longer could an Irishman celebrate his religion anywhere but in secret caves and fields, or educate his children but in hedgerow schools taught by priests marked for death should they be captured. Yet the daughter of the manor attended a church of stained glass windows and high steeples paid for by the compulsory tithes of his people to a religion not their own, and she listened to a pastor not banned by pain of death from his own country nor hunted down by bloodhounds like an animal. She rode to that church in a carriage made fine with wood polished to a high gleam by hands as gnarled and as sore with labor as those of his father. And she, this oppressor's daughter, wore silks and satins such as his mother would never know.

It was her guardian, true, who had ordered him whipped for the taking of what had once been his people's, who stood there, bored, waiting for the punishment to be meted out. The boy hated him for the injustice of it, for the shame, for the insult of deeming him not significant enough nor man enough to wield the whip himself, and for the pain he knew would come. Yet he but acted in her name. It was the FitzGeralds, not Lord Cartland, who held his country in captivity. And she had dared plead for him, beg for him.

The boy's eyes blurred with his hate and impotence, then he blinked and pressed his mouth hard against the block. He would allow her no regret for a deed that was but one of countless such wrought by the oppressor. No pity, he vowed, would he accept from the daughter of the foreigner. No whimper would he make to unite them in her helplessness. He would not scream, not for apples fallen to an earth that had once been his. But he did. And he hated her all the more for it.

One

Caitrin FitzGerald leaned against the ship's rail, gazing out at the New World, but it offered her none of the haven promised to so many others. For her it was a snare carefully and deliberately set by her uncle.

Her uncle! she mocked silently. So Lord Cartland styled himself and it was as his niece that he always introduced her. And she always denied the relationship, her words quirked to suggest a less moral association, leaving him to explain to politely raised eyebrows that he was, actually, the brother of her mother's second husband and her legal guardian. Somehow her disavowal, that hint of an illicit, debased connection, always flustered him, this man who seemed to have no weakness, no vulnerability, no blood in his veins. It was the only means she had ever discovered to embarrass him, to drive a splinter, no matter how fragile, into his haughty composure. She paid for it each time with the withdrawal of her few privileges, but it was worth it. She had so few opportunities to express all her years of carefully nurtured hate.

Sighing, Caitrin stared at Long Island as the ship drifted up its length, not seeing the thick forests or the smoke that plumed above isolated farms. Her ears were deaf to the luffing of the sails high above her and to the excited voices about her as she wondered again how life would have been for her had her father lived. Her mother, in the long, slow months of her dying, had talked of the man seldom mentioned before. She spoke of a man strong enough to temper justice with mercy, a man beloved by his people, a man who secretly practiced a faith that could have, had it been discovered, deprived him of his estate and of all rights in a country where to be Catholic was to be less than human. But he had died when Caitrin was so young that all she could remember was his laughing green eyes, his bright streaked hair. Only when she gazed into a mirror, into eyes so like his, could she summon a memory of him. Her mother had been content enough with her second husband, her desire for love and laughter having died with James FitzGerald. And William Cartland had been a good man, staid and upright, ruling his wife's people with a firm and just, if unimaginative hand.

But he, too, had died, leaving a widow no longer young and a stepdaughter not yet eight years old. Then Harold Cartland, finding the widow's determination not to remarry—certainly not to him—stronger than his own will, had had himself appointed guardian of the estate . . . and of Caitrin.

Her eyes clouding, Caitrin thought again of how it had been Harold Cartland's ruthless, rigid dominance that had driven her mother to her death. It was but one of many crimes she held against him, she thought, remembering her mother's hesitant suggestions to him for mercy, for understanding of the

12

people, his answering display of profits that climbed higher each year under his management. Her mother had never given up, each effort drawing from her the strength she used to defy him in her quiet, frail way. Only once, though, had Caitrin asked him for compassion, and sometimes it seemed she could still hear the screams of a thirteen-year-old boy she had been powerless to help, could still see his hate-filled eyes. Ever after, she had set her jaw against any beseeching word. She bent no more than necessary, giving only as much as her guardian could take, never more. Then he had announced his intention to attend to business in the American colonies.

Caitrin straightened, suddenly aware that her hip was cocked in an unladylike angle and her elbows were resting on the rail, her chin propped in her hands. To rest the face so was not only ungenteel but it created wrinkles. Or so she had been told time after time at Miss Primm's Academy for Young Females in Dublin, where her uncle had sent her in the vain hope that a veneer of gentility would soften her obstinacy. Then she propped her chin again.

"Wrinkles and the Missus Primm be damned!" she whispered to a seagull gliding past.

Harold Cartland had announced his journey with a face as indifferent as he greeted everything. He calmly appointed a bailiff to his niece's estate—one, he was careful to determine, as relentless as himself—and packed his bags.

Trying to hide her joy, Caitrin had watched his preparations. She had less than a year until she reached eighteen, until she could fire the bailiff and gather the manor's reins into her own hands.

Then he informed her that she was to go with him. Guessing at her half-formed plans to run away, to disappear until he was forced to leave without her, he had forbidden her the stables, placing a guard on her.

Biting her lip angrily, Caitrin tossed back a strand of hair from her eyes and saw the city of New York for the first time. Large warehouses crowded its many wharfs. Men were engaged in bustling activity at the fort at the tip of Manhattan Island. There were, she knew, some twenty thousand or more people in this city at the edge of the world. Perhaps, if she were to stay here, she might be able to find someone to help her, to stand with her against her guardian. But Cartland was not to stay in New York. He was to go to some isolated fort deep in the wilderness, and she with him. She could not remember the fort's name; the news had seemed the final blow to all her hopes, and defeated for the moment, she had closed her ears to all else he had told her. There was nothing she could do, no place she could run to where he could not find her, such were his connections, his influence.

Lifting her face to the wind rising from the land, she welcomed the breeze on her hot cheeks. It brought with it the scent of pine trees, of grass drying in the heat of July, and the stench of civilization, acrid smoke, rotten garbage, swine running free in the streets.

The breeze whipped her hair back across her face, stinging her eyes. It was time to go below, to smooth her hair into the high, elaborate style society demanded. At least, once they left civilization—or what she heard passed for such in New York—she would be able to brush the powder from her hair, to discard the stays that stabbed her with each move she made, each breath she took. And in New York, there were dignitaries to meet, crown officials to be

14

introduced to as Cartland's niece, and the opportunity once more to see his composure slip for just that fraction of a second. Revenge, no matter how paltry, still tasted sweet. And it was all she had.

With one last glance at the shore awaiting her, Caitrin went to her quarters below.

Two

Closing the cabin door behind her, Caitrin leaned against it and gazed at the cramped quarters that had been her home for the past month. There were two bunks, one above the other, a small table, an armless chair. Even with their trunks stored under the bunk, she and Anna had scarcely enough room to turn around, their panniered skirts making it almost impossible to pass each other. The *Humber* was, after all, a warship with few comforts. The delicate rug of brick-red and Persian blue on the floor and the small mirror on the wall were welcome concessions to her rank and sex. A narrow shelf below the mirror held her cosmetics and the few Anna Redmond used. But Anna Redmond was absent, and the room seemed larger and more appealing. She had had so few private moments during the long voyage. Even when the other passengers had been struck with sea-sickness, Anna Redmond, too, had remained healthy and watchful.

Caitrin had returned from Miss Primm's to find her old nurse gone, replaced by Anna Redmond. Ona, her uncle explained, had become too old to properly attend her, and she needed a woman to train

17

her in the manners appropriate for a female of her rank. Caitrin had accepted the news of Ona's exile with a calm face, refusing him the satisfaction of knowing he had deprived her of one of the few people she loved and trusted.

Yet Caitrin would have hated Anna Redmond even if she had not replaced Ona. She was less companion than spy and guard. Lord Cartland had hoped his niece would accept Anna as a confidante, thus making himself privy to her every thought and emotion. But Caitrin used her solely as the lady companion he had introduced her as, sometimes making the woman cater to her every deliberately perverse whim. Yet Anna did everything flawlessly. That she accepted Caitrin's demands and tantrums with an indulgent smile only drove the girl to devise more exacting chores. But, most often, Caitrin ignored her, aware that this was the one thing the woman hated.

Nor was Anna only a lady's companion. Anna was also Lord Cartland's mistress. And cold comfort they must have from each other, Caitrin thought, frigid, canting puritan that Anna was.

Wondering if they emitted the rasp of two dry sticks rubbed against each other when they came together, Caitrin giggled and pushed herself away from the door. Moving easily with the gentle heave and roll of the ship, she walked to the mirror and studied herself. Tendrils of hair escaped the pins that held back her curls . . . curls streaked pale gold, deep auburn, strawberry-blond where the wind had blown the powder from them. And her scalp itched! There had been only salt water to wash it in during the long voyage. A bath seemed a luxury she hadn't had in years and would be her first request as soon as she set foot on solid earth. And she would wear her hair as she wished, with no powder to dull it. If her uncle and Anna Redmond saw such a need to bring the modes of civilized England to colonial bumpkins, let them do so and leave her to her comfort! There was little they could do when confronted with such small rebellions. Caitrin smiled, beginning to replace the errant strands.

Her mouth was filled with hairpins, her hands still tucking and twisting when she heard a tap on the door. It wasn't until she grunted permission to enter that she remembered Anna never knocked, that she was always suddenly opening doors as though to catch Caitrin at some forbidden deed or thought. Swinging about in alarm, she relaxed when she recognized Ashley Cartland. Her gaze flicked disdainfully over him before she turned back to the mirror.

It always amazed her that members of a family could appear so similar. The Cartlands all had narrow hatchet faces, pale blue eyes, thin, lipless mouths. Only in strengths and weaknesses did the mold vary. Caitrin's stepfather's features had been softened by a lazy good nature. Ashley's mother's had been pinched and sallow with avarice and narrow thoughts. Ashley, Caitrin told herself, would be an exact replica of his uncle were it not for the weakness about his mouth. What was cold intelligence in one was greedy cunning in the other. But Ashley's features were now wan with illness.

"To what purpose do you so honor me?" Caitrin asked, not bothering to feign interest.

"I've seen little of you, Caitrin," he answered, voice beguiling. "You've scarcely spoken to me, your own cousin, the whole voyage, though you have had time enough for the officers ever surrounding you!"

Caitrin shrugged and returned to her hair.

19

"You are no blood kin to me, nor would I have it so! And you have been retching your guts into a chamber pot the whole voyage. Would you have had me hold your head and wipe your dripping mouth? If so, I trust your disappointment was no ruder than your manners! I did not invite you here, and you may leave!"

Ashley stared at her proud back, eyes narrowed in fury. His uncle was right. Caitrin had all the faults of her Irish forebears, all their lack of the social graces and delicate amenities that conceal so much and make life so pleasant. She had the uncouth mouth of a croppie, no matter the lessons pounded into her, the examples set for her. But he had come to her with a purpose. The art of seduction was not unknown to him, and rape, if she pushed him to it, was as good a way to settle the problem of her stubbornness as any.

"Caitrin," he whispered, stepping to her, his hands running from her shoulders to her elbows and back. His lips grazed the soft flesh of her neck. She stiffened in shock. Never had he dared touch her so before and her mind reeled, seeking a reason for it. Nor did she move away. Indeed, there was little place for her to go. "Caitrin," he repeated, "don't reject me! Don't let your dislike of our uncle keep us apart! In your thwarting of him, you but deny us the pleasures, the love we could have of each other. Bed with me now and we can face the world with a deed accomplished. We could be married in New York. He has enough influence, even in this benighted place, to have the banns waived. Say you will, Caitrin!"

His hands felt clammy through the thin fabric of her gown. His lips were dry as a rasp on her neck, reptilian. His hands moved to cup her high, round breasts.

"Caitrin," he whispered, his hot breath touching

20

her ear, "I want you! I want to possess you . . . your soft mouth, your sweet breasts . . ."

"My broad acres!" she hissed, spinning around to face him, her back to the wall. "Get out of here! Go back to your uncle and his leman and tell them I will not be ordered, nor coerced, and certainly not seduced! You think me a fool? You think I don't know he sent you here as a pimp sends a whore, and had you succeeded, you were to carry my inheritance back to him as your wage? And does he think me fool enough not to know why he brought me here to the edge of the world? I'm to be eighteen in seven months, and no longer will he be able to control my lands, my fortune! And he would have me marry you and put it all back into his hands? No! Never! And if he takes me to the last, farthest outpost in this heathenish land, he'll succeed no more than he would at home. Tell him that! Now, be gone and tell the grand pimp master you have failed—again!"

Ashley only leaned back against the wall, smiling pityingly at her.

"But you are the fool, my sweet," he drawled in the languid accent of the Dublin fop. "He has bent strong, important men to his will, and you think to defy him? When he speaks, heads of state obey! Don't let his low title deceive you. He will bend you or break you, and the choice is yours. Be wise and go with him. The rewards are far greater than any disadvantage you seem to imagine. He cares for his own, watches over them, spares them all discomfort and inconvenience."

"Until they are sucked dry, then he discards them!" she spat.

"Only those with aught left to give, those who think to fool him, to cheat him," Ashley replied, then his demeaning amusement vanished. "Don't be a

21

fool, Caitrin! Give in! You are no longer in Ireland with nosy neighbors and those shirttail relatives of yours, as meddlesome as they are powerless. Out there," he told her, waving a pale, limp hand toward the approaching land, "there are preachers aplenty who would be deafened enough by a few gold pieces not to notice if the bride protested force. Nor would they notice a forged signature on a wedding license. There are innkeepers who would ignore the screams of a new bride—some men, after all, like their bed-sport rough. There are ways, Caitrin, to force you, and once married, with a brat in your belly, who would dare to come between a man and his wife, no matter her tears and accusations?"

Pausing, Ashley studied her for a sign of fear, of yielding, but saw only obstinacy. Her head was held high, proud, her small chin jutting, her delicate jaw set. His eyes shifted under her contemptuous gaze before he continued.

"And there are other methods, cousin, to deal with a reluctant woman. Laudanum, given long enough, renders one dependent on it. Soon enough she'll do anything, promise anything for it. Yet it is used often enough, and who would object to a fond, concerned uncle administering it to a hysterical niece? And he carries a large supply in his chest. Think on it. Do you think he came to this barbaric place with no purpose or that his purpose concerns you? Hardly, but your presence will not be allowed to inconvenience him."

Caitrin stared at him, dismay visible for the first time on her features.

"Why?" she asked, "Why does he want me and my land? He's used it for ten years and well he milked it! He has wealth enough to satisfy any man! Why does he want me and mine?"

22

"Why?" Ashley repeated, an amused smile tilting his thin lips. "Because he never releases what he once holds, and he allows no one to stand against him, not for long. You've done so for a longer time than most. He's indulged you. So, make it easy for all of us. Bed with me now. Wed with me tomorrow, and we'll all be the happier for it . . . you as much as the rest of us."

"No!" she said, eyes glinting, her chin lifting in defiance. "Never! And I want you gone! Now!"

"Do you hope, sweet cousin," Ashley chuckled, "to find a man to protect you here in this savage land? Then you are a fool! There is not an officer aboard this accursed scow who has not heard you were caught in bed with a stable boy. What matter that it is but a lie devised by our uncle? Few men are so greedy or so easily swayed by a pretty face as to wed a woman reeking of manure. But I, I tell them, understand your childish propensity for foolish escapades and am willing to forgive you, to trust you, to wed you."

Outrage flared in Caitrin's eyes, then her full mouth quirked up in wry amusement. "I should have known he did something like that by the advances made me recently. But you insult me. Believe me, I would much prefer bedding a stable boy than you! And now," she told him, her light, lilting accent slipping easily into the soft brogue she knew he hated, "'tis time, I'm thinking, you went from me. Aye, and isn't it long enough I've wasted on the likes of you and more?"

"No," he answered, straightening up from his indolent pose, his face suddenly hard, his eyes dropping over her. "I haven't accomplished what I came to do. Your games, sweet cousin, are done. It is time you submitted, time you ceased to deny us. Don't think to scream. All who would hear are above, more interested in what waits on shore than your dubious virtue. And fighting will but make the deed less pleasant for you, more exciting for me."

Ashley felt omnipotent at the fear he saw flicker in her wide eyes. He saw her quick appraisal of the distance to the door and was there before her, with a swiftness she had not thought possible. Catching her shoulder, he swung her away from him as he gripped the front of her gown, ripping it to her waist, then he jerked her into his arms. His elbows held her arms pinned. One hand twisted her head back as she tried to bite him, the other gripped a wrist as he pushed her against the wall, the shelf cutting painfully into the small of her back. His weight held her immobile as his mouth searched for hers. Sobbing rage and refusal, Caitrin turned her head from side to side until his fingers twisted into her hair and his mouth pressed down. His lips were hard, cutting the tender inner flesh, then his tongue forced her mouth open, thrusting into it. She heard her own whimpered protests and forced herself to be quiet, unresisting, as her mind searched frantically for a means of escape. Behind her on the shelf, she remembered, was a small pair of silver scissors inlaid with gold.

Ashley chuckled at Caitrin's softening, thinking she had resigned herself. And why would she not submit as easily as had the tenant wenches at home? They all pleaded and begged, then gave in. Releasing her wrist, he pulled up her skirts, his hand moving cold and hurtful over the smooth flesh of her thigh.

Caitrin held herself motionless, the effort shaking her, as his spider-thin, relentless fingers sought her softness. His defiling mouth moved from hers, leaving a snail's trail of slime, a line of bruises down her neck to the high roundness of her breasts. She

24

heard his murmur of "Ah, how sweet they are, cousin mine!"

Her body quiet, she stared at the ceiling, eyes narrowed as she reached slowly, carefully, behind her, seeking the scissors. Her fingers stumbled over a steel curling iron, a packet of hairspins, fumbled over a box of beauty patches, a bottle of perfume, then she felt it fall to the side with a clatter. Holding her breath, forcing her mind away from his violating hands, Caitrin prayed that he hadn't heard the betraying sound. Then her hand closed over the scissors.

But, single-minded and confident of success, Ashley had drawn back from her to loosen his breeches. She ceased her searching, waiting until she knew his swollen manhood had leaped free, until he pressed against her again. With her free hand, she drew his head to her breast, blinding him, and felt his groan of pleasure as her other hand twisted on the scissors. Carefully, she separated the blades, pushing them back to the handles. Trailing her hand up his back and over his shoulder, she pressed the point of one blade into the side of Ashley's neck where the vulnerable artery pulsed.

"You will leave me now," she whispered.

His body went slack and his head lifted from her breast. His mouth was still parted and moist, but disbelief had leaped into his eyes. The urgent swell of his manhood went flaccid against her thigh.

"Caitrin?" Ashley whispered, not yet accepting the loss of what he had been so confident would be his.

"You will leave me now," she repeated, pressing the weapon harder into his neck. He stared into her unrelenting eyes. Her desire, her need to strike, was clear as she returned his gaze, and he slowly backed

25

away from her. She followed, the scissors against his throat, her free hand tugging down her skirts.

"Arrange yourself," she ordered, her glance disdainful on his unbuttoned trousers, "and leave me! Tell Cartland you failed . . . that I will not be seduced nor raped, not by such a spineless thing as you! Go!"

Ashley backed away from the loathing in her eyes, his own glinting with the fury of humiliation as his hands secured his breeches. His shoulders jarred against the door and his fingers searched for the latch. Finding it, he jerked the door open.

"You frigid bitch!" he whispered, and then was gone.

In shock, Caitrin stared weakly at the closed door. Her legs shook as she went to it and dropped the bar. Leaning against it, she felt its cool, inanimate strength, then turned. Her step was steady as she went to the bunk and kneeled, searching beneath it for the chamber pot. Pulling it to her, she vomited away the filth she felt in her flesh, the soil in her soul. Purged at last, she stripped off her torn dress and tossed it into a corner. Crawling into the bunk, she pulled the blanket over her and began to shake spasmodically in fear. Cartland, she knew, would try again to control her, and perhaps next time he would be more successful.

It seemed hours before Caitrin heard the decisive rap on her door, but it could have been only a short time since she had curled into a ball, seeking comfort from her own heartbeat. Forcing herself up, she threw a shawl over her shoulders. Going to the door, she lifted the bar, knowing full well who stood there. Vindictive anticipation faded from Anna Redmond's

26

pale eyes as she studied the impassive features of her charge. Though Ashley had failed in his rape, she had hoped, at least, to find Caitrin weeping and marked by violence and shame. But the girl only regarded her visitor with an eyebrow lifted in bored query.

"I came to see if you needed me," Anna said at last, swallowing her disappointment. "We have docked and I thought you might not have noticed."

Caitrin tipped her head. The deck beneath her no longer fell and lifted in a rhythm that had been a part of her existence for so long.

"So we have," she agreed in a soft brogue. "And wasn't I sleeping and missing all the excitement? Won't I be needing your skillful fingers if I'm to be ready to go ashore with you?" Caitrin smiled, enjoying the other woman's frustrated rage. "You do have such skillful fingers, you know, Anna," she complimented. "Does my uncle find them so?"

Her eyes danced at the flush of rage on Anna's sallow features and her lips parted, curving higher as her thrust went home.

"Why, thank you, Caitrin," Anna replied, hate knotting her chest as her mouth arranged itself into an aching smile. "Shall we start on your hair?"

Three

Caitrin retreated into a curtained alcove, seeking to escape the smoke-laden air, the babble of voices determined to impress their English guests by volume, if not by content. She was wearier than she had thought. More than anything, she longed to crawl into bed and sleep. Sleep had become her only relief from the pressures about her, and too often it only resulted in nightmares. Now, she still had dinner to sit through, and it had been with such pride in their provincial plentitude that her hostess had listed the dishes for her—roast goose, turkey, leg of pork, boiled beef, mutton chops, fried tripe, venison, pigeons, three different potatoes, cabbage, hominy, onions, beets, and carrots. Somehow the naming of each, ticked off on chubby fingers, stimulated nausea more than appetite.

The colonials also consumed alcohol with a will not necessarily equaled by their ability to control it. Many of the men smoked pipes, filling the air with raw tobacco fumes, while others delicately dipped snuff, punctuating their conversations with massive sneezes into fragile lace handkerchiefs. Caitrin had never before seen snuff used by women, but it was a habit ugly enough, she was certain, to catch on in Europe.

Frowning and leaning her head back against the wall, Caitrin tried to remember the name of the lady who had so honored her by offering her snuff. Bayard? De Peyster? Hamilton? There had been so many names attached to unfamiliar features that none made sense.

Now, she was tired of conversation, of men eyeing her with lecherous eyes, telling her Ashley's lies had done their work. She was tired of struggling with names and faces that would not merge. Her fatigue had made her petty and spiteful, she knew. Closing her eyes, she sighed, hoping to remain undiscovered in her little corner for a few minutes more.

How long, she wondered, would she feel abused and soiled? She bit her lip, blinking back tears that could too easily dissolve her remaining strength. She needed every ounce of it and more. She needed all her wits and could not afford to lose them in foolish emotions. She needed to hoard her hate and pride, to hone them into a weapon as much against her own weakness as against her uncle. It would be too easy to give in, to take the comforts he offered, to place in his hands all cares, all worries, to live her life as an extension of his. But the price was too great. He wanted her soul, her mind, her spirit. He would turn her into a puppet dancing only on his strings, thinking only his thoughts, living only for his approval, until she became as unfeeling, as coldly cruel, as stiff as he was. The very thought filled her with terror, and she forced her mind to her arrival in New York.

Later, she would try to figure out why Harold Cartland had chosen just that time to send Ashley to her, try to predict what to next expect. Later, when she felt less bruised and defiled, she would use the memories of Ashley's hard hands, his sullying tongue, to build her hate, turning his attempted rape into a shield.

New York was not the primitive settlement she had expected. Seen from the ship, the city had offered a view of tall steeples. Mansions of two and three stories lined the tree-shaded streets leading up from the wharves. Large buildings of commerce commanded the waterfront. The tall ships filling the harbor had saluted the new arrivals, joining the homage sounding from the fort that dominated the western tip of Manhattan. The scent of early summer lingered under the smell of salt from the sea, of sewage, and of smoke.

Riding to the governor's house, one part of Caitrin's mind was still stunned by Ashley's attack. The other had watched her flirt with the handsome aide of Governor Delancey who rode next to her carriage. His admiring courtesies would change to scarcely concealed leers, she knew, when the rumors spread by Ashley and her uncle reached him. For the moment, though, she could only enjoy his honest attentions.

During the short journey, he had pointed out the city's landmarks—the high steeple of the New Dutch Church, of Trinity Church, the rising scaffolds of King's College, the high dome of City Hall. He showed her what he called the most beautiful home in America, William Walton's residence. It stood, a handsome home, three stories high and built of yellow Holland brick, its roof covered with tiles. And he apologized. It, along with many other homes, put to shame the governor's house. So she had found, but the small chamber she was given, with its ornate ceiling, silk canopied bed, bright rugs, and dark

31

woodwork, was welcome after the tiny cabin shared with Anna and an occasional rat. And it was, as her guide rushed to assure her, the center of New York's society. Seeking her approval and expecting the scorn of most Englishmen, he told her of the culture to be found. There was gambling in all the better homes. Horse races were run at the slightest whim, along with cockfights, too, if she liked them; many ladies did not. In the summer there were picnics on the Hudson, in the winter ice-skating parties. Several theaters were occasionally honored by companies from England.

Caitrin had smiled and nodded, watching him brighten at her uncondescending attention. But she was not to stay in the city he painted so proudly. Nor could she recall his name or his features.

But one face leaped into her memory out of the hundreds of curious who had lined the streets, that of a young man leaning against a cart filled with brick. Red dust darkened his blond hair and had settled into the laugh lines about his broad mouth. He wore no hose and his breeches were rough woven. Tossing back a lock of hair from his eyes, he stared at her, his gaze frankly admiring. Meeting her haughty glare, he puckered his lips in a soundless whistle of approval. And she had laughed back at him.

Caitrin smiled. Had such happened at home, he would have been horsewhipped. Perhaps in this land where even a common laborer could be so impudent, she would find a man strong enough to defy her uncle, bold enough to challenge his power. Then she put the hope away; to dream so could only weaken her. But the thought of such a man, with bold eyes and a thumb on his nose for danger, stirred something within her, a hurt and a need she had not felt before and did not dare acknowledge.

Why, she wondered once again, had her guardian come to the colonies he so disdained? It certainly was not from loyalty to England; the only fealty he gave was to himself. Perhaps heads would roll in his wake. They so often did. Nor was it a secret that King George II and his advisors were unhappy with conditions in the colonies. The French threat loomed larger each day, and the lack of unity among the colonies created a situation as dangerous to themselves as it was to England's hold on the New World. Nor was the mother country pleased by the many military defeats; and Lord Cartland's word was enough to send a general home in disgrace.

Whatever his design, she decided, he would gain from it—financially, most likely. One thing she realized was that he had not wanted to take her with him into the wilderness. Ashley's intended rape of her and the marriage that was to follow had been designed to remove her from his hands, leaving her in New York while settling her inheritance into her husband's grasp. And there must be a reason he wanted to leave her behind, something he did not want her to see. But knowing his purpose could only strengthen her and she vowed to search it out. For the first time, hope rose in her and a small smile tilted her lips.

William Johnson leaned against the wall, watching the gossiping men and women with hazel eyes turned grey with disgust and anger. They romped and played, poised and flirted as though no savage war raged but two hundred miles from them, a war threatening New York City itself, should luck favor the French. As it was, the scale was precariously balanced, tipping one way then the other, and all patriotism, faith in God, and one's own sect aside, it could go either way. Yet that pompous ass of a governor, Delancey, had called him back from his men, when all that held the uneasy alliance of his Indians and the army together was the glue of his presence. To discuss matters of urgency, the message had read, when all Delancey wanted was to draw him into the bickering over funds, to be assured all would be well, and to have him meet another nabob fresh from England, there to tell the colonials how to fight a war they had waged for nigh on ninety years. It had happened too often. Time and again, after years of ceaseless parleying with his Iroquois, some limp-wristed, lisping fool from London would open his mouth and destroy all his efforts.

Now many of England's Indian allies were gone. The Six Nations were hopelessly divided, some siding with the French, some futilely seeking to remain neutral, some still loyal to their white father across the sea. And he couldn't blame any of them. He was totally disgusted with the government's vacillations, unrealistic demands, and broken promises. And here he was at a party, a curse on all of them, when he should be with his command, with his Molly.

He had come to the colonies as a young boy, an indentured servant to his uncle and little better than a slave. Now, his uncle's land's were his and he was one of the wealthiest men in North America. King George had appointed him Secretary of Indian Affairs for the Six Nations and their allies, making him accountable only to the king himself. Yet most people held him in contempt for his lack of fashion and education, for his friendship with the natives.

All but the women. Most of them were eager to share his bed, most of them had. But his head hurt with an ache only Molly's brown fingers could ease. He felt the impending return of the fever that periodically shook him and only the remedies of his wife's people could ease it. The pox was flaring again and he silently cursed the woman who had given it to him. But it could have been any one or several of the hundreds he had bedded, the mother of any one of his hundreds of children.

Yet even thinking of them stirred his lust and he grinned, acknowledging his greatest weakness. He liked women, in or out of bed. He wanted a woman now, to take his mind off his duties, to draw his anger with inane fools from him. William Johnson looked around the drawing room. All the women he might desire he had either bedded before or had found too virtuous for quick conquest. White women took bed play too seriously, often involving him with tears and recriminations that took all flavor from the sport, that robbed him of the joy he took, the joy he tried to give.

But there had been a new face there, an unusually lovely one even with her brittle, nervous laugh. And he had heard the tag end of a rumor of an affair with a stable boy. She was Lord Cartland's niece, and whatever that worthy's purpose in the colonies, William Johnson wanted to know of it.

But she wasn't Cartland's niece, he recalled, seeing the shadow of a pale green skirt in a curtained alcove. He had introduced her so and her denial had hinted of a more illicit relationship. If the tightening of his face, the flick of fury in his pale eyes, was what she sought, she had been rewarded. Johnson had seen, too, the satisfied tilt of her mouth. Whatever her reason for anger, whether he had denied her a new dress or had brought her from the dissipations of London and Dublin to the New World's dull society, he, Johnson, could use her resentment.

Nor was there a family resemblance. Cartland was

narrow-featured, cold, and had dismissed him with a disdainful glance as no more than another ill-dressed, ill-mannered country bumpkin. He would not have been surprised if Cartland's mistress had not drawn back her skirts to avoid whatever contamination she thought he carried. His nephew, too, a Dublin dandy from his languid pose to his curled and powdered wig, his suit of apricot satin and the beauty patch on his cheek, had lifted one eyebrow in hauteur before turning away. A bad mistake, that, all of it. Johnson was not a man who readily forgave such snubs, even from an Englishman. Cartland had the air of a man with nefarious plans, and Johnson had the means, the power to thwart them, once he discovered what they were. He did not like combining business with pleasure, but high-strung women talked, especially in bed, and this one appeared soiled, pampered, pettish. An angry woman talked even more.

Moving, he chose a site where he could study her undetected as she leaned against the wall, head back, eyes closed. In repose, her face was even lovelier than he had remembered, with its flaring eyebrows, small, straight nose, high cheekbones, delicate jaw, and small, firm chin. Her mouth was meant to be kissed, with its finely chiseled upper lip a trifle longer than the full, pouty lower one. And he had noted her eyes earlier, eyes that in their fringe of long, dark lashes would change with her moods, now gold, now green. She had not powdered hair that any Indian brave would gladly kill for nor did she wear any beauty patches, and Johnson wondered if she did so to spite her guardian and his mistress or if she disliked artifice. Probably spite, he decided, if she was the wayward, spoiled wench she seemed. But her gown of a soft white fabric sprigged with a deep green,

trimmed with lace and green ribbons on its sleeves
and hem, with a petticoat of that same shade, would
have every man in the chamber hoping her taken by a
sneezing fit. It was cut square and so low at the bodice
that with but a bit of wishful thinking, a man could
swear he saw the shadow of coral-tinted nipples. And
the lacing at the front of her bodice, the tightness of
her stays, only lifted her breasts higher, rounder,
tempting a man's eyes, his hands. Nor did she wear a
modesty piece, that scrap of lace tucked in by more
modest women to conceal the more generous of their
curves.

Was she, Johnson wondered, so dissipated, so
brazen, that she sought to tantalize every man there?
Or was it but one more attempt to defy, to thwart her
guardian? But he would not know by watching her,
and moving toward the alcove, he coughed lightly.

Startled, Caitrin jerked with fright and her eyes
flew wide. One hand clutched at the drapery behind
her and the other lifted as though to ward him off. In
her eyes was the expression of an animal cornered but
determined to fight to the death. She stared at him,
seeing a man in his early forties, over six feet tall,
with unpowdered dark red hair. His clothing was ill
fitted and out of style even by colonial standards, the
shoulders of his coat too tight, the sleeves too short,
the legs of his breeches too wide. Yet he seemed a man
with a way with women about him. But he was not a
threat to her, and Johnson saw relief flood Caitrin's
features as she recognized him. Regretting his intru-
sion, he wanted to apologize, to beat a retreat, but
there was information he needed and he smiled dis-
armingly.

"Lady FitzGerald, I did not mean to frighten you,
but I'm surprised to find so lovely a woman alone
with no fops about her."

Her chin lifted, her features hardening with anger, and she regarded him with a cool stare.

"I had but sought a moment's solitude," she stated, but he made no motion to leave and she sighed, too well-bred to be truly rude—yet. "Sir William Johnson, is it? I cannot remember so many new faces, new names."

"But you remembered mine," he told her. "I am flattered and honored."

"'Tis that you were late," she answered bluntly, turning to gaze indifferently at the huddles of gossiping people. "More so than is even fashionable."

Johnson's mouth quirked in irritation. She needed to be turned over someone's knee. She was but a spoiled brat, no matter that she jumped at small noises. She needed to be spanked, and there were more ways of doing so than with the flat of one's hand.

"Do you know," he asked, "that there are rumors concerning you and a Dublin stable boy?"

Her eyes flew back to him, her face turning stark, and her small white teeth fastened into her lower lip as she fought to control her tears. Suddenly, she reminded Johnson of his daughter, his favorite among many girl-children, when she had come to him, dark eyes filled with tears, her full lower lip quivering provocatively in her child's face. "What?" she had pleaded, "is a half-breed bastard?" There was the same bewildered grief in this woman's stricken eyes. Then her gaze dropped and he wanted to draw her into his arms. He wanted to comfort her as he had his daughter, telling her of his love, of her value, of her beauty, telling her it would be all right. But he could not nor did he know the cause of her fear, her sorrow, her bewilderment. Helpless before her unshed tears, her pain, he could only stare in admiration as she visibly gathered composure back about herself. When her gaze lifted again, her eyes were dry and he saw pride in her features, pride in her strength, in her lineage, in the blood of bold, unyielding men and women flowing in her veins. Then, as though she sensed his compassion, his empathy, her features opened to him, her small, rueful smile telling him she trusted him, moving their relationship far beyond mere flirtation.

"I know," she sighed. "My cousin spreads them. My guardian wished me to wed Ashley and thinks, perhaps, to keep other men from me. Or perhaps he hopes to drive me to obedience by the insults dealt me."

"And you don't want your cousin?"

"I don't! And he but wants me for my lands, my inheritance! Nor would I have him, lickspittle, limp-wristed, weak-spined fop that he is!"

Johnson grinned at her vehemence, then sobered.

"Has his plans for a marriage aught to do with his visit to the colonies?" he asked, surprising her.

Caitrin's gaze grew pensive, then she shook her head, saying, "I don't know, and the dear knows I've pondered it. I only know his presence will benefit only himself and harm others. 'Tis always so. But why do you ask?"

"I don't like unpleasant surprises and Cartland strikes me as a man who deals them. He is as twisted as a burned snake."

Her mouth quirked in wry agreement before she drew within herself once more at the mention of her guardian.

"Lady FitzGerald," he offered impulsively, "should you ever need aid, come to me or send me word."

"I thank you," she answered, knowing him sincere. "But my uncle is a powerful man. 'Tis best

39

that I rely only on myself. I've no wish to endanger others."

"And I, too, am powerful, and this is my arena." He did not boast, Caitrin saw. Her head tilted in acceptance and she offered him her hand. He held it, his mind already elsewhere. "Where in Ireland are you from?" he asked.

"Leitrim, near Sligo." Then the mischievous imp so often destroying her best intentions pounced on her tongue. "You're Irish, too, I wager. I had noticed your brogue before, though now you've lost it. Is it something you use only when planning seduction?"

A grin tilted his mouth. Yes, he decided, he liked her. And he would receive far more answers from her with honest questions than with any sort of flirtation.

"I am, but the brogue I use only in the presence of a beautiful woman from home herself. But I've another reason. There is a man here in the New World," he told her, "from Leitrim by his accent, though he has never said. You might know him; queerer things have happened. He calls himself Roarke O'Conner. He's tall, my height or more, with black hair and blue eyes. And handsome—or so I'm told by the sighing of my women. He's bold in his gaze and quiet, but with a chip on his shoulder. Would you know him or of him?"

Caitrin's brow puckered at the thought of black hair and blue eyes, then she shook her head, unable to put a face or a name to the memory.

"No," she said at last, "I don't know him. We've O'Conners among our tenants but no Roarke. 'Tis an unusual name and I would remember him, I think. He concerns you?"

"He does. 'Tis more a case of what he doesn't do than what he does. He is a woods loper—a coureur de bois, the French call them. He brings furs to my post, excellent furs. He talks a bit, but never of himself, and listens more, drinks a little and never gets drunk. He works alone and never mentions the Indians he lives and trades with, but many woods lopers are loners and more closemouthed. Still, I don't trust a man who never gets drunk. And there is something about the man, something driving him I don't understand. Most of them live from bottle to bottle, squaw to squaw, and 'twas but a chance that you might know him." He shrugged the hope away and straightened away from the wall he leaned against. His eyes grew intent on her features as he made a sudden decision. "But I've a favor to ask of you," he stated. "A favor that could prove dangerous to you. 'Tis your uncle. He concerns me, worries me. He's up to no good, but what he plots I don't know. . . ."

"And you wish me to spy for you," Caitrin interrupted. Her features grew hard as she returned his apologetic gaze. Her chin was lifted and her jaw set, but her eyes held forlorn pain. The friendship, the protection he had offered, was but a ploy to use her as so many others tried to do, and she cursed herself for the foolish hope she had allowed that it might be otherwise with him.

Johnson saw the despair and hurt in her eyes, and he reached out to touch her. She jerked away as though his hand would defile her, her jaw hardening further, and his arm dropped.

"Aye," he admitted, holding her defiant gaze, "I thought to use you. This country has been good to me. I love it, aye, and its people." He glanced around at the posturing, gossiping throng, gentry and nouveau riche alike, and for a second an askew grin tweaked his mouth. "Well, most of its people," he admitted, then his features became earnest once

41

more. "There is little I would not do to protect those I do respect and value, Indian and colonial alike. I would use my own mother to do so, but I would request her permission, her compliance first, just as I've now asked yours. Whatever plots your guardian weaves, I cannot protect anyone unless I know what web he spins and what flies he had caught in the strands of it. Nor can I watch him. But you can."

"Your people are not mine," she shot back, "nor is your country! Nor do I wish to be used . . . to be put in jeopardy while being so . . . to protect people not mine from a threat that may be aught but a figment of your imagination. So just why should I spy for you? Tell me!"

"To protect yourself," Johnson responded, his eyes refusing to yield before her irate gaze. "When I first approached you, aye, I thought to use you unwittingly, to trick you, perhaps, thinking you but a spoiled, priggish brat. But I was wrong, both in my intention and in my prejudgment. Instead, I found you a strong, proud woman. But it is your pride, your strength, that is the greatest threat to Cartland. If you unintentionally get in his way, he'll not hesitate to harm you. You know that, and how can you protect yourself, how can I protect you, if we do not know his plans, do not know how to avoid stepping on his toes?"

Caitrin studied Johnson's concerned, earnest features. She could see no insincerity in them, but still he was asking her to do something dangerous, deceitful, no matter that her stepuncle was a man without morals, and she asked, "What is it you would have me do?"

"Nothing that would put you in peril," he told her. "Nothing! I would want your word on that. I want no sneaking around corners, no peeking in keyholes. I want you to do aught but keep your ears and eyes open to where he goes and with whom he meets. That will tell me much. Nor do I want you to write aught down. 'Twould be dangerous to you. Only when you can send me news should you put pen to paper.''

"How would I get a letter to you?"

"One or another of my people would contact you from time to time. He'll identify himself. Or, if you should see one of Robert Roger's rangers, you could trust him to get word to me. Whether you agree to help me or not, I want you to send me a message should you ever need me.''

Caitrin nodded her understanding, then stared down at the hands she held twisted before her. The knuckles were white with tension. She had been asked to do something possibly dangerous, but not to do so could imperil her even more. Then her gaze lifted to meet Johnson's again. She trusted him, that she knew, and she did not trust easily. Whatever she agreed to, she was not alone anymore. This man cared for her, would do his best to protect her. Whether or not he could did not really matter. And she would be defying her guardian, would, perhaps, be instrumental in bringing him down. She laughed softly at the thought and held her hand out to Johnson.

"Aye," she told him as her fingers were enveloped in his fist, "I'll do it, and with pleasure!"

He grinned back as he bowed to kiss her hand, then tilted his head at the sound of the dinner bell.

"Will you sit with me at table?" he asked.

"Caitrin is to sit with her betrothed," Lord Cartland stated, and they turned together to face him. He looked from his niece to Johnson, his narrow visage expressionless. "My ward is betrothed to my nephew, Sir Ashley Harwood," he explained.

"We are honored, William," Caitrin commented, tapping his forearm with her fan, her features once again molded into the proper social ennui. "My guardian has chosen us as the first to hear the happy news of a nonexistent betrothal."

"My niece," Harold Cartland said through tightly set lips, "is somewhat hysterical from time to time."

"A malady often observed in women forced into a way of life against their own better judgment and will, a life perhaps repugnant to them," Johnson observed.

The other man stared at him with frosted eyes, then held out his arm to his niece. Indecisive, she turned between them. Was it worth the price to defy her uncle? Not yet, she decided, and she placed her hand over Cartland's while her eyes spoke her regrets.

"I enjoyed our conversation, Lady FitzGerald," Johnson told her, bowing, while his eyes reminded her of his promise, their agreement. "Thank you."

"The pleasure was mine, William," she answered. "And perhaps we'll meet again, perhaps at Fort William Henry."

"You mean to take her into the wilderness?" Johnson, astonished, demanded of Cartland. "'Tis no place for a woman, even one raised to its dangers! Hundreds have been killed or taken into captivity this last year alone. And there isn't a warrior alive who wouldn't give ten years of his life to have that hair hanging in his lodge."

His glance took in the streaked curls cascading down Caitrin's back, but Cartland's remained coldly fixed on William Johnson.

"Caitrin is my ward. Her welfare is in my hands and in my heart. She goes where I go."

William Johnson held his icy stare for a moment,

realizing further argument would be futile. It would only antagonize the Irish peer further, and Johnson wondered again about Cartland's purpose in America. "Your servant, sir," he said abruptly, bowing before he turned away. And if he did not discover that purpose until too late, if her guardian did take her into the wilderness, perhaps there would be little else he could do but pity Caitrin FitzGerald.

Four

Three weeks later, Lord Cartland left New York, taking with him his ward, his nephew, Anna Redmond, and a small company of soldiers reporting to Fort William Henry. For Caitrin, it was a relief to leave behind the city and its exhausting and endless round of entertainment, as its social leaders hopelessly vied to compete with Europe.

Although New York was now six days and one hundred seventy-five miles behind, cobwebs of fatigue still blurred her brain. The journey up the Hudson by sloop had been peaceful, but the nights had been spent on shore partaking of the hospitality of various manor owners. Caitrin was expected to be gay and charming, and she had been so. She repeated again gossip long cold from England and Ireland and, now, New York City. The women demanded news of the latest fashions and dance steps, while the men had withdrawn to their pipes and porter. Twice, her guardian had slipped away to covertly closet with his host of the evening. Trapped with the women, Caitrin wondered and worried about his clandestine behavior. Whatever Cartland's purpose, William Johnson would be interested in the names of the men

47

involved, that she knew, and she committed them to memory.

Captivated by the river's ever-changing vistas, she had watched the contrast of wilderness, the soaring cliffs of the Palisades, the distant blue haze of the Catskills, for hours at a time. The slumbering heights of the Highlands and the scattered marks of civilization intrigued her.

The Hudson was a river of lakes, of heavily wooded islands. In many places, a primeval forest of chestnut, oak, and hickory crept down to the water's edge. In others, wide valleys rich in fruit, vegetables, and grain stretched into the distance. Mansions that rivaled those of Ireland dominated the heights, and neat houses, the Dutch influence visible in their half doors and stepped gables, dotted the farmlands and formed villages. Their boat met others descending the river, passing canoes paddled by bearded, buckskinned woodsmen and half-clothed Indians. The Indians fascinated her. Some were dressed in odd bits of the white men's clothes, while others wore only breechclouts, their faces barbaric and sinister behind paint and tribal tattoos.

Yet the dark, brooding soul of the wilderness weighed on each breath she took. Only the Indians seemed to truly belong, and even they moved as temporary players against the solid prop of wilderness and mountains. The sloop's passage opened vistas of breathtaking, intimidating magnificence. Still, too much death and suffering occurred within its grandeur, Caitrin thought, as though the purpose of its dense forests was to conceal from God's eye the evil perpetrated in His name. Perhaps He was not finished with it. Perhaps He might, on a whim, level it with one pass of His hand and recreate it in a proportion more suitable to man.

Shuddering, Caitrin put the thought from her mind and gazed at the approaching town of Albany. Sloops, whaleboats, and canoes covered its waterfront. Tiled houses sat with their brick-gabled ends toward the broad, tree-shaded streets running up from the Hudson. Bustling people crawled about like insects on a disturbed anthill. Propping her chin in her hands, Caitrin wondered what diversion her hosts of the coming evening would require of her— and whom her guardian would meet that night.

Roarke O'Conner squirmed, rubbing the itch between his shoulder blades against the rough brick corner of the tavern's wall. Silently, he cursed all insect-infested public houses, then, the itch alleviated, he settled back into a drunken slouch, broad shoulders slumped unevenly. One leg was bent at a loose angle, the other outstretched as a precarious prop for his long, slim frame. Scratching the coarse stubble of his three-day beard, he lifted an almost-empty jug to his lips and gulped, shamming thirsty swallows as his clear, penetrating eyes scanned the scene before him.

It appeared as though all of Albany had flocked to the waterfront to greet its prodigious guest and, if he knew the people at all, they would be impressed. The tighter Lord Cartland's nostrils pinched, the more they would truckle. The more imperiously he lifted his narrow head or waved his slim white hands, the more they would cheer. They streamed past him to the docks—bewigged nabobs with their powdered and bejeweled wives; solid, heavyset patroons with their fat hausfraus; soldiers of the crown in scarlet;

men of the provincial militia in buckskins or blue and buff; bateau men; Indians; and always, the whores.

Tempted as he was, he would not follow the river of humanity flowing past in a babble of Dutch, English, and several Indian tongues. The prestigious visitor would come past him. He had waited so long that a few minutes more would not matter. The scars on his back suddenly itched as they had not done for years. Roarke writhed against the wall again, then settled back, his jug cradled lovingly in the crook of his arm.

He should have been on his way to New France days ago. But he wanted to set eyes on Lord Harold Cartland again, wanted to see how the last ten years had touched him. The information he had for General Montcalm could wait the few hours more. It had taken months to garner. He had gone to New York, to Boston, as far south as Philadelphia, to places no Frenchman dared appear. But a seldom-speaking, soft-brogued Irishman would be welcomed anywhere—except in Ireland. He could buy a round of drinks and listen to soldiers, to amateur politicians, to whores far gone in the cups. A frontiersman clad in buckskins, a bottle in one hand and a flintlock dangling from the other, seldom drew suspicion and no one thought to question his politics. Nor did they see, somehow, the hate so strong he wondered why it wasn't obvious to all.

They talked of furs and therefore of Indians, and from Indians to war. It was but a small step more to secret campaign plans, of movements of men, how many, by whom, to where. It was information Montcalm would pay well for, whenever he received it. The general would wait. Roarke, himself, had learned well to wait—and how to use that time.

Still, for all the hate he hoarded, had nursed to a dull, unquenchable glow that only total revenge would put out, Roarke hoped he would not find Lord Cartland changed. Time or disease should have no part in the vengeance he had waited for so long.

For ten years, from the day he had slipped away from his home, his family, his back still weeping and raw from the whip, he had planned and dreamed. Then, he had used his hate to drive himself up into the shrouds, to retain his grip on wet and flying lines, each motion wounding anew the flayed muscles of his back and shoulders as he worked his way before the mast across the Atlantic. Once in the New World, he had known only one thing: his revenge required money, a large sum of it. To kill a man from ambush, even to slip a knife between his ribs, telling him face to face as he did so who he was and why he was dealing him death, would not be enough. Only complete destruction would satisfy his hate. He needed to see the man writhe, to rob him of his estates, his power, his position. He wanted to watch him scrabble as, one by one, his truckling toadies and wealthy supporters deserted him, turned their backs on him.

That took money and a way to acquire it fast enough that nature would not, with a more merciful death, rob him of his vengeance. He had found it in furs, had learned the ways of the woods, of Indians, of the traders, as quickly as his thirst for revenge could take it all in. Shilling by shilling, pound by pound, letting them work themselves for him, they had added up. He had allowed himself no pleasures, no liquor to dull the edge of his hate or purpose, no women other than an occasional Indian wench to ease the tight ache of enmity within him. He had become a loner, going into a wilderness no other white man had set foot in, trading with Indians regardless of their alliances, French or English. Slowly, his wealth increased, feeding on itself and growing. Until war once more loomed. Then, he found the French paid a man well who could go into English forts and cities . . . who could judge at a glance the importance of blood-smeared papers taken from the pouch of a dead English soldier . . . who could hold tribes there when they, blood sated, wanted to go home to celebrate their newly acquired scalps, their loot, their terrified prisoners. The tribes were often indecisive as to which side to support in a war between the thieves of their lands and the well-paid tribes brought under the French flag.

He, too, had paid. He paid with the loss of a bit more of his soul each time he stood by and watched the torture of men and women luckless enough to fall into Indian hands. More died at the end of his war hatchet, from the muzzle of his flintlock, than the blood victims.

Then, last autumn, he had earned enough to destroy the powerful Lord Cartland. How he would do so he did not know. That would come to him in its time, as had his wealth. And there was a whisper of a rumor that Cartland was overextended, that he faced debt. But no more would the screams of the tortured ring in his ears, no more would he paint himself for war and dance with all the frenzy of the savages about him. No more would he wield a war hatchet. He had enough to buy Lord Cartland's lands, lands that had once been the O'Conner's, if in Ireland a Roman Catholic could own land. But he would not deny his faith. He would win his revenge on his own terms, giving up no part of himself. His faith was the one thing that he had kept inviolate. Perhaps he would break Cartland at the gambling tables, perhaps in the courts of law. He had money enough to buy false witnesses, to purchase his way into the secrets of the powerful, to use them against themselves. Such men did not reach the pinnacle of power without leaving a stench behind.

He had money enough, too, to buy a girlchild turned woman, to wipe all trace of pity from her eyes, to use her, possess her, then discard her, kick her aside as the useless thing she would become. *He had enough money to buy all the apples in the world.*

The hate he bore Cartland was a cold, hard thing, oddly impersonal, as impersonal as Cartland's whipping of him had been. But the daughter of the manor, the girlchild of a people who were but ravaging mercenaries when his had owned immense herds of cattle, had ruled vast lands, had dared to pity him. She had dared to plead for mercy for him, the daughter of those people who had taken all from his, who had held them in oppression for countless generations. Hate for her filled his throat with bile, his heart and groin with a strange lust.

Then, at a party in Montreal where even Governor Vandreuil held in esteem a man as useful as Roarke O'Conner, he had heard the breathing of a name. Amid the laughter and wails of the gambling men and women, among the aimless chatter and gossip, over the swell of music and the shifting of dancing feet, he had heard the whisper of Lord Cartland's name. That, and the news Montcalm needed, had directed him south. Whatever intrigue drew the Irish peer to the New World, he had come to Roarke. But his revenge still had to wait. Now Roarke only wanted to see him once again, his vision unblurred by the pain and humiliation dealt a child not yet a man.

Shifting his position, he wondered if he would have hated Cartland so had he wielded the whip himself. He did not think so. Settling back once more, Roarke again became nothing more than another unwashed, drunken woods loper. He could hear the boom of cannon in salute, the roar of the crowd in welcome. Then they were there, and Roarke found himself unprepared for the hate that rose like vomit in his throat, blinding him, shaking the jug lifted to his suddenly numbed lips. He swallowed and found himself once more in control, his body dead to all but his purpose, his vision so clear he thought he had never truly seen before.

Lord Cartland rode in a carriage, a young man beside him whose features proclaimed him a family member. Facing him, her back to Roarke, was a woman with a set, stiff back and powdered hair. He ignored the young man and the woman, his eyes searching Cartland's features. There was no change in the narrow face. Time had not coarsened the woman-fine complexion or sagged the clear, white skin. The pale eyes were still cold and contemptuous. Only the faint, disdainful sneer had deepened, grooving permanent furrows down past the corners of the lipless mouth.

Roarke's lips relaxed into a satisfied smile; his prey was only his, unshared with time and the diseases that plagued more mortal men. His gaze moved back to the woman and dismissed her. That graceless back, that high, imperious nose, could not belong to the one he sought.

Then he saw her riding behind the carriage, her riding habit the same dark green as she had worn in the orchard, the color of rain-drenched apple trees. As he had wanted Cartland unchanged, he had hoped to find her altered. He had wanted her thick hair to have dulled, to have dimmed to a dingy brown so drab and thin that even powder could not enhance it. Instead, it had become streaked in a mixture of gold, auburn, and chestnut, such as he had never seen before. He had imagined her poreless, translucent complexion ravaged by dissipation, and hoped to see the cankers of venereal disease eating at the full, red mouth. Her large, slanting eyes that shone first green, then amber, which had once met his with such demeaning hurt and pity, should have become hard and disdainful. Yet he could see only pride where haughtiness should be, only a joy for life where he had hoped to find scorn and apathy. And Cartland was taking her into the wilderness, endangering the life of someone so alive, so beautiful! Roarke felt an irrational rage and concern at the Irish peer's stupidity, and he pushed it down.

He stared at her, willing her to turn to him, to look at him. Then he dropped his eyes. No, he did not want her to see him so—not as a drunken, filthy woods loper, jug dangling from one nerveless finger, a three-day stubble of beard on his cheeks. His pride was too great, his hate too deep for the girlchild who had dashed to her uncle to betray a croppie boy stealing apples from an orchard that had once been his. If Montcalm could wait a few more hours, he could wait another day or two, Roarke thought, his mind forming plans.

And the Cartland party had passed, gone to the mayor's mansion. The only signs of their having been there were the excited babble of the crowd, the throbbing of Roarke's heart, and appropriately enough, he thought, a still-steaming pile of horse droppings in the street. Nor did he have time for musing. There was a tailor to visit, a cobbler.

The butler opened the door of the mayor's mansion to his imperious banging of the heavy brass knocker. Ignoring the servant's request for his name, Roarke handed him his tricorn with a withering glance down a haughtily lifted nose and moved languidly toward the loud humming of voices. It led him to a large, crowded drawing room. Weaving his way through the throng, he nodded to one curious glance, lifted a vaguely acknowledging eyebrow to another. But Lord Cartland and his niece were not yet there. Accepting a fluted glass of sherry from a passing tray, he positioned himself against a wall to wait and watch. The residents of Albany would assume he was traveling with the Irish peer, and Cartland would think he was a denizen of Albany. Bored, drunken eyes lifted to the ornately plastered ceiling, together with a disdainfully tilted mouth, should give him privacy.

But why he was there at all Roarke could not say. He had already accomplished his purpose in Albany. He had seen Cartland and had found him unchanged, had seen Lady FitzGerald and had found her beautiful. And time would bring them to him; his own resolution would make it so. Yet he was endangering himself and his mission to see Cartland and his niece one more time. He had waited too long to be such a fool now, when his revenge was but a few more weeks, a few more months away.

56

And he was so uncomfortable! He had lived too long in buckskins to be at ease attired as an over-dressed nabob. He hadn't had time to outfit himself with a wig. His hair had been set in lard in two small rolls on each side of his head. The remainder was in a queue, tied, after powdering, with a blue satin ribbon to match his pumps. It was hot in the crowded chamber room, and the lard threatened to melt in rivulets down his forehead and the back of his neck. He patted at it with a fragile handkerchief trimmed with lace. Blue satin garters at his knees cut off the circulation in his legs. The pumps he wore, with their high, bejeweled heels, were too large for his feet and the paper he had stuffed into them pinched his toes. Like his embroidered blue velvet waistcoat, the shoes had been custom ordered and the original customer had not returned for them. As the shoes were too large, the jacket was too small. The froths of lace at Roarke's hands disguised the short sleeves, but the jacket pulled tight across his back and broad shoulders. But he was at least indistinguishable from the several dozen other macaronis mingling with the gentry and the solid burghers of Albany.

Roarke resisted the urge to fidget, to shove his way from the room. Suddenly, all he wanted was to leave, to be in the tall, deep forests on his way to Mont-calm. Then the flow of conversation about him ebbed to a low, vibrating hum. Albany's august guests had entered the drawing room.

If Lord Cartland was impressed by his reception, he did not show it. A superior smile curled his lipless mouth and his gaze rarely made the effort of focusing on the person with whom he was speaking. Anna Redmond stood on his right, her face stingy with disdain, her nose pitched as though the odor of the chamber was not quite to her approval. On his left, Caitrin gracefully maneuvered her wide panniers and train through the press of people. The deep apricot of her silk sacque dress drew out the multicolored streaks of her hair. She smiled and nodded, but her features were tight with fatigue and strain. Taking a glass of wine offered her by a red-coated officer, she touched his sleeve with her fan, her features animated as she laughed at something he said. Whatever Roarke's need for revenge, he could not deny her beauty, her warmth, and he felt an inexplicable surge of jealousy as his eyes narrowed on her.

As though feeling his intent stare, Caitrin turned, searching the mass of people, and he deliberately straightened away from the wall, drawing her attention. She met his gaze, her own aloof then changing, becoming puzzled with an ungraspable memory.

He saw her brow furrow as her eyes questioned his, and suddenly he wanted her as he had never wanted a woman before. He wanted her beneath him, stripped of all civilized demeanor, his body degrading her with a lust she would respond to, her thighs opening to him, her hips surging up against him, her hands beating a tattoo of need on his scarred back. He wanted her at his feet whimpering for more, her face distorted by desire. He wanted to open her to a passion so strong it would be perverted by its own intensity, would deform her beauty into a mask of degradation, until the clear, bewildered eyes searching his were jaded with sexual corruption and the features that stirred in him the unbidden emotion of a more gentle desire were unrecognizable. He wanted to slam his seed into her until the slim, graceful body he craved, her hair veiling them as her mouth sought his, was distended and heavy with his bastard child, no longer capable of stirring desire within him.

Then he would discard her, pass her on to other hands, make of her a whore until she became a slovenly, shuffling slut unwanted by any man. Holy Mother! he wanted to feel her hair silken in his hands, her mouth soft and parted on his, her body lifted and accepting beneath him. He wanted to move within her until a moan of passion fluttered her throat, until he carried her with him to complete fulfillment, until he held her cradled against him, their needs sated and at rest. He wanted to see the children who would come of such passion at her breast or cuddled between them in a feather bed.

He saw her read the hate, the revengeful lust, the overwhelming need in his eyes; he saw her bewilderment turn to fear. Then the fear was gone, replaced by a responding need that turned Roarke's knees weak beneath him before she turned away.

Caitrin drew her lower lip between her teeth, biting down against the unfamiliar sensations gripping her. Never before had she felt the flood of weakness that somehow carried its own strength. Her body was no longer hers; it belonged to the blood singing through her veins, to the painful, demanding throb that ached deep within her, stirred to life by the consuming desire in the eyes of a man she did not know. Yet she felt she should. There was something familiar, something she should remember about the eyes that had regarded her with such virulent lust, with a hate she could not comprehend.

And she knew what he had aroused in her. It was a need she had not thought to know, a need not belonging to the ordered life laid out before her—

marriage arranged to match land and fortunes, a loveless bedding tolerated for the required children. Her only demand in a husband was that he not be of her guardian's choosing or for his advancement. The emotions shaking her had no place in such a marriage, could only weaken her. And the hate she had seen beneath the lust in his eyes terrified her even as she felt drawn by it, responsible for it. It promised far more passion than all the empty words of love and seduction whispered in drawing rooms, while dancing, on the sweeping lawns of Ireland lighted only by the stars. No soft, cool kiss she had exchanged in mild flirtations had touched her as had the demanding, hating eyes of a man she did not know.

Breathing deeply, Caitrin tried to quiet her body's need, to slow her mind's whirling. Then she looked back, her stare cool and objective.

The lust she had seen in his gaze was gone, replaced by a cold, blank enmity. And his eyes were clear, unmarked by the liquor in the glass he lifted in mocking salute. His steady gaze was a lie given to the slouched drunkenness of his posture. He was tall and slim, his blue eyes a startling contrast to the deep tan of his skin, the white powder on his hair. He did not belong here, among people of pallid complexions and delicate mannerisms. He was a woods loper, a coureur de bois as the French named them, Caitrin guessed. He was Roarke O'Conner, she suddenly, somehow knew, and William Johnson was right to wonder about him. There was a latent power in his lithe frame that spoke of a purpose held tightly in leash. There was a cold, relentless intent in his eyes that, for some reason she should understand, threatened her. Yet beneath the hate she sensed a deep, unhealed hurt.

Caitrin dropped her gaze to the glass held loosely in a hand with an effeminately cocked finger. When her eyes met his once more, one eyebrow was lifted in a derisive manner. Her smile deepened as apprehension leapt to his features. Then she looked away. Yet her hand still shook on her own glass and she knew he saw her tremors.

Roarke watched as Caitrin turned back to her companion, tapping him on his sleeve with her fan. He heard her light laugh lift above the surrounding babble and his worried eyes narrowed on her slim back. She had seen through his drunken ruse. The citizens of Albany were edgy; the war was too close and they would not deal lightly with a possible French agent should she mention him. But, somehow, he didn't think she would. She was no longer the child running to her guardian with tales of a thief in the apple orchard.

Nor did Caitrin look at him again. Yet his gaze seemed ever on her, drawing her around to look at him, to read the hate and need in his eyes one more time. She conversed and laughed, her features feeling stiff and false with her need to turn one more time to the deep blue eyes so filled with conflicting emotions. She smiled and flirted, while every moment she felt, in each cell of her body, the compelling gaze of the tall, slim man who had become the only other truly living person in the room. All others were but mannequins.

At last, Caitrin could bear no more. The air was heavy with smoke and the odor of seldom-bathed bodies. Perspiration trickled into the cleavages of the powdered bosoms around her. It beaded the powdered faces of the men pressing in on her. A plump, over-dressed woman was telling her of the licentiousness of William Johnson, of his many illegitimate children, her eyes avid with disapproval and a salacious interest. Caitrin smiled politely, her eyes on the tallow melting down from the woman's lard-set hair. Dropping her gaze, she watched a heart-shaped beauty patch float slowly, inexorably downward on a film of perspiration, over the woman's large bust to the cleavage between. Jerking her eyes away, she turned to a man discussing the virtues of bullbaiting versus cockfighting. Sweat blotched the powder on his crimson, porcine features, flowing from under his ill-fitting wig and into his tiny eyes. He blinked, then wiped at it with a filthy lace-trimmed handkerchief. Caitrin swallowed hard.

"Forgive me," she gulped. "I've really no knowledge or opinion of either."

Smiling an apology, she glanced quickly around but did not see Roarke O'Conner. With a sigh of half relief and half disappointment, she made her way through the throng, eyes downcast to avoid further entrapment. Without a respite from the heat and the press of people, the forceful gaze she felt ever on her, she would faint, and she made her way outside.

Roarke moved after her. A solid Dutch burgher with suet-heavy jowls grabbed his arm and drunkenly peered into his face. Something must be done, he insisted, to protect the populace from the French and their savage allies. They would be down on the colonies any time now, murdering people in their beds, men, women, children, and he was a man of property! He could lose it all! Lord Cartland must be apprised of the situation. Roarke looked disdainfully down at the damp hand on his velvet sleeve and the burgher hastily removed it. Perhaps, Roarke suggested, the French and their Indians could be bribed.

Or perhaps he might convert to papistry. Surely his property was worth the price of his soul. The man's jowls quivered in indignation and he let Roarke pass with a "Humph!" Roarke's mouth curled up in cynical amusement as he again sought the door Caitrin had departed through. Ignoring the interested, coquettish glances of several women, he followed Caitrin and his purpose. And he saw that he was not the only man to do so.

The evening was cool on Caitrin's upturned face as she strolled between rows of rosebushes. Their fragrance filled her head, and the stars in the night sky seemed close enough to touch. It seemed almost as if she were home in Ireland. A smile tipped her lips as she remembered a similar evening there, but then she had not strolled an aisle of roses alone. George Browne had been with her, his sweet smile and laughing eyes soft on her face. His voice had been beguiling with its brogue lilting beneath the affected drawl of the Irish Ascendancy. Yet even as he claimed his affection for her, his honorable intentions, she reminded herself that he was a second son with no property, no title. And perhaps her guardian was right in saying he was but after her estates, her fortune. George Browne, too, had soon joined the army, and Caitrin often wondered who had bought his commission. The Brownes, for all their lands, their position, were in financial straits, and she suspected her stepuncle. Even as she resented his interference, she knew it was for the best. Still, the soft words, the tender kiss, was a sweet memory. Then she sensed she was no longer alone, that someone walked with her, and she knew who it was. Yet she did not turn, her skirts swaying as she continued her aimless stroll. And the intruder moved with her. At last she reached out and caressed a half-opened rose, then turned around.

But it was not Roarke O'Conner she confronted. He stood in the shadows, watching, his light blue suit but one of several shafts of light from the full moon. He saw Caitrin's chin lift in surprise at the sight of the trespasser in her solitude.

Caitrin recognized him as one of the many dandies who had smiled at her suggestively, whose leers told her Ashley's lies had done their work. He now stood too close to her, his too-red mouth curved into a smug smile. Drawing her skirts close, she stepped back, outrage in every line of her body. Yet the fop ignored her disdain and lack of greeting. Instead, he plucked a rose and held it out to her. Caitrin did not deign to glance at it.

"A rose for a rose," he said, his smile a smirk, and Caitrin's lip curled at his trite cliche.

"I came out to be alone," she stated coldly.

"Ah, but a beautiful woman should never be alone," he told her fatuously. "Nor does she need to be."

"And if she prefers it so?"

"But you really don't, do you?" he grinned as he drew the rose suggestively down her arm. "Not a woman like you."

"And what kind of woman is that?" she asked, one arched eyebrow lifted.

"A woman," he smirked, still drawing the rose up and down her arm as her flesh gathered goose bumps from the loathsome contact, "who has been in the confines of a warship for months, with no privacy—and none since—for getting what she needs."

"And you think you will provide surcease from those needs?" she challenged, chin lifting.

Certain of his conquest, his smile widened. "I do. 'Tis said I've ways to please a lady."

"And you may please me by leaving!" Caitrin hissed, jerking her arm away.

At her words, rage replaced his leer. Grabbing her wrists, he jerked her against him, grinding his pelvis into hers. Her knee drove up but he held her too close for her to find her target, and she clamped her teeth into the flesh of his jaw. Yelping in pain, he pushed her away, his fist aimed at her face. Moving silently, swiftly, Roarke grabbed Caitrin's wrist, swinging her away from her attacker, and took the upraised fist in his other hand. Releasing Caitrin, he tightened his fingers over the other man's clenched hand, squeezing hard, forcing him to his knees as he sobbed his agony. Putting a foot on his shoulder, Roarke released the fist and shoved him over to his back. A cold smile curled his mouth as he gazed down at the man clutching his injured hand, tears flowing down his face, smearing his powder.

"'Tis my suggestion, boyo," Roarke drawled, nudging him with his toe, "that you do as the lady asked and rid us of your company . . . now."

Hunching over his hand, the man stood and backed away, eyes glinting rage. "I would call you out, sir," he hissed from a safe distance, "but I'm too much a gentleman to fight a duel over a woman who lies down with stable boys!"

A derisive smile marked Roarke's lips as the man scuttled away, then he turned to Caitrin. He had seen the man leave the drawing room after her, his purpose obvious. When he had followed them out, he had told himself he was merely curious. He'd watched the man approach her, had heard every word with the intent of seeing the seduction played through to the end, but he had not expected the feeling of outraged jealousy roiling in his belly or for her to fight. Nor, having seen so much killing and torture, should the sight of a woman being raped bother him. It was because it was Caitrin, he told himself. No matter how many men she had been with, his plans for revenge did not allow that another hurt her or bring her down first. He wanted her exclusively his in that. Yet rescuing her had put him in jeopardy. He could not afford to be noticed, to be questioned. Yet he lied to himself. He could have come to the aid of any woman in danger. But only Caitrin, he knew, could create such fury in him toward her attacker and such concern for her safety, and Roarke pushed the unwanted thought away.

He studied her for a long moment, seeing only pride in her uplifted face as she waited for him to speak. Nor did she flutter, offering explanations or accusations. There was no fear now in the eyes that refused to lower before his cold smile. It was as though she trusted him completely. But he could not accept such trust, not from her. And she so serene, so beautiful, as though the life she led, the perversion of her class, even the recent assault, had not, could not, toughen her. But he knew the gentleness, the innocence of her, were lies.

"A stable boy?" he mocked, echoing the words of her attacker. And she did not try to give him a denial or an excuse. Instead, she flinched as though from an invisible blow, drawing in her breath in a gasp. For a second, her eyes glistened with tears, then she closed them, squeezing tight. When she opened them again, the tears were gone. Bending over from a waist Roarke knew his hands could span, she picked up the rose her attacker had let fall and examined its bruised petals.

"'Tis sad, isn't it, to see something innocent or helpless injured for an evil purpose, even a rose," she said, voice round on a hidden hurt. Then she smiled bitterly. "A stable boy? Aye, 'tis said of me."

She looked away, her profile delicate in the moonlight, her throat a slim column of alabaster. When she turned back, her chin was lifted in dignity. Nor did she speak or offer an explanation, and Roarke's hand moved to trace the fragile line of her jaw, seemingly of its own volition. A deep, hard ache gripped his groin in a desire to hold her, to comfort her, in a rage to take her, to humble her. Then his fingers sank into the silken hair at the back of her neck as he drew her to him. His mouth touched hers in a kiss as soft as the brush of a butterfly wing, tasting her sweetness, her fragility, breathing her breath. He wanted to hold her forever, to love her with his flesh, his soul, to punish her with his body even as he protected her always from the evil of his own hate and anger. The need to simultaneously love her gently and to hurt her, to destroy the core of innocence in her, tore his heart, his mind, his body apart. She did not fight him nor did she respond. Her lips remained soft and motionless under his, as though she waited, for what he did not know. Releasing her mouth, he held her closer as he shook with the emotions warring within him. Then he heard her whisper as she revealed the pain and the steel beneath her delicate exterior.

"Is it your intent, too, to rape me, Roarke O'Conner?" Caitrin asked.

Roarke jerked her head back to stare into her face. She winced, yet her jaw was hard with defi-

67

ance, her mouth set.

"You bitch!" he spat out. "And do you think I would follow after a stable boy? Nor would I have to take you in force! I'm thinking you would lie down easily enough for me!"

To prove his point, his mouth took hers again, this time in a brutal kiss. His lips ravaged hers, drawing in her lower lip to suck at it, to bite at it, creating an unbidden flutter of desire deep within her. His tongue took her mouth, raping its softness, its sweetness, and he heard her unconscious moan, a plea to be released, to be taken. He felt Caitrin's ineffectual fists beating at his back, then the blows weakened as she fought the unaccustomed sensations surging through her. A curious warmth suffused her veins, spreading its gentle fire, turning her knees to water beneath her as a part of her mind wondered, Why this man with his lustful, hate-filled eyes? Why should it be this man, a stranger somehow so familiar, an unidentified man somehow so well-known to her, it seemed, with one kiss, that his blood called to flow with hers, his very bone to weld against hers, no matter his threat, his scorn. Her arms crept up to encircle his neck, seeking the support her trembling knees could not give, and her mouth, at last, responded to his. Her lips opened, growing soft under a demand that became gentle with the lifting of her tongue to his, with the faint sob shaking her throat beneath his fingertips. The giving of her, the sweetness of her, shook Roarke to the depths of his being, and he knew he groaned in reply, knew he could take her then, have her there, with the fragrance of roses in their nostrils, with the cool of the smooth lawn beneath their bodies. But to take her so would be to lose himself to her. And he shoved her from him, his face diffused with fury.

"Aye," he said, his laugh raging at himself, at her, "I could have you, and you willing enough!"

Turning, he left her, skirting the house as he went. He had seen what he had stayed in Albany for, and Montcalm was waiting. By dawn he was miles away, his moccasined feet taking him north. Nor did he wonder, for a long time, how she had known his name. It had seemed but natural that she did.

Five

Albany was some three days and forty miles behind them, yet thoughts of Roarke O'Conner still haunted Caitrin. Refusing to think of his kiss, his painful words, she could only puzzle over his hate-filled, lusting eyes, trying to make sense of his obvious enmity. The lust she aroused in him, she felt, was as unwelcome to him as her responding need was to her. It threatened each of them, no matter how diverse their purposes. She had known him before, but that memory eluded her, as though she would find it too disturbing. Somehow, too, she sensed that Roarke O'Conner's malice was directed at her guardian. Perhaps, she told herself, it only touched her because she was, however unwilling, a part of Harold Cartland. Yet, she knew she lied; his enmity for her was too personal. Nor could she ask her guardian about a man named Roarke O'Conner. It was as though to speak of him would betray a trust, a covenant made long before. And whatever his purpose she sensed it was clandestine.

Those few people in Albany to whom she had casually mentioned his name had looked blank and had shrugged, denying any knowledge of a Roarke

O'Conner. Yet William Johnson knew him, and considered him important enough, dangerous enough, to ask her about him. She considered his every possible motive for playing a drunken nabob. He might be an agent for the French, but the idea was too odious, too outrageous. It insulted her pride, her self-esteem, and was denied by the unacknowledged need he had aroused in her. Yet the suspicion kept returning with the thought that perhaps his people were not hers and a man was only a traitor if he turned on his own.

There were many Irishmen in the French forces but they were men from generations before, their very names distorted to fit the French tongue. And he was too young to have been one of those thousands who had fled Ireland to fight the English under foreign flags. Most of them were long dead, leaving only their sons and grandsons to battle under the lily flag of France. Were he one of their descendents, he would not speak with a brogue. The English had recently so graciously opened her armies to the Irish Catholic and it was under the banner of George II of England that Irishmen now died. If Roarke O'Conner had been driven from his home by hunger or futility, it would have been to the British army he would have turned. So she argued with herself, trying to find another reason for his behavior, his disguise. Whatever it was, it could only be counter to the well-being of the good, staid citizens of Albany and the colonies.

The journey north had taken them through forest and farmland. The farms and small villages were more scattered, the inhabitants more wary. Each town had a stockade. Each farmhouse was fortified. The people were alert and their eyes flicked past

Caitrin, searching the fields and forests beyond her even as they spoke. No man went about without a musket, and the women kept their children close at hand.

Breathing in the fear, Caitrin, too, became apprehensive, her eyes ever on the woods and thickets. She doubted their small company of untried English soldiers would be of much use. She had heard too many stories of the suddenness of Indian attack, of its ability to inspire terror. The soldiers, too, were nervous and jumpy, and their young, unblooded officer was more concerned with the impression his red uniform and carefully powdered wig made on her than with the column. In his nasal London drawl, he expressed contempt for Indians and for the provincial soldiers who fought them. Their abilities, he assured her, were vastly overrated. Caitrin doubted that he was, in fact, truly aware of any danger. If so, he was the only one who wasn't. Even Lord Cartland carried himself more stiffly, his pale eyes colder than ever, while Anna Redmond, her reproving tongue silent for once, stayed as close to her lover as his chilly lack of welcome allowed. Ashley went about with white lips and trembling hands.

Yet, for all their fear, Caitrin thought herself the only person to welcome the company of thirty rangers joining them at Saratoga. The English officer eyed their shabby and woods-stained green uniforms with a haughtily lifted eyebrow, offering only his fingertips in a handshake he was certain would soil the immaculate white lace at his cuffs. Lord Cartland had greeted their officer, Captain Robert Rogers, with the same contempt he viewed everything in this primitive land, ignoring the captain's mocking grin. Only when Rogers's eyes settled on Caitrin did his nonchalant smile fade into disapproval. Then his gaze flicked over her in appreciation and his grin widened again. It was a grin that seemed to invite her into a select circle mocking the fools about them.

With only a word of warning to Ashley and the English officer to put away their snuffboxes, he mounted. Indians, he told them, had an uncanny sense of smell. Then, posting men to the rear, to the front, and fanning out to the sides, he led them out, pushing them into a fast, mile-consuming pace.

It wasn't until afternoon that Caitrin rode forward and drew her horse in beside Rogers. He greeted her with a grin, then continued his survey of the rough road ahead as she studied him.

William Johnson had told her of this tall, stocky man, and others had delighted in recounting the exploits of him and his rangers as though they were their own. He hated Indians, having seen too much of death and destruction at too young an age not to. He had carved his small group of men into a force that fought with all the skill of his enemies, whose feats were among the few victories in a war plagued by blunders and defeats. He took his rangers in under the very noses of the French and out again, seldom losing men, taking scalps from heads within shouting distance of French forts. Winter's deep snows and cutting cold didn't halt them. They but donned ice skates or snowshoes and continued. Just as Caitrin, after an hour's silence, was wondering if he was naturally laconic or if the life he led had made him so, his eyes touched hers before returning to their searching.

"William Johnson wrote me about you. Said you had spunk," he commented. "He said I might be running into you, but he didn't say if your uncle's a natural-born fool or if he has a reason for bringing

74

you with him."

Caitrin shrugged. "He's no fool, and he'd tell you I'm his responsibility, that he's concerned for me, does not trust my care to another."

"That man loves no one, not even himself, and I wouldn't trust him to guard a piss pot without stealing the turd!" Rogers commented, turning his profile to her, displaying the strength of his firm lips, solid jaw, and the nose that descended straight from his forehead with no break in the bridge. That this man who had not exchanged a word with Lord Cartland should so accurately sum him up amazed her. And his brief words, too, had been meant as a warning.

"Lady FitzGerald, are you?" he asked after a moment.

"Caitrin," she answered.

"Mistress Cat," he corrected, grinning. "We don't put much store by titles and such here, leastwise those not earned. 'Tis a hard place," he added irrelevantly, "especially for a woman gently bred."

His glance appraised her again, then he settled more comfortably in his saddle, his eyes once more on the road ahead, and began to talk. Indians did not rape, he said, not normally. To take a woman before the age of thirty weakened them, and until they were properly purified, white women would defile them. So if a woman was captured, she did not have that to fear. Should someone be captured, the best thing to do was to close his or her mind to fear, to not think of what might come, but to concentrate on the moment. If someone could sustain the grueling march to wherever he or she was taken, that person had a chance to survive. To fall, to stumble, to lag behind, to weaken, was to lose that chance. If they held their minds to each forward step, if they ignored the

75

possible, probable brutal deaths of other captives, they might live. But to show too much strength was also a danger. Indians admired courage, liked to test it.

For a moment, Rogers's monologue ceased, his mouth closed on the ways in which courage was tested. If someone survived to reach the village, he said, that person's chances to live increased a bit.

Glancing at Caitrin's unusual hair, Rogers privately thought her chances would be next to nothing. Still, the Indians were fickle and there was always a possibility. And she might never be captured and his words better used to cool his porridge. He hoped so, but she should not be here at all.

In a village, he said, it was even more important to keep your head. A man was sure to see things that would, at the least, cause him to spew his guts. At the most, they'd drive him crazy. A lot went that way. Do what was ordered. Do not do anything stupid or foolhardy. Hang on by your fingernails and let the others do the same. You cannot help them nor they you. Pity was as sure a way to death as any other. A captive, too, might be taken north. The French paid a bounty for captured English; it encouraged the Indians to take more. And a woman might be taken by a coureur de bois, a half-breed or quarter-breed Frenchman. If she did not fight him, if she tried to please him, she might live. But do not think them any less savage than Indians. If anything, they were more bloodthirsty, more cruel.

Nor should anyone try to escape. To do so was considered either courageous or defiant. The resulting death, should the person be recaptured, would be long and painful.

Rogers's voice droned on and Caitrin listened, storing away each word. He was not one for idle conversation. He was considering the possibility of the worst happening and was preparing her for it. He was trying to raise the chances of her survival, if captured, from totally hopeless to a faint possibility.

The rest of the afternoon passed quickly, Caitrin taking in his every word. They dismounted and walked a long while. His long stride seemed tireless and she forced hers to match it, ignoring muscles aching with the unaccustomed exercise. Somehow, with the heat of the lowering sun on her back, its rays casting deep lavender shadows across the narrow track, she could not believe she would ever have cause to thank him. It was too peaceful. A soft breeze rose with the approaching evening and stirred the leaves to a faint rustle. Grasshoppers flew from underfoot, their wings beating a hot rattle. And still he walked and talked, and Caitrin listened.

At last, he ordered a halt and took her arm with a grin, leading her to a log where her body gave out beneath her, her legs shaking. Her eyes blank with fatigue, she watched the erection of the small tents to be used by Cartland's party. Caitrin only roused to accept a bowl of stew from Rogers, and suddenly famished, she began to eat. He, too, dipped his spoon into his steaming bowl, then halted, the utensil half-way to his lips as he listened to a sound she could not hear.

"Company coming," he stated. "Be here in a few minutes, and just in time for supper."

Then he returned to his meal. A few minutes later, Caitrin heard a sentry's challenge and a reply. Her eyes on the dozen or so Indians silently entering the campsite, she did not notice the man with them until Rogers greeted him with a slapping, pounding hug and a stream of welcoming obscenities. Then William Johnson turned and bowed, the courtly

77

gesture strange with the scarlet jacket he wore over buckskin leggings.

"I regret," he told her, "that your guardian did not see fit to leave you in New York, though 'tis happy I am to see your pretty face."

She tried not to reveal her curiosity and apprehension as Johnson introduced her to his Indians. Her eyes carefully averted from their ornately carved and knobbed war hatchets, Caitrin solemnly shook each dark hand. She met each pair of black eyes, not letting her gaze wander to the paint smearing each brown visage. The oldest, his sparse hair white, his tall form still straight, studied her the longest while she tried not to stare at the scar running from the corner of his mouth almost to his ear. When he turned back to Johnson, his words were an emphatic, guttural flow.

"Tiyanoga tells you, girl," Johnson translated, "to cover your hair. Its temptation is too strong."

"Thank him, and tell him I will heed him."

Tiyanoga held her gaze a moment more, then inclined his head slightly. Turning on his heel, he strolled away to join his comrades at their fire.

Caitrin watched his dignified departure, then sat back down. Somehow she had found little in William Johnson's Indians to frighten her. As though reading her thought, he nodded toward Tiyanoga.

"Do not," he warned, accepting a bowl of stew, "judge all Indians by my Mohawks and my Mohawks by their behavior now. They can be as savage as any, though these, now that they have met you, would not harm you, not as long as I've their friendship."

Sitting down next to her, Johnson spoke between bites of stew, bringing Rogers up to date on the latest stupidities of His Majesty's representatives. Study-

78

ing him, a concerned Caitrin noted that he had aged in the last few days. Illness had deepened the lines about his mouth and eyes, and fatigue blurred his features. He was traveling constantly, meeting with the Iroquois, trying to hold their allegiance. Accepted as one of their own, he was expected to exhort, demand, cajole in hours-long poetic pleas for their trust and loyalty, painting himself as they did, dancing himself into a frenzy that knew no exhaustion as they did, then bedding the women they offered him. And feeding his fatigue was the knowledge that the loyalty he courted could well be betrayed by the very people who needed the Iroquois the most. It lent a bitterness to his frustrated, invective words that Rogers acknowledged; however much they differed toward the Indian, they shared mutual respect, a dislike of bureaucracy, and a strong friendship.

At last, anger vented, the conversation became general. The men relaxed, drinking cups of rum. After regarding her a moment, Johnson poured some for Caitrin.

They regaled her with gossip of the affairs and stupidities of the personages she had met. Under prompting from Johnson, Rogers lost his reserve, treating her to dry, understated stories of frontier exploits. She soon realized his phrase "this man I know" referred to himself, "these men I know" to his men. Lounging back on a bedroll, his cup balanced on his flat belly, William Johnson, fatigue at bay, told her of Indian customs and beliefs, showing Caitrin another aspect of a people Rogers considered savage. Soon she forgot her own aches and fatigue. She was so caught up in their stories that she jumped when Lord Cartland spoke her name.

"Caitrin," he repeated, his features disapproving "it is time to retire."

"I'll stay up a while," she answered. "I'm not yet tired."

Cartland stared at her as she turned back to her companions. His ward, he decided, as he strolled away, mouth tight, had become infected with the lax and casual behavior so prevalent in this barbaric land. She had lost all respect for her station, consorting with upstarts and unwashed woodsmen. His grip on her was slipping and he would have to regain it. She no longer even bothered to defy but went her own way, brushing him off as she would one of the gnats infesting this heathenish land. There was no deliberate defiance in her refusal to retire as there would have been a month ago. She had not even considered that he might object to her companions. She had simply given his suggestion no thought at all.

Silently, he cursed Ashley's bungled attempt at rape; she would not have so easily resisted him. The thought intrigued him, then he discarded it. He had no need for passion. Anna Redmond, with her detached acceptance, satisfied what physical lust plagued him. Still, Caitrin would have to be brought back into line. He had had to bring her with him; she was too large a threat at his back and would deliberately destroy him if she could. She had no appreciation for what he had done for her, of the life of leisure and polish he had tried to give her. Rage seethed through him as he thought of the two louts she chose to honor with her company. He had seen their amused expressions at her defiance, knew they did not respect or fear him as they should, as did so many. He could feel their eyes on his back as he walked away, the contempt beneath their smug smiles.

Caitrin, too, watched him leave.

"He met twice with men. Both times they closeted themselves for hours," she told Johnson, giving him

80

the names of the men involved and the places where they met.

Johnson squinted in thought before stating, "They are all greedy, in debt or both, and fit company for Cartland. None would hesitate to kill his mother should it profit him. It but confirms my suspicions but does not tell me what they are about."

Caitrin sighed, pleating the cloth of her riding habit with her fingers to hide her disappointment. Her eyes were pensive and a frown creased her brow.

"Something else troubles you, girl," he guessed.

"I may have seen the man you asked me about, in Albany it was," she said regretfully, feeling like a traitor. Yet she knew she could trust Johnson.

"Roarke O'Conner?" Johnson asked, concerned to hear that the Irishman might be so far away from his trapping grounds. "Describe him for me."

"He is tall, slim, with black hair and blue eyes. He was dressed as a dandy, but there was something about him, something different from most nabobs. I would know. God knows, I've seen enough of them. And he was behaving as though drunk, but he was sober, I swear."

"That's the lad, all right. I'll keep an eye out for him, if he is still about," Johnson told her, then he grinned. "Liked him, did you, girl?" he asked, his grin growing at her blush.

"I did," she admitted, "but he frightened me."

"Why?" Johnson asked, squinting at her. Roarke O'Conner frightened many women even as he attracted them, but not to the degree Caitrin felt.

"I don't know," she lied, remembering the need Roarke had aroused in her and his hurtful words, even as the memory of his kiss assaulted her. "There was something about him. I felt I should know him, but I cannot remember from where. And it seems important that I do. Perhaps 'tis but a foolish female notion.''

"Why do I think you not a woman to suffer from such?" Johnson wondered.

Caitrin laughed at the compliment even as she shook her head to deny it. "I think I'll go to bed," she yawned, her fatigue and the rum suddenly overpowering her. "I think Robert Rogers has a hiking trip planned for me tomorrow, and early, too."

Lord Cartland heard the murmur of voices bidding his ward good night. He listened to the sound of her settling into her tent, yet he could not sleep. So he thought.

Six

When Caitrin crawled from her tent the next morning, William Johnson and his Mohawks were gone, and she decided it was for the best. She was in no mood for company and could only respond to Rogers's bright greeting with a groan. She ached from head to toe.

Stumbling back to the log where she had sat the night before, she accepted a slab of corn bread and a bowl of stew and began to eat. The meal, she noticed petulantly, was from the night before, and Caitrin forced the unappetizing food down. A ranger saddled her bay mare and she wondered how she would ever force herself onto her back—certainly not with dignity.

But there was no need for concern. When the column was ready to set off, Rogers approached, leading his long-legged, rangy grey and her mare.

"A bit sore, are you?" he asked, eyes dancing.

"You are," Caitrin retorted, "a man given to gross understatement."

"So I've been told," he laughed amiably as he scratched the stubble of his beard. "And the best way to loosen up is to walk it off."

Caitrin stared at him, incredulous. Then her chin lifted in the stubborn set her guardian knew too well and she stood, accepting the reins of her mare.

He was right, she discovered. Her muscles began to loosen as the sun's rays burned away the wet chill of morning. He held the pace down until her step lengthened into a swinging, mile-eating stride. His eyes were even more alert on the surrounding forest. William Henry, Caitrin knew, was the last fort on the English-Canadian border. Beyond, at the north tip of Lake George, as Fort William Henry sat on the south, at the Ticonderoga Narrows, was Fort Carillon—and the French. If there was a chance for an Indian attack, it was on this wilderness road. But the company arrived at William Henry without incident. Aware of the renewed faltering of Caitrin's steps, Rogers allowed her to mount again.

"You'll do, girl," he told her, boosting her up.

Caitrin smiled at him, aware it was not a compliment to be given lightly, not by him.

"Will you stay here?" she asked.

"No, I'm off to Lord Loudoun, to Louisburg. I don't favor forts, anyway. My men fight better when they're not penned up like cattle for the slaughter."

Then he reddened at the too-apt analogy.

"Fort William Henry is as safe as any other," he hastened to explain. "There are over two thousand men here, plus the women and children, and Fort Edward is less than a day's march away. What with the men there and the militia in Albany and New York, there's little cause for worry." But he had not called the men at William Henry soldiers. Caitrin pictured an assortment of everything from English and provincial soldiers to bateau men and woodsmen, and she wondered how many of them could be counted on to fight. And why, if it was as safe as

84

Rogers said, had so many people, himself included, disapproved of her presence there?

The fort, Caitrin thought as she rode through its gates, was a canker in the depths of the wilderness. Its rough, raw presence defiled the blue waters and wooded shores of the lake. The forest around the fort had been stripped and burned, the earth laid open and as raw as a wound for a distance far beyond the range of a musket shot. The trees and brush so cleared had been heaped into an impregnable, soot-blackened barrier at the foot of the remaining trees. The fort was an irregular square of embankments of gravel surmounted by a rampart of heavy logs laid in tiers and filled with earth. The lake offered protection on the north, a marsh to the east, and ditches filled with wooden spikes on the west and south. The blockhouse was of stone but the other buildings were all of log. In the encampment surrounding the fort were the latrines, kitchens, graves, and butchering sites, with no obvious design or concern for their neighbors, and Caitrin smelled the filth long before she saw it.

Caitrin gazed about at the mass of humanity, moving about on errands known only to themselves, at the cattle and pigs mingling with the populace, and she bleakly wondered how long she would be there. The odor of unwashed people, of excrement, of poorly disposed of offal, was overpowering, and she tried to convince herself that she would become accustomed to it, would soon not notice the stench.

Lord Cartland seemed to notice nothing. He gazed haughtily over the scene, even his narrow nostrils not quivering at the odors. Ashley, though, was pale, his eyes darting about above the lace handkerchief pressed against his mouth and nose. Even Anna Redmond had lost much of her aloof disdain. Her colorless lips were set tighter still and a scowl creased her forehead. Again Caitrin wondered about her guardian's purpose there. She had observed his disdainful appraisal of William Henry's fortifications, had seen a slight smile of satisfaction, and she found it was much easier to connect him, rather than Roarke O'Conner, with treachery. Whatever it was, she doubted Ashley or Anna knew much more than she did. She hoped, too, that she would know soon. Living in constant apprehension was nerve-racking, and living in this pesthole would make it no easier. The confusion of man and animal, of loud nasal twangs, of foul odors, of visible filth, overwhelmed her. Suddenly, she longed for the clean green landscapes of home, for the fresh odor of the sea and newly turned earth, for the lilting brogues of her people. Then she dismounted to meet the fort's commander and his officers.

Lieutenant Colonel Munro was a regular British officer. With him were several more men dressed in the king's scarlet. Studying him, Caitrin wondered if fatigue was a chronic condition of wilderness command. But there was a reason for his weariness and the lines about his eyes and mouth. He had taken over the fort from Major Eyre and had since been plagued with deserting men, as well as those bedridden with dysentery and smallpox. Often more than half his fighting force was ill. Now he had to keep his command in battle readiness while boredom assailed them all. Still, Caitrin told herself, Rogers had said Munro had over two thousand men. That included sailors and mechanics, true, but it certainly looked like enough, in these confined quarters, to hold the French and Indians at bay.

*   *   *

Caitrin found life at the fort tedious. There was little, she was told, for a lady to do . . . a lady who should not be there at all. Setting her chin, she observed the life about her, searching for a place for herself within it. In a community so large, there had to be something to occupy her. If Ashley had slandered her—and she was certain he had—there was little indication of it in the attitudes of officers eager to walk her about the stockade's battlements. Perhaps its lack was due to a tendency to judge someone more by his actions than by rumor or birth. Perhaps it was because many viewed Ashley's priggish manner and aloof posturing with amusement. Whatever the reason, she was happy to be free of slurring comments and insulting innuendos. Perhaps, too, they were afraid of the disruptions an attractive woman could create among so many males. They were men aware that any moment might be their last and tempers were stretched to the breaking point, yet each day was passed in boredom. Still, she could only look out at the lake, could walk around the battlements just so many times. And the view of the encampment, if colorful, was far from intriguing.

There were quiet evenings passed in the officers' quarters and meals with a menu that held little variety. They were certainly not enough to occupy her time. So Caitrin turned to the enlisted men's women and children.

Among them was work enough to fill her days and more. There were always sick children to be nursed and mothers to be relieved for a few moments to attend to others of their large broods or to seek fresh air and a quiet moment. Soon there were always children clustered about Caitrin as she told stories and taught them games quiet enough not to disturb their nervous mothers. The mothers and children, too, radiated the fear gripping all in the fort; any diversion was welcome.

Commandeering a small corner of the barracks, Caitrin set out to teach the children at least the basics of reading and writing and math. Interspersing her lessons with tales and songs from her own childhood, she held their attention for hours each morning. Sometimes, drained of all energy by the effort of controlling and keeping the interest of twenty-seven children, Caitrin wondered if she would be allowed time enough to teach them anything at all, so persuasive were the rumors of an imminent French attack.

And it was a task her guardian could not deny her. But he did try to take it from her. He told her it was unhealthy, that the people lived in a squalor encouraging disease and infestation, that she was endangering all of the better class of the garrison. His advice and orders ignored, he had gone to Lieutenant Colonel Munro, demanding that he order her to stay away from the encampment. Munro, concealing his dislike of the Irish peer, told him he had no control over civilians, nor could Cartland call the lieutenant colonel a liar.

So Caitrin and her uncle went their own ways. Cartland ignored her, the tightening of his lipless mouth, the added chill in his eyes, the only sign of his rage. But Caitrin watched him. He seemed to be waiting for something. He seemed so tense she thought that, were she to touch him, he would hum. He kept to himself, a silent, condemnatory specter, a solitary, rejecting figure untouched by the tension within the fort. Even a bored Ashley had condescended to enter the limited society, losing a touch of his hauteur. Anna Redmond, though, continued to hold herself aloof, every rigid inch of her stating her scorn of the New World and its relaxed ways, of the company within which she found herself.

Lord Cartland's long, twice daily tour of the stockade walls piqued Caitrin's curiosity. It always took him, at last, to a point overlooking Lake George. There he would stand gazing out over the view, waiting, she sensed, for the French. As they all did, no matter the hope that General Montcalm would go to Louisburg to meet the force Lord Loudoun took to attack that stronghold. But there was only a vague impatience in Cartland's watching. And Caitrin knew, whatever his plans, whether he accomplished them or not, he would not let her go easily. Should he succeed in them, he would draw her along with him, and if he failed, he would hold all the more tightly to her. Then she put her guardian from her mind. On July 27, the French came.

Seven

Rising early that morning, Caitrin dressed quietly so as not to wake Anna. The last thing she wanted, her temper never at its best when pulled out of a warm bed, even by her own curiosity, was to deal with the other woman's demands for information. Even Anna Redmond was touched by the fear holding them all, not sharing Lord Cartland's confidences as she infrequently shared his bed.

Still, Caitrin told herself, toes curling away from the plank floor's chill as she drew on her dress, if Anna wanted to know what was happening, let her find out for herself! She hadn't the time to tell her.

As it was, she thought, securing her hose and slipping her feet into narrow slippers, surely even Anna had heard of the activity on Lake George, of the enemy patrols. A soldier, straying too far from the fort, had been killed and scalped. Several English patrols had been ambushed, two returning with dead and wounded, the other not returning at all. The bodies found later were mutilated and one man had been taken captive, his fate assumed to be horrible. Munro was sending a detachment to reconnoiter the French posts, and Caitrin wanted to see the departure

91

of the flotilla of three hundred men.

The sun had not yet risen when she threw a shawl over her shoulders and closed the door on a sleeping Anna. The chill of early morning had not yet given over to the heat of July, but the dew had laid to rest some of the stench.

Climbing the stairs to the walkway around the stockade, Caitrin glanced back at the people flowing out the wide main gates. She was thankful for a view of the wallwalk, yet she wished she could join in their gossip and share their laughter, no matter how nervous it was.

The lake below was concealed by a mist obscuring the distant shores, the mountains beyond rising from it like islands in the fog. Wrapping her shawl closer, Caitrin stared down at the activity.

Three hundred men of the provincial army were preparing their keel boats, while their families, friends, and the curious pressed close, hampering them. Voices rose, excited, fearful, cut with broken bits of laughter, individual words soaring above the babble, some obscene, some bragging, some fearful. Then the boats were pushed from shore, helped by the many hands staying behind. They floated out into the mirror-smooth lake, the ripples settling into the calm water as though into oil, and Caitrin heard the shouts wishing them good luck, good-bye, good hunting. Then the voices died abruptly, queerly, into a fearful hush, and Caitrin waited, watching as Colonel Parker split his force, each segment disappearing into the mist. Then they were swallowed up as though by the water of the lake itself, and Caitrin shivered with a sudden foreboding.

It was the cold of early dawn that soaked into everything, she insisted to herself. Making her way to the dining hall, she wondered what breakfast would be;

92

probably corn bread and salt pork again. She sometimes thought that the colonial hogs, as stubborn and stiff-necked as the people, did not produce such delicacies as chops or bacon, out of sheer perversity, perhaps. But some beef had been slaughtered to keep it out of French hands, should they come, and she walked faster.

The morning passed slowly. The very air pressed down, holding time at a halt. People spoke in hushed tones, their ears attuned to the news to come more than to the moment's conversation. They stood in silent groups, coming together then scattering, seeking word, hope, relief from fear.

Caitrin, too, was waiting, listening, jumping at any chance noise. But this was not her war, she told herself. Nor were these people hers. Soon, when she turned eighteen, she would return to Ireland. There, the French would not threaten her, nor could her guardian. But she knew she would suffer as much in a siege as anyone, and a war hatchet respected no nationality or sex.

She shivered, thinking of those who still maintained a facade of optimism. There were, they said, two thousand men at the fort and another twenty-four hundred, at Fort Edward, fourteen miles away. Two thousand militiamen waited at Saratoga and four thousand more below Albany. After all, Fort William Henry could easily hold out against any force Montcalm might send long enough for reinforcements to arrive. But there was a touch of hysteria in the hope; fate had a way of tipping the hand in the best of situations. There had been too many blunders in this war. Whether caused by English arrogance or by simple cowardice, the victims were just as dead.

Closing her ears to both hope and fear—and her own apprehensions—Caitrin went about her tasks.

But her students would not cooperate. Touched by their elders' fears, they turned dull and vague or uncontrollable.

At last, Caitrin gave up, closing her book, telling them to return their few slates. Nor was she needed in the married men's quarters. Even the most fretful of the infants had grown quiet, as though waiting. The usually harried women sat in stiff, unwelcoming groups. For the first time since coming to the New World, she felt the invisible barrier of class and nationality. And she was unmarried, childless. She could not comprehend the mind-dulling fear of a wife for her husband, a mother for her children. Needing the women although they did not need her, Caitrin sat with them a while, listening as they did to the hum of flies in the dust-moted air, to the strum of apprehension played by their own pulses, to the shout announcing the return of the men that did not come. Then she left, unable to bear the pain of their patience. And they were not even aware she had gone.

The men in the infirmary were quiet, too, responding to her attentions with polite smiles that did not reach their eyes. There was no whining from the chronically ill, no groans from the injured or dying as they, too, listened. And Caitrin left them also.

In the light, she was surprised that the sun had risen so high. Sentries walked the fort's southern walls, while the northernmost were crowded with officers and enlisted men alike. Ignoring the need to join them, she strolled aimlessly about the stockade, meeting only those whose duties could not wait. She found the silence heavier than the usual clamor, missed the warm jostle of passing men, their nods and greetings. Even the cattle stood motionless, only their tails flicking at the flies worrying them. The pigs lay quiet in their favorite wallows.

Three times Caitrin wandered to the classroom, to the women, to the infirmary. The women waited, the bedridden lay uncomplaining. The classroom was deserted. Lunchtime came and went unnoticed. She wasn't hungry. Her stomach felt tight, her throat tense.

It was during her fourth tour that a shout was raised. It hung on the air, a solitary lifted cry from a sentry with eyes more keen than most. Then it was repeated from a thousand mouths before it fell to a roaring babble.

Picking up her skirts, Caitrin ran, climbing the stairs to the wall two at a time. Elbowing her way through the pack of people, automatically smiling at those she so offended, she ducked around the last shoulder and was at the wall. She stared into the distance, a hand shading her eyes as she searched the blue waters. Then she saw the boats, specks that grew draggingly larger. Only a third of those setting out in the early dawn were left, but behind them, like a cloud of gnats, was a swarm of canoes manned by thousands of Indians, and the impotent spectators held their breaths and hopes.

Only the artillery moved, leaping to their guns should the Indians come close enough. The rest strained forward in a useless effort to speed the boats toward them. They saw them slowly pull ahead, the men striving with all their strength and panic at the oars, the canoes dropping back. The watchers relaxed with a collective sigh. Only as they shouted their hurrah did they think of the other two hundred men, the thought driving the cheer back into silence.

They waited as the boats grew larger, as the terror in the faces of the men rowing them became clearer. As the first boat beached, a voice demanding news broke the quiet, then a hundred more joined it before they fell silent once more. Then the story was told, the single speaker's gasping words clear in the hush.

Colonel Parker had split his force, three boats leading, three more following, then the main flotilla, the last hundred men trailing behind. The first boats had just cleared Sabbath Day Point when, no warning shot fired, they were surrounded by canoes and captured, the three boats behind them taken in the same way. When the main force started around the point, they were met by a mass of canoes, a hail of bullets, and war whoops. Panicking, some fought back. Others leaped into the water in an attempt to swim away and were killed as they floundered amid oars, paddles, and swinging hatchets. It was soon over, the last boats arriving only early enough to see the water red with blood, to hear the last screams of the dying. There had been men captured; that they had seen, but they were certain to be tortured and killed. And there was nothing they, these last hundred, could have done that would not have been suicidal.

Caitrin listened, fear and grief catching in her throat. When the grim recital was done, her voice did not join the babble of rage and terror. Instead, she turned, unaware tears streamed down her face, and pushed her way back through the crowd. The women, the children, the ill and wounded, would need her now.

Then her eyes settled on her guardian. There was a light of satisfaction quickly suppressed in his face when his eyes met hers. Then he looked away disdainfully. Only when she turned away did his gaze follow her retreating form, his thin lips curled into a smile.

Eight

The next days passed in preparation. Whatever time the defenders had was too short. Fort Edward had been attacked. One hundred fifty Indians and Canadians had driven the pickets in, killing eleven and taking one prisoner. The apprehension suffocating Fort William Henry was gone, leaving behind a calm acceptance. The defenders went about their duties hurriedly, steadily. Caitrin still held her school, now to keep the children entertained more than to impart learning. The class, too, was reduced, the older children needed to help on the defenses. In the afternoons, she went to Miles Whitworth, the regimental surgeon, to fold bandages from any material available. Her jaw set against regret, she sacrificed dresses, petticoats trimmed with lace, her warm, lovely shawls, keeping only her riding habit and two simple cotton gowns. Nor was the thought of the trunks stored in New York a comfort, and she wondered when or if she would ever open them again, revealing their contents of fashion and frill. Gritting her teeth as she reduced each garment to long swatches, she couldn't but doubt that the delicate fabrics could ever bind wounds or stanch pulsing blood.

Each morning and each evening she walked the circumference of the wallwalk. The lake and the forest looked so peaceful, so undefiled by blood and war, but they would not remain so.

Nor did the French come as she expected, the view one moment serene, undefiled, the next filled with white uniforms and screaming, naked savages. On the night of August 2, Lieutenant Colonel Munro sent out two patrol boats. Unknowing, they moved directly toward the hidden French encampment. The enemy could easily hear the dipping of their oars and their voices as they called from boat to boat; the night was so clear, the water so smooth. They were almost past the French when an undistinguishable dark bulk was spotted and they drew closer. At first they thought the large bateaux abandoned, then they heard the bleating of sheep. As swiftly as they began to row away, the Indians on shore launched their canoes, screaming in pursuit. The patrol boats held their distance, then a quarter of a mile from the fort, they began to tire, and the Indians opened fire. Returning it, the English killed one Indian and wounded another. Taking advantage of the enemy's confusion, they again picked up their oars, fear giving them a burst of energy. As they reached shore, the fusillade from the fort drove the Indians back.

It was the musket fire that woke Caitrin. Above the throb of distant drums, she could hear the hesitant breathing from the other bed and she smiled into the dark. Anna Redmond, too, was awake, was afraid. There was little she herself could do yet, Caitrin decided, listening. To join the mob streaming from their beds would only add to the confusion, and she went back to sleep. Later, they would need her.

*　　*　　*

98

The French and Indians had not yet appeared the next morning, so Caitrin went to breakfast. Only after eating did she join the observers on the wall-walk. She was in time to see French boats appear, crowded with white uniforms gleaming against the blue waters, firearms and decorations glinting in the sun. She watched, thinking how unreal it seemed, how difficult it was to believe those men bore her malice. But their virulence was not for her. It would be easier to understand and somehow less frightening if it was. She was only a captive in someone else's drama. Captured by the French, she would be offered the protection due her rank and sex, but there was none they could give her from an impersonal bombardment soon to come. Glancing at the grim faces about her, Caitrin set her jaw and went to her classroom.

The children were attentive, as though to lose themselves in tasks where adult fears could not touch them. Only when the sound of distant musket fire intruded did their eyes become wide. The fort's answer calmed them, these children of war and wilderness, and their heads dropped once more. To comfort herself as much as them, she held them until it was the normal time to be dismissed. Caitrin watched them go, but there were no customary shouts and scramblings on their release. Then she sighed. She, too, felt subdued by fear.

But Lieutenant Colonel Munro had sent word to General Webb at Fort Edward, she reminded herself. Soon reinforcements would arrive, perhaps before the French could set up heavy artillery. In the meantime, she would hold no more school, not until the siege was over, and perhaps not even then.

Caitrin left the infirmary in the middle of the afternoon for a brief rest. A lull came in the firing as she walked to her quarters and she stopped a soldier to ask why. The French, he said, had called a truce. One of their officers was approaching the gates.

Climbing to the wallwalk, Caitrin saw a blind-folded French officer being led into the fort. Farther away, in the enemy lines, there was a mass of white uniforms, of Indians edging forward then back, scenting blood, eager for it, yet hesitant to take the first claim, like birds of prey on a still-stirring corpse. Shuddering, she looked away to a small group of French who waited some distance ahead of their troops. Above them waved a scarlet flag, its hue blood-red against the forest, and she touched the arm of the English officer next to her. Robert Mitchell turned, lowering his spyglass, the scowl distorting his handsome features disappearing as he recognized her.

"Hardly the same as the moonlight walks we took up here, is it?" he asked cockily.

Caitrin smiled back at his brash impudence, then asked, "Why do they use a red flag?"

"It's their flag of truce. Since their national flag is white, it saves confusion."

Looking back at it, Caitrin bit her lip. Its bright color somehow made the scene more grotesque.

"Would you like to look," Robert asked, handing her the spyglass, "while there's the opportunity?"

As she lifted the glass to her eye, the distant scene sprang forward. The French appeared so ordinary, so surprisingly normal. Somehow she had thought they would all be of one mold, exact replicas in their white uniforms. But they looked scarcely different from the English; only their complexions were a shade darker. Turning to the Indians, she gasped at the dark faces, the naked bodies made hideous with tattoos and paints of black, white, and red in bold swatches or intricate designs. Their heads were shaved, the remaining scalp lock adorned with feathers and fur. Their ears were pierced, the lobes stretched and drooping to their shoulders with the weight of brass wire and glass beads. They grimaced and gestured, leaping in and out of the view of the spyglass almost as though they sensed her gaze. Caitrin's hand shook and she gripped the glass tighter, focusing it on the Frenchmen awaiting the courier's return. She studied each face, wondering which one was Montcalm, which one his aide, Captain Bougainville. Then she moved the glass to a buckskinned figure standing at the group's edge, apart yet aloof.

Before she saw the features, she recognized the proud stance, the lifted head. He stood casually, long legs straddled wide, hands resting on narrow hips, a flintlock cradled in the crook of his arm.

Holding the glass in trembling hands, she studied the face in the circle of the lens, a circle dominating her whole vision, her whole being. The handsome features, the high bridged nose tilted slightly off center as though once broken, were the same. The firm, full mouth made for laughter, for kisses, was held so grimly that a muscle twitched at its corner. The eyes were a startling blue beneath black brows and his hair gleamed ebony.

Then the eyes were returning her gaze, staring at her, a strong lust and need beneath the rage and a long banked hatred that glinted in them. Caitrin jerked the glass down before she realized that he could not read the fear and dismay on her face, not at that distance. He only knew her by the streaked hair flaming in the sun. Lifting the glass again, she stared at him, saw his eyes narrow on her, a faint, contemptuous smile curling his lip before he looked away, dismissing her, to watch the return of Montcalm's messenger.

Slowly, Caitrin lowered the glass, nausea rising, knees shaking. Her fingers gripped the rough edge of the wall for support. She felt somehow betrayed and violated, seeing among the French the man whose glance had so aroused her, awakened her, knowing that her suppressed doubts and suspicions were true, that she had become somehow love-blind and foolish. His memory had stayed with her, had haunted her. Several times she had awakened from a dream of him, an ache of emptiness and want throbbing within her. The hate in his eyes had only raised her desire, creating an urge to smooth it away, to watch it disappear with a need responding to hers. Now, with a loathing that swelled her throat, that pushed back her shame, her desire, she answered his hate.

Feeling a touch on her arm, Caitrin jerked from her thoughts. Robert Mitchell repeated her name, his merry eyes now concerned on her blanched features.

"Terrifying, aren't they?" he commented lightly, inclining his head toward the Indians. "Perhaps I should not have let you look."

"They're grotesque," she agreed, her smile threatening to crack her lips. "But General Webb's men will be here soon, and I have to go to the infirmary."

"Maybe I'll see you there," he called after her.

"I hope not!" she answered, managing a light laugh over her shoulder.

But Webb's reinforcements did not come that day. Indecisive, immobile with fear, he ignored the first two dispatches from Munro informing him that the road was still open and matter-of-factly stating the serious nature of their situation. The third appeal was still controlled, its desperation dignified, admitting that the road between the forts was now blocked,

102

yet not condemning Webb. This the general answered, not from his own pen but from that of his aide-de-camp. It read:

> *"The General has ordered me to acquaint you he does not think it prudent to attempt a junction or assist you till reinforced by the militia of the colonies, for the immediate march of which repeated expresses have been sent. The General has learned that the French are in complete possession of the road between our forts. A Canadian prisoner just brought in and questioned has reported the French force in men and cannon very great, with upwards of eleven thousand troops who have surrounded the fort entirely for a distance of five miles. The General wishes you to be informed of these details so that, if the militia he has sent for arrives too late for him to march to your aid, the commander of Fort William Henry had better see to obtaining the best terms of surrender he can get."*

It would be three days before Munro discovered that the letter had fallen into enemy hands.

Nine

The day after the French appeared, Caitrin awoke stiff and sore, as though she had been beaten by invisible hands. It was her body's reaction, her very bones' reaction, to fear and tension. General Webb had not yet come. She would have been awakened by the exuberant greeting of the sentries, by the guns of the French, if he had.

Looking in her small mirror, Caitrin saw that apprehension had tightened her features, had drawn faint lines about her mouth. Anna Redmond's face, too, showed fear. Her skin was ashen, as though unwilling to admit her terror. Ashley's hand had shaken so at supper that the food had flopped from his fork, spattering the tablecloth. The others had simply averted their eyes. Only Lord Cartland seemed untouched. A faint smile lighted his eyes, a smile she could only recall noticing when he had seen a business associate beaten down, a recalcitrant tenant broken under the whip.

Caitrin wondered why the thought of him with a whip teased her memory, then she put it from her mind. Her step contained a calm confidence, a purpose, as she left her quarters. Whatever happened in the future, she was needed now. For a moment, a memory of blue eyes taunted her and she shoved it away, anger firming her jaw.

All day she worked. All day the wounded came, a few by themselves, more carried by comrades. She wiped brows, smiled until her mouth ached, changed bandages and sheets, her nose no longer curling at the stench of blood and gore. She forced whiskey and laudanum down pain-tight throats, offering oblivion to men soon to be under Miles Whitworth's knife. She watched the surgeon dress wounds and administer medicines from his rapidly diminishing stores, her mind cataloging every movement, each measurement. Too soon, she would be doing it herself, releasing him to more urgent cases. Only taking a moment to eat the meals brought her, she worked on until late in the night, when Miles sent her to her quarters. His smile was grateful and weary as she left, his request that she return in the morning following her tired footsteps.

It was a loud boom followed by the sound of crashing, flying wood, of screaming, of running feet that woke her from an exhausted sleep. The French had planted their artillery, was her first thought as she jerked up, her eyes flying to Anna. She was staring back. For a moment they were united by terror, then Caitrin jumped from bed. Moving quickly, she dressed, then was gone, slamming the door behind her. How Anna passed the day, whether in the safest part of the fort with the women and children she so derided or in the chill comfort of Lord Cartland, Caitrin did not care.

Flinging the infirmary door open, she tossed her cloak on a peg and turned to meet Miles Wentworth's red-rimmed, anguished eyes. He stared up at her as he bent over a man who tossed and turned in fever.

"Get out!" he shouted.

Caitrin stared at him, stunned.

"Get out!" he repeated.

"Why?" she whispered, her lips stiff with hurt.

Miles Whitworth's hand waved in rage, in futility. With the gesture, he seemed to cast away all hope, making mere chafe of their efforts.

"Smallpox," he answered, instilling in the words all the terror and torment the dreaded disease inspired. Caitrin's face went stark with disbelief and shock as she saw God's hand in a monstrous, cruel joke, and she wondered if they were truly cursed. "Now there are two enemies, one within the gates, one without," she thought. "May God and all his saints have mercy on us!"

"I've had cowpox," she said at last. "If you've had cowpox, you don't get the other. You know that."

"You would lie to help me, wouldn't you?" Whitworth accused. "Are you lying?"

"I would lie, yes," she agreed, "but I'm not."

Miles studied her a long moment before belief came.

"Then welcome to hell," he said, his harsh words denying the vast gratitude and relief in his face. Tying on an apron, Caitrin began her day. They had worked for over three hours when, suddenly, the bombardment ceased. The groans, curses, and delirious babbling of the wounded and ill surged up in the abrupt hush. Caitrin and Miles stared at each other, but only for a moment. They would find the answers to the question in each other's eyes too soon. Whether the silence meant the arrival of Webb, a truce, or a surrender, the men needed them, and they returned to their gory task. Whatever the cease-fire meant to the world outside, in their hell it was a blessed moment of relief, a time when no more wounded came, a time to possibly gain on the men still requiring their care. And it would be too brief a time. The shells fell again within the hour.

All day they worked, Caitrin ever at his hand yet finding time to bind wounds too slight for his harried attention, to cool fever-dry brows with rags soaked in vinegar. Adding her strength to that of the orderlies, she held down the victims of his knife. Her stomach in her throat, she held shattered arms or legs as the doctor amputated. Her own teeth were gritted in an effort to not scream with the unconscious patient as he cauterized each wound with a red-hot iron. Too often the body beneath her sweating grip leaped from the table to fall back dead. Too often they died before ever reaching the knife. And all day the artillery resounded, the fort guns answering the French until the few moments of silence seemed louder, more threatening than the bombardment. And always with them was the fear that the walls might be breached.

It was mid afternoon when a man was brought in, flesh laid bare and rippling where his jaw should have been. Miles had long since trusted Caitrin's judgment and she knew this one would go under the knife, hating herself for the decision even as she made it. Her hand was steady as she poured the whiskey and she wondered at it; her whole body trembled with fatigue and an unrelenting pity she had no time to weep out. Turning, she reached for the laudanum and found only empty vials.

"The laudanum," she whispered. "Where is it?"

Somehow Miles Whitworth heard her through the bedlam and looked up from the wound he probed. His hand left a bright banner of blood as he wiped away the sweat from his forehead. Closing his eyes, he fought fatigue and desolation.

"Gone," he stated. "We'll make do with whiskey."

"No!" she whispered, staring at him, stunned by the ignominy of what he suggested. Then she shook her head. "No, I know where there is more!"

Whirling, forgetting to remove her blood-soaked apron, she fled the room. Not seeing the shattered and flaming buildings, not smelling the acrid scent of gunpowder, of burning wood, she ran, skirts above her knees. She didn't notice the shells falling around her, didn't know her arm had been grabbed until her feet were almost jerked out from under her. The soldier's face was black with gunpowder, his eyes red-rimmed and blinking. He gestured toward the French line, lips moving. They formed the word *guns* and she laughed, shaking her head.

"I can't hear you!" she shouted. "The guns!"

Laughing at the inanity, she ran on. The soldier stared after her, then shrugged. He had better things to do than chase after a crazy, hysterical female.

Lord Cartland was where she had expected him. A glass of sherry in his hand, a book in his lap, he was sitting in the one comfortable chair in the officer's quarters. Oblivious to the danger, his very posture stated his immunity. As his ward entered and closed the door behind her, he looked up and lifted a perfect eyebrow sarcastically.

"The angel of mercy has deigned to visit me," he commented, his words an attempt to strip her work of dignity and purpose, to reduce her again to a worthless woman of smiling manners and false courtesies. "I do wish, though, my dear, that you had thought to bathe. You smell of the charnel house."

"That is where I've been—or in hell."

"Surely you exaggerate, my dear, and such degrading labor is hardly worthy of your attention or rank. Surely there are women of low birth to do such work. Changing bedpans and all. Disgusting."

Caitrin stared at him. There was no time to be drawn into an argument. No time to explain the conditions of the infirmary. Nor would he have cared.

"You have laudanum," she stated. "We need it."

"Ah," he answered, twirling the stem of his wineglass. "I had thought there was a purpose for your visit, but you are mistaken. I've no laudanum. I've no need for it. I haven't headaches or other such frivolity." He dismissed such weakness with a shrug as beneath him, and Caitrin wanted to scream that men were dying, that they suffered from far greater torment than a headache. "But why would you think I have laudanum?" he asked, only mild curiosity in his tone.

"Ashley told me."

"Your cousin, my dear, as you well know, is given to lying," he laughed disdainfully, dismissing Ashley.

Caitrin did know and her hopes slumped. Yet it seemed but hours before that Ashley had attempted rape, had told her of Cartland's supply of medicines.

"Did you know," Lord Cartland asked casually, his eyes amused on her dejected face, "did you hear, in that pesthole in which you insist on burying yourself, that General Montcalm sent another envoy?"

Suddenly wary, Caitrin lifted her chin, meeting him stare for stare. Beneath his amusement, he was gloating and she refused to ask the purpose of the French messenger. It could not be good; her guardian's obvious pleasure told her that. Nor did she need to ask. His news gave him too much delight for him to keep silent.

"It seems the French intercepted a message from General Webb and very courteously delivered it to our valiant Lieutenant Colonel Munro. Webb has decided not to honor us with his presence or that of his men."

Caitrin held his gaze, refusing to let him see her despair. There were still wounded to tend, ill to comfort. She dared not think of what the news meant, not yet. She pushed all thought of it from her mind and turned to the door. Her hand was resting on the latch when another thought came to her and she turned back.

"Do you know a man with the French, Roarke O'Conner by name? A dark man, black-haired, blue-eyed?"

For the first time, concern flicked in his eyes and a scowl of genuine puzzlement creased his forehead.

"No," he answered after a moment. "Should I?"

"Perhaps not," she told him, "but he knows you."

Not waiting to see his reaction, she left, closing the door behind her, then leaning against it. He had been truly bewildered by her mention of Roarke O'Conner, that she had seen, but he had lied about the laudanum. As she had turned back from the door, she had caught a smile of amusement curling his narrow lips.

Caitrin laughed softly as she picked up her skirts and ran to the infirmary, head lowered, shoulders hunched against the shells and noise. She would need help with what she wanted to do.

"The three of us," Caitrin thought, keeping watch as two orderlies ripped at the lock of the door with a crowbar, "must look like three demons from hell, attempting to breach the side door of heaven!" The men were coated with blood and gore, flecks and flots of it in their hair and in the stubble of their bearded faces. Their fingernails were black with it, and she knew she looked little better. "And this must be the door to heaven, if heaven means oblivion from pain."

Then, with a splintering creak, the lock gave way and the door swung open. It was a simple matter to break the padlock on the trunk. It popped open at the crowbar's first shove.

Throwing back the lid, Caitrin kneeled down and gestured to the men to guard the door. With no regard to delicate fabric, she tossed clothing aside as she searched. Lord Cartland would know she had burglarized his quarters, would know what she had taken the moment he saw the broken door. She would face that later. Pulling out the last embroideried waistcoat, she stared down at the layers of vials lining the trunk's bottom. They had been there after all. She scooped them into her apron, then not wanting to miss a single one, she groped about and felt a corner of something sticking out of the trunk's lining. Pulling it out, she found a silk-wrapped parcel in her hand.

Caitrin stared at it, her skin crawling as though she held a serpent. Then, overcoming her repugnance, she unfolded several crackling sheets of parchment.

They were bills of sale for land in New York. Manor after manor, estates, judging by the acreage listed, that were worth a fortune, William Johnson's among them. Lord Cartland's name was inscribed as purchaser on each, those of the men he had closeted himself with on the journey to Albany beneath his. Francois Bigot, Intendant of New France, Joseph Cadet, Commissary General, Varin, Commissionary of Marines, and Bigot's deputy at Montreal

112

were there, listed as owners, as sellers. The sale date was blank.

Nausea swelled Caitrin's throat as she considered what she had discovered. Bigot was greedy, a generous gambler. He loved luxury, wallowed in it, insisted on sharing it. His tastes were expensive, his debts large enough, certainly, for him and his confederates not to hesitate to sell land he did not own for a pittance of its value. It was only a matter of finding a buyer. But few in New France had money enough; the taxes imposed by Bigot, much of the revenue going into his own coffers, saw to that. So he had looked elsewhere for someone unscrupulous enough, gambler enough, to buy land in a country not yet defeated. And he had found Lord Cartland. But her guardian was not such a gambler as to wager where he did not consider the odds in his favor. He would have to have great confidence in French victory. Nor would he place himself in a position as perilous as that of traitor. All he did was legal or bordering so close to it that it would take a score of lawyers and a judge as wise as Solomon a century to unravel. Such would be the case with the evidence she held was he anywhere but in a fort besieged by French and savages. These English and colonials would not hesitate to hang him were they to see the bills of sale, the contempt he held for them in each line. And rightly so, she thought. This, too, was what William Johnson was looking for, but there was no way to get them to him. For a moment, Caitrin was tempted to take the parchments to Munro, then knew she could not. As much as she loathed her guardian, as much as she feared him, she could not be responsible for his death.

Yet, as she refolded the papers, she wondered if she would one day regret her decision. Lord Cartland was wealthy, but the sums paid to Bigot were enormous. To collect them he would have had to mortgage all he owned and, perhaps, her property as well. If he lost the gamble or if he had not been able to touch her estates, she would be more valuable to him than ever. She would be all he had left.

Shuddering, Caitrin placed the silk-wrapped packet back exactly as she had found it. He might suspect she had seen it, but he could not prove it. Still, he would wonder, would watch her carefully once he discovered the laudanum missing, and her eyes would betray her knowledge. It was too odious for her to conceal. There was little she could do but face him later, and Caitrin left the scattered garments where they lay. Gathering the corners of her apron up to protect the laudanum, she left the chamber, her mind already back on the wounded and ill.

Miles looked up from the man he was tending to see her triumphant smile. His own grin momentarily wiped the fatigue from his features, turning his face into that of a mischievous boy. Washing away the blood that encrusted his arms to his elbows, he came to her.

"Good girl," he said, eyes feasting on the laudanum as he helped her empty her apron. "We'll deal with Cartland when the time comes. Has there been word from General Webb?"

So completely had she forced the news from her mind, that she could not remember what her guardian had told her.

"Webb is not coming," she said at last, her voice calm. "The French intercepted a letter from him and delivered it this morning."

Their eyes held a moment, then he shrugged. "We have work to do. That we'll deal with later."

*   *   *

It went on forever. The wounded kept arriving. With them came the men with headaches so severe they could not see, with fevers so high Caitrin's fingers burned when she touched them, with backaches so crippling they staggered . . . the smallpox victims.

She worked through the day and into the night, caught sleep where she could and worked again. She now moved in a state where all was clear, where each motion was perfect. She felt as though there was no effort beyond her ability, no thought too abstract to understand. She felt as though they worked in a world alone, with no one out there who knew or cared whether the defenders of Fort William Henry lived or died. She saw the men, ill, wounded, dying, saw the ones who still fought, their wives and children as puppets moved by careless governments, puppets placed in a playroom or on a lawn then discarded, as a spoiled child would discard a toy. As the toy would be destroyed by rain, by a carelessly placed foot, or stolen, so would they be smashed, drowned in a rain of blood or taken into captivity. And no one cared. Had Caitrin known that two thousand men of the New York militia were now on their way to Fort Edward, she would have only shrugged, faith and hope gone. Nor did she miss them; they only weakened her.

Had she heard William Johnson's furious, profane tirade as he argued with General Webb, calling him a coward, begging him to at least give him the men so he, himself, might take them to Fort William Henry, she would have only smiled, knowing Webb's refusal certain. It could not be otherwise.

Had she seen him in a rage so profound that he stood before Webb and, button by button, braid and epaulets, sleeve by sleeve, insult by insult, tore his English uniform jacket from himself, throwing after

115

the shreds of red and white his waistcoat, shirt, buckskin leggings, moccasins, and smallclothes, until he was naked, then, hawking deeply, spitting in the middle of the general's desk, she would have admired him for his fury, would have understood it though far from passion herself. But she would have smiled, too, gently mocking his tantrum. The wheels were in motion and all the wrath of William Johnson could not halt them. If she had sensed his intense grief and sorrow, the humiliation he felt as an Englishman, she would have longed to hold him, to comfort him. But it was useless, she would have told him; all emotions were, as was all resistance to the circling of the wheel.

And she would have been right. At seven in the morning of August 9, 1757, Fort William Henry raised a white flag and Colonel Young stepped from the battered gates, back straight and head high, concealing his grief and shame, his rage at the betrayal, as he walked to meet the French.

Ten

Caitrin did not hear of the capitulation until twelve hours after the deed was done. Late the previous night, Miles had found her in a heap on the filthy floor next to a man moaning with fever, a vinegar-soaked rag in her hand. Her face was so white, the dark circles under her eyes so pronounced, that the surgeon felt a surge of fear. Squatting down, he groped for her pulse and found it even. With a sigh of gratitude, he picked her up and carried her to a corner. She would wake soon enough . . . too soon, he thought bitterly.

But Caitrin didn't awaken when the guns began again. Nor did he wake her. Exhausted as she was, she would have been of little use, no matter that he needed her. Two hours later, the bombardment ceased for good.

When Robert Mitchell entered the infirmary, it was late in the morning and still she slept. The English officer's boyish face had aged with war. His merry eyes were already death-weary, but they widened as he gazed about. The sawdust-strewn floor was stained with blood between the thin mattresses on which men moaned and sobbed in pain and fever.

117

Amputated limbs were tossed, crawling with flies, into a barrel near the gore-coated table. The surgeon himself seemed to be the arch demon of some unbelievable hell. Blood, some bright, some old and flecking rust, clung to the stubble of his beard, was matted in the thatch of dark hair on his naked chest, was smeared over his face. Even his eyes were bloody with fatigue as he studied Robert's nausea-pale features. Whitworth's voice, too, seemed strained, emerging in a harsh whisper.

"I'll thank you not to spew or faint, Lieutenant, I've mess and bodies enough here and don't need another. Why the silence out there?"

Robert Mitchell's gaze ceased its fascinated roving. He blinked and gulped, then instantly regretted it, the fetid odor bringing vomit to his throat. Swallowing hard, he said, "Lieutenant Colonel Munro called a truce. Colonel Young is asking for terms right now. Where is the Lady FitzGerald?"

Whitworth stared at him, dreading whatever terms the French would give them.

"Over there," Whitworth answered, nodding toward a dark corner. His mouth turned grim as he wondered what terms the French would give them. "Take her to her quarters and let her sleep. Post a guard outside her door with orders not to let anyone in, including that harpy who shares her room and her guardian."

Robert lifted Caitrin in his arms, his nose closed against her stench. She, too, was coated with blood and gore. Her usually glossy hair was heavy and dark with sweat. Her thick, dark eyelashes were spread like fans over cheeks smeared with tears and grime, and they did not so much as flutter as he picked her up. Beneath the dirt, her skin was pale and waxlike, and he wondered if this was the same woman who had

118

strolled the wallwalk with him, voice soft and lilting, eyes sparkling green or amber as she flirted. Then he carried her away.

It was late in the afternoon when Caitrin awoke. For a moment she lay in bed, absorbing the comfort and peace, then jerked up, the room strangely unfamiliar. Staring about, she realized where she was. But it was not where she belonged. She stood, one hand braced against the wall as her head spun. But Miles needed her and Caitrin stepped to the door. She jerked it open, then jumped back as the man who leaned against it fell through. His arms flailing like windmills, he fought to maintain his balance, stumbling forward then back before he stood swaying, while Caitrin giggled for the first time in what seemed like forever.

"What are you doing here?" she demanded, fear of her guardian replacing her humor.

"The bloodletter, Whitworth, ordered me here," he explained, sheepishly scratching his ear. "You're to sleep and I'm to let no one in."

"And I've had visitors?"

"Aye, ma'am, that harridan who says 'tis her room, too, and that cold, long-nosed bastard Lord Cartland." Then he blushed and scratched his ear, his eyes looking everywhere but at her. His language may not have been proper, he realized, but his sentiments were true and his own. Cartland had but looked through him once with those icy eyes and that had been enough. "I'm sorry, ma'am, for the cussing," he apologized, "but I don't like the man, neither."

"And haven't I heard such before . . . and applied to him?" Caitrin answered, smiling back at his abashed, agreeing grin. Then she sobered. "What time is it?"

"Almost dark, Ma'am."

"Why did you let me sleep so long?" she accused, heading once more to the door. But the soldier grabbed her arm, halting her.

"The bloodletter told me to. And he told me, when you wake, you're to be brought food and a hot bath. Until then, you're not to be allowed out."

"But he needs me," she stated.

He shook his head regretfully, then said, "He doesn't, not now. We've surrendered this morning."

"What terms do they give us?" she asked, the sudden fear and apprehension in her eyes reflecting his.

"We're to be released. They'll hold an officer hostage and send the rest of us to Fort Edward, and we have to swear not to fight again for eighteen months. They're taking our firearms and leaving us our baggage, such as we can carry. We've got to return all our French prisoners . . . the Indians, too." His eyes dropped to stare at the tips of his moccasined feet, avoiding hers. He had his doubts in the French pledge of protection. "They're to give us an escort protecting us from the savages. They say we have the Indians' word not to harm us . . . for whatever good that is."

"You think there'll be trouble?"

"I don't know, Ma'am. You can't get Indians to fight, keep 'em up with promises, then not come through. They'll be mad as hornets when they see all that booty, the scalps, the prisoners walking away from 'em." His eyes back on hers, he shrugged. "Aye, and maybe I'm wrong. It might come to nothing. I just don't trust 'em . . . lost too many of my own, my friends to 'em. Now, I'll see to your water."

Hunger satisfied, her hair once more shining and silken, her body clean, Caitrin began to dress. Then her eyes rested on her rumpled bed, and she succumbed to its promise of oblivion once more. Sometime in the night she awoke to angry voices outside her door. She recognized the stridence of Anna Redmond, the contempt of her guardian, then the nasal, immovable drawl of her guard. Chuckling, she snuggled deeper into the blankets and drifted off again.

The sun had not yet risen when Caitrin returned to the infirmary. She had put on her riding habit, in case they would march to Fort Edward that day. Her riding shoes, too, with their stout black leather and silver buckles were suitable for walking. She discarded as useless the dress she had worn in the infirmary, and the other she bundled in her last shawl with her hairbrush, a few cosmetics, and a pair of slippers. With only a glance to be certain she had not forgotten anything, Caitrin left the room that had been hers for over two months, wondering if she would ever see it again.

A guard was still at her door, a different one, but his steady eyes and firm chin were the same. Going with her, he tried to protect her from the jostling men and women who ran about collecting their possessions and streaming to the gates to wait. They were to go to the English encampment outside the fort itself, her escort explained, and they all wanted to be first, to get the best quarters. Then he left her at the infirmary door.

Caitrin blinked in the dim light, not believing it the same place from which Robert Mitchell had carried her. Fresh sawdust concealed the floor. The

121

barrel of severed limbs was gone to the graveyard. The table had been sandstoned clean, no trace of its macabre purpose remaining. The moans of the fevered and wounded seemed subdued, perhaps, Caitrin thought, due to the women and children about them. Even the stubble of Miles Whitworth's beard was gone. A fresh wig was on his head, clean clothes were on his body. His eyes, too, were clear with the sleep he had at last claimed.

"We leave soon," he greeted her, "when our escort arrives, the wounded with us. Will you go with us or with your family," he asked, his eyes laughing, telling her he knew her answer.

"With you, of course," she smiled back, then asked, suddenly concerned, "And the men with smallpox?"

"They stay behind, their families with them. We're told they will be well taken care of. Right now, see that the men on litters are comfortable. Some will need laudanum. You'll know the ones."

Caitrin turned to the task, using work to suppress her fear for those to be left behind. She had heard the surgeon's mistrust of the French promise in his voice, but she was as powerless as he was. And she knew Miles well enough to realize he had already tried every available means of protecting them.

It was a fear-haunted line filing out of Fort William Henry to the entrenched camp some eight hundred yards away. Although there were those who saw only relief at the end of the fighting, most felt exposed and vulnerable among the white uniforms of the French and the paint of the Indians. Caitrin walked beside Miles, her eyes straight ahead. She did not want to see the painted warriors who danced and grimaced or stood solidly threatening, their obsidian eyes the only thing alive about them. More, she did not want to meet the gaze of a blue-eyed man or see the triumph he must feel to see her so defeated. Then she put her pride aside at the surgeon's request for help. Some of the wounded could go no farther and he was demanding that the French surgeon be sent for. Together, the two men went through the line of injured men. Seventeen were selected to stay behind in several small huts, in the French surgeon's charge. To try to take them farther would be to chance killing them; Miles had no choice. Then why, he wondered, did he have the gut-deep feeling he was condemning them to certain death?

They would be safe and comfortable, Miles assured Caitrin, not meeting her eyes. Sensing her doubt, her desire to go back to the wounded, he gripped her arm, moving her along with him to the encampment.

The entrenched camp was a bedlam of confused and frightened men and women. The French bombardment had turned the trenches, the log buildings, the parade ground, into a lunar landscape of pits and craters. Many of the buildings still burned, the smoke stinging the nose and eyes. There were no trees, no grass, no living thing but the prisoners themselves, only dirt and the stench of gunpowder, of smoke, of the decaying animals. Outside the flimsy barricades were the savages, their thwarted rage and blood lust seeming to float on the air with a threatening menace that only stretched raw nerves even tauter. Impotent in defeat, the men bickered and fought over camp-sites. The women quarreled over blankets, ripping them from each other's hands, often turning into shrieking harpies, pushing and scratching. Then the officers moved in, pulling them apart, breaking up the fighting men, and some order was achieved.

Caitrin stayed with Whitworth and the wounded in makeshift huts, wondering if she, too, would have battled for a favored shelter or a warmer blanket. The veneer of gentility was thin, the urge for survival strong. Then, the wounded as comfortable as possible, she settled down to tend the women's scratched faces, the men's bruises, their bleeding and broken knuckles.

Once she thought she heard a scream, barely audible, a high-pitched and terror-stricken shriek floating on a shifting breeze, then it was abruptly cut off. Not certain it did not come from inside her own skull, Caitrin looked at Whitworth. He did not glance up from the man he tended, but the quieting of his hands, the tilt of his head, told her that he had heard it too. Her eyes then moved from him to the woman before her and their gazes held, reading the possibility they both refused to admit. Then, having exposed too much, they looked away, Caitrin returning to her washing of the four furrows on the woman's cheek.

Harold Cartland came, as she knew he sometime would. Caitrin was helping the surgeon set a broken arm. He stood there, clothes immaculate, narrow nose pinched against the stench. The only sign of his nervousness and anger was the striking of his walking stick against the shining black leather of his boots.

Caitrin scarcely glanced at him, then returned to her task. Even the flies swarming about her, crawling over the wounded, did not seem to dare trouble him, she thought. Then, the bone set, the splints wrapped, she settled back on her heels in a very unladylike manner and stared up at her guardian.

"You wanted something?" she asked. "Perhaps you have a hangnail or an ingrown hair?"

"Yes, I want something," he said, the full force of

his icy gaze on her. "I want the laudanum you stole."

"And what laudanum might that be?" Caitrin smiled, finding that his rage and cool contempt no longer frightened her. "You told me you had none. Can I steal something that does not exist?"

He stared at her, the soft chuckle from Miles Whitworth lifting a faint flush to his sallow cheeks, and his lips tightened. She was right, he knew, a frustration he seldom experienced feeding his wrath.

"And the other?" he demanded at last, his gaze never leaving her face. "Did you see the other?"

He saw the flick of fear and repugnance in her eyes before she lowered them, noted the guilty flush she could not control, and he knew then that she had opened the concealed packet, had read the papers.

"There was no laudanum, so what else could there have been?" she asked, aware that the blush betrayed her. But only the curl of Lord Cartland's lip showed his satisfaction. She wouldn't speak of it to anyone, he knew. She was too soft, as were all of her sex. She lacked the ability to brush all obstacles aside to reach a goal, to remove a threat, to ignore the ethics of lesser humans. It was her one weakness. Laughing abruptly, a silver blade of sound freezing the air, he slapped his walking stick once more against his boot before turning contemptuously away. Soon enough, he would control the little bitch once more.

Coming toward her, Robert Mitchell turned to stare after Lord Cartland, almost stumbling over a log as he did so. Catching himself, he stepped over it, squatting next to Caitrin, and handed her a bowl.

"Breakfast," he told her. "They call it cornmeal mush. These colonials can do the most atrocious things to the noble maize."

Smiling, Caitrin dipped her spoon into it, hunger overcoming distaste. Then she realized he was not eating, that his eyes were on her retreating guardian.

"Did you know he has approached several of Montcalm's aides-de-camp, demanding to see the general?" he asked. "Montcalm has shown the good taste to refuse him." Then, remembering Caitrin's relationship to Cartland, he stammered an apology, his flustered gaze falling to the bowl he held.

"There is no love lost between my guardian and myself," she smiled. "Or secrets to be told either. I don't know why he wants to see Montcalm."

The lie filled her with an uncomfortable guilt and Caitrin attacked her breakfast again, wondering why Lord Cartland wanted to see the French general. Perhaps he hoped to stay with the French, to go to Montreal with them. If so, he would try to take her with him, would once more have her under his control. She could only hope Montcalm would not accept him; the general was said to be an honest man, and he would have no use for nefarious plots and schemes. If he had orders to accept the Irish peer, he would have granted him an interview.

Caitrin's brow was still furrowed as she sent Robert Mitchell away. She liked him, she told herself ruefully, would have even considered him as a possible husband, but he was a younger son of an English earl and, as such, had chosen the army as a career. Lord Cartland knew too many men in the War Office, and he could break a promising young officer far too easily. Then she returned to her nursing, ignoring the sudden memory of blue eyes. There were too many more important things to worry about than the wounded affections of one Robert Mitchell, or the hate and lust in the eyes of Roarke O'Conner. There were some who felt that the French could not hold the Indians back, that they would come. And, late that morning, they did.

They could be heard swarming down the road from the fort long before they were seen. There was a hunger now to their howling that chilled the soul, that said blood lust had been aroused but not sated. On whom, the English did not know, but they, themselves, might be the next victims.

Caitrin's hands quieted as her eyes sought out the savages she could not see through the hut's walls. She gazed blindly for several moment's, listening to the pounding of fear in her chest. Then she glanced about. Through the door she could see women drawing their children closer even as they moved nearer to their men. But the men were impotent, stiff in their wary, frustrated stances as they clutched ammunitionless muskets, the gunpowder gone with their bayonets to the French. Then, setting her jaw, she returned her attention to the man she was nursing.

The militiaman had not winced when Caitrin pulled the bandages from the tender flesh of his wound but now he gripped her hand. She looked at him, but there was no pain in his face. He was staring at her.

"Ma'am," he advised, "you had best cover that hair, and with no fancy, frilly cap, neither." He was but repeating Robert Rogers's advice, but she had nothing to use. His brow creased, the soldier propped himself up on his elbow, listening to the war cries growing louder, then he looked at her again. "Use those," he told her, nodding at the soiled, blood-encrusted bandages she had removed from his wound. "Maybe they'll think you got no hair under them . . . got nothing but a patch of skull."

Caitrin wrapped her braids tightly about her head. Then, nose wrinkling, she covered her hair turban fashion with the long strips of cloth, she realized ruefully, that had been torn from one of her fine lawn petticoats. Tying it securely, she looked at the soldier. He grinned, revealing the gap where his

127

front teeth had once been, and nodded. The blotches of dried blood overlapped perfectly at the side of her head, giving the appearance of a real wound.

"You'll do, ma'am. Wouldn't tempt even an Abnaki."

Wondering how long she would have to endure the bandage, Caitrin smiled back, then finished dressing his wound. Her hands were gentle, but her attention was on the wild yells that came yet closer. Then the shrieking died on a last, wavering, nerve-crawling note. Giving the soldier a smile of thanks, Caitrin went to Miles to see what he next wanted of her and, she knew, to seek what little protection and comfort he could give her. His eyes were startled when he looked up and saw her strange headdress, and she giggled. He nodded his approval, then moved his head one time in an abrupt shake, acknowledging death's victory over his limited skills. Closing the dead man's eyes, he stood. His arm about her shoulder, he walked her to the door.

Indians and bush lopers, now silent, shoved their way into the English camp, easily brushing aside the compliant French guards. They moved quietly at first, frightening in their silence, in the way their avid eyes touched everything and everyone about them. Their every glance claimed what they wanted, what they would take. Little had been left for them at the deserted fort. Even the rum casks were stoved in to keep them out of their hands, and they were eager for booty. Traces of blood on the mouths of some, fresh scalps at the belts or in the hands of others, were grisly testimony to the fate of the smallpoxed men left at the fort, of their wives and children. Some of the scalps were old and rotting; even the English dead buried in shallow graves beside the fort had not been spared. Too soon they grew bolder, encouraged by the weaponless men, by the cringing women. They stalked about, brandishing tomahawks or knives, pinching the cheeks or buttocks of the men, licking their lips and rubbing their stomachs in a gruesome pantomime all understood. It was the women they took the most delight in, fondling their long hair, eyes gleaming. They grinned at the terror-struck mothers while caressing the heads of children.

Repulsed yet fascinated, Caitrin watched, moving closer to Miles Whitworth. An Indian approached, others behind him, faces and naked bodies painted and tattooed in grotesque designs. Beads and brass wires stretched their earlobes to their shoulders. Their noses were distorted by the polished bones or smooth rocks thrust through, and their eyes were gleeful and greedy as they searched for other, better amusement.

It was more with disgust than with fear that Caitrin returned the stare of their leader as he stopped before her. He grinned, delighted in her reaction, then he reached out and touched her bandaged head with blood-stained fingers. Tilting her head back, she glared at him, then remembered Robert Rogers's warning not to show too much courage. Reluctantly, she swallowed back her spittle but refused to flinch as he waved a bloody scalp in her face. Laughing, he pointed to her head, then to the scalp, offering it as a replacement for the one he thought she had lost. Then abruptly, childishly, he lost interest and pushed past her into the hut.

She turned with Miles, as determined as he was not to see the wounded harmed. Then she halted. A few feet from her, leaning against a post, was Roarke O'Conner. His flintlock was slung in the crook of his arm. His hatchet was in his belt, yet there was a watchful quality to his pose that denied his casual stance. His eyes touched her bandage, narrowed on it, then he smiled at the ruse before his gaze turned cold on her face. Caitrin held his emotionless stare, her own features impassive and uncaring, as Miles Whitworth's hand urging her, she entered the hut. The Indians had spread out through the crowded room. They threatened the injured men with tomahawks, pretended to thrust their knives into wounds. But it was scalps, prisoners, rum they wanted. They opened bottles of medicine, sniffed disgustedly, and tossed them away, scattering their precious contents. At last they left to seek a more rewarding, exciting game. Flinging the scalp once more into Caitrin's face, the leader followed them.

It was only when the shadow of the last passed out the door that Caitrin's knees began to shake with fear. Tightening her jaw, she pushed the terror away as a luxury she could ill afford and began to pick up the shards of glass, grateful for Miles's insight. He had seen her fear and rage, and he had been wise enough to let her fight it herself. He did not pat her shoulder clumsily or tell her everything would be all right, as so many men might have done. He knew that might not be so. His unspoken words had told her, too, that he shared her fear. He had, Caitrin thought as she sucked a cut thumb, even been wise enough to leave her the task of disposing of the broken bottles. He did not know it was the cold blue eyes of Roarke O'Conner that frightened her the most.

Unchallenged, the Indians grew bolder. Tempers held tightly in check, the men took it. There was little else they could do. One motion of defense, one violent reaction, would bring certain massacre. Yet rage and fear had reached such a peak in the English, the Indians had become so audacious that had Montcalm arrived even moments later that afternoon, the trap of tension holding the English and colonials would have surely sprung.

His rather high-pitched voice lifted in anger above the shrieking, and Caitrin went outside to see the famous French general. Roarke O'Conner, too, was out there, to watch, to gloat, why, she did not know.

Montcalm was a small man whose force of character negated his slight stature. He was not handsome. His nose was too large, too Roman, his forehead too high, but his was a face that drew people to him. His voice rang as he chastised the Indians and bush lopers for the breaking of their word. It went deep with contempt as he scorned their taunting of defenseless men, women, and children. Then it fell soft, reminding them of their pledge, of the sacredness of it, as he cajoled them on their honor as warriors. At last, first one by one, then in groups, they left the encampment. There was offended pride in the stride of some, shame in the step of others, but they all went reluctantly.

Montcalm watched them go, his mobile mouth grimly set, then he turned his mount after them, only to be confronted by Lord Cartland.

"Marquis de Montcalm," Cartland requested, his head tilted arrogantly yet still with the disadvantage of a man afoot addressing one on horseback, "I wish to speak with you—privately."

"Who are you?" Montcalm asked. He noted the thin white hand Cartland waved, the contemptuous gesture deriding everyone but himself and the general. The French commander's mouth tightened in disgust. "And what business do you believe you have with me?"

"I am Lord Harold Cartland of County Leitrim, Ireland. I believe you have had cause to hear of me."

"Your reputation, sir, has indeed preceded you. Even honest men have heard your name." Montcalm's narrow nostrils twitched with scorn. "I cannot think, though, of any business involving you that might concern me."

He urged his horse forward, but Cartland pressed closer. His action amazed Caitrin. Never before had she seen him debase himself and she could only guess that the stakes in the game he played were higher than she had thought. Only the angry, frustrated prisoners kept him from publicly stating his purpose. He might think them rabble, but he was still aware they would tear him to pieces if Montcalm were to refuse him protection in the name of Pierre de Vaudreuil, Governor General of New France.

"I am an Irish peer," he stated. "I've the most influential connections in England. During peace they extend to the highest individuals in the courts of France. I would have a word with you in private."

"If you have such high connections, monsieur, then your value as a hostage would be dubious," he rasped. "And what you were yesterday, who you knew then, does not concern me! Today you are a prisoner of war, no more and no less than all these about you, no more entitled to preferential treatment than the lowest of them! I am doing all that is possible to keep you alive. Be thankful for that and expect no more!"

He pushed his horse disdainfully toward Cartland and ordered Captain St. Luc de la Corne, the "General of the Indians," to surround the encampment with his Canadians. A sigh of relief from the prisoners greeted the sight of men in Canadian uniform forming a protective cordon around them. Yet there were whispered reminders that the Canadians, for all their white blood, their civilized uniforms, were often as bad, if not worse, than the savages they were supposed to restrain. Nor did

Caitrin join in the relief or doubt. She was noting the flush of rage on her guardian's powdered cheeks, the effort he took to control his temper. Never had she seen him so demeaned . . . and publicly! She gloried in it, knowing he couldn't, at that moment, vent his fury on her.

Yet Caitrin was ever conscious of the man standing behind her. In the hut she had sensed he was outside, watching, waiting. For what, she did not know. She felt threatened by his presence even as it somehow reassured her, stirring a wanting and need in her she did not wish to confront. She felt invisible strings tugging at her, pulling her around to face him. Fighting them, she held her eyes on her guardian as he walked away without a glance at her.

At last she reluctantly turned, knowing she had to; there was no other way to return to the hut. A small smile at the idea of backing toward it tilted her mouth, then was gone. She did not want to face him, yet her eyes were drawn to him. But Roarke O'Conner's gaze was on the tent Lord Cartland had entered, one eyebrow cocked in question. He, too, was puzzled by her guardian's actions, and he had to have even less knowledge of them than she did. But what his interest was she could not guess. Then his eyes moved to her, as cold and as impersonal as a winter sky. They held to her features, studying each with no sign of approval or disfavor, with only an icy appraisal before they moved down her slim, proud frame. His gaze traveled slowly, assessing her, stripping her, leaving her exposed in a way she had never known yet disturbing her in a fashion not completely unpleasant. When his eyes returned to her face, his lips curled in disdainful approval. His smile made of her only an object to be used and discarded in a way Ashley's attempted rape could never have done.

It mocked her even as his eyes told her he wanted her, demanding her response.

Seeing the blush flaming her face even as her chin tilted arrogantly, Roarke's smile broadened. His eyes followed her as she brushed angrily past him, holding her skirts aside as though the slightest contact with him would contaminate her. He frightened her. He puzzled her, and he found cruel satisfaction in the thought. She could not understand his purpose, his interest in her. But she had responded to the touch of his eyes. He had aroused her. One corner of his mouth curved higher before his smile abruptly faded. She had touched him, too, had opened something within him he had to defeat before it conquered him. Then he followed the Indians out of the encampment.

Even with the cordon of guards, the prisoners passed an uneasy night. Caitrin tossed in a dream-troubled sleep. Roarke O'Conner's gaze mocked her. He would reach for her, face soft and wanting as she could only hope to one day see it. Her own body would melt in a desire so intense it hurt, then he would laugh, triumph contorting his features into those of her guardian. Lord Cartland stalked her through a forest so dark and deep she could not see, yet all things were visible to him as Robert Rogers's voice twanged at her with advice always proving wrong. Her legs turned to stone, her throat closed tight as she realized she was at last under his total control. A dozen times she jerked awake to the nightmare-spawned shrieks of Indians.

When, at dawn, the war cries and the screams of their victims became real, Caitrin sat up, certain she was awake but not convinced of the reality of the cries. Then they made a perfect, horrible sense that drove all caution from her as she rose in one motion and leaped barefoot to the door. Miles Whitworth lunged for her from his pallet and missed, then she was gone, skirts lifted high on her slim, long legs as she sped across the encampment. The Canadian guards, eyes turned avidly, wistfully toward the screams, did not notice Caitrin until she had burst through them. They shouted after her, too surprised to give chase until she had far outdistanced them.

Her throat ached with sobs of rage and frustration, with her exertion. Her outraged mind drove her on against all fear and caution. Her only thought was for the seventeen wounded men Miles Whitworth had been forced to abandon. The only sound in her ears beyond the pounding of her heart was their dying screams. Caitrin, stride lengthening further, only sensed the man leaping to cut her off from her goal. He reached for her and she tried to dodge, then fingers grasped like steel on her shoulder. Stumbling and almost falling, she twisted like a cat in Roarke's arms to face him. Not recognizing him in her blind rage, she fought to be free, beating at his face, striking out with all her frenzied strength. Holding her wrist, Roarke swung her away from him, his free hand descending in an arc against her cheek. Her frantic sobs were cut off by the blow, her breath taken from her in a gasp. For a moment, her knees gave way and Roarke grabbed her other wrist, jerking her back to her feet. She swayed there at the end of his arms, eyes closed against the tears that flowed unchecked down her face, the print of his hand vivid red on her cheek.

"You stupid little bitch!" he hissed from between teeth clenched with fear for her, with rage at her recklessness. Slowly, Caitrin's eyes opened and she blinked, vision clearing. She stared at him, seeing his grimly set face, the white muscle that twitched at the corner of his mouth, the rage and fear in his eyes.

"Let me go!" she whispered. "They need me! They are being killed and they need me!"

Roarke stared at her, features tightening further, and he shook his head in disbelief at her stupidity. Seeing his refusal, Caitrin's head fell back on her slim neck.

"Please!" she sobbed. "I nursed them, washed them, cleaned them as though they were babies! I changed their bandages, washed their wounds! I held them when they were under the knife! Their pain was mine! I even stole for them! They belong to me!" Seeing no softening in his grim features, Caitrin twisted her hands in Roarke's grasp, holding them up to his inspection. "See my hands?" she whispered plaintively. "They were soft, beautiful once! And now the men they tended are dying, are being killed! Let me go to them!"

Roarke's grip only tightened as he shook his head, staring at the red and roughened hands, at the ripped nails. His fingers dug into her wrists as he fought the urge to pull her to him, to hold her as she sobbed her anguish against him. She was so small, he thought irrelevantly. If he were to hold his arm out level from his shoulder, she could walk under it without the top of her head touching him. Somehow he had thought she was taller. There was such pride in her walk, such grace in her high held head and slim back. Yet, for all her small stature, there was steel in her, too. His jaw clenched, Roarke battled his desire to strike her once more, then again. He wanted to wipe the grief from her face and replace it with pain, striking out, too, against the emotions roiling within him. Instead, he drew her into his arms, holding her close. His mouth pressed against her neck, feeling the pulse leaping beneath his lips. He held her so, rocking her, calming her, cuddling her. He felt her arms creep around him, felt a sob swell her throat. Her name came unbidden to his lips, a gentle croon, and he ground his teeth against it. A need to protect her, to shelter her always, twisted in his belly, shaking him with its intensity, and he groaned, rejecting it. He wanted to tell her the men were dead, that no one could have saved them, that he would have done so for her if it had been even a little bit less impossible. Then he thrust her away from him, into the arms of Miles Whitworth.

"Take her," he ordered, "and, by the Holy Virgin, watch her! The stupid little bitch will find herself dead and without a scalp yet if you don't! And, for God's sake, get her out of here!"

He turned on his moccasined heel, an acute, inexplicable jealousy welling in him at the sight of Caitrin in the arms of the English surgeon. Then he swung back.

"Her head," he stated, "it's not injured." Nor had he ever thought it was, but he had to ask.

"It's not," Miles agreed, wondering at the rage and hate and need beneath Roarke's concern—and at an Irishman's presence with the French.

But Roarke only nodded his thanks. A strange elation filled him as he strolled away. The worry he had felt since first seeing Caitrin's bound head was gone. It was just, after all, he insisted to himself, that she had not been wounded. No one had the right to give her pain but himself, no one else the right to destroy her as he intended to do.

Eleven

It was an exhausted, frightened column that trod the long Lyman road to Fort Edward. An advance guard of Canadian colony regulars led the way, and a hundred yards or so behind were the three hundred French regulars promised by Montcalm. But on both sides, in step with the prisoners, were the Indians and bush lopers. Blood lust aroused by the slaughter of the seventeen wounded men, the savages had once again descended on the camp. Fresh scalps swinging from their belts and no longer content with taunting and teasing, they began to plunder the English goods. The Indians were difficult to control, the French captain explained with a shrug, and he advised the English to give up their baggage. The savages, after all, felt justifiably deprived of the spoils of war. Hoping to appease them, Munro and his officers agreed. Yet capitulating only excited the Indians further, and the discovery of rum in a canteen created a mad scrabbling for more.

Now, fear-driven, the English moved as quickly as they could. The Indians and bush lopers crowded in about them, snatching hats, coats, muskets, and deliberately impeding the march.

Caitrin walked beside the wagons containing the wounded, aware that the Indians were not menacing her or the wounded as they were the others. It was a comfortless thought. They knew as well as she did that the wounded could not escape. Nor was there relief in being at the rear of the column. The French soldiers were close, true, but Fort Edward was farther away.

A high-pitched scream broke over the rattle of the column, quickly followed by more. Her foot braced on a protruding board on the wagon's floor, Caitrin pulled herself up and stared at the long line of defenseless people. Her eyes widened in disbelief and her hand moved to her mouth to press back a responding cry. The repressed whimpers vibrated against her fingers as she watched the Indians converging on the helpless women and children. She stared, unable to move, as a dozen, a score, half a hundred victims were borne off into the woods flanking the road. Their hapless screams mingled with the triumphant shouts of the Indians. The savages appeared, she thought irrelevantly, like ants swarming over a helpless, trapped creature who had inadvertently disturbed their hill, only to disappear beneath their sheer numbers. Then her mind leaped free of its stupor, searching frantically for a place to hide the body it contained. The woods? Under the wagon? There was no safe place. For a second, it considered propelling the slim form it found itself trapped in into the wagon, burrowing it under the bodies of the wounded. Caught there by indecision, by fear, Caitrin clung to the wagon's side as the attack became an inundating, concerted living thing. Indians swarmed over the wagon she stood on, inexplicibly ignoring her as they tomahawked and scalped the wounded.

Too frightened to move, Caitrin could only stare around her, with no place to go. Her eyes leaped about, searching for anyone, any place that might offer even a moment's safety. They fell on a man struggling to reach her, on desperate blue eyes in a face set in furious determination. His gaze holding hers, he forced his way through the swarming savages between them. But she had looked back to Miles Whitworth. She saw his grizzled head as he fought the Indians pressing in about him. His features were set in rage as he swung his musket about him, protecting the wounded at his back. The foolishness of his courage brought a hysterical giggle to Caitrin's throat, for the savages had already gone over the wagon's sides and front. The wounded he was defending were all dead. Then a hatchet was swung at his head and he went down, disappearing under the sleek, painted wave of Indians.

A tide of hatred rose over Caitrin. The threat of Roarke forgotten along with a fear for her own life, she leapt from the wagon. Her hands beat at the tattooed and painted faces, pounding into naked backs as she forced her way to Miles Whitworth. Perhaps surprised by her attack, perhaps deeming her insignificant and interested in more valuable booty, they parted for her.

Roarke saw her jump, saw her turbaned head disappear into the mass of Indians, and he redoubled his efforts to reach her. He knew he sobbed with anger and fear as he raised his flintlock, beating aside anyone in his way. He saw her just out of his reach, saw her final, insane thrust to reach her goal, then her shoulder was seized by a sinewy, dark hand and she was jerked to her knees, vanishing from his sight. An undulating cry of triumphant ripped from the throat of the warrior who claimed her. The long

141

bandage binding Caitrin's head was tossed high in the air, floating back down over the insane scene like a banner at a grisly festival. Roarke stared at it, fear engulfing him, and his flintlock slammed viciously into the back of the Indian blocking him. He saw the glorious gleaming of her hair, the terror on her features as she swung at the face of her captor, then she was yanked back to her knees.

"Caitrin!"

The wild, grief-torn cry ripped from Roarke's throat. He lunged forward between the bodies separating them, his hand outstretched to her. Roarke's cry penetrated her numbing fear and she reached toward him. Their fingertips touched, were forced apart by the weight of the frenzied warriors about them, then touched again, straining toward each other. Then her hand was tight in his, surprising him by its slim strength, and he pulled her off her knees toward him. He saw the hatchet rise, saw it swing down toward her head. His free arm lifted to it, catching the wrist of the Indian on his forearm, then his elbow smashed into the warrior's face, knocking him backward. Even as he lifted his flintlock to swing it butt end into the gaping mouth of Caitrin's captor, he saw the joy and trust on her features turn to disbelief. Her wide eyes were fixed on something behind him. Her lips formed a plea, then he heard a hollow thud over his right ear, saw himself pitching forward into a swirling mass of darkness. His fingers grasped Caitrin's once more, tightening as though to reassure her, then he felt her soft hand slip from his before all went black.

Stupefied, Caitrin stared up at the French soldier standing over Roarke O'Conner's prone body. He lifted the musket he had used to strike Roarke down, proudly showing it to her.

142

"These bush lopers," he explained, "are worse than the damned savages. They disgust me!"

Then he turned on his heel, his repugnance assuaged, and walked away. Caitrin watched him go, feeling herself in a nightmare. But it was no dream. Ruthless fingers tightened in her silken hair, twisting her to her feet. A cruel hand yanked her arm high up behind her back and propelled her into the forest. The screams and curses of the slaughter faded behind her.

Roarke swam in waters that pushed darkly in on him, holding him down. High above, he could see the wavering surface, sunlight bright on it, and he forced himself up. His body spiraled as he rose, lungs gasping for air, his head aching for it. He heard himself moan, felt his head lifted and the lip of a mug pressed to his mouth. Rum scorched his dry throat and he blindly thrust the mug aside, jerking up.

Sitting there with his throbbing head in his hands, Roarke tried to remember what had happened. For a moment, he could only feel an intense urge to rise, to be about on an imperative errand. He was needed. Someone who had trusted him was gone, was in danger. Then the memory of green eyes turning amber with joy, with complete faith, pushed his confusion aside. He remembered slim fingers that had grasped his, clinging with the trust that he would draw her from the maelstrom of horror. Then her features had filled with terror again.

Not realizing he groaned her name, Roarke swung his legs over the edge of the cot, his head spinning. Hands pushed him back and a mocking voice laughed.

"She must be much woman, your little English

whore, that you call to her in your sleep . . . that you attack the whole Cayuga nation for her!"

Roarke blinked against the blinding pounding within his skull and sat up again, his head in his hands.

"What happened?"

"You were playing the cavalier gallant, it seems, and tried to rescue the fair damsel from the hands of the red demons. A French officer," the speaker paused to spit his disgust, then continued, "misunderstood your intention—or so he claimed—and leveled you with the butt of his musket."

Roarke screwed his eyes tight, then opened them again. The ferret-faced, dark features of Jacques Leverett swam before his vision, then cleared, his stained teeth small and pointed in his thin mouth. Jacques grinned his delight in seeing his rival brought low and in such a comic fashion. Briefly, Roarke wondered if he could trust Jacques's word. The half-breed coureur de bois would not hesitate to lie in his jealous hatred. Things came too easily to Roarke—the best furs, the comeliest squaws, while Jacques's efforts, for no explicable reason, always turned sour. But truth or not, he had to have Caitrin back. She had been so near his grasp, had been, for such a short time, within his hand. Yet why he had gone for her and not to Lord Cartland, Roarke did not attempt to understand. Thrusting the memory of Caitrin's terror-struck face aside, Roarke stood up. He swayed, everything going black once more, then his head cleared.

"Who got her?" he demanded.

"A Cayuga," Jacques shrugged, disinterested. "Don't know. Don't care. And I was too busy," he explained, holding up two scalps, one a woman's. "Maybe Pierre Sorel, he know. Him it was kept your hair on your head when I would have let it go."

Leaning over to pick up his flintlock and his tomahawk, Roarke felt another wave of dizziness assail him. She had trusted him, had turned to him, and he had lost her. The thought raised a taste of vomit to his throat and he pushed it back. He walked to the door as Jacques mocked behind him, *"Ami,* you should not be about so soon after such a blow! And on an errand of love! She, no doubt, is dead by now, anyway. Is it not so? But if she isn't and you find her, give her a good roll in the blankets for me!"

Roarke glanced back at Jacques, ignoring the taunt. Then a chill shook him and he seemed to awaken as though from a dream. Reality returned, and he welcomed it. Somehow, he realized, he had allowed Caitrin's green eyes, her proud features, her helpless plight, his remorse at his failure to save her, to weaken him, to wean him from his purpose, his hate, and his jaw tightened in rage at himself. He had been stupid, had allowed her to make a fool of him. Now, he needed all his strength and wits to rescue her, to once again take up his cause, his need for vengeance. He used his carefully nurtured thirst for revenge, his hate for the pity in the eyes of a girlchild whose family had so harmed his, to drive back the fear the words of the coureur de bois had revived. He cursed Caitrin for being at Fort William Henry, for so seducing him from his resolve. Remembering Jacques's perverted pleasures, his sadistic cruelty toward women, he grinned.

"Mon ami," he replied, the wolfishness of his smile, the relentless light in his eye, chilling Jacques, "I will do even better. When I tire of her, when I have her big with brat, I'll give her to you. If you still want her. You like the sluts big with brat, don't you?"

Not waiting for Jacques to answer, Roarke ducked

out the hut's low door. The hazy sun of summer was low on the horizon and he had already lost too much time. He needed every moment and even then he might still be too late. If he had been robbed of his vengeance, he could only hope Caitrin's death had been quick. The prayer, he knew, was counter to his own desire to hurt her, to punish her, but so were the unwanted emotions he fought. If he were to be denied his revenge, he wanted no one else to touch her, to hurt her.

Twelve

The ground leaped up to meet Caitrin's every step, jarring her, tripping her. How many miles they had traveled she could not guess. They had not halted since the massacre early that morning, except for the killing of the woman. Now the sun was low, casting her captor's shadow back behind him. It darkened the path before her, hiding the exposed roots, the smallest obstacles so easily tripping her. And it took so little to throw her off balance, to send her stumbling into the back of the warrior who led her tethered by her neck like an animal. Each time she did so, he knocked her flat with a blow to her head, stunning her. Then he would stand over her, yanking at her bonds, his misshapen features torn between hope that she would not rise and his desire to return to his people with a captive. The temptation to lie there, to submit to death, was strong, the uncertainty of her fate robbing her of hope. Then Robert Rogers's voice would lift her up, reminding her again that if she could survive the march, her chances to live increased. And her survival instinct was strong, as was the memory of the woman who had not done so.

Caitrin had not known she was in the long file, not until she had heard her fall. Caitrin's captor had paused to see the sport, forcing her around to watch, also. His small eyes lighted with glee as they twitched from the scene to Caitrin's face, then back, promising her the same fate.

The woman lay there, broken, her only protest a sobbing grunt as a foot landed against her ribs, against breasts still swollen with milk for a stillborn child, into a belly still tender from childbirth. Her captor, furious with her passivity and mocked by the laughs of his comrades, hefted the woman half up by her hair, brandishing his tomahawk in her face. But she only stared at it dully. Suddenly bored with the game, he raised the hatchet, swinging it into her skull. Sensing his intent, Caitrin jerked her head away, eyes squeezing shut. Her captor laughed, twisting his fingers into her hair and forcing her head back around. Unable to look away, Caitrin closed her mind to what her eyes could not help but see. Ignore the misfortunes, the pain of others, Rogers had stressed, and she did.

The hatchet descended with a hollow crack, then the savage drew his knife in a circle about the dead woman's head. Yanking the scalp from it, he exposed a naked skull blotched pink and white, beads of blood salted over it. Taking such trophies, Caitrin reminded herself dispassionately, was not new. Four hundred years before, the English had offered a bounty for Welsh scalps, man, woman, or child, and William Johnson had told her that the Indians had not taken them until taught by the white man. It did not make the sight less horrid.

Then the hand twisting her hair let go and Caitrin fell to her knees. Bracing herself by her arms, she vomited up her disgust. Her body convulsed, straining to rid itself of the poison her eyes had fed it, the spasms ripping at her long after she was empty. She heard the jeers of the Indians, then felt her captor's foot on the back of her neck. He pushed her forward, pressing her face into the vile mess she had spewed up. Rage filled her then, a rage so strong it rendered her powerless for a long moment. She waited for strength to return, her slim frame shaking with the desire to rise, to attack the savage faces about her with all her force and fury. The brief defiance would be worth being borne down under the weight of a score of tomahawks in her head. But she might not be allowed a swift death. An act of courage, of defiance, Rogers had told her, was admired, was tested with torture. Her body cramped with suppressed rage, she forced herself to rise slowly to her feet. Then the fist of her captor slammed her back to the earth. She rose again; there was nothing else to do.

The Indians watched her hopefully, expectantly, but she only stripped off her many hampering petticoats and wiped the smear of vomit from her face. Disappointed, they led her off again, the pace they set harder, faster, as though to punish her for frustrating their hopes.

But the hate and rage sustained Caitrin, and she fed it with each branch her captor deliberately let slap back into her face, with each time he jerked her off her feet. He showed an uncanny talent for sensing each time her balance was precarious, yanking on her tether, stepping quickly aside as she sprawled full force to the earth, breath knocked from her. Then she was beaten for clumsiness. The first few times he took her by surprise, bloodying her nose, filling her mouth with dirt, scraping the skin from her face, but she quickly learned to catch herself on her hands. Soon they were bruised, torn, and bleeding, embed-

ded with bits of twigs and dirt, followed by her forearms, her elbows. Then she learned to fall on her
shoulder.

As the day wore on, Caitrin's rage and hate was
drowned beneath passive acceptance. Soon only a
vital urge from the depths of her soul drove her to rise
time after time, putting one foot in front of the other.
That, and the memory of the horrid, teeth-on-edge
sound of a scalp being taken, like that of a grisly
canvas cloth being ripped.

Yet she was thankful the Indians had increased the
pace. No longer was her captor allowed to torment
her, thereby delaying the others. Whatever their goal,
she reasoned numbly, it would bring her rest. Or
perhaps death, but that, too, would bring peace.

The sun dropped at last behind the tall, dark trees
and they came to a clearing in the forest. This was
where they were to pass the night and Caitrin
dropped to her knees, pillowing her swollen face in
her bruised arms. But her dry throat, her gasping
breath, cried for water, and she dragged herself to the
creek. Once there, though, her shaking hand lifted
with precious water, she was jerked back. Only after
the warriors drank could she. Soon, thirst assuaged,
face washed, she collapsed beneath a tree, refusing to
hope that she might be fed. Then her captor tossed
her a small cake of dried meat, fat, and berries. Her
hand shook as she lifted it to her mouth and a well-
aimed toe struck her hand, knocking the cake away.
She stared after it and her captor grinned as he
ground the pemmican into the earth under his heel.

Uncontrolled tears rolled down her cheeks, smearing the grease and blood the cold water of the stream
had not removed, as the delighted laughter of the
warriors buffeted her ears. Then a harsh voice lobbed
off their mirth.

"Ga-no-a-o-a!"

The speaker was tall and broad-shouldered. The scars at the side of his face, on his wide chest, and rippling down his left arm, the scalps at his belt, spoke of his courage and prowess. The ornate tattooing and painting of his body, now blurred with sweat and the blood of others, the gold in his stretched earlobes, his elaborate headdress, displayed his status as chief. His black eyes gleamed with contempt as he stared at Caitrin's captor. She could not understand his guttural rush, but there was scorn in its very intonation. Her captor cringed under the abusive tirade, then his huge chin lifted in blustering defiance. He strutted where he stood, hopping from one foot to the other as he spoke, his clenched fist waving at her in a possessive, terrifying gesture. The chief spoke once more and the others tittered. Their laughter drove Ga-no-a-o-a into a fury she was certain would be directed at her, then he shrunk before her eyes. The glance he threw her held pure hatred as the chief spoke again. Ga-no-a-o-a scowled, trying to show his disconcern, and raised an empty pouch. The chief's lip curled in contempt before he reached into his own war bag and tossed a cake of pemmican into Caitrin's lap.

Her hand closed over it, fearful that it, too, would be snatched away. She looked at the chief, her lips moving in gratitude. But he had not come to her defense; he had only chosen to chastise her captor. Hunger suddenly gone, Caitrin forced the pemmican into a stomach spasmodic with fear. Her mind became alert with terror and she studied her captor as she ate. It was her ill luck, she suddenly realized, to fall captive to their clown, their laughingstock, and he was all the more dangerous for it. He was small compared to the other Cayugas, with short, bandy

151

legs and a too-large trunk. His neck was long and thin, his round head sitting on it like a ball on a stick. One eye was cast to the side. His jaws were too big, the top of his head too large. Beneath his capering facade, resentment and hatred roiled. She had seen it in his brief defiance of his chief, in the angry glance he cast her way. In his twisted thinking, he blamed her for the role he had always played, although she had only just come to him. Now he, too, had a scapegoat, someone he could torment as he was tormented. One jeer too many could turn him on her with the swiftness of a striking snake. There was no way to predict his behavior, no pattern to guide her. To try to placate or please him would be thought weakness and he would hate her for it, but if she did not do so, she would be punished as lazy or insolent. She was his slave but a slave was not, Rogers had told her, always valued for his labor. A scalp held as much importance as did a living captive. Her only material value was the bounty offered by the French. But she had yet another value to him: She could be used to gain status with his people. It was this thought that most terrified her and she shook spasmodically with the fear. The Iroquois greatly admired a man who turned his captive over to the tribe for their entertainment, thus displaying disdain for possession, contempt for wealth, and pride in his prowess as a warrior. And the tribe's pleasure was in the torture of the captive. An Indian, so condemned, took pride in the testing of his courage, his endurance, his immunity to pain. He sang as the flames, so placed that they only blistered and charred, consumed him slowly. To honor him, to display their esteem, his torturers prolonged his agony all the more. The white man, though, resisted and railed against the honor and the Indians, to show their contempt, but stretched his suffering even further. As a woman, though, she would not be burned alive, not at the stack. She would be given to the women. And squaws put their men to shame in their ability to devise varied, painful forms of death. They knew where nerves sang at the slightest touch, where not to cut arteries, allowing the victim to mercifully bleed to death. They knew how best to apply burning splinters, sharp knives, to a captive spread-eagle and naked on the ground. Rogers had spared her such stories but the women at Fort William Henry had spoken of it, shivering in horrified fascination.

And Ga-no-a-o-a had so little to lose, so much to gain in giving over a captive. That he would, despite his gesture, still be an underdog, would only baffle and embitter him.

But thinking of it did no good, and Caitrin gulped air into fear-tight lungs, trying to control her shaking, which gradually ceased. The fear roaring in her ears calmed and she heard the whimper of a child. Never, Rogers had emphasized, allow compassion to weaken you. If you want to live, ignore the agony and terror of others. But a child cried. Opening her swollen eyes, ignoring the mad scene of Indians capering in the firelight, Caitrin saw a small, terrified figure trying to press himself into the foot of a tree. For a moment, she struggled to remember his name; the classes she had taught were a lifetime ago.

"Tommy!" she whispered, then she repeated it louder.

He blinked like a baby owl in the firelight, joy filling his pinched face as he recognized her. He was crawling crablike to her, casting glances about, when Ga-no-a-o-a grabbed him, dragging him back to his tree. Another warrior leaped forward, face contorted with resentment at Ga-no-a-o-a's interference with his captive. Then the chief intervened once more, waving Tommy to Caitrin. He scuttled to her, his grateful arms encircling her with a gasp. She rocked him, his head pillowed on her shoulder. She whispered to him, her fingers caressing his baby-damp hair, telling him he was too big a boy for such loving, almost a man he was, but just this once would do no harm. Even big grown men need such from time to time. She sang softly to him, a lullaby her mother had sung to her. She sang of a castle, of the peace within its war-battered walls. Her soft voice pleaded for the pity of Holy Mary, asking that all ill pass them by. Her words counseling patience to a child yet too young to take up the work of his warrior father fell on the sleep-deaf ear of the boy she cradled. Nor could he have understood them; the Irish that flowed over her tongue was unfamiliar, but the comfort of her arms was enough.

The next morning, his captor led the boy away on a different path. Caitrin watched him, knowing it was for herself she grieved. The boy would survive. The Iroquois lost too many warriors to kill a child who could one day replenish their ranks, and he would be adopted into the tribe if not rescued first. But she needed him. She had needed something on which to dwell, beyond a future offering only terror. To wonder where she would be now, what would have happened to her if the hand that had gripped hers had held, if Roarke O'Conner had claimed her, could only weaken her. She could see no further back than that; all else was too distant in the past to consider.

For four more days, they marched. Like an animal, Caitrin was fed and watered twice a day, and ignored as the Indians grew more intent on their journey's end. They became preoccupied with the exploits they would brag on, with the dances of triumph they would perform. Their guard on the prisoners grew more lax. They knew too well how bewildered an Englishman could become in the dark, thick forest. And the prisoners knew too well the punishment meted out to those who tried to escape.

Ga-no-a-o-a, too, made plans for his moment of triumph. There was still malevolent hatred in his eyes when he looked at Caitrin, but he seldom abused her. Her numb mind did no more than drive each foot forward, more from habit now than from fear of death or torture.

The sun's dying rays glistened on the river beside the village when they arrived. Caitrin scarcely heard the barking of the scrawny, slinking dogs, the shouts of the children. Her eyes were blurred to the scattered bark-covered log houses she was driven past. The women's shoves and blows seemed but a continuation of her nightmare journey. When she was pushed forward to be presented to Ga-no-a-o-a's wife, she stumbled over an out thrust moccasin and fell once more. She tried to rise out of long habit, but a foot pressed into her back held her down.

Ga-no-a-o-a's voice, loud and boastful, was answered by one shrill with scorn. Her captor's wife was not as pleased as he had hoped, and Caitrin sensed that she would bear the brunt of her displeasure. Then she was jerked to her feet and a fist slammed against her head. Ga-no-a-o-a, the imp still living in Caitrin's mind whispered, even lacked the strength of his wife. Her ears ringing, her knees turned boneless, she was shoved into a house and pushed into a

155

corner. A large hand thrust a bowl of succotash at her, then she was left alone. The entertainment outside promised more amusement than the tormenting of an exhausted and spiritless woman.

Caitrin ate more from fear of offending than from hunger. Then, meal finished, she fell into a deep sleep. She did not hear the man tortured at the stake. His screams were but the shadows of nightmares flitting over her bruised and swollen features. Several times brutal hands tried to rouse her enough to witness his suffering. But she only moaned in her slumber, curling her body to protect her belly from the kicks aimed there. She was spared the fear that would have been hers had she seen the rage Ga-no-a-o-a's wife took out on him. The passivity of the captive he had presented her did not please his wife.

But captives, scalps, and stories of glory were not all that the triumphant Cayuga brought home with them. They brought an enemy more deadly than the white man, than the harshest winter. They brought smallpox.

Thirteen

A rough hand shook her and Caitrin whimpered an objection. In her dreams she knew what awaited her and she fought to retain her grip on sleep. Then she was lifted up by cruel fingers twisted in her hair. A stinging slap jerked her about, and sobbing a protest, she opened her eyes.

A woman, tall, broad, and muscular even among women known for their unusual height, stood over her. A lumpy nose divided a long face made ugly with years of frustration and resentment. Her arms were as big around as Caitrin's thighs and her enormous breasts, covered only by a multitude of beads, hung to her thick waist. Seeing the foot lifted to aim a blow into her ribs, Caitrin scrambled to her feet. Pleased, Nun-da-wa-o stood back, hamlike hands on huge hips, sneering contempt as she surveyed her slave. Sensing entertainment, the other women of the longhouse crowded about. Their black eyes gleamed pleasure, flicking from Nun-da-wa-o's dissatisfied features to the captive's frightened ones. Her audience captured, Nun-da-wa-o lifted her voice in a jeering castigation of her husband's many failures as a warrior, as a hunter. His every misfortune was recited and relished in great detail. His ancestry as a Cayuga was doubted, his parentage placed on the possible union of a toad and a whooping crane. Even his abilities as a husband were ridiculed with obscene gestures measuring the size of his manhood and his lack of skill in the use of it. Then Nun-da-wa-o turned her scathing attention to the pitiful captive he had dared bring her, further proof of his poor prowess as a warrior. With jabbing fingers, she pointed to the fragile bones of Caitrin's wrists, to her small shoulders, to her lack of height.

Caitrin cowered under the ridicule, then the pride and anger that had sustained her so often in her life lifted her head. She straightened her shoulders. Her small jaw was set haughtily as her eyes, amber with disdain, stared back at Nun-da-wa-o.

The calm defiance did not halt the squaw's jeering, but the disparaging tone gradually became boastful. The words still belittled, but they turned back on themselves. Now they pointed out through ridicule attributes surely visible to all. The mocking of Caitrin's slim body but emphasized the strength that had carried her on a journey where many stronger women perished. The jeers at skin so pale, so delicate, only called attention to the punishment so small and fragile a woman had endured.

Then Nun-da-wa-o caught her large nose between her fingers, face wrinkled at Caitrin's odor. As though by signal, the women jumped on the captive, tearing her clothes from her. To their delight, she fought back, but their numbers bore her down and stripped her naked in seconds. Their victim now nude, the women stepped back to relish the scorned modesty all white women displayed. Caitrin's hands fluttered, trying to cover her nakedness. She cringed under their mocking glee, then her rage surged back.

Her hands dropped and her chin lifted. The women's laughter acknowledged her pride. Their taunts pointed out the whiteness of her skin, the high roundness of her breasts, the pink of her nipples, the tiny waist sloping into slim hips. The very difference of her trim figure pleasing them, they stripped off their own few garments to compare length of leg, size of waist, width of shoulders. Then they pushed her out the door of the longhouse to the river to bathe.

Her skin scoured raw, her scalp tingling, Caitrin lay back on the soft grass of the riverbank. The sun warmed her naked body, and she could hear the gossiping women around her. The scene's very serenity frightened her, threatened to lull her into lethargy. She had quickly learned that the whims of Indians changed with the blink of an eye. Their admiration of the hair streaked with the colors of autumn could too soon turn to jeers as they mimicked the taking of a scalp. Their toleration could become cruel abuse in the flash of a second. And the deceptive peace was shattered with the first thought of chores left undone. Instantly, she was blamed. She was jerked to her feet and propelled back to the village by a score of angry, shoving, pummeling hands as she fought to keep her balance. To fall would bring a dozen feet slamming into her ribs, her belly, her head. Then, suddenly, in one accord, they halted their wild race. Their shrill voices lifted in delight as, with one mind, they yanked her about to see the blackened, burnt figure at the stake.

At first, Caitrin thought it a fingerless, toeless, earless effigy. Then, as a moan issued from its broken and blistered lips, she realized it was human and still alive.

Her head swam. Vomit rose to her throat. Only the dozen cruelly tight hands held her to her feet. Caitrin blinked, forcing her dizziness away, her sudden fear and disgust giving her strength. Too often, as a child, she had cringed under her guardian's contemptuous abuse as he tried to break her with scorn and insult. Then she had learned to fight back with the only weapons she had, her disdain and hatred and impassive features allowing no fear or pain to show itself. She learned, too, to close her mind, to allow no emotion to touch her, to break her.

It was this lesson that came to her aid as she faced the figure at the stake. He, she realized, was an Englishman, his face painted black, who been with her on the trail. He had told her, an affected London drawl in his conspiratorial whisper, that she had nothing to fear, that the Iroquois did not rape. His condescending warning had drawn several blows for her from Ga-no-a-o-a. She had resented him and his disdain of women then, and she used that resentment to further dull the nausea and fear assaulting her. Her mouth curved into a wry, scornful smile as she wondered if he still thought rape all there was to fear. She now knew, too, why his face had been painted black. It was the mark of death, a harbinger of the soot that now coated his twisted features. Only a twitching at the corner of her eye betrayed agitation when a warrior leaped forward to jam a pointed stick into the charred flesh of the figure's groin. His single, high-pitched scream vibrated along her own nerve endings, but her features remained unaffected. Then she remembered Rogers's warning not to display excessive courage, and her stoicism plunged back into abject terror as the jeering of the women quieted. They seemed to back away from her in silent respect even as they stood motionless.

Yet there was no other way she could behave. She had learned no other way to face adversity than with lifted chin and challenging eyes. Lord Cartland had taught her too well and too early for her to forget now. She could not cringe, not for long. Nor could she allow herself to conjure up a future of even more painful forms of torture than could the fertile minds of the squaws. That way lay insanity, and she needed all her wits about her to survive. The slightest error would bring certain death.

So Caitrin drew a mantle of impassive strength about her. She sat and watched the continued torture with calm, shuttered eyes. His diminishing screams, the horror of what her brain would not allow her eyes to witness, could not touch her as the sun rose to its zenith, then fell slowly into the trees. Only at his death late in the night, when she was returned to the dark security of her corner, did Caitrin allow the horror to overcome her. Secure from pitiless, avid eyes, she shook with silent sobs of compassion and fear.

The next morning Caitrin's mask was again in place and she set about learning all Nun-da-wa-o would teach her, encouraged by kicks and blows. Her hands cramped about a pestle, she pounded hard kernels of corn to a fine powder in a mortar. Her back aching, her face sunburned, she bent for endless hours to weed countless rows of corn and beans with a short-handled hoe. She blinked back fatigue in the dim and wavering firelight as she stitched bead after bead in intricate, whorled designs on buckskin.

Sometimes her efforts pleased Nun-da-wa-o. More often they did not. Her errors were explained only by a blow to her head, a foot in her ribs, then she was left alone to puzzle out her mistake herself.

Caitrin took the kicks and blows as she tried to

161

discern what behavior was acceptable. She knew to smile when Nun-da-wa-o pointed to distant mountains, then to herself before her hands shaped a pyramid. "Great Hill" was her name and it was apt. Pointing to Ga-no-a-o-a, Nun-da-wa-o mimed lifting her head in her hands and placing it on the upright pole of a drying rack. "Head on a Pole" he was, with his long, skinny neck and huge head. The women tittered behind their hands, their eyes malicious, but Caitrin's features were impassive as she nodded understanding. To have joined in their mockery of a warrior would have brought her blows and kicks, no matter that they had invited her.

Beyond a few names, Caitrin could make little sense of the Cayuga tongue. French had come easily to her. She had spoken Irish Gaelic before English, but she was not encouraged to speak this language. If she pointed to an object, the women would name it, their eyes darting first to Nun-da-wa-o for approval. Their reluctance boded Caitrin little good. It only reaffirmed her lack of place in the tribe, her possible lack of any future at all. But learn the language she must, Caitrin told herself. There was an order beneath the veneer of confusion in the village. Everyone and everything had a purpose, a place.

The children were tolerated in a way unknown in the white world. Seldom were they corporally punished, then only lightly and not by a parent but usually by an aunt or an uncle. Ridicule was occasionally used for discipline, along with the threat of the supernatural, as the banshee was used in Ireland. But whatever deterrent was employed, it was gentle and without anger. The children were the future of the tribe and respected as such. The men were accorded a deference or disdain determined by their prowess as hunters and warriors, by their wisdom as leaders and sachems. The place of each was understood and respected. The same was true of the women. Even the scrawny, mangy dogs were assured their place, whether only into a cooking pot.

Only she, herself, Caitrin thought, belonged nowhere, because Nun-da-wa-o had not yet decided what she would do with her captive. It was the Indian woman's speculative deliberation that frightened Caitrin the most, that made her the brunt of all the Indians' fickle moods.

Nun-da-wa-o felt demeaned by her husband. His many failures reflected on her, had turned her bitter. Ga-no-a-o-a had not even sired a child for her. She yearned for respect, for a status she was certain should have been hers. Until Ga-no-a-o-a had brought Caitrin to her, she had seen no way of acquiring either. Then, suddenly, her ambition was no longer a bleak hope but a question of how best to use her captive toward her desired ends. To send Caitrin to Montreal for the French bounty would gain her fine kettles, bands of wampum, jugs of rum. These things she had once craved, had envied in the hands of others. Now she knew they could not earn her what she wanted; they were but by-products of it. Caitrin, as her slave, was a living testimony to Ga-no-a-o-a's abilities as a warrior, yet her capture was viewed more as an exception to his bad luck than an example of his prowess. She was more a reminder of his failures, bringing Nun-da-wa-o ridicule instead of respect as her husband's misfortunes continued. Still, it was not every woman who could brag of a slave to order about, to vent frustrations upon. That gave Nun-da-wa-o an esteem no one could deny. And there could, one day, be the honor of offering her up as a member of the tribe, a womb to bear sons to the Iroquois—if any warrior would take so small a female, if such a puny creature could bear children at all.

Then there was a way to grasp all the respect, praise, and honor in one win-all, lose-all lunge. She could offer her slave up for torture. Such a gesture, demonstrating disdain for the French and their material goods, her contempt for what little wealth she had, would be admired by all. Her captive, though slight, was strong and hardworking. To give her up could put Nun-da-wa-o's name on the tip of all tongues, garner her all the esteem she craved. Such a gesture would be spoken of throughout the Iroquois nation, the very mention of her name shaming anyone not Cayuga—if the white girl did not fail her, shame her, if the pride in Caitrin's tilted chin, the courage in her eyes, was not sham. But if it was, if the girl faced death badly, begging, cringing, crying, then the gesture, the opportunity, would be wasted. She would have gambled and lost and be left with nothing.

So Nun-da-wa-o weighed, measured, balanced. And Caitrin felt her speculative eyes on her, eyes that drew a knot of fear in her belly. She knew the Indian woman's thoughts almost as though they were whispered in her ear. Her hands shook whenever the women's gazes fell on her. When she saw their exchanged glances, the question in their eyes, her throat would tighten with her terror. To run away could only result in recapture and a certain death, whereas while she lived, she could still hope. But for what, Caitrin did not know.

A hand gently shook the dream of relentless, never-gaining, never-slackening pursuers from Caitrin. She blinked, bewildered by the unaccustomed, tender

164

awakening. Then her eyes met the sympathetic gaze of Nun-da-wa-o and she knew that the Indian woman had reached her decision. And she knew what it was.

An intense feeling of relief surged through her; the agonizing uncertainty was over. Then, overpowering it, came terror.

Closing her eyes, blocking out Nun-da-wa-o's compassionate features, she let fear overwhelm her, let herself flow with it, drown in it for a long moment. Then, biting down hard on her lip, she forced quiet the moans constricting her throat, the wailing protests in her soul. Wrapping herself in a mantle of impassive submission, Caitrin insulated her mind from the pain that would be hers, just as she had willed away the agony of the man at the stake. When her eyes lifted again to Nun-da-wa-o's solicitous admiration, they were dead, as though her soul had already deserted her.

For the first time, she ate with the other women and was offered the best of the pot. She went with them to the river to bathe, ignoring their gentle concern. Their sudden courtesy was not for her, a part of her mind acknowledged, but for the value she represented to Nun-da-wa-o. She passively accepted their careful grooming of her, and only when they returned to the longhouse, only when Nun-da-wa-o approached her with a small pot of paint, did terror break through the barrier erected against it. For a moment, a scream against the nightmare she was living rose from the pit of her belly, but her throat closed convulsively over it. Her lungs screamed for the breath her fear denied them, then Caitrin became inert. Her mind closing like a sprung trap to all about her, she submitted to the painting of her face. It was black paint, she knew, although her eyes were

165

closed, the paint of cut-ta-ho-tha, the mark of the condemned. The women prepared her carefully, as they would a bride. They combed her gleaming hair until each long strand hung in waves down her back. Exquisitely beaded moccasins were found for her slim, high arched feet. A laboriously embroidered skirt of doeskin was wrapped about her waist. Several long strands of beads, each ending in a silver metal, hung around her neck and between her naked breasts. And Caitrin didn't need to be told that there would be no work for her that day. It was her day of honor, and the squaws led her out of the longhouse to sit, hands idle in her lap, in the sun. It was, she thought, as though this was her wedding day.

There was no watch set on her. There was no need. Each warrior, each squaw, each child was a guard. Even the scrawny, flea-infested dogs watched her, heads cocked, tongues lolling as their lips curled in what appeared to Caitrin to be mocking amusement. They seemed to sense, perhaps smell, the terror she, herself, could not face and were ever ready to give raucous alarm should she try to run. Nor was there a way of escape besides the one the women would, once their chores were done, prepare for her. She could only hope it would be short.

Resting her head back on the longhouse wall against which she sat, Caitrin let the sun warm her features. It felt warmer than usual, she noted objectively, as though the black paint drew its rays, and a deluge of grief assailed her. She could not rail or weep against the death awaiting her; she refused to let herself consider it. She mourned instead for the many things she had not yet done, would now never do. She had never given herself to a man in love, had not sat with him, his head in her lap, before a fire on a cold winter's night. She knew so little of passion, of gentleness. Only two men had touched her at all, one in attempted rape, another with eyes of lust and rage. She would never bear a child or feel its mouth tugging at her breast. She would never again see her home, hear the lilt of her people's voices or the drip of rain from wet eaves, smell apple trees after a summer storm. The small things of life were to be taken from her and Caitrin's thoughts revolted against the injustice of it. For the first time, she allowed herself to consider what would have happened had she married Ashley, had she stayed safe in New York City. For the first time, she regretted her stubbornness, her defiance, thinking the loss of her spirit, her soul, worth her life. Once more, she remembered imploring blue eyes as a hand gripped hers. She could almost feel the fingers tighten, then the reassuring hold was gone, the determined gaze with it. She wondered again what would have happened, where she would be had Roarke O'Conner held to her, if he had claimed her. For all the denial of the hate and fury in his eyes, there was lust there, along with need, she thought. Somehow, strangely, it was the thought of him that brought her the strongest grief, the greatest pride. He became the image of all that might have been. But if he lived, he would come for her, that she knew, somehow, in her soul, and a faint smile formed about her lips. It would be of no matter what drove him.

But it was senseless conjecture, Caitrin scolded herself. He was no doubt dead. If his head had not been broken by the musket stock, he would have surely been scalped by the Indians attacking the English prisoners. They were seldom concerned over the nationality of a war trophy. In that way they were more liberal than the French or English. It was funny, she told herself, how easily, how lightly, she had come to look on death.

Then, her thoughts unacceptable, her mind reeled into apathy. Her eyes were closed yet she could still hear the men in idle, gossiping groups, the children and dogs racing about, through and around the scattered groups of adults. And the women talked as they worked, their voices lifting in excited laughter. They were discussing her, were guessing and arguing about her behavior when she faced death. Then Caitrin's mind repelled all impression, all emotion, and she sought a deep, dreamless sleep.

Fourteen

But it was not the female captive who was on everyone's tongue. Another subject held their interest—
the arrival of a man late the night before. It was not
his purpose that whetted their curiosity. That, with
their long experience of white men, they understood.
He had to want something. What it was, they
assumed, was to summon them again to the war
between the pale strangers. The only question was
whether or not to go. There would be more scalps,
more captives and booty, and if coming battles were
as one-sided as the last, it would be well worth the
cost and effort. Still, they had but returned home.
They had hardly had time enough to mourn their few
dead, to celebrate their victory. There were exploits to
tell, deeds to relate again and again, until sucked dry.
There was booty to gloat over yet a while, to exhibit
to admiring eyes, respectfully grazing fingertips.
There was plunder enough yet remaining to trade for
rum and gunpowder. The general accord was that
they would put off Roarke O'Conner and the white
father in Montreal with indefinite promises and
vague words. They would entertain him with
speeches glorifying both him and themselves, their

shared feats. They would reassure him of their respect and friendship, saying much, pledging nothing. The war was, all told, between the white tribes, and it was a foolish, greedy man who hunted when the beams of his longhouse groaned with meat. Whatever words were said between the tall coureur de bois and the others in the council lodge, no promises would be made, not yet.

But Roarke had not come with a call to war and his purpose was almost done. Only once more, he told himself wearily, would he have to tell his tale, then, win or lose, he would be finished.

The first time he had told it, over two weeks before, the words had come haltingly. So much of it was an ancient story, but the wrongs still ached, the wounds still bled. But now, with so much practice, the tale ran smoothly. Perhaps too smoothly. The Indians were accomplished, eloquent narrators and could easily suspect lies in a story told too facilely. Not that he lied. He did not. His tale's few untruths were but interjected to make an ancient, foreign story comprehensible to the Iroquois mind. But he would, Roarke admitted to himself, lie his way to the very foot of the throne of the Almighty to gain his purpose. Still, he had to hold his tongue as steady over the half-truths as the truth. There had to be sorrow in his voice, along with rage, hate. It had to be told as though it had happened yesterday, with the grief and shame still roiling within him.

But he was so tired! For seven days he had followed a twisting trail, seldom resting or eating. His injured head still ached with dizziness. He had ignored the pain and the vertigo as he traced the Indians west, traveling fast, faster than a quarry burdened with booty and captives. He had had only his pack, his rifle, his determination. With Jacques Leverett's word that Caitrin had been taken by a Cayuga as his only clue, Roarke had gone from village to village seeking her, telling his story.

It was the Indians' hospitality that delayed him the most. There was gossip to exchange, tales of prowess to hear before he could ask his questions and listen for truth in their answers. He was required to smoke countless pipes of tobacco, to perspire away fatigue in innumerable sweat houses. Sometimes he thought he saw mockery in the dark eyes of his hosts. They seemed to sense his anxiety, his impatience, his urgency, and delighted in unobtrusively thwarting him. Then, after all the rituals, they would send him on and not, he knew, the shortest way. They knew who held Caitrin and deliberately sent him in circles, when a straight line, when one name, would have saved him days. Whatever empathy his tale aroused, it was not enough to overpower the delight taken in making a fool of a white man. Nor was Caitrin's captor a warrior known to Roarke.

Briefly, Roarke wondered if it was to his advantage or against it that Ga-no-a-o-a was so obscure a warrior. It depended on whether the man was young and unproven or if he was older and simply luckless and inept. Only when he saw them would he know how to deal with Caitrin's captor and his wife.

The door at one end of the council house opened, a narrow beam of sunlight flashing through the darkness, and Roarke looked up. His face was smooth, he knew, and displayed none of the hope and fear he felt. Nor did he allow it to show disappointment as two young warriors entered and slipped quietly to a near corner. Then his eyes dropped again as he waited. His hosts had confirmed that the Englishwoman with hair the shades of autumn was with them, but they could not give her to him, despite his shame and

171

need for revenge. Only the warrior who had taken her could do so, along with the warrior's wife. They sent for Ga-no-a-o-a, his wife, and their captive.

Accepting a pipe, Roarke inhaled its harsh smoke and held it a long moment. Its stinging ached his chest and dizzied him before burning away the cobwebs of fatigue. Exhaling, elbows on his knees as he sat cross-legged on the bench, Roarke passed the pipe on to Ha-ne-a-ha. The old man took it, his wise eyes studying Roarke. If anyone could see falsehood in his tale, could read confusion beneath his avowed need for retribution, it was the ancient sachem. The middle finger of his right hand was missing, and perhaps it was its absence that gave Ha-ne-a-ha his wisdom. He had had reason enough to dwell on variant perversities of human nature since the day he had, as a boy, laid his finger on a chopping block and dared his brother to whack it off. His stupidity had followed him in his name, A Finger Lying, and served to remind him of his own foolishness and to forgive it in others. But the finger was not really gone. Roarke's eyes dropped from the sagacious gaze of Ha-ne-a-ha to the medicine pouch that rested on the sagging, wrinkled flesh of the sachem's chest. In the buckskin bag, so legend had it, was the missing digit. The youth stupid enough to so lose it was now an honored sachem, his judgment and pronouncements famous. But the brother had died young, on his first war party, his name long since forgotten. There must be, Roarke mused, a moral somewhere in the story but he could not see beyond the waiting.

Blinking in the dim, smoky light, he glanced at the chiefs and minor sachems arranged about Ha-ne-a-ha. Other than O-da-wa-an-do, the tall, thickset war chief, and the sachem, few were important beyond

172

the village itself. Still, he had to go carefully.

Briefly, he wondered what he would do when—and if—he got Caitrin away. Where could he take her? The English colonies might not be safe for him; too many had seen him with the French at Fort William Henry. To go to the French could make Caitrin a hostage, and she might be taken from him. So much, too, depended on whether Lord Cartland still lived and if he was with the French or English. But that, Roarke decided, he would think about when—and if—he got her.

Inhaling from the pipe once more, he studied the council house. Although similar to other Iroquois lodgings, it was a male refuge from the matriarchal longhouses. It was rectangular and built of bark set clapboard fashion on the walls and roof and fastened with laths. Approximately twenty-four feet across and over sixty feet long, it was but half the length of many such structures. A door was at either end. It had sleeping berths on both sides and running its length. Above were storage shelves. Firepits ran down the central aisle and smoke holes were cut in the middle of the peaked roof over them. On some of the sleeping berths were mats of skins and blankets. Weapons hung on the walls and several war shields rested against upright support poles, but no bark barrels filled with beans and charred or dried ears of corn were in the corners. Golden dust motes danced in the oblong beams of sun cast through the smoke holes. The blue haze of smoke, the scattered weapons, the silence, spoke of a pagan sanctity. There was a fraternal bond disallowing shrill female voices, the wailing of infants. Even the dog slinking in with two warriors settled into the heavy quiet. No infants toddled into the rarefied atmosphere, but preadolescent boys were welcome and were struck breathless with awe. About Roarke, too, the curious warriors waited.

All eyes, Roarke's with them, swung to Ga-no-a-o-a when he entered, then to Nun-da-wa-o, and a soft sigh brushed the silence. The men relaxed again, all but Roarke. His throat tightened with apprehension. He knew Caitrin was in the village but he had not dared to ask how she was, if she had been harmed. And he wondered if the sight of her would again bring him that unaccountable mixture of lust and hate. He sought her small, slim figure, hidden then revealed as Nun-da-wa-o sat down with a heaving sigh. Caitrin, eyes downcast, settled down next to the squaw, feet tucked under her and to the side as she had been taught with blows and kicks, a position suitable for a female. Roarke saw the paint that smeared her features. His breath was torn from him. His knee jerked convulsively once before he could control the betraying spasm. Had he come half a day later, she would have been dead. Or a burned, cut, bleeding, blistered, featureless, mindless thing he could only help with a bullet to her brain. Yet, even as his stomach heaved, an overpowering lust consumed him.

The black paint contrasted sensuously with the bright torch of Caitrin's hair. It whitened the pale, naked flesh of her neck and shoulders, of her breasts. The paint hiding her features, the barbaric beads and metals resting between her rose-tinted nipples turned her into an effigy of a woman, into a body to be used, a receptacle of lust, of sperm. The pagan ornaments, the cut-ta-ho-tha, robbed her of identity. They turned her into a thing neutered yet somehow so totally female that Roarke ached with lust.

Breathing deeply, he drove down his need with the

174

reminder that the life of the woman—and his—rested, at that moment, in her hands. A sign of relief or recognition, a sob of joy, and his long search, his carefully contrived tale, would be for nothing. But Caitrin betrayed no emotion and Roarke wondered if she felt anything at all. Her eyes aimlessly roamed about the council lodge, then touched him. They were curiously dull, as though no one lived behind them. They brushed Roarke's face indifferently, before moving on. There was no fear or grief or hope in their opaque depths, and Roarke despairingly thought that perhaps she had sought refuge in insanity.

Then her gaze wandered back to him. She frowned, Roarke guessed, in an effort to bring her mind back from whichever limbo she had lost it in. A flick of some unidentifiable emotion stirred in the depths of her death-dark eyes, then the faintest of smiles, a smile of proud acknowledgement, tipped her lips before her gaze dropped again. Her chin lifting in a gesture of her old pride, she settled back to wait, only limitless, calm patience on her features. Whatever reaction Roarke had expected and feared, it had not been Caitrin's calm acceptance of his presence as her due. It was as though his efforts to find her, to save her, was something entitled her by right or rank, by her noble name and blood. Any other reaction could have cost them their lives, but still his jaw tightened in rage, a muscle jerking at the corner of his mouth.

When Roarke again faced Ha-ne-a-ha, all concern and need for Caitrin was gone. Only hate and the desire for vengeance, to wound as he had been wounded, to strip from her her pride as he had once lost his, remained. Once again, Caitrin became the source of all the wrong done his people and himself. He took the pipe again, inhaling the acrid smoke as he waited for the tobacco to calm him, allowing the time as he did so to build into suspense.

Sight seemed to come to Caitrin through the very pores of her skin, as though she had no need for the eyes she held downcast. Even as she stared at the hands clasped tightly in her lap, she saw the avid, dark faces turned toward her. All the details of the council house, even the cold enmity on Roarke's features, were clear although she dared not glance up. The incredulous hope raging in her would be too visible to the black eyes drilling into the shield about her emotions. Her wits, dulled by a fear too long sustained, seemed as slow and as stumbling as a toddler's first steps, but some instinct warned her to remain impassive.

When Nun-da-wa-o had led her into the council house, Caitrin was a puppet. To think, to wonder, would have been to touch incomprehensible terror. For a brief second, she had not recognized Roarke, her brain failing to accept the impossible message of her eyes. Then the sight of him was so unbelievable she was stupefied, was stunned long enough for the urge for survival to conceal the whirlwind of joy assaulting her. Only a brief flare of incredulous hope struck her before a shutter of indifference fell again over her mind. And the joy she had felt was shattered too quickly by the hate she sensed in Roarke. But whatever its cause, whatever she might have done to deserve his enmity, he was there, and it seemed strangely right that he was. Whatever his intention, it would take her from the death promised her. Whatever his purpose, he wanted her alive, that she knew. And alive, no matter how tenuous or precarious, she had a chance. For what, she did not know, had not yet considered. Survival itself seemed such a miracle that she could not think beyond it. Death was still too near, her life still in the hands of a mocked and misshapen misfit, of a bitter, frustrated woman who had the fragrance of her people's admiration in her nostrils. So much rested in the words and actions of the man sitting so casually in the center of the room and Caitrin dared not trust enough to allow herself hope. She knew too well the swift changes of mood that ruled her captors. She bore too many cuts and bruises as evidence of their fickleness. The tenuous balance of their moods weighed on the air of the dimly lighted dwelling, an invisible, stifling dust. Suspense passed from person to person. Dark eyes flicked from the captive's black-smeared face to the scorned, abused man who held her, then on to the mountain of a woman who had found a way out of shame. The gazes passed on to the white man sitting opposite the sachem. Only he seemed untroubled, unconcerned.

Roarke's head remained bowed. The words he had repeated so many times in the last days suddenly had new meaning, endowed once more with the rage of a man driven unjustly from his home, with the grief of an exile from the earth he loved.

"Many seasons ago," he began, and his audience leaned forward to hear his soft words, "long before the eyes of your grandfather's grandfather first opened on the goodness of the earth, aye, and his grandfather before him, there was a land, an island, beyond the shining sea. There, The Maker so multiplied the deer and elk that none of His people knew hunger. As here, when the chill wind first blows across the land, the sun in this land would darken in the sky with the passing of geese and ducks. The trout and salmon filled each stream and river, their sweet flesh there for the taking by any man with hunger upon him. It was land truly blessed. And as

177

its earth, its waters, its skies were fruitful, so were its people great. The wisdom of its sachems was marveled at by men many days distant from its shores. Its teachers journeyed over all the world east of the sun's rising to bring their teachings to other peoples. The deeds of their heros are still whispered of, so brave, so dauntless were they. The beauty and gentleness of its women were legend throughout the world; men came in great canoes from far across its seas to look on their forms and faces.

"In that time there was peace in the land. So rich in precious metals, so skillful were its craftsmen, that all persons wore exquisite ornaments of gold, silver, and bronze. So wise were its leaders, none knew injustice. So did the Maker bless this land, none knew need; no man knew greed.

"But there was envy in the hearts of those across the narrow strip of sea but a day's journey away by war canoe," Roarke whispered, long nurtured anger straining his voice. "They looked on the green island of plenty, of peace and wealth, and they lusted to plunder it, to defile its soil with the blood of its people. So they came, the same men who now come to the land of the longhouses, the men of the red-coats. To a land smaller than the earth walked by the manflesh eaters, the Abnaki, the land named Maine by the white man, they came in their great numbers, with strange, powerful weapons."

Roarke paused, the eyes he held downcast lifting to stare unseeing above the heads of his rapt listeners. His jaw tightened and he breathed in deeply before continuing, his words round with anguish.

"As the redcoat washes in waves over the land of the Iroquois, claiming a few grains of earth with each surge forward, releasing always less than was taken with each ebbing away, so they washed over the land

178

of the Irish. For more years than the most ancient crone can remember in legends told them by their greatfathers, the people fought to hold the earth given them by the Maker, but too many were the red-coated ones. So they became defeated by the weight of their numbers, by their false promises, the warriors of the land, the sons of the warriors, and their sons after them. Yet the people fought on until one day of sorrow and shame, no more could they fight. They were unmanned by their need to preserve the seed of but one man, so few had they become, that it might swell with child the womb of one woman. They wished to hear again the birth cry of a child in a land where wolves, grown fat on human flesh, stalked between the longhouses, where the bark of the dog fox could be heard at the door of each lodge. So the people accepted the yoke of slavery. No more could a man lift his eyes to follow the flight of the eagle without the bite of his master's whip driving his gaze once more to the earth . . . earth no longer his but another's. No more could he tell his children of the glory once theirs; to speak so was forbidden. No more could his sons seek wisdom at the feet of the sachems, for the wise ones were dead or driven from the land.

"So came the time of sorrow and want. The eyes of each man avoided those of another in their shame. The men sought no more as hunters the deer and elk, the trout and salmon, the fowl of the air. No more did they go against their enemies, battle hatchets in their belts, the battle cries of their clans on their lips. The women gave birth in grief, for no more could they rear a child to aught but slavery. With the strangers came a chill wind and they learned to shudder with the cold, their teeth chattering in their sockets with it. For the first time they knew hunger, for they fed on no more than the leaving of their master's tables, and the hungry wailing of their children keened in their ears. No more were the people proud and wise, for need teaches greed and hunger. Slaves know no wisdom, for servitude lends itself only to cunning. There is no pride in the subjugated, for a foot on the neck bends the head to the earth and those who eat of dirt know only a blustering vanity blown away in the breeze of their own boasting. And as the people ate of servitude, those few unbowed warriors left the land. As flights of wild geese, they flew away to fight the redcoated strangers in other lands, under other war chiefs, leaving the people unprotected and without chiefs of wisdom and strength to lead them."

The bitter, angry recital paused. For a moment, he could see again the thin, zealous features of the priest who had taught him angry pride, his people's history in one of the forbidden hedge schools. Yet the priest would not have countenanced a hate so long nurtured, would have seen it as a disease turning back on its host. Nor would he have condoned the vengeful demeaning of a woman—or a lie. Yet if the stealing of a shirtful of apples became a deed of defiance when related, what harm? Roarke argued with himself. And if he did lie, was it not less a sin than if he left Caitrin to die, if he had not come to her at all? Under the weight of his gaze, under the pull of the long, heavy silence, Caitrin lifted her eyes to his. For a moment, he saw fear and hope mingled in their green depths, then, refusing to flinch before his contemptuous gaze, they turned haughty and cold. It was the response he needed, and he used it to mollify the guilt and shame his memories summoned. He sensed strength in her that only bent beneath adversity and vowed he would break it, whetting his long-nourished fury. Yet something stirred within him as he studied her proud, vulnerable features, something threatening him, and he used a bitter hate to smother its small flame.

Roarke's voice had adopted, during his long recital, the cadence of the shanachie, the Irish bard, and Caitrin recognized it, knew he spoke of their country's past. When he began to speak again, his eyes still trapping her, she knew, by the keening edge to his utterance, that he spoke of a more recent, more personal wrong. The harshness in his words told her that, whatever crime he recited, she was the one he accused. Even as Caitrin felt these things, she grew more bewildered and her bewilderment fed her fear.

"Yet, time without number," Roarke continued, his voice a keen, "through the long years, young men were born who strived to cast away the bonds of thralldom, for the hatchings of eagles cannot become titmice. Always there grew to manhood youths who refused to bow their heads, who defied their conquerors, for the blood of warriors does not breed men with the coward's heart. Such a one greeted the morning twenty and three years ago, and tasting the rankness of slavery on his first breath, he rejected it in a wail of outrage and fury. The remembered deeds of his people was his drink as he grew, the wrongs done them, his food. Perhaps it was too rich for a boy so quick to anger, so anguished by his people's despair. Perhaps the bread of hate should have been leavened with the salt of patience, of discretion. As the arrow released over soon will miss its mark, so did the man-child fly, and fall, his wings not yet feathered full. Yet his deeds of defiance were a man's deeds, and when snared, he stood as a man, scornful and in contempt of his captor. Though he faced torture as a man, the usurper of his lands, his rights derided him as an infant still pissing his breechcloth. He refused, too, to sully his hands with the chastising of a child,

181

passing the foul task into the hands of an underling, a soul of mud so low that, had the youth not been tied, he would not dare approach him with an appeal for alms. To view the humiliation of the manchild, the usurper ordered his foster daughter to watch him whipped as you would a two-year-old. It was the pity in her eyes that the manchild found to be his greatest shame. That a female should look on him with condescending compassion, a child so young she had not yet greeted the moon with her menses, was the greatest ignobility of all, and long did the youth harbor hate and desire for revenge in his breast.

"It was the pity in the eyes of his family that drove him from his home. It was the need for vengeance that gave his exile purpose. It grew with him as he reached manhood in the land of the noble people of the longhouses, who welcomed him. Many years, long years, he gathered weapons to him, strength of arm, fleetness of foot, keenness of eye. He also gathered the weapon most valued by the white man, long bands of wampum, the most certain path to his goal. It was this labor which ate away the young days of the manchild, chewing them with the teeth of bitterness, swallowing them down a throat dry with hate and shame. Then, suddenly, his vengeance was in his hand, only to be lost through his fingers as water into sand, leaving only arid grains of rage, frustration, and despair. The usurper of his birthright, of his youth and pride, was killed, not in shame as he deserved, but with rank and honor. And with his death was gone, so thought the youth-grownman, all chance for revenge, for the regaining of his despoiled pride. But then there came to him the girlchild-grown-woman who had dared pity him. She came but, his vengeance at his very fingertips, he lost her to a mighty warrior of the Iroquois. So once more

182

he seeks revenge, this time in the search of a woman."

Throat dry, Roarke stopped speaking. He surveyed the faces turned to his and sensed the excitement beneath their expressionless facades. They knew now why he was there and who he sought, but they, as he, needed it said. But Roarke could not read their sympathies; his gamble would be to the end. His gaze then rested on the misshapen features of Ga-no-a-o-a, studying him.

"I seek a woman with hair streaked the colors of the trees in the season of the fallen leaf."

Ga-no-a-o-a's tongue flicked over wet lips as his cunning eyes twitched, seeming to turn about in his head, seeking Caitrin and Nun-da-wa-o behind him. This jerking glance warned Roarke of his dangerous weakness and of his wife's strength. Ga-no-a-o-a was tasting of the heady hemp of power for the first time and he liked it. He held something another wanted and he could easily, maliciously destroy it, denying another as he was so often denied. Or he could decide to be magnanimous, shaming his tormentors. There was no way to guess his decision and no way to influence it.

But the woman was less a gamble; her pride and hunger made her manipulatable. And through her, perhaps, the man. Yet he dared not insult Ga-no-a-o-a. He could only address Nun-da-wa-o through her husband.

"The Cayugas are a proud, noble people," Roarke stated, voice calm and emotionless. "They do not traffic in the booty harvested in war; such is but a token of their prowess and is not for barter. They do not sell their captives as does the gluttonous white man. To ask such of an Iroquois would be such insult as must be washed out in blood. Such booty must only be given up as a gift, for there can be no

183

price set on a man's valor. But the esteem of his people would be without measure should a warrior of the mighty Cayuga offer such a prize to another's revenge. He would know respect and distinction without end."

Pausing, Roarke studied Ga-no-a-o-a and Nun-da-wa-o. Only a deep blush betrayed her agitation. But the man's face was avid and gloating. His eyes, the cocked one vainly trying to align itself with the other, scurried around the longhouse, lighting nowhere as it sought an answer to his dilemma. Then insult warred with greed as Roarke drew strings of wampum as long as himself from his pouch. His gaze covetously caressed the long, wide bands of white and purple, not the white man's cheap glass ones but the invaluable beads painstakingly made of the shell of mussel and conch, and his wide lower lip fell moistly slack.

"This paltry gift," Roarke explained, waving a careless hand over the five priceless belts, "is but a token of the honor deserved by such a selfless warrior of the Cayugas."

Ga-no-a-o-a slurped up his lower lip and his wavering eyes at last met Roarke's. They ridiculed the white man's transparent efforts and desperate need.

"She is marked for death," he stated, his eyes full with the pleasure of tormenting another. "It is a compromise that should suit all, satisfying your thirst for revenge as it honors me as a warrior."

Roarke showed none of his dismay as he lowered his eyes. So desperate and determined had he been to find Caitrin, he had not considered the possibility that her captor would not give her up. Ga-no-a-o-a's refusal had twisted all his arguments and flattery back on himself. He thought of kidnapping her, then

184

rejected it; it would cost them both their lives. Even if he could somehow delay the torture until the next day, attempting to steal her away that night, the odds on their being captured were so high only a driven, frantic man would consider it. Lifting his cold gaze to Ga-no-a-o-a's gloating features, Roarke fought the urge to smash the ugly, insolent face into an unrecognizable pulp. He dared not look at Caitrin as he grappled with an argument he knew was flimsy and probably futile; surely his despair would burst into tears of frustration. If he failed, he would, he realized, try to kidnap Caitrin, no matter the odds. If he could not, then he would end it swiftly for her, with his hatchet to the back of her head, though he, too, would die for it, and not easily. He knew too well how ably the squaws could administer agony, and no one would hurt her but himself. But Nun-da-wa-o's voice drove back the words teetering on the tip of his tongue. She could see all she dreamed of tossed away with her husband's spiteful refusal.

"May a mere woman speak?" she asked, addressing Ha-ne-a-ha, meeting his eyes past the shoulder of her husband. The sachem nodded and she turned to Roarke.

"The fledging warrior of the people of the land east of the rising sun was greatly wronged," she stated. "The dishonor done him deserves great vengeance, but is not the death of the woman of the bright hair at the hands of the Iroquois enough?"

Heartfelt relief sloughed through Roarke as he understood the chance Nun-da-wa-o gave him. He reached for it, knowing he would have no other. His eyes held hers, yet his voice rose as he addressed all within the council lodge, echoing in the pent-up silence.

"You give her only death," he told them angrily.

185

"Do not the Iroquois show esteem when they paint a face with the cut-ta-ho-tha? Does not such a death test the courage and strength of the victim? Yet you tell me to exalt in the respect you show her, to find vengeance in her dignification? Think you I am a fool for the blue of my eyes, my pale skin? I came for justice and you but offer me a dry pap! You shame a guest of the people of the longhouse!" The rows of dark eyes fell before Roarke's, and he knew he had a chance even as cold sweat slid down his sides and back. "I would take my revenge in a way that would shame her as I was shamed, would drive her from her people's scornful gazes as I was driven. Far more dreaded than death by white women is rape, is being taken by a man before their coming together has been blessed by a priest, a black robe. I would so take her, though 'tis contrary to the ways of both your people and mine. And to bear a child without such a blessing is a humiliation a white woman would rather die than face. I would get her with child. I would force her to confront her people so. Her people are as kings in the land that was once mine. They walk with arrogance over the necks of my people. I would, by sending her to them so disgraced, force them to taste of the shame they once forced through my clenched teeth, and then my thirst for vengeance would be slaked. Would the people of the proud longhouse deny me such?"

Once more his gaze met the eyes of the occupants of the dark structure. In them he read their aversion. He saw their disbelieving contempt for the twisted, cruel ways of the white man, and he thought he had gone too far, that he had surely lost. Then his eyes rested again on Nun-da-wa-o. The squaw met his gaze squarely, her eyes reflecting her incredulous disgust. She wanted, more than anything, to have the per-

186

verted white man gone, and the woman with him. Yet the respect she had long coveted was now within her grasp and she reached out, taking it. Her fingers closed over a long, wide band of wampum; no more than one would she allow herself, and she drew it to her.

"I would keep this," she stated, rising to her full height and bulk, "that no one doubt my honor or speak of me with disrespect. You may have the woman to do with as you will. Though your way sickens me, she, too, is of your race."

Roarke bowed his head to her, then looked at Caitrin. The silence drew her eyes up to his and Roarke's mouth quirked in a harsh, triumphant smile. The realization that she was now his, that her life was saved, stirred beneath her apathy. Joyful relief flared up, only to be drowned in her bewilderment, and Roarke's smile broadened, taunting her bewildered fear. Then he turned to Nun-da-wa-o.

"Prepare her for me," he requested, "as you would a bride."

The Indian woman stared at him, her repugnance clear, then she nodded. The little one with the bright hair was no longer hers. This man of hate now possessed her and could do with her as he willed. Yet she wondered if the girl would not have met less pain and suffering under the knives of the women than at the hands of this man with eyes as cold and dead as winter.

Fifteen

The cut-ta-ho-tha had been washed from Caitrin's face. Her long hair was combed until no tangle remained, its smooth length rippling down her back. The soft, beautifully ornamented doeskin skirt, leggings, and moccasins she had been dressed in early that morning in honor of her impending death were taken from her, then returned after she was again bathed. The strings of beads and metals again hung cool between her naked breasts.

Her grooming complete, the women guided her to a single-family longhouse set slightly apart from the village. With them they had brought household goods, soft furs and crimson trade blankets for the benchlike bed against the wall, a broom made of twigs that now, its sweeping done, leaned beside the opened door of bark boards hung on wood hinges. Several bags of pemmican hung from the rafters along with ears of corn—bright spots of white, red, and yellow against the high, dark shadows. Earthen pots containing charred corn and dried beans were set in a corner with a mortar and pestle and an assortment of bark trays and dishes.

Within moments, the Indian women had transformed a naked, shell-like structure into a place of comfort and warmth. But it was not meant, Caitrin recognized, as a place for a woman alone, nor had she been brought there as their prisoner.

If she had any doubt as to who would share it with her, it was dispelled when Nun-da-wa-o brought Roarke's flintlock, powder horn, and bullet pouch. A beautifully embroidered and beaded pouch, too, was there, the items a bold statement of male purpose and domination in a longhouse of the matriarchal Iroquois. From where she sat before the small fire, her feet tucked properly under her, Caitrin studied them. The flintlock, she knew, was loaded; Robert Mitchell had taught her to load and shoot one during the peaceful lull before the fall of William Henry. It had been more for amusement than for anything else, yet it might yet prove a valuable lesson. If nothing else, it gave her the ability to control her own death. The most debilitating aspect of being held a captive, she had found, was the total lack of any authority over her own life.

A corner of her full mouth tilted in a wry smile as she remembered the laughter that had accompanied her shooting lessons and the young man who had flirted with her. It all seemed so long before, though it had been no more than a few weeks.

Then she caught her lower lip between her teeth. She did not think she could take her own life; she had fought too hard to keep it. Perhaps only being used as her guardian would have done had he been able, turning her into a soulless, prideless thing, could turn her to suicide. But perhaps not even then, so strong had she found the vapor of life within her. Still, it was good to have the means to do so at hand, the means to deny the use of herself to others.

The four belts of wampum were still in his pouch, she knew. After hours of nervousness and apprehension, she rose to her feet. She prowled the small room, checking the contents of each deerskin bag, each bark and earthen bowl. Roarke's pouch she saved for last, inhibited by respect for his privacy, but curiosity and anxiety overpowered her restraint. Other than the wampum, there had been little in it, and it was for something, anything to give her insight into its owner, that she searched. There was his razor, so often honed that its blade was narrow and bowed, its bone handle stained and molded to fit the palm perfectly from many years of use. The razor's very age told her that it had been old when Roarke received it, most likely from his father. Such things were handed down from generation to generation, and Roarke's possession of it was evidence that, for whatever reason he had left Ireland, his father and his family had regretted his going.

There was little else in the pouch: a thin sliver of hard, fine soap smelling faintly of violets and dried meat; a smaller bag of charred corn and maple sugar; a comb similar to thousands traded to the Indians by both the French and English. They gave her no clue to the man who had bought her from Ga-no-a-o-a.

Yet however few its contents, the pouch itself told her a bit more about the tall man who had haunted her since her arrival in the colonies. Some woman, an Indian, had cared enough for him to spend hours in flickering firelight to make such an exquisite object.

Rejecting a strange whisper of jealousy, Caitrin told herself that all she needed to know of Roarke O'Conner was how best to use him for her own survival. Nor could she learn anything more until he came to her.

But he seemed to take forever. The stew of zuccinni, squirrel, and beans had become a glutinous mass. The fire it warmed over was only a glow of blackened coals. The women had gone hours before, taking with them their gentle hands, their soft smiles that seemed to plead forgiveness for a crime she could only guess at, and their pity. That those women who would have administered to her a hideous death but a few hours before now pitied her should drive her insane, Caitrin thought. She did not know what Roarke O'Conner had said in the council house, had only seen the sudden aversion in every dark face. The women's sympathy was not the compassion they had displayed toward someone condemned to death, but rather the pity for someone doomed to a terrible fate.

Yet Caitrin could feel no fear. There was curiosity and a strange excitement, a humiliated anger at having been bargained for like a sack of beans, a packet of tobacco, though it had kept her from death. But she felt no gratitude. He had saved her for his own purpose, and not from mercy. Apprehension was within her, though, for she did not know why he hated yet wanted her. She was nervous but there was none of the repulsion she still felt when she thought of Ashley's assault. The man she waited for, a man she did not even know, offered her nothing, not even the promise of survival beyond the night. Yet she had refused Ashley as she would not refuse Roarke O'Conner. Her virtue, she had come to realize, was a small price to pay for life. The women who prattled of death before dishonor, who scorned any of their sex who submitted rather than die, could never have been in a position to make the choice. If they ever were, they would make the same decision she did, no matter how odious the man.

Seven Basic Ingredients for Good Financial Planning

❶ The best way to learn decision-making is to practice making decisions. You have a 50% chance of being right the first time!

❷ Find the black hole of mysterious cash drain. Everyone is entitled to the occasional splurge, just know what it is and decide if it's worth it.

❸ Jumble belongs in a jumble sale. Organizing yourself and your paperwork is a giant step toward effective action.

❹ Owning your own dwelling is cheaper than renting. Once in the real estate market, stay in it until you are ready to finance a great retirement home.

❺ Put not all thy eggs in one basket. Diversity is the soup of life.

❻ Remember the miracle of compound interest: 10% doubles in seven years, 15% in five years. It's a miracle if you're earning it, and a nightmare if you're paying it.

❼ You can manage your money better than any government or pension-plan bureaucracy. Get your hands on it as soon as prudently possible.

THE KITCHEN TABLE MONEY PLAN

---

by Barbara McNeill & Robert Collins $14.95

Grab your own piece of the pie

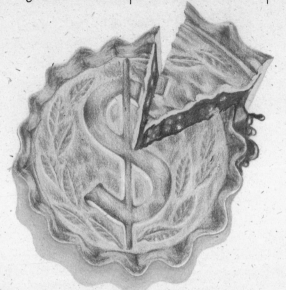

Financial planning that's easy to swallow

THE KITCHEN TABLE
MONEY PLAN

by Barbara McNeill & Robert Collins $14.95

 HarperCollins*Publishers*Ltd

4 FREE BOOKS

FREE BOOKS

TO GET YOUR 4 FREE BOOKS WORTH $18.00 — MAIL IN THE FREE BOOK CERTIFICATE T O D A Y

Fill in the Free Book Certificate below, and we'll send your FREE BOOKS to you as soon as we receive it.

If the certificate is missing below, write to: Zebra Home Subscription Service, Inc., P.O. Box 5214, 120 Brighton Road, Clifton, New Jersey 07015-5214.

FREE BOOK CERTIFICATE

4 FREE BOOKS

ZEBRA HOME SUBSCRIPTION SERVICE, INC.

YES! Please start my subscription to Zebra Historical Romances and send me my first 4 books absolutely FREE. I understand that each month I may preview four new Zebra Historical Romances free for 10 days. If I'm not satisfied with them, I may return the four books within 10 days and owe nothing. Otherwise, I will pay the low preferred subscriber's price of just $3.75 each; a total of $15.00, *a savings off the publisher's price of $3.00.* I may return any shipment and I may cancel this subscription at any time. There is no obligation to buy any shipment and there are no shipping, handling or other hidden charges. Regardless of what I decide, the four free books are mine to keep.

NAME

ADDRESS   APT

CITY   STATE   ZIP

(   )
TELEPHONE

SIGNATURE   (if under 18, parent or guardian must sign)

Terms, offer and prices subject to change without notice. Subscription subject to acceptance by Zebra Books. Zebra Books reserves the right to reject any order or cancel any subscription.

GET
FOUR
FREE
BOOKS
(AN $18.00 VALUE)

Leaning forward, Caitrin poked the coals to a brighter glow as she admitted she lied to herself. She did not want to refuse him. Roarke O'Conner fascinated her somehow. He attracted her, for all his hard, relentless features and demeaning glance. And thinking of him disturbed her in a way that was somehow pleasant. Remembering the way his eyes had touched her in disdainful appraisal and lust, with a need she had sensed beneath his mask of hate, she felt the stirring of a strange warmth within her. Whatever his reason for coming after her, for rescuing her, he also wanted her; he felt the same perturbing, reluctant desire she did.

Catching her lower lip between her teeth, she sat back again on her heels, confused by her conflicting emotions. Then her chin lifted and all expression fled her features, her face becoming impassive.

The door creaked, then Roarke O'Conner entered, sidling soundlessly into the room. Caitrin stared at him, her nose wrinkling against the reek of raw trade brandy. His face was obscured by shadow, but she knew if he was not drunk, he had certainly been drinking. For a brief moment, a shrewish anger flowed over Caitrin, startling her. Words demanding to know where he had been and with whom, sharp words of reproach, leaped to her lips and she bit them back. Such a reaction, like that of a harpy wife, was stupid and irrational, she agreed to the imp in her mind that jeered at her for so betraying herself. It was his sudden appearance after she had waited so long for him, she excused herself.

"There is stew," she blurted out. "It is overcooked but still edible if you are hungry."

But Roarke did not seem to hear her petulant tone. Stepping out from the shadow, he stared at Caitrin, his face stark, a mask of some rigid, unyielding material not flesh. Whatever the alcohol's effect, it was now gone. But the hours he had spent healing with liquor the rankling wound of want and compassion had not been wasted. He no longer felt even lust, only a relentless resolution. For a second the bewildering problem of how to cold-bloodedly commence a rape glinted his eyes with a self-disparaging humor, then they turned to ice. Whatever need and hurt Caitrin had sensed beneath his shell of hate and contempt was gone, leaving no mercy or desire to soften him. For the first time, she feared him. Sudden terror suffocated her. Her throat worked with a single, hard gulp as she took one involuntary, shaky step away from the cold purpose in Roarke's eyes as his gaze dropped over her. His eyes lingered in detached, demeaning appraisal on her high, round breasts, brushing with an insulting glance over her naked nipples, then moving significantly lower before lifting again to her face. A smile jerked a corner of his mouth and one eyebrow was cocked in insolent query as he saw the indignant lift of her chin, her flush of outraged anger and fear. The intended affront of his gaze had touched more than the surface of her flesh and her humiliated fury, the bewildered apprehension in her eyes tasting sweet in his mouth.

"Thank you," he mocked, "but I've no appetite, not for the meal you suggest."

He paused before speaking again, the deepening of his brogue deliberately derisive.

"Yet you do understand what it is I would have of you, do you not, Lady FitzGerald? What hunger I would have you satisfy?"

Caitrin did not answer, only her pride holding her

194

gaze steady before his. Submit, Robert Rogers had told her, and she clung to the thought in an effort to control her urge to run from his relentless intent. To give ground before him would make his intentions easier to fulfill, would be to have him on her like a hawk on a rabbit. He wanted her to fall back before him, and her chin lifted higher in a gesture of the disdain she could no longer feel.

Roarke's derisive smile twisted higher as he acknowledged her attempt at defiance, then it was gone. Stepping away from the wall he had leaned so casually against, he unfastened his belt and tossed it to the shelf above the bed, the long knife in its sheath clanging as it struck the wall. His gaze never left hers as his buckskin shirt, his moccasins, and his leggings followed the belt, and he was stripped to his breech-clout. She held his eyes, unwilling to give him the satisfaction of looking away, of dropping her gaze over his body. But she saw it at the periphery of her vision. It gleamed gold, scarcely more pale than his face. Its very masculinity, the breadth of his shoulders, the hard muscles that rippled across it, the narrowness of his hips, forced on her the awareness of her own curves and turns, the soft texture of her skin, the fragile purpose of its feminine shaping. It aroused in her a painful sensation of vulnerability that was totally different from the terror she had felt before. It was a sensation gone as swiftly as it had assaulted her, yet it had, for a brief moment, parted her lips and flickered in her eyes.

Seeing it, Roarke drew his breath in in a hiss, then, his hands hanging loosely at his sides, his fingers slightly crooked, he approached her. There was something predatory in his slow, ambling steps, in the tilt of his head. He stepped soundlessly over the earthen floor, his movement containing a feline grace. He seemed to stalk her, his eyes never leaving her face, holding her trapped.

It seemed to Caitrin as if she watched him approach for an eternity, yet no more than a few feet separated them. Her lungs ached with the holding of her breath. Her fingernails bit into her palms. Then he was before her, staring down at her, holding her under his relentless, consuming gaze. The muscles of his jaw twitched with satisfaction as he saw her trembling effort to stand fast before him and he chuckled when her eyes at last fell under his.

He gently lifted the strands of beads over her head and placed them on a shelf, his cold gaze still on Caitrin's downcast face. Its calculating intention refuting the tenderness of his caress, Roarke touched her. His hands brushed over the mass of her silken hair. His fingers sank deep into it, gathering it into glistening skeins. Its cool, satin texture, so different from that of Indian women's, surprised him, tempting him to bury his face in its soft masses, to breathe in its sweet odor, but his eyes did not soften. He took her face in his hands, tilting it up to his and gazing into it, the weight of his eyes heavy on her lowered lids. His thumbs touched her delicate jaw, their pressure barely felt, then his fingers grazed the arch of her eyebrows and over her closed eyes. His fingertips brushed the thick fringe of her lashes before one hand skimmed her cheek as it sank back into the hair at the nape of her neck, leaving a path of tingling flesh in its wake. Then the other hand traced down the straight line of her nose and over her lips, touching them lightly, stroking the full lower one with the ball of his thumb as though the sight alone could not prove its provocative fullness.

But Roarke was looking at the perfection of the face he held in his hands as only the stage on which Caitrin's emotions played. He had felt the flutter of her eyelids under his fingertips, the almost imperceptible trembling of her full, soft lips, the repressed desire of her mouth to part beneath the passing of his thumb. He could almost see the battle that waged within her. Her fear was there, urging her to whirl away from under his arms, to escape the threat of him. It fought with her determination to face him, to never back down before him.

And beneath her fear and determination was a rising tide of need and desire. Its presence almost invisible on her rigidly held features, he watched as it grew slowly and inexorably no matter the will she held against it, the sight stirring an unwanted, equal need in him. He watched it swell as his fingers left her mouth to follow the curved jut of her small chin to her round throat. The beat of her pulse leaped at his touch and Roarke smiled faintly, his eyes still on her face as his hand dropped lower. His fingers brushed out over the fragile curve of her collarbone, then back, before tracing their way down the line to her navel. His thumbs pressed into its shallow depth as his fingers encircled her waist. Their pressure painful on the small of her back, he forced her hips to tilt up against his swollen manhood and saw her features tauten further. Still, she refused to look at him.

He had felt the faint flicker of anticipation as his hand traced a path between her breasts and the slight sigh of relief that followed when it failed to stray to them. Now his lips quirked as his hand wandered back up the delicate cage of her ribs, Caitrin stiffening once more under his touch.

His eyes clinging in satisfaction to her features,

197

Roarke ignored the grip of need that pounded in his loins, swelling his throat with a lump he could not swallow. He drew his thumbs lightly along the underside of her breasts and saw her flinch slightly. He traced their firm, full roundness with his forefinger, his touch as faint as a breath, then drew his palms lightly over the pink nipples. Even as Roarke heard her almost inaudible gasp of impotent anger, he felt the nipples budding beneath his palm. He could sense, as though they were his own, the nerves twitching under the light circling of his hand, nerves tugging into being a reluctant, bitterly fought desire.

Caitrin's battle against the need his touch aroused was so intense she began to shake. Her eyes were no longer closed to shut out his features but in a vain attempt to concentrate better against the hurtful ache rising in her. They were tight with her effort and the muscles of her neck jumped under the fingers that held her caught.

"You tremble, Lady FitzGerald, under my hand," Roarke drawled, the gentle caress of his voice menacing. "Do you think I mean you harm?"

Her breath, a gasping implosion of anger that he should so ridicule her, overrode her fear. Her eyes flew open, sparking a golden fire as they met his. Her head jerked back in a gesture of contempt and pride, to meet the hard, unyielding cage of his hand.

"You play with me!" she hissed from beneath clenched teeth. "I'll not—"

It was the warning grip of his fingers in her hair that cut off her outraged words. She stared at him, her hands clenched at her sides, her body shaking in her attempt to control the fury surging through it, her eyes amber in rage. Then her gaze dropped. With a visible force of will, she ordered her body relaxed, her temper down. When her eyes lifted once more, they were expressionless and her features were tranquil. Only the haughty tilt of her chin remained.

"There is a service I would ask of you, sir, as the gentleman you are," she stated, her voice as cool and socially smooth as though they gossiped in the finest of Dublin's drawing rooms.

Roarke stared at her, astonished at her audacity. Caitrin felt a hysterical giggle lodge in her throat, trapped there by instant regret for her foolhardy tongue. Then he smiled, the admiration in his eyes chilling her more than his rage had yet done.

"Think you your position, mistress, one from which to bargain?" he drawled.

Caitrin did not answer, her eyes refusing to flinch from his, and his mocking smile widened.

"And what service would you ask of me?" he taunted. "And with what would you pay for it that is not already for my taking?"

"Ga-no-a-o-a has something of mine. Would you have him cheat you of the full value of your purchase?"

"And would you have us both at the torture stake? What it is that you value more than your own life—or mine?" he asked in languid curiosity.

"He has my mother's rosary," Caitrin stated, her request seeming suddenly ludicrous. The whole situation was insane and she wished he would finish what it was he had come to her for, then allow her a rest undisturbed by fear when he was done. It had been only a few moments before, the imp in her mind reminded her, that she had admitted herself willing to sacrifice her virtue for an opportunity to sleep secure in the knowledge of a man there to protect her. But it was not to be, not just yet. Roarke O'Conner,

Caitrin saw by the gleam in his eyes, was not yet finished with his tormenting of her.

"You would have us both dead for a string of beads and a crucifix, would you, mistress?" he taunted, his tongue twisting the respectful term of address into another, less honorable one. "And you a Protestant. Think you an evening's sampling of the favors it is said you pass about so generously and indiscriminately worth such a price? Have you developed skills with your experience so wanton as to replace the charm of your long lost innocence?"

Caitrin stared at him, not seeing his hope that she would deny his aspersions. Her eyes were wide and stunned, then a cold, proud veil of disdain dropped over her features. It was almost funny, she thought, hurt welling up in her, that Ashley's lies would reach even into the depths of the New World's forests. And it was ridiculous that she should care so much that the man who had bought her for a band of wampum should believe them. Then she struck back.

"Perhaps you had best go to those I so honored for any references you seek of my abilities!"

Caitrin saw his eyes go stark with a pain she did not understand. An ache of disappointment swelled his throat, threatening him, and he twisted it into a burning, blind hate. Whatever the hopes he had concealed even from himself, he had known he would not find her untouched, yet his unreasoning hurt that she was not, that she did not attempt to deny his taunts, overpowered his passion and need, perverting them into a desire to inflict pain. Suddenly, he knew it was not lust that caused a man to rape; it was hate and a need to see a woman debased and destroyed. The hate stripped his features to the bone with purpose, and Caitrin flinched away from it.

"But what do you want of me?" she whispered, her eyes bewildered and frightened. "I don't understand! I just don't understand!"

"I want," he rasped, "to know you hurt and feel shame! I want you totally degraded and debased, no pride left in you! I want to see you big with my brat and hating your burden! I want to see you wholly wanton, so stripped of self-respect that you would spread your legs to any man for a coin and a prick to scratch your itch, and all at my command! I want you totally broken and by my hand. Only when I see you so will I let you go back to your guardian, if he still lives, because I want him, too, to see you a crippled, twisted thing! And you will carry a message to him from me, along with my bastard! You will tell Lord Cartland I will break him, too, if I have to track him to hell to do so!"

Her head moved back and forth in denial, and he saw the fear and bewilderment grow in her eyes, feeding his hate and fury. Her lips repeated, "Why? Why?" the fear becoming shadowed with pain as his fingers twisted deeper into her hair.

His other hand was, in contrast, almost gentle as it tugged at the fastening of her skirt and eased it over her hips. Fingers spread, his hand slid lovingly down her back as he watched her mesmerized fear become terror. Cupping the roundness of her buttocks in the palm of his hand, Roarke tilted her up to press against him as her terror became blind panic. But it was not until his lips touched hers that the fear released her and she began to fight. A sob of protest and panic shuddered her slim body, and her head twisted in a vain attempt to escape the hard, brutal mouth that crushed her lips against her teeth, cutting the tender flesh. Her hands beat against his ribs and back so hard she could hear the hollow drum of her blows, but his grip did not ease. Unable to breathe, the taste of her own blood copper on her tongue, Caitrin frantically pounded at the side of his head, then her fingers grasped his hair and jerked with all her strength.

He only laughed, mocking her efforts, his mouth leaving her lips to press a searing path of bruises on the hollow of her throat. He felt the futile blows of her knee against his thighs, the kicks against his shins that could only hurt her naked feet more than they did him. Then he tossed her to the bed, the force of the fall knocking her breath from her.

Caitrin lay there, gasping for air, as Roarke jerked off his breechclout. Her eyes flew wide at the sight of him, then he was on her, a hand pinning her wrists above her head, one knee pressing up between her legs. She could hear her own sobs and her body seemed to fight without direction from her. Yet it was as though she did not struggle at all against the weight holding her down and the hands that ruthlessly explored her. His knee forced her thighs open to him, the rasp of his breathing in her ear. The salt of her blood and his sweat was in her mouth. She could feel the throbbing, hard strength of him and knew it was useless to fight any longer. No longer caring, her body sagged beneath him and he drove against her once and again, seeking an entrance that was denied him. His back tensed, his muscles knotting, then his long, hard body relaxed over her as the realization came to him. His lips moved in her hair with the whisper of her name. The hand that had held her head released her, to blindly stumble over the features of her face.

"Caitrin?" he whispered again, his tone incredulous. Slowly, he lifted his head to gaze into her contemptuous face and a shudder caught deep within him. His fingers brushed over her eyes, closing them, shutting away the unforgiving hate he saw in them. Then they traced over her straight nose, the line of her jaw, her bruised lips.

"Ah, girl, girl," he whispered, his tongue rounding the words into a keening caress of sorrow as he fought to control his body's demanding need. Then he realized the battle was lost, and he shook his head in regret and useless refusal. His hand closed gently over her eyes and turned her face to touch his as his head lowered to her hair. Whispering her name once more in a plea for forgiveness, he felt her whimper of pain once, then again, as the fragile membrane of her maidenhead parted to permit him entry. He heard the groan that seemed to erupt from the depths of him, his need mindlessly driving his body on in a rhythm that sought and found an empty animal release too easily and quickly attained.

His passion spent, Roarke held Caitrin beneath him, not wanting to release her, not yet. How was it, he wondered, that emptiness could choke him, for he felt hollow yet his throat closed on the nothingness. He was suffocating on his desolate triumph. He had taken her in an act that either exalted or debased its participants, yet she had somehow eluded him. There was nothing that he could do to destroy or demean her, not if she did not allow it. It was her strength. Only Caitrin could pass such strength into his grasp . . . and only as a gift.

A sigh of intense relief that he had not so harmed her, that he had not been able to degrade her, shook him, and his arms clasped tighter about Caitrin. Physically, yes, he had hurt her, had taken her virginity, had, perhaps, given her a child, but he had not touched her soul. And he did not want to, not by force, and he wondered when it had become so, when his consuming revenge had changed into an unadmitted, unacknowledged need. He had waited so long, had twisted his very soul to the goal of seeing Lord Cartland destroyed along with the woman he now held in his arms. But, somehow, sometime in those years, the memory of Caitrin's girlchild face, her green eyes, had supplanted his hatred for her guardian, although he had refused to let the hate go. He had been waiting for her to grow up, he knew suddenly, to become a woman, yes, but not for the lies he had told himself. He had eagerly sought sight of her that day in Albany and yet had told himself he wished her grown up ugly and hard. A small, unadmitted part of him had held her memory as a talisman of the home from which he had been driven.

He had had to believe the rumors concerning her promiscuity; the decadence and disdain for virtue in Dublin's aristocracy was too well known for her to be otherwise. He had wanted her in spite of the gossip, his first sight of her in Albany breathing life into a secret hope he had nurtured even as the whip of Lord Cartland's lackey striped his back. But he had denied it, had repressed it even as a part of him prayed for her safety when he saw Montcalm's artillery had shattered the walls of Fort William Henry. He told himself he prayed that he would not lose his chance for revenge. He had felt a stunned, despairing anguish when her fingers were pulled from his, yet he still lied, still told himself it was for the chance for retribution he felt slip from his grasp. He had awakened from the musket blow to his head filled with grief and fear, yet still unable to admit his need.

He had not faced it even as he came after Caitrin, his hope she was alive lifting his feet when they would have faltered with fatigue. He had felt, even then, that he would know, somehow, if she was dead. There would have been a vacuum in his heart. It was his pride that could not admit to the bond he sensed between them.

Somehow, sometime, the girlchild had become a woman, and as she grew, an ocean between them, a part of him had grown with her. He needed her, needed more than the unresisting shell of her in his arms, yet he knew, even now, that his pride would not, could not let him admit it, not to her.

Feeling Caitrin stir beneath him, he clasped her tighter still, not willing yet to let her go. His fingers brushed over the smooth skin of her face, then blindly began to untangle strands of her hair. The tip of his tongue traced the convolutions of her ear, before his mouth searched out and rested in the hollow of her throat. But it was as if he caressed only the flesh of her, her soul being far withdrawn from him.

She should, Caitrin told herself, feel more than she did. There should be shame, grief, anger, yet all she felt was tired, too tired to even straighten her cramped fingers from their clasp on the hair at the back of Roarke's neck. She should feel dirty, defiled, and all she could summon was weary fatigue . . . that and a small sense of disappointment. The pain that he had so hurt her, that he had wanted to do so, his reasons for it were things she would examine another time, a time when it no longer mattered.

Somehow it seemed she was always disappointed in one thing or another. The famous people she had met were always, in some way, flawed. No party she attended, no experience, was ever as exciting as anticipated. Even fear, she had found, could only reach a certain peak, a point where it became an audible hum in the ears. Then the nerves could no longer support it, the mind seeking release in stupor. And this, this being raped, this animal act whose very mention stirred such fear and revulsion, had also proven to be a negligible thing. There had been pain but certainly no more than she could bear. Then she had felt nothing; his assault had been over so quickly, the very position and motion of the act so ridiculous. And emotionally, somehow, he had not touched her. She had drawn away from any hurt or shame he could have dealt her.

And it was good that she could do so, Caitrin insisted to herself, yet she wondered if that was a flaw in her . . . if, perhaps, she could not feel as others did . . . if something essential was lacking in her. Pushing the thought away, she scowled, seeking the source of a nagging, annoying memory she knew was important. It brushed her mind with teasing wings as fragile as a moth's, then she felt Roarke's hands again lifting her, tossing her back into the bed. She felt him over her, his weight bearing down on her as her hands beat at his shoulders, her fingernails digging into and scoring with crimson gouges the ridged, scarred flesh of his back . . . the scars!

Knowing what she would find, Caitrin hesitated a long moment, suddenly strangely frightened. Roarke's fingers were quiet in her hair, his body tense over her as though he, too, was afraid as her hands began to search. She stared, unseeing, up at the roof's shadowed beams, her fingers groping over the rough ridges that marred Roarke's back. She felt the hard muscles that quivered under her hand as though they sought to escape her touch. From below his waist to his shoulders her hand moved, then slowly down again, her fingers like those of the blind, reading each scar, counting them.

Then Caitrin closed her eyes, her body sagging with a despairing grief and understanding she thought would tear her apart as she began at last to sob. And in her nose was the fragrance of apples.

Caitrin heard Roarke's aching whisper of protest against the anguish that shook her. She wept the tears he had never been able to release, and in doing so, she somehow brought him ease; she drew the festering hate and revenge from him.

His hands wandered over her, trying to draw her closer still, trying to quiet her body's racking shudders. He murmured her name over and over, his voice a moan. His mouth pressed against her hair, her face, trying to soothe her weeping. Then he found her lips. He heard her gasping sob at the touch, felt her recoil. Then she grew quiet, her body acquiescent and expectant under his.

Drawing back, Roarke gazed at Caitrin's sorrow-blotched features, then gently pressed his lips to her swollen eyelids. He whispered her name again and she opened her eyes to meet his. She stared at him, a pucker between her brows as she tried to read in his eyes what his lips could not say. Her fingers brushed lightly along his jaw to his mouth. He had taken time to shave, she realized with wonder, before coming to her. A man intending rape, yet he had shaved! As though seeking an answer to all her questions, her fingertips touched his lips before curling into the close-cropped hair at the back of his neck. Then she drew his mouth down to hers.

Suddenly needing and wanting her as he had never

207

needed a woman before, Roarke felt her whimper of surrender as his mouth claimed hers. Her lips parted at his command, and her tongue met and clung to his in a kiss so sweet with the desire to give, with her yearning to take, that he thought he would burst with it. Her hips tilted under his, blindly seeking and finding the shaft of his manhood, tumescent with his need.

There was a moment's pain as abused tissues yielded to him, then an aching warmth shook Caitrin. She heard his groan, felt the shudder of it in his throat, and knew she sobbed in response. The imp in her mind mocked her need to give to the man who had, so shortly before, taken her with rape, even as her body absorbed Roarke in total abandonment, her hips eagerly meeting each urgent thrust. Then the imp was gone, driven away by passion. Roarke seemed to become a part of her, the taste of him on her tongue, the weight of him in her flesh, his moan echoing in her throat, the very pulse of him singing in her veins. Her sob shaking her, Caitrin knew she called to him, pleaded with him, begging for release, for the gift of him, and she found that pride was alien to the place of overwhelming ecstasy where he had brought her. She felt the blood that rushed within her, felt every muscle in him urging her, lifting her to heights of pleasure she had not known possible. Then his seed jerked out of him, flooding her. The fire of it burst through her veins in a tide of crimson heat that carried her on its crest. A sob of triumph swelled her throat as she laughed back at the imp in her mind. Beneath the passion shattering fragments of her brain, she clung to one thought before being swept into a swirling darkness: There was no disappointment on the other side of the fulfillment given her by Roarke.

Roarke cradled Caitrin's languid form in his arms. She quivered slightly from a weeping he sensed was of joy. He held her, his face pressed against hers as his lips moved in a prayer of fervent gratitude. Somehow, in some incredible way, regardless of all his blundering, his insane, stubborn clinging to a hate long lost, in spite of the hurt he had given her, she had become his. She had given herself to him in a way no woman had ever done before. She had touched his soul with hers and in so doing had become as essential to him as the air he breathed, and he would never, could never, release her.

Sixteen

Caitrin stretched in her sleep, then moaned as stiff, sore muscles and tissue complained. Moaning again, she reached out, seeking Roarke's warmth and finding only empty blankets. Her eyes flying open, she sat up in dismay.

The longhouse was empty, and a wave of fear and desolation swept over her. Perhaps it had all been a game with him after all. Perhaps he had only meant to use her for the night and would, that morning, return her to the squaws! And the morning was almost gone. Perhaps the women waited outside, waited for his nod of consent, prepared to enter and paint her face once more for death.

Staring at the door, her jaw clenched against the sudden fear, her fingernails cutting into her palms, Caitrin knew that should the women come once more for her, she would not be able to bear it. Having collected her courage once to face such a death had sapped her of all strength and fortitude. She had calmly, numbly accepted its inevitability because since her capture, she had expected little else; it had seemed only logical. To not only be miraculously snatched from death to find unknown tenderness and

211

passion, but to also find promise of a future she had never dared to dream of before, to be shown hope only to have it burst apart, would destroy her. She would become a cringing, sobbing, pleading thing. He had said he wanted her destroyed and perhaps this was how he had chosen to do so. Perhaps the very raising of her hopes, only to cast them down again, was the revenge he wanted.

Her gaze still on the flimsy door, her knees too weak to carry her there, Caitrin felt anguished wails breaking against the knuckles pressed to her mouth. It seemed she could hear the expectant laughter of approaching women then, jerked by a shred of hope, her eyes leaped to the walls of the cabin. Then her shoulders slumped in overwhelming relief and she bit her lip against a sob of joy.

Roarke's flintlock and hunting shirt were still there. And where he had tossed them were the shirt and leggings he had discarded the night before. He would not have deserted her to wander naked but for his breechclout through the village.

Caitrin's laugh was tinged with hysteria as she settled back into her warm nest of furs and blankets. She curled up in them, missing his presence although she had known it only one night. If his bladder was as full as hers, then she could well understand why he had gone out. She needed to, also, but wanted to savor the warmth of the bed a moment longer. And once out of their longhouse, Iroquois men seldom returned until night; he would be forced to squat with the warriors to pass the day in gossip and boasting. Or perhaps he joined them on a hunt or in fishing.

But she wished he hadn't left so soon; she wanted the warmth and comfort of him. The strength Caitrin had sensed in Roarke when she first saw him in Albany had not proven false. The eyes that had aroused a hitherto unknown need had not lied in their promise of passion. But her desire, she knew, trying to analyze it, went far beyond lust. He filled her with a need to comfort, to give, to take, to cling even as she supported. She wanted to bring him joy, love, a child. But lust, she decided, was enough to think on now.

The corners of her mouth turned up in a soft smile as she thought of the night before. Sometime in the late night, a nightmare had tormented her. A dream had stalked her with blackened faces, with circling, grotesquely painted figures brandishing fingers of flame. And into it had strolled an arrogant man whose blue eyes had stared at her with indifferent contempt before he turned, disinterested, away from her beseeching hands. She had sobbed with terror, with a sense of insufferable betrayal, then Roarke had awakened her. He had held her, his hands soothing away her fear, until her arms had found their way about his neck, until she pressed tightly to him, suddenly wanting more than comfort.

And Roarke had given her much more. Caitrin smiled, remembering. His hands had wandered over her gently, seeking out places where the nerves quivered close under her skin. His lips, his tongue, caressed her mouth, her shoulders, her ears, the nape of her neck, kissing, nipping, teasing. They roamed down to her breasts, a triumphant chuckle in his throat as her back arched at the touch of his mouth. She moaned then with the rapture of it, the mouth that tugged at her with a pleasure-pain she could not bear yet did not want to end. His hand, suddenly rough with passion, sought the moist heat of her and felt her wince. He stopped then, his body taut as he fought to control his own passion, then relaxed.

Gently, slowly, three times, his mouth pressed in the hollow of her throat, he stroked her with his hand until she became no more than a vessel for the intense, throbbing pleasure that flowed from the knot of her womb, coaxed by his fingers. And, each time, he laughed exultantly, sharing the ecstasy he gave her as she begged for him to stop, to never stop. He, at the end, caressed the length of her, gentling her, bringing her down from the heights of fulfillment. Then Roarke brought her hand to his turgid shaft. He let her feel it harden, guiding her curious fingers over the velvet smoothness of its head, its distended, corded veins. Cupping her fingers within his, he curled her hand about the crinkled sack with its shifting, ovoid contents, their weight surprisingly heavy in her palm.

"There," he whispered, boyishly proud and boasting, "are the children I will have with you!"

Then Roarke drew her hand back to the shaft, showing her how to caress him to the ecstasy he had given her, letting her know the pleasure she gave him, the power of her touch.

She laughed softly, eyes gleaming.

"Ah," she chuckled, "I have, indeed, become wanton!"

Then, frowning, Caitrin repeated her words, listened to the echo of them, the proud joy she felt gone, her tone stark and flat with pain.

"He would make of me a wanton," she whispered a third time, remembering the words he had spoken in hate and rage. "And well he had succeeded!"

Inexplicable grief rose in her. Never would she know if Roarke O'Conner had held her in love or in hate. Never could she trust him. His raging words of revenge would always be between them. Never could she dare give to him, not as she had done in the too-short hours of love that were all they could ever share. Always she would wonder, "Is this the way to his revenge?" And, no matter his protestations or his denials or deeds, she would always question his motives, doubt his purpose.

Never again would she dare to open herself to him. The thought of a lifetime without the joy she had so briefly tasted filled her first with an intense sorrow, then with a cold, brittle fury. Suddenly, she hated him with all the passion and rage remaining in her. He had dared to show her joy, only to snatch it away. He had told her his intentions, yet she had allowed him to strip her of her pride, to use her. She had whispered of her need for him like a bitch in heat, and the thought of how he must have secretly gloated filled her with shame and fury.

But no more, she whispered to the taunting, crowing imp in her mind. Soon her need to relieve herself would drive her from the security of the longhouse, and she would have to face him and the people of the village. Surely all would know of her humiliation. Perhaps he had bragged of his prowess, of his ability to stir virgins to rut, to bring them to beg for more. If not, surely her cries of passion had been audible to all who had not slept. But there was nothing she could do now but gather her dignity, shattered as surely as her maidenhead, and walk with what remained of her pride. Her hate would hold her head high, no matter her shame. And never again would she allow Roarke O'Conner to so claim her. She was his slave; he had purchased her and she would obey him, giving all he asked but no more. She dared not give him reason to be rid of her, not yet, not here, but never again would she meet him in passion. Never again would she allow him to touch her soul. She would hone her hate against him. With it she would suffocate the need she felt for him. She would use it to deny her love. And, perhaps, in lying to herself, she would come, too, to believe it.

Trapped by Iroquois custom, Roarke sat with a handful of warriors and watched the ever-shifting fortune of the deer button game. Their eyes intent, the squatting men crowed or groaned dramatically as luck favored first one then the other player.

It was a stupid game, especially for grown men, Roarke thought churlishly, conveniently forgetting the hours he, himself, had spent engrossed in it. He watched, feigning interest, as one player tossed eight buttons of elk horn, burnt black on one side. The warrior gave a high-pitched hoot when seven of the buttons turned up black, his supporters adding their glee to his. After taking two beans from the other player's cache, he tossed again, turning up, to his friends' moans, five blacks and three whites. His opponent, chortling, picked up the buttons. And the game would go on, each player trying for six or more buttons of one color with each toss, until the stake was totally in the hands of one or the other. It was a game that could continue for days. All else— hunting, fishing, war—would be forgotten.

Nor could Roarke escape. From the moment he had set foot outside, he had been trapped in Iroquois hospitality. Greeted with friendly shouts, he was escorted to the river for a morning swim. From there he had been accompanied to the sweat house, then back to the river. Entertaining him with gossip, they had basked in the sun with him for an hour and more, until the game of deer buttons became irresistible.

And they had never considered that he might want

to do otherwise. That he might prefer the company of a woman would be not only astonishing but impossible.

To seek Caitrin out, to pass time alone with her, would be to lose their respect, could lead them to question his masculinity. More dangerous, it could raise doubts concerning his reasons for wanting her. There had been skepticism and a wry, tolerant humor in the wise old eyes of Ha-ne-a-ha, but others would be less pleased to be the victims of his purpose. Roarke had not noticed any trace of revulsion for him in the morning, though he knew they could not understand the perverted ways of the white man, either in women or war. It would be insane to rouse their mistrust for a few hours with Caitrin when, the Most Holy Father and all the saints grant it, he would have her for a lifetime. He wanted her safely away from the village, but to leave too quickly would appear like flight. Perhaps it was no more than concern for Caitrin that lifted the hair at the back of his neck each time he heard a high-pitched shout or a loud sound. He had become like an old broody hen with one chick. Or perhaps it was the warrior at the sweat house, eyes glazed with fever and complaining of a back and headache. But they could not run, not yet, and in the meantime their presence in the village was too perilous for Roarke's liking.

He knew his eyes strayed too often in the direction Caitrin must go to bathe in the river. And the attention he gave the game lacked convincing zest. But his companions' excitement was too great for them to notice his own disinterest.

Yet, dangerous as it was, he still wanted to be reassured that she was his by the sweet, yielding passion of her mouth. He had thought to wake her that morning, but the violet shadows under her eyes,

217

her deep sleep, had held him back. He contented himself with smoothing her shimmering hair back from her face, with pressing his lips softly to the blue vein that pulsed under the transparent skin at her temple. So fragile she seemed. Too fragile, he thought, to contain the strength she did.

It was not only the taste of surrender on her mouth that Roarke wanted. He wanted to talk to her, to tell her the thoughts he had never shared with anyone, to listen to hers. There was, really, so little he knew about her. Suddenly, he could see a life beyond the culmination of revenge. Suddenly, there were years ahead of him that he had never considered before, years to marry, to breed children of a beloved woman, to build instead of destroy. There was Caitrin and he wanted to make plans, to discuss with her the life they would know together.

There was land in the New World for the taking. Not here, not in the blood-drenched country that had been the battlefield between the French and English for so long, but farther south in the Carolinas, in Georgia. There was land down there, where he was not known as a white man turned savage or as a traitor. There, winter was a lady bred to the bone who trailed veils of mist and magnolias in her ambling wake, so he had heard. There winter's breath was not a knife to the lungs but a soft sigh that leavened with life limbs gone languid in the long, lazy summers.

And there, unlike so many of the New England colonies, a man could be of the Roman faith, could attend the church of his choice without facing the bigotry of his neighbors or paying a higher tax than they did as cost for the privilege.

Or they could go to Canada. He would always be accepted among the French, and Caitrin, as his wife

218

and an Irishwoman, would be welcome. He had money enough now to do either. But Canada would be impossible if England won the war. And such plans were a waste of time until he had Caitrin away from the village, until he found an immediate refuge for them both.

The deer horn buttons were scattered once more on the scarlet blanket. The men around him hooted but Roarke frowned, their shouts scarcely intruding on his thoughts. He could make all the plans he wished, but Caitrin was an heiress. There were people and land in Ireland that belonged to her, and for all that his wealth might appear immense to him, he saw it with the eyes of an Irish croppie who had not seen a shilling from one year to the next until he was thirteen years old. No matter the lands he might possess or the proud blood of the woman he bedded, in Ireland he would always be an Irish croppie. A night of love with him could not change that for Caitrin, though he wanted to offer her so much more. Even married to him, she might want to return to her estates. Not only was her wealth there but so were her responsibilities. But, with a papist husband she would not, according to the Penal Laws, be allowed to keep her lands. She would be forced to sell them at but a fraction of their worth. Nor could he repudiate his faith—or even pretend to do so—and even if he did, he would never be accepted. Nor could he become a drawling, gesturing nabob greeting a fortune lost or won at cards with a languidly lifted eyebrow, a man who even pursued his neighbor's wife lethargically. The savages, crowing and wailing over their game, were less alien to him. In Ireland, he would be, instead, brother to the croppie standing akimbo at the passing of the foreign lord, legs straddled, cap on head, and chip on shoulder. That a fist in the face would be the croppie's reward was incidental.

For all that he yearned to see his home again, Roarke knew he could never do so. And if Caitrin did not chose to share his exile? Could he let her go? He did not think so. The very thought drove his nails into his palms, his knuckles whitening. His jaw clenched, the muscles jerking, and Roarke forced it to relax. His features could too easily reveal his agitation.

He blinked, his vision clearing, and saw Caitrin following the path to the river. The sight of her raised a new fear: He had not warned her of the peril of exhibiting the joy they had shared. But there was no danger, he saw. Caitrin walked with a free, fetterless stride, her head held proudly, her chin lifted. Her face was set and when her eyes met his, they remained impersonal and impassive. Then, before they moved on, cold contempt shuddered in their depths, chilling him, shaking him.

It was late when Roarke returned to the longhouse. The last of the early autumn twilight had long since faded. The deer button game had lasted forever, fortune favoring first one player then the other. As a guest, food was served to him by shyly smiling women, denying him hunger as an excuse to seek out Caitrin. When the gambling at last ended, Roarke had been forced to lounge in the council house and listen to gossip and stories of feats of heroism. Only after hours of seemingly rapt attention interlarded by several prodigious yawns, only the first faked, did he dare excuse himself as tired.

But sleep was not in his thoughts as he ducked through the door into the cabin. Hours of frustration had whetted his hurt to a cold anger. Yet in the back

220

of his mind hope that he had been mistaken in what he had seen in Caitrin's eyes still lingered.

He was not wrong, he realized when he saw Caitrin in the feeble light of the longhouse's interior. She had not stayed up for him with food as she had the night before nor had she gone to bed. She sat on its edge, asleep, her feet drawn under her, obviously waiting for him. Her head rested on the support pole she leaned against. And no longer did she display her breasts in the unabashed manner of the Iroquois women. A scarlet blanket was wrapped about her, secured with a cheap and tarnished trade brooch. It was this deliberate concealing of the breasts he had kissed and caressed that told Roarke his fears were real.

His eyes still on Caitrin's face, he squatted to feed the fire. He wanted to see her clearly. He had to be able to read each nuance on her face, to see if she lied, to know why she had withdrawn from him. When the light of the fire danced high, he kneeled before her, gazing at her sleep-gentle face. Firelight touched the tips of her eyelashes with gold and licked at her hair with copper. Her mouth trembled into a faint smile at some dream, then it was chased away by a frown that tucked her brows into a pucker of anxiety. Roarke touched her mouth with a gentle finger, wanting to press away her fears with the frown he smoothed.

"Wake up, little girl," he whispered. "Wake up, Caitrin," he whispered. "Wake up."

Her eyelids fluttered, then opened slowly, reluctantly. For a brief moment joy leaped in their green depths, then they closed against him, growing opaque. Her face grew hard with a forbidding haughter as she drew away from the post she leaned against.

221

"Did you want something? . . . What am I to call you? Sir? My lord? Master?" she asked sarcastically.

His mouth tightened and his blue eyes turned to ice, but Roarke's voice was calm.

"My name will do, my given name," he answered. Then his eyes dropped over her significantly. "Considering how close we have been. And I will call you Caitrin," he added, his head bobbing once in a mocking mimic of a toadying servant, before his voice hardened, "if your ladyship will be gracious enough to allow me such intimacy."

Caitrin stared at him, her face unreadable as hurt raged through her. It seemed he deliberately derided the night they had shared. Then her chin lifted.

"Do I have any choice? Haven't you the strength to use my name as freely and as familiarly as you did my body, whatever my objection?"

Roarke's eyes held to her indignant face as he wondered if the pain he sensed beneath her rage was real or only a figment of his hope.

"Aye," he answered at last, "I've the strength, but I do not wish it so. I do not wish to hurt you."

"Then take me to New York!"

Roarke's features hardened and she laughed.

"I thought not! It is revenge that drives you, naught else! So you told me, but I let your kisses and soft words deny your warning! Not now, never again! I'll not aid you in your twisted plans!"

Roarke knew then that Caitrin hurt. Her pain reached for him in the words that begged for a denial, yet he knew there was no way she would let him soothe her, let him ease the grief he had given her.

"You would not believe me were I to tell you otherwise, would you?"

Caitrin's proud, closed face was his answer and Roarke at last looked away, afraid his eyes would betray his own need and hurt. When his gaze returned to hers, his own features were set. He cupped her face in his hands, his eyes cold blue flame as they searched hers.

"If you'll not believe me in one," he told her, his voice a soft, beguiling caress, "then I'll not give you cause to credit me in the other."

He lowered his head, his mouth moving over Caitrin's in a whispering, pleading kiss. His lips, his tongue, beseeched a response, nibbling, sucking at hers, begging and promising as they clung with a searing passion or grazed light as a feather's fall. His mouth tugged at the hurt and need in her with a rending pledge she did not dare trust, and as a weapon against her clamoring desire to submit to her aching want, she summoned hate. She used it to etch in her mind each word of revenge and hate he had spoken, each moment of his rape the night before. Her will became an impregnable wall against him and she held her body passive as he lowered her to her back, his body over hers.

He could, she knew, too easily turn her resistance to passion if she fought, so closely was the battle waging within her between her will and her need. Caitrin thought she would surely burst with her desire to respond, to give to him, no matter the lies she felt in his aching kiss. His hands roamed over her, touching, caressing, loving as he tried to reach her need, her passion. Then, at last, as though no longer capable of trying to reach her, Roarke entered her. He ignored her gasp of pain as torn, dry flesh parted to him, his body moving over her gently, carefully, passionlessly. His culmination of desire was little more than a shudder, then Roarke lay over her, his hands still cupping her face, his mouth buried in her hair.

"You've come a long way, haven't you, croppie

boy?" Caitrin asked, her question striking out at her need to cradle him, to whisper words of love, to soothe him as she would a hurt child. "Ten years ago you stole apples. Now you rape women."

Roarke lifted his head. The last remnant of passion fled his eyes as they met hers, turning stark. He stared at her a moment before his face dropped into her fragrant hair once more, his body heaving with a single, quickly finished tremor of pain. Then he pushed himself from her and stood up.

It took Roarke only a moment to draw on his breechclout and moccasins, his face a rigid mask. When he turned back to lean over Caitrin, he twisted his hand in her hair and pulled her mouth up to his. His mouth bruised her lips, yet its message of love and rage and grief was undeniable. Then he released her and his hand whipped into her face. The blow spun her away from him, sprawling her across the bed, and when she at last raised her head to look at him, he was gone.

Inanely, she wondered where he would spend the night.

Seventeen

It was only a few hours later when Roarke came back. Caitrin slept curled up in a ball, her face smeared with dried tears, the print of his hand still visible on her cheek. For a brief second he wanted to cuddle her, to whisper to her. Then his face hardened. There was no time now for words of love, no time to try to convince her of his feelings, his intentions. He shook her roughly and she whimpered. He shook her again and her eyes opened, bewildered. Then her features hardened and she jerked away from him.

"Why don't you seek out a squaw," she suggested. "Perhaps you'll find her more compliant and your bed sport better."

Roarke lifted Caitrin and swung her to her feet, shaking her.

"We haven't time to play games, to argue, to fight! Get dressed!"

Turning, he began to gather his possessions, stuffing them into a backpack. When he looked at Caitrin again, she had not moved. Her chin lifted, she stared at him defiantly. For a brief moment, Roarke's fist clenched with the desire to knock her into movement, into obedience, then his hand relaxed. Going to her, he touched her nipple with a gentle finger and her chin lifted higher.

"You have beautiful breasts, beautiful nipples," he told her softly. "I would hate to see pine splinters thrust through them and set on fire. You have the longest eyelashes I've ever seen. I would hate to see the eyelids cut from you so you cannot close them to the torture done you. And your hair, never have I seen hair like yours. Nor have they." His head jerked toward the village. "And they would just as soon have it from your head as not, especially now."

"Now?" she repeated, bewildered.

"We have to leave, and we have to leave now! There is no time!"

"But why?" she asked stupidly.

"Smallpox!" Roarke hissed into her face.

"But I've had cowpox. I can't get smallpox," Caitrin said inanely, wondering how many times she would have to explain that fact in this benighted country.

Roarke snorted.

"Aye, but the Indians haven't even cows! Nor have they had smallpox, not until the white man came. Do you know what smallpox does to Indians? It decimates them! It can wipe them out, all of them! And when they realize what is happening, they will figure we brought it with us! They'll come for us, those healthy enough! Now, get moving. Get dressed! Help me pack. Take all the food you can lay hands on! We might have but a few hour's head start. There's a cave I know. We'll hole up in it . . . if we make it there!"

"But the children," Caitrin argued, not moving as Roarke turned back to his packing. "Who will take care of the children?"

Again Roarke's fist clenched in frustration. Then he relaxed and drew Caitrin's unresisting body into his arms.

"There is no help for the children, Caitrin. They'll be the first to go, then the old. The warriors will be the last, and 'tis them we have to fear. Now, move!"

She stared at him a moment more, then turned to do his bidding. Her hands shook suddenly as the danger hit her. A basket dropped from her nerveless fingers and she stared at the dried beans scattered over the floor.

"Leave it!" Roarke ordered as he tossed her a buckskin shirt. "There should be food at the cave . . . if bears haven't found it. Put that on and braid your hair."

Finished with his packing, he looked at Caitrin and his mouth quirked into a smile. She looked lost in the shirt twice her size.

Lost, he thought, and like a bewildered child.

He longed to comfort her, to tell her everything would be all right. But it might not be so. His mouth was set in grim lines as he settled a backpack on his broad shoulders and helped Caitrin with a smaller one. Last, he dropped his bullet pouch and powder horn over his shoulder and lifted his flintlock from the wall. Taking Caitrin's hand, he drew her cautiously out of the longhouse. But she tugged back against his hand.

"You?" she whispered, her eyes clinging to his features. "Have you had smallpox?"

He studied her upturned face before shaking his head.

"We'll deal with that if it happens," he told her. And, Holy Mother of God, how could it not happen? he wondered. How many hours had he sat and gossiped with warriors now shaking with fever? How

227

many hours had he sat in the sweat house with men now racked with back and headaches? But that would be dealt with later.

The village lay quiet as Roarke drew Caitrin from shadow to shadow. A dog barked and he drew her into deeper shade, waiting until it quieted. If there was movement, if anyone was awake, it would be women tending their sick warriors in the family cubicles of the longhouses. He had lied to Caitrin. The first to fall ill were those warriors who had been at Fort William Henry, those who had massacred the smallpox victims, who had looted their possessions, who had dug up the dead. But it would be the children who would be next, who would die the quickest. And he, too, had been at Fort William Henry. He shook the thought from him and led Caitrin into a forest without light.

They traveled without respite until the sun was high over head. It seemed to Caitrin that Roarke pushed her harder than even the Indians had done. Her back and shoulders ached from the weight of the backpack. Her legs shook from fatigue when he finally called a halt near a small creek. Sinking to her knees, Caitrin dropped her head to her arms in front of her. Never, she thought, would she move again, no matter how many Indians were behind her. Then she felt Roarke take her backpack from her, felt his hands kneading pain back into muscles long since gone numb. She cried with it, trying to push him from her, but he held her down until his hands massaged the pain into a warm glow of comfort.

Taking off her moccasins, he carried her to the creek and dropped her swollen feet into icy water. She gasped from the cold but he held her there until all feeling was gone. Drying her feet with his hands, rubbing them gently, he at last looked up at her.

"Sorry if I hurt you, but you have to be able to walk. We have at least another day's travel, a day and a half, perhaps, depending on how fast we can move. You've done well, much better than I thought you would. But it won't get any easier and we have to move fast. They've missed us by now. And I won't be able to help you, to carry you."

Caitrin's chin lifted angrily.

"And you think I would ask it of you?"

Roarke's mouth tipped into a satisfied grin. She would keep up. His challenge would hold her to her feet long beyond the time any other woman would drop. He already knew her stubbornness well enough to realize that—and to use it. Then he sobered.

"Put your moccasins on," he ordered, handing her a piece of jerky. "'Tis time to go."

They walked until after dark, until Caitrin could barely make out the blur of Roarke's buckskin shirt in front of her. Only her anger kept her on her feet, but she collapsed when he at last called a halt, her legs giving out under her. Shaking her out of her stupor, Roarke handed her pemmican and dried fruit, insisting that she eat and drink.

"No fire," he told her. "They can smell smoke for miles."

Caitrin did not care. All she wanted was to sleep forever. But Roarke would not let her. Again he dipped her swollen, bruised feet in a creek, then chafed them warm. Then he forced her to walk deep into the forest away from the creek.

"They'll look for us by water," he explained, and all Caitrin could think was, Damn the Indians and damn Roarke O'Conner, too, as he spread blankets for her to lie down on. Nor did she do more than murmur a weak protest when he crawled in next to her, drawing her into his arms.

Sometime during the night it began to rain. They woke in sodden blankets, and Caitrin thought her teeth would never stop chattering, not even long enough for her to chew the jerky Roarke gave her. Her shoulders and spine ached. Her legs and feet were cramped, swollen, and weak. Her fingers, toes, and nose were numb from the cold, from the rain that continued to pour down. Nor did it help when Roarke looked up at the sky with a satisfied expression.

"Good weather," he commented. "Our tracks are washed out by now and they'll be easier to hide today."

Then he grinned at her.

"Though, you, Catkin, look like a drowned kitten."

Then his smile disappeared as his eyes wandered over her. Her hair was slicked to her head with rain, exaggerating her large eyes, the line of her jaw. Her wide mouth was chapped a vivid red, and her lower lip trembled from the cold and damp. His gaze dropped lower, to the buckskin shirt that was clinging to her body with its wetness. It molded her high, round breasts and outlined the cradle of her hips, the thrust of her pelvic arch. Her nipples were full and proud with the cold. Suddenly, he wanted to lie her down in the moss and mud, to strip the shirt from her, to taste her mouth, the sweetness of her tongue. He wanted to warm her body with his, to draw her nipples into his mouth, feeling their chill turn to heat under his tongue. He wanted to take her there in the cold and wet, to enter her, to bring her to need and warmth and surrender.

But there was disdain on Caitrin's features when Roarke's eyes returned to her face. Beneath the scorn, too, he saw her fatigue, the sheer will she used to hold onto her remaining strength.

"Is my lust so obvious, then?" he asked, mocking her.

"It is," she answered, her chin lifting higher. Her back straightened, thrusting her breasts forward, and her hands moved to the straps of her backpack, as though to remove it.

"Anna Redmond, my stepuncle's whore, has told me that a lady would rather die than submit to undesired attentions, which I've difficulty reconciling with her relationship to Lord Cartland. Then she and my uncle sent my cousin to rape me, to force me into marriage with him. It did not work, as you well know." She shrugged. "Myself, I've learned to love life too much to not fight for it, no matter"—her eyes dropped significantly over him—"how odious the task I'm expected to perform. And I, too, seek revenge against my stepuncle. I, too, may have the means to acquire it. So what would you have me do? What do you want of me? Shall I lie down? The ground is cold, but you'll find me so, too."

Roarke stared at her, need in his eyes. I want you, he thought, as you were the other night, open to me, giving to me, taking me with a warmth and desire I never thought could be.

Then his vision blurred with an intense headache. The tightness in his back, in the very bones of his legs, was not from travel fatigue. He should have known better than to hope it was. He had walked much longer, much farther, had slept too many nights in the cold and rain to have hoped it was so. He blinked hard against the pain and it receded a bit.

But how long he could keep it at bay, he did not know.

"We travel," he told Caitrin. "The price of your survival we will barter for later."

Turning on his heel, he plunged into the forest. Caitrin stared after him a moment, her jaw jutted, then followed.

Roarke pushed her harder that day, the bone-deep ache in his back, his legs, his head, the fever he felt building ever at his heels. No longer did he pause to let her catch her breath. No longer did he gallantly hold back branches that would have slapped her if she did not catch them. As unremitting as the rain was, he doubted that the Indians still followed; ill, they would prefer their longhouses to revenge. Still, twice he led her into streams, following them for miles without respite, until her feet were blocks of ice. She slipped and fell three times on moss-slick stones, soaking herself. Each time, he reached back and jerked her to her feet without a word. Each time, she stumbled on after him. A hundred times she thought she could not go on. Her feet were swollen and blistered inside her moccasins. Her legs felt like blocks of wood. The pack cut into her back, its straps into her shoulders. Her mind ceased to function, her only goal the swinging fringe on the hem of Roarke's buckskin shirt. Only because it moved did she move. When it stopped suddenly, she ran into Roarke, staggered, and fell to her knees. He did not seem to notice her as he gazed around, then he jerked her to her feet and dived into the underbrush, pulling her after him.

Soon they were climbing a steep, heavily forested slope that tipped and tilted under Caitrin's feet. The rain increased, something she had not thought possible, making the ground treacherous underfoot.

When Roarke at last halted, she collapsed to her knees, not asking why, only grateful for the respite.

"Stay!" he ordered.

Like he would a dog, she thought, too exhausted to even mutter a protest or feel concern that he deserted her. She only wanted to stay there forever. Dropping her head into her lap, she fell instantly asleep, the rain pelting down on her.

When Roarke came back, he gazed at her dejected form for a long minute. His eyes were held to the white triangle at the nape of her neck. It looked so vulnerable, with the tendrils of damp hair slicked to it by the rain. He thought of carrying her, then his vision blurred with fever and he knew he could not. Ignoring her protests, he shook her awake and dragged her to her feet. Pulling her behind him, he dragged her up a steep slope, dropped to his knees behind the huge trunk of a pine tree, and disappeared. She stared after him, bewildered, then dropped to her knees to follow him through a low, short tunnel into a cave.

Blinking, Caitrin stared around in amazement. A fire in the middle of the chamber illuminated the vague form of two tunnels and the fantastic shapes of pillars of stone. Stacked against the vaulted walls were heaps of furs and trade goods, baskets, and buckskin bags of food. Deeper into the cave was a large pile of firewood, enough, she thought, to last for months. Then all she wanted to do was curl into a pile of fur and crimson trade blankets and sleep.

But Roarke would not let her. Ignoring her protests, he stripped her naked. Standing her before the fire, he dried her skin and hair, scrubbing her into a rosy glow. Then he carried her to a nest of blankets and furs. She was asleep before he put her down, but not before a numbed section of her mind wanted to cling to him, to ease her chill against him, to absorb the incredible warmth of his skin.

When Caitrin at last woke, the fire had burned down to a faint glow. For a moment, she could not remember where she was and panic brought her to her feet. She was in a cave, she realized, the cave Roarke had said would give them safety. He was there, too, sleeping apart from her. Suddenly, she wanted to go to him, to curl into his warmth, then anger replaced the unwanted desire. He slept, leaving her unguarded in an unfamiliar place. And the fire had almost died. If it had, she would have been alone in total darkness, and she suppressed an urge to kick Roarke awake.

Instead, Caitrin built up the fire, feeding it kindling, then logs, making as much noise as possible as she did so. But Roarke, who could wake at the snap of a twig, the drop of an acorn, slept on. Hungry and thirsty and still exhausted, she kicked a pile of logs, sending them crashing down, and still he did not wake.

She stared at him, wondering if he was playing a game. Perhaps he hoped she would go to him, lean over him, shake him. Then he would grab her, pull her down and into the blankets with him. A strange warmth stirred low in her belly and she pushed it down with memories of Roarke's rape, his humiliation of her. Then fear gripped her as she remembered the heat of him when he carried her to her bed the night before, the way he had hunched and straightened his shoulders as though to ease an ache, the way he had rubbed the back of his neck. Cautiously approaching Roarke, she peered down at him. He was curled into a ball, as though to protect his stomach. And she knew he always slept on his back, alert even in sleep. She studied his face, though she knew it was too soon for pimples to form, then she placed a hand on his forehead. He was burning hot, and he tossed and moaned as though her light touch was painful. Moving her hand, she found a pulse that beat an erratic rhythm.

Hunkering back on her heels, she studied him. Judging from the sensitivity of his skin, he was within two or three days of the eruption of pimples. Which meant that he had been ill for several days. When he drove her so hard, he had also been driving himself against the racking pain, against the weakness and fever that would have prostrated most men, to get her to safety. Once the pimples erupted, the fever should fall, the aching diminish. Then the pimples would become blisters, the blisters pustules. It was during the pustule stage that the fever went up again, that most people, four out of every ten, died. Or they died during the stage he was in now. And blindness. Some became blind from lesions on the eye.

Caitrin's mind flinched away from the thought of Roarke dying and the inexplicable grief she would feel. Instead, she faced fear. To be trapped in the wilderness alone with only the brief woods lore Robert Rogers had taught her was too terrifying to contemplate. Or with Roarke blind. To leave him would be impossible; she owed him too much. But she must deal with the present now.

She had to eat. She had to find water, not only for herself but to bathe Roarke, to try to reduce his fever.

Caves, she remembered, often have water. After all, that was how most caves were formed, with water. It accounted, too, for the strange rock formations she

235

could glimpse beyond the firelight.

For a second, claustrophobia at the thought of leaving the fire and Roarke, of exploring the dark, close tunnels, held her immobile. Then she shook it off. Tightening her jaw, she took a torch and an empty tin jug and headed down a dark tunnel. But people get lost in caves, Caitrin thought, never to be found, and she stopped abruptly. The torchlight wavered on the glistening walls as she held it in a shaking hand. Turning slowly, she peered back and could see the glow of the fire. It gave her courage and she could hear the faint trickle of water. Holding the torch higher, she moved deeper into the tunnel and found a small stream that ended in a deep pool. High above it was a faint patch of light, a natural flue for the fire's smoke. Filling the pot, she went back to the main chamber and Roarke.

Eighteen

Then began days and weeks of fear and fatigue. She sponged Roarke with wet cloths that turned warm as they touched his skin, until she thought her arms would drop off. Patiently, she wiped his fever-encrusted lips, trying to keep them moist. Cradling his head in her arms, she spooned a broth of jerky, dried beans, and corn into his mouth and gave him water as often as he would take it. She had to keep his strength up now, she knew, no matter how he fought her in his delirium. When the pustules rose at their worst, they would invade his mouth and throat. Swallowing would become painful, perhaps impossible. She dared sleep only in bits and snatches. Her fear of the fire dying and leaving her in total darkness haunted her. Anxiously, she waited for pimples to form, to change to pustules. The number of pustules often determined how ill the patient was. The fewer the pustules, the greater the chance of survival. In extreme cases, a patient could become a dripping, unrecognizable mass of pus. Death, then, was inevitable.

Occasionally, Roarke would rouse from his delirium, too exhausted from fever to speak. Each time, his lips formed a faint smile. Once he clasped her hand, pressing its soft palm against his mouth, his eyes touching every feature of her face. Then he lapsed into unconsciousness again, moaning incoherently.

On the third day, Caitrin woke with a start. She had slept too long and the fire was almost out. Hastily, she fed it, then went to Roarke. But he was quiet, sleeping easily. She felt his forehead and found his fever down. Anxiously, she studied him inch by inch. A few reddish spots marred his forehead. More were on his hands and forearms, and scattered across his chest. Faint reddish spots stained his feet and legs, but they were altogether light.

Gratefully, she dropped her head to his chest and began to cry. A hand touched her hair, began to caress her head, and she looked up.

"Am I to die, then?"

Caitrin stared at Roarke as he smiled gently at her. Carefully, he wiped the tears from her face.

"I don't know," she whispered honestly. "I don't think so, but I don't know."

Pulling away from him, she sat up. Studying her, Roarke could see the fatigue that drew dark smudges under her eyes. She only looked more beautiful, more fragile. But the fragility was deceptive, he knew.

"Generally," she said at last, "the fewer the pox, the better the chance. You haven't developed many pox, at least not yet, and I don't think you'll get too many more. But it doesn't always hold true."

Sighing with weariness, she ran her hand through her thick hair, lifting it back from her tearstained face, and asked, "What do you know of smallpox?"

"Very little," Roarke answered. "Only enough to know to avoid it at all costs—or almost all costs. Sometimes, though, there are exceptions to even the

238

most hard-cast rules, sometimes even a woman."

His eyes held Caitrin's as she scowled and lifted her chin in rejection of his comment.

"Would you get me something to eat," he asked at last, "then tell me about smallpox?"

Suddenly ravenous, Roarke ate two bowls of the jerky and succotash stew Caitrin gave him. Yet he watched her as he ate, amazed that he was also hungry for her. She moved about the fire, cleaning up. When she went back to the pool, jug in hand, his gaze did not waver from the dark tunnel until she came back. At last, she sat down next to him. Her voice was neutral.

"Smallpox begins, as you know, with a high fever and body aches. Some people die during that stage. Then, a few days later, pimples form. As yours have. Soon—tomorrow or in a couple of days—the pimples will form blisters. A couple of days or more after that, the blisters become pustules. With the pustules, the fever comes again. It is during that time that most people die. If they survive, then it is a matter only of recuperation, of waiting for strength to come back, for the scabs to form and fall off."

Reaching out, Roarke took Caitrin's hand, ignoring her tugs to free it.

"You look like a schoolteacher sitting there reciting an obscure history lesson—the Visigoths' invasion of Spain or the Trojan War—and not the course of a disease that may or may not kill me."

He ignored her renewed attempts to jerk her hand away and asked, "Will you still love me if I'm badly pockmarked?"

He laughed softly as she flushed angrily. Teasing was not an aspect of Roarke's that she was familiar with, and it discomfited her. It threatened her with that deep, aching coil of warmth in the pit of her belly, with the feeling she could trust him . . . but she could not. At last, he relented and released her hand.

"You're weary, girl, aren't you?" he asked softly as he traced the line of her jaw with his finger. Tears of fatigue formed in her eyes and she blinked them back as he said, "You've done well . . . better than anyone could expect. You're a woman any man would want by his side, would be proud to have in his bed. I would have you in my bed now, if only to watch you sleep, but I want you to go to your own. You need to rest if this thing is to prostrate me again. I promise I'll not touch you."

Caitrin held his gaze and knew she could trust him. Gratefully, she crawled into her pile of furs and blankets and slept for twelve hours.

Roarke was dozing when she woke but the fire had been fed, the water jug filled, and a stew was set aside, still warm. Caitrin grinned wryly to herself as she ate. Roarke was definitely a better cook than she was, at least with jerky and succotash. But then, she had never had the need to learn. Finished with her meal, she began to comb and braid her hair. When she next looked at Roarke, he was awake and watching her. There was a faint smile about his lips that somehow disconcerted her.

"May I have a bowl of that stew?" Roarke asked. "And come talk to me while I eat."

Caitrin could think of no excuse not to go to him. There was nothing else to do in the cave but sit next to him, and no graceful reason not to. Still, he did not say anything and she shifted where she sat.

"How did you find this cave?" she asked at last.

Sitting cross-legged on the floor, Roarke put aside his bowl. The pimples on his face, arms, and feet had deepened in color, were beginning to form blisters. His features were gaunt from the high fever. Dark circles had settled under his eyes but his gaze was bright blue as he regarded her.

"I wounded a bear and followed him in here. It had been his den."

Caitrin stared back at him, eyes wide.

"But that was a stupid thing to do!"

Roarke grinned in wry agreement.

"Aye, I know, but I've a soft spot for wounded creatures. And 'twould be a sin to have let him die a death of agony."

Did he sense her own inner wounds? Caitrin wondered. There was something in his eyes, in the tone of his voice, that said he did. Then she put the disconcerting thought aside as he continued.

"I would never have found this otherwise and decided it would make an excellent storehouse for trade goods. And a better lair in case of trouble. I thank God for my foresight."

His gaze was intent on her and Caitrin felt a flush rise.

"I keep a boulder rolled over the entrance when I'm not here—to keep another bear from finding it. That was what I was doing when I left you on the trail—rolling the boulder away and lighting the fire. I did not want to do that to you—leave you alone in the dark with no idea where you were or what to do. I apologize for it."

Nonplussed Caitrin dropped her gaze from his. She did not know what to say, how to thank him. He was the last man she would ever choose to be indebted to. But he, too, owed her and would owe her more should he survive the smallpox. Whatever their differences, they had to be amiable to each other if they were to survive. And Roarke, she knew, sensed her discomfiture.

"You said," he mentioned finally, "that you, too,

241

bear Lord Cartland a grudge, that you might have means to gain vengeance."

The fingers that had been braiding and unbraiding the fringe of her buckskin shirt ceased their fiddling, and Caitrin, startled that he would remember her rash words, stared at Roarke. But she found, in his steady blue eyes, the knowledge that she could trust him—in that.

"I found documents," she told him at last, "in his trunk, deeds they were, to properties along the Hudson. William Johnson's was one of them. He— my uncle—and several other men were listed as buyers. The owners were listed as Frenchmen, one of them Bigot."

Roarke's eyes narrowed.

"So that is what he was doing at William Henry! He's cast his lot with the French! And his fortune!"

But Caitrin did not share his glee. She shook her head.

"No, not his fortune. He has friends in high places. He had political power but little wealth. What wealth he used would have to be mine. Which is why he brought me with him. I would have come of age while he was gone, and he knows me well enough to realize I would have immediately taken control of my properties, would have found money missing. Which is why he wanted me to marry Ashley, why he sent him to rape me."

A surge of anger assailed Roarke at the thought of another man's hands on Caitrin or another man in bed with her. To suppress it, he grinned.

"If he's used it, if he's lost it, then at least you'll know 'tis not for your money I want you."

A flush rose over Caitrin's features and her chin lifted.

"Aye, but you never said you wanted me for my

money. 'Twas vengeance as I remember it!"

Roarke sobered before her anger, wondering how long he would regret his careless words of vindication.

"Then we'll talk of revenge, plan revenge. I only wish to God we knew where Cartland is now, with the French or the English. 'Twould help determine where we are to go after I get well. The English may give me a too warm welcome, if I was seen by the wrong people at Fort William Henry, and the French would hold you for hostage. Yet it is the English who would like word of Cartland's treachery."

Slowly, Caitrin's high color died.

"And what did you do for the French that the English might want you?"

Roarke met her eyes with a steady gaze.

"I gathered information."

"Then the English might assume you a spy."

"Aye, they might."

"And were you . . . are you?"

"Aye, but first I'm a woods loper. I sold my furs to whomever paid the highest. If I heard word of aught that the French might use, aye, I sold it, too. And vengeance can be expensive . . . the kind of vengeance I seek."

Caitrin stared at him. It seemed she could feel again beneath her fingertips the scars that marred his back. And where in a man so driven, she wondered, could there be room for a woman, for love? How could she be anything but a tool for his vengeance? How could a woman ever trust him to want her for any other purpose? A surge of grief engulfed her and she drove it back with anger at herself for even thinking there might be anything else between them. It was revenge he wanted and so did she. And that was enough. She could be with him for that, stay with

243

him for that, and then be done with him, as he would be done with her.

"And what were you doing at Fort William Henry?" she asked.

"Cartland was there. You were there. I could not very well be with the English. You had seen me in Albany, had seen something in me, I thought, beyond aught but another woods loper. I thought you might seek answers to questions I did not want asked. Nor did I want to be penned inside the fort, tethered, unable to move, and fast. 'Tis well I was not, for the French would have assumed I was playing a double game."

Caitrin grinned wryly.

"Straddling a fence," she observed, "can be adverse to a man's health."

Roarke smiled back ruefully.

"Aye, and to any children he might think to have."

A flush rose over Caitrin's cheeks and she looked down.

"I've no idea where my uncle might be," she said at last. "He wanted to go to the French, that I know. I saw him trying to speak to General Montcalm in private."

"Did he?"

"Not that I saw. He even evoked Bigot's name, which seemed to please Montcalm not at all."

"It wouldn't. Montcalm is an honest man and despises those who are not. He would have no part of a plot such as exists between Cartland and Bigot. I doubt he even knows of it. And I doubt Cartland is in New France. Montcalm would see to that."

"Wherever he is," Caitrin observed, "he'll be on his feet. He's like a cat in that."

"Aye, but even cats have only nine lives." His eyebrows meshed in thought. At last, he looked at her.

"I think we'll go to Montreal. The French will most likely see you as Irish before English; there are many Irishmen in the French army. If you play the part of Cartland's niece but are ignorant of his plot, you should be safe. Perhaps we'll learn enough to hang the man. And I know Montreal . . . the place, the people. If it should prove dangerous, we can escape more easily from there than from the English."

He did not see Caitrin's dismay at the picture of Lord Cartland hanging, neck in noose, wigless, lifeless, bald, elegant buckled shoes pigeon-toed and dangling, head askew. As much as she wanted revenge, as much as she feared him, the picture was disturbing and she shook the thought from her. There was no room for pity, not for Cartland. He'd not hesitate to destroy her if he thought she threatened him. And she did, by her knowledge, by her very existence. Her very survival could depend on destroying him before he destroyed her. If it was revenge Roarke wanted, then so did she. Soon, within hours perhaps, his fever would rise again, prostrating him, and she turned her mind back to his intriguing plan. And how, she wondered, was she to send a message to William Johnson from New France?

Soon, too soon, the smallpox struck Roarke once more. It seemed as though she had had no time at all to rest, to regain her own strength, before the long hours, the long days of nursing Roarke began again. With it came the effort of forcing liquids down a throat raw with open sores. Nor did fear for his death abate, although the pimples that dotted his face, his arms, and legs were light. There still remained a one in four chance that he might die.

"Will you still love me if I'm badly pockmarked?" he had asked, and the question teased her with its flippancy. It prodded her into an anger that suppressed any doubts she might have had that, perhaps, he might not have been teasing her. Sometimes, she even told herself, she wished he would die, would end the confusion that tore her thoughts apart.

But slowly, too slowly, Roarke's fever dropped. The pimples formed pustules, then foul-smelling scabs, which within a couple of weeks began to fall off, leaving a few brownish scars scattered over his arms, legs, and forehead. Slowly, Roarke began to recoup his strength.

Yet it seemed to Caitrin, considering the lightness of Roarke's case, that he malingered, that he was in no hurry to leave the sanctuary of the cave. Yet each day they stayed, each day he became stronger, threatened her. She had cradled him in her arms to feed him, had bathed every inch of his body, had attended his most personal needs. Now, she no longer even handed him a bowl of food, a mug of water, but instead set it down near him. Carefully, she maintained a distance between them beyond arm's length, avoiding even his most accidental touch and refusing to meet his gaze. At night she lay in her bed, eyes open in the dark, listening to his soft snores.

Yet the barriers she had erected against him were no longer easily maintained. No matter how she fought, she found herself relaxing with him, enjoying his company. Her body had an awareness of its own that she could not deny. Against her will, he held her enthralled with stories of the coureurs de bois, the Indians, the societies of Quebec and Montreal. Fight as she might, she found herself smiling at his teasing, his jokes. And she told him of her childhood, of the deaths of her parents, of a child

246

growing up lonely amidst a multitude of servants. She told him things she had never told anyone, things she thought long forgotten. But she did not speak of the priest who had slipped up the back stairs to give her mother last rites, the same man who had instructed her in the Catholic Church. It was too dangerous a secret to trust to anyone. And if Roarke wondered why she had asked for the return of her mother's rosary, he did not ask. Yet always, she held his words of revenge as a wall between them.

And they would leave soon, she told herself. Nor could it be soon enough. Then they would be united only by their mutual purpose.

Then, one night when Caitrin had begun to feel as though there were no world beyond the one she shared with Roarke, he set aside his supper bowl and studied her. His gaze seemed to drink in every aspect of her features, then he shrugged and looked away.

"We leave tomorrow," he stated.

Startled by her sudden regret, Caitrin gulped back tears. For a long moment, she sat with her hands in her lap, staring at them, trying to sort out her conflicting emotions. Then she began to clean the dishes. Standing up, too, Roarke started to pack.

It seemed to Caitrin that they were finished too soon. Taking a trade blanket with her, she went back to the pool to bathe. When she returned, Roarke was sitting by the fire, cleaning his flintlock. Sitting opposite him, wrapped in a scarlet blanket, she began to comb her hair, letting the flames dry it. The warmth and the rhythm of the comb soothed her, drawing her into a trance.

Lost within herself, she was not aware that Roarke, setting aside his flintlock, had stood up. Then he was behind her. His hand was over hers, and he took the comb from her.

She stiffened. Her head came up slowly. Eyes wide, she stared at the far wall as his hand gently lifted her hair and draped it over her shoulder and down her breasts. He drew her earlobe into his mouth, sucking it. Then his lips traced slowly from beneath her ear down the line of her neck to her shoulder, and she shivered.

"No," she whispered, as much against the sudden sensations as against the kiss itself. "No!"

"Yes," he breathed against her skin, his voice hoarse. "Oh, God, yes! I've waited too long! Lie down with me!"

"No!" she repeated as his mouth pressed into the hollow of her collarbone. "Oh, Holy Mother of God, no!"

Her head swept from side to side in negation, then dropped back to rest against his shoulder, her lips pressing against the pulse in his neck as his hands moved around her beneath the blanket. He caressed her breasts, scarcely touching them, his mouth feeling the quake of desire in her throat. His thumbs touched her nipples, lightly at first, then deeper, and he felt her moan beneath his lips.

Reluctantly, she lifted her mouth to his. He took it, felt her lips part, her tongue rise to meet his, draw back, then lift again, taking, giving. His groan answered hers and he drank of her as though he would never let her go, even as he turned her toward him, as he lay her down on the scarlet blanket, his body covering her. Taking her face in his hands, he drew back to look at her, to touch her lips with a trembling finger before his mouth claimed hers again, stronger, deeper. Then his lips traced along the line of her jaw to her throat and down, drinking of her fragrance, her skin, until the warmth of his breath grazed her nipple. His tongue touched it

248

lightly, felt it rise with the moisture and his breath, then he drew it in, felt it engorge within his mouth.

Caitrin's body arched closer as his lips drew a compelling warmth into the depths of her that grew and grew, until she thought it would surely burst, surely consume her with its sweetness. She knew her head tossed from side to side, that her fingers wove through his hair, fluttering helplessly over his shoulders, stiffening and relaxing with the pleasure. Her legs parted beneath him and opened. Her body pressed up against him. She heard her gasps of need and a part of her stood back, remembering her resolution, saw her wanton in her lust, and mocked her unrestrained abandonment.

But it did not matter. The only thing that mattered was Roarke over her, his weight upon her, his mouth on her breast drawing such incredible pleasure and need from within her.

Then his mouth left her nipple, brushed softly down the line of her, caressed her navel, then moved lower. His tongue parted her, tasted her, pressed against the core of her. A moan burst from her throat, then the intense pleasure of it drew her abruptly back within herself.

"No!" she gasped. "No!"

Twisting suddenly, kicking out in desperation, she flipped away from under Roarke like a landed fish. He caught her ankle as she crawled away, pulling her back under him. Stunned, she stared at him a moment, then began to fight. Her body jerked under his and her fists swung at his face. One connected with his ear before he caught and held her pinned beneath him, legs sprawled. Her wrists secure, he shook his head to clear it of its ringing and looked down at her, laughing.

She looked back, gaze defiant, jaw set in that

obstinacy he was coming to know too well. But beneath the contempt in her eyes was a hint of passion, of laughter. Slowly, he lowered his head to touch her mouth with the tip of his tongue and she jerked away. Drawing back, he grinned down at her, then sobered as he moved against her. He watched her face as he found the heat, the wet of her, as he pressed deep into her. Gently, slowly, he drew back, then pressed again, watching her defiance turn to wonder. Her head fell back to move from side to side as her fingers twined with his. A moan shook her throat as her body rose to him, opened to take him more fully. Her gaze narrowed in concentration, turning inward even as it held to his face. Then her eyes closed as deep shudders overtook her, as the bubble of heat and need burst within her, spread through her, only to build and burst again and again. It seemed to her that the intense pleasure would never end, would flow and ebb and flow again until it melted her into nothingness. Then, through it, she heard Roarke gasp her name, once, twice. She forced her eyes open to see his face racked with ecstasy as he drove his seed deep within her. She heard his shout of triumph as her body took him, held him, shuddered beneath him one more time.

Roarke slowly lifted his head and cradled Caitrin's face in his hands. Gently, he wiped away her tears.

"Ah, Catkin," he whispered, "don't cry. There's no cause for tears. Do you know how rare it is, this thing with us? People search for it all their lives and never find it. Never before have I had this with a woman. Never, I know, would I find it again."

Caitrin snuffled and gulped and allowed him to smooth her tear-damp hair from her face, to draw her closer. She allowed him to tuck her against him, spoon fashion, and listened to his soft snoring as he dropped off to sleep.

But Caitrin's eyes were wide on the fire. Suddenly, more than anything in the world, she did not want to leave the sanctuary of the cave, the safety of Roarke's body curled around hers. It was as though nothing could threaten her there. For the first time since her stepfather had died, she felt protected, secure, and she snuggled closer to Roarke.

The idea of eating nothing but dried corn and beans and pemmican for the rest of her life was absurd, though. Picturing Roarke and herself, years later, with skin like mushrooms and blind as moles from living underground, Caitrin giggled to herself.

Then her humor faded. Always, it seemed, she had stood as a buffer between her uncle and her mother, until her mother's death. Then she had defied him for herself, to protect her own integrity, her own identity. And she had waited, anticipating the day when she would come of age, when she could order him gone from her and her people. But she had never confronted him, had never set out to deliberately destroy him as Roarke wanted her to do, and she found herself afraid. She knew how powerful he was and how far he would go to protect himself. Never had she known someone to defy him and win. And she and Roarke had such flimsy weapons, some papers she had read, Roarke's fortune. Papers could be destroyed or Cartland could have her declared insane. Witnesses could be bought, and who would doubt the instability of a woman captured by Indians, condemned to torture, rescued by a half-savage woods loper, then hidden in a cave with a smallpox victim? And what kind of fortune could a woods loper acquire large enough to destroy Lord Cartland and all his resources? But why was he involved in such a perilous scheme? He was a man who loved to gamble, though, whether at cards or in business, the larger the stakes the better. Perhaps this was nothing but another gamble. But if he lost, then he would be more dangerous than ever.

Caitrin's mind whirled with possibilities, and she sighed and closed her eyes. Briefly, she wished she and Roarke could just disappear. Already there must be those who assumed her dead, and there must be any number of places they could hide in this vast land where they could live without fear.

But he wanted revenge. He had told her so, had told her he would use her to accomplish it, would even get her with child to do so.

Caitrin's eyes flew open. Suddenly, she felt cold, sullied by the lovemaking that had left her so warm, so desired a few moments before. Anger flared through her at her own stupidity, at the body that had betrayed her with its need, its passion. She remembered Roarke over her, felt again his seed being driven into her. Perhaps she was already pregnant. Slowly, her hand pressed against her belly. Was it her fertile time? Mentally, she counted back to her last flow and realized she had not had one since she had been captured at Fort William Henry. But anxiety would do that, she argued, although she had never missed one before. Her hand moved to her breasts. They were fuller, tender, the nipples more sensitive, but lovemaking could make them that way. And the slight nausea she had felt in the last few weeks, that could be caused by the constant fear she had lived with, the unrelenting diet of dried beans and corn and pemmican.

But Caitrin knew she was searching for hope. She was pregnant, well over a month pregnant.

Frantically, she wondered what she could do. But there was nothing. And many women bore illegitimate children. Almost half of all women were pregnant when they married, that she knew. And there was no stigma in it. But those were women of the lower classes, the merchant classes. Nor was she to be married, not to Roarke. That was not his intention, not a part of his revenge. Nor would she accept him, not now, not ever, not after he had used her so. Or the women of her class had abortions. She had heard enough drawing room gossip to know that. But she recoiled from the thought. Even if it was not forbidden by her faith, she did not think she could do it. She had come too close to death, had fought too hard to live to deny life to a child, no matter how detested the father. Feverishly, her thoughts swept on. She had two, maybe three months before she would show, four or five if she laced tightly. Perhaps in that time their plans would be fulfilled and she and Roarke parted forever; he need never know she carried his child. Never, she swore, if she could in any way avoid it, would she give him that satisfaction, that aspect of his vengeance. And never, she vowed, would she ever again give herself to him in passion and abandonment. Her jaw set, Caitrin fell asleep.

Caitrin woke to the feel of Roarke's mouth on the nape of her neck. His lips nibbled at her and she sighed in pleasure. Then her eyes flew open and she stiffened away from him as he turned her to face him. She looked up at him, eyes cold and defiant. He stared back at her, puzzled, then brought his mouth down to hers to kiss away her anger, whatever its cause. But her lips were slack and ungiving. At last, he drew back to look at her, but her gaze was focused beyond him. Cradling her face in his hands, he studied her impassive features, looking for a clue to her enmity without success. Softly, gently, his eyes touched her every feature. His calloused fingertips followed his gaze, tracing her jaw, chin, the straight line of her nose, her eyebrows, as though they could read what his eyes could not. With the ball of his thumb, he grazed her full lips, then touched her eyelids, closing their blank animosity away from his view. Soft as a falling leaf, his lips touched them, then moved to her mouth. Gently, they tried to coax passion from her frigidity. His tongue traced her lips, then parted them, seeking her tongue, pleading with it without response.

His mouth moved down, found the pulse in her slim neck, but its beat remained slow and steady. His hands sought the soft fullness of her breasts, his thumbs touched her nipples, their rough ridges drawing the tender flesh to erectness. His mouth drew them in, one after the other, and he felt them engorge, but there was no responding need on Caitrin's features. His lips nipped the flesh around her navel, then he pushed her legs apart to open her to his mouth. She lay unresisting, exposed to him, her eyes blank on the high ceiling as his hot tongue parted her, sought the core of her. He moistened her, felt her flesh become swollen under his tender attention, but she did not move to press his mouth closer, did not sigh or moan, did not run pleading fingers through his hair or clasp his hands to draw him up and over her, into her. At last he moved, his mouth tracing his way back, to gaze into her face. But there was no softening there. Jaw clenched, Roarke took her head between his hands.

"Catkin!" he whispered, his voice broken with urgency. "Catkin! Why? What happened? Tell me!"

At last her eyes focused on his and she lifted one eyebrow in derision.

"Hadn't you better get on with it," she asked, "if we are to leave today? Vengeance, after all, will not wait forever."

Roarke stared down at her unyielding features for a long moment, knowing that the revenge he had built for so long no longer mattered. If this woman would but ask, he would turn his back on it with no regret, if she would but touch his face, open her body, her passion to him, if she would but join herself to him in love again. But it was revenge, too, that she sought, and Roarke could see no beginning for them, no life for them together until he had given it to her.

He longed to wipe the apathy from her features, to stir her to emotion, any emotion. Instead, he drove into her, pounded into her. She lay patiently beneath his onslaught until he reared over her, his face contorting as he flowed into her. His head dropped down next to hers, his shoulders shuddering with the emptiness of his release.

"Are you finished?" Caitrin asked, and Roarke lifted his head to look at her. His eyes held a bleak desolation that swiftly became murderous rage. Jerking himself away from her, he rolled to his back, shaking with his need to strike out, to batter her into response, any response. At last he stood, ignoring Caitrin, and finished packing.

Nineteen

The pace Roarke set was steady. Still not completely recuperated, he did not push himself or Caitrin. For the most part, they traveled in a heavy silence neither sought to ease. Only when giving her instruction did Roarke speak and Caitrin swallowed back a thousand questions that leaped to her mind.

She had long since lost any sense of direction or location. They were headed northeast, she thought. She wanted to ask where they were, the name of each mountain she saw, each river they crossed. Summer had ended while they were in the cave and early autumn had touched the forest with an artist's pallet gone mad, with vivid colors she had never seen in Ireland. She longed to ask the name of each crimson tree, each russet or golden shrub, every unfamiliar bird she saw, each autumn flower. But she kept her mouth clenched against each question until her jaw ached. Each night, Roarke set out snares, ending at last the unremitting diet of pemmican, and Caitrin had to bite her lip against a request to be shown how to set traps of her own.

They scrupulously avoided the slightest of touches, of eye contact, and slept apart. After their meal,

Roarke insisted that they move on until darkness overtook them, before they bedded down with no fire. The woods were full of Indians, he curtly explained, and she believed him. Too many times he had halted her, signaling her to caution, quiet. Twice, they had slipped into the underbrush, hiding as a column of half-naked savages walked past.

Yet Caitrin was ever aware of him lying an arm's length from her. The nights had turned crisp and she huddled in her blankets, shivering. But she knew it was more than cold that shook her. It was the need to wake Roarke, to curl into the warmth of his body, to feel the security of his arms around her, his body's warmth over her in lovemaking. A part of her wanted to tell him of the child she carried, of her need for him, to beg him to take her somewhere, anywhere safe, to let go of his hate. She shook with the need, and the soft whisper of his slumber mocked her. She knew that at the snap of a twig, the hoot of an owl, he would be instantly out of his blankets and alert. His easy sleep taunted her, seemed to express contempt for her desire, her weakness.

Then, one morning, she woke and he was gone. Fighting panic, she told herself he would not have brought her this far to desert her. He needed her, after all, for his revenge. Nor could she do anything but wait.

It seemed forever before, with no sound, he was there. Without a word, she put on her pack and followed him. Soon, she caught a glimpse of blue through the thick foliage, then the St. Lawrence River was at her feet.

She stared at the rampaging rapids in dismay and her fear only increased when Roarke pulled a small canoe from its hiding place. But he did not notice her consternation as he stowed their bedrolls and packs in the canoe. Then he reached to hand her in but she did not move. Only her eyes shifted from the frail craft to the raging river and back.

He studied her, his eyes narrowed like a wolf's on a rabbit. Caitrin had never complained, had never allowed worry or dismay to show. She had followed him unhesitantly, never allowing fear or consternation to open a door between them.

But now she was shaking with it. Suddenly, he wanted to take her in her terror, to turn it toward him, to rape her mouth with his, to force her to the earth and open her to him, and he knew she would respond. She would fight him as she could not fight the river and perhaps her fear would turn to an answering passion.

And he wanted to take her in his arms as he would a frightened child, to cradle her against him to assuage her fear, to tell her everything would be all right.

But it might not be. The river was dangerous and not all who traveled this stretch of it survived. And as treacherous as it was here, it only became more perilous closer to Montreal. Yet to continue by foot could add weeks to their journey with, still, the threat of Indians. It was much easier, too, to slip into Montreal unnoticed from upriver than from across.

"Do you swim?" he asked her.

Caitrin's eyes flew to his and she took one step back from the river's edge, shaking her head. Then she turned to run.

Roarke leaped after her and caught her shoulders, spinning her around and into his arms. She fought him wildly, blindly, and he caught her hands, forcing them behind her back.

"Catkin!" he rasped, shaking her. "Catkin!"

She gasped, trying to drag breath into terror-paralyzed lungs. Her head dropped to his chest as she sobbed. He held her, gently rubbing her back until her weeping eased. More than anything, he wanted to take her mouth with his, to taste her tears, to turn them to passion. He shook with the need to lower her to the earth, to transform her terror to trust with his body, with his desire. But he knew that to do so would, somehow, be to take advantage of her, would turn her further away from him.

"Catkin," he whispered, "I won't lie to you. The river is dangerous, aye, but not so much as the woods. There are Indians about, and many more the closer we get to Montreal. And coureurs de bois, who would ask too many questions. Who would gossip too much. Montreal would know we are on our way long before we reached there. I've done this run many times and I would not take you down it if I did not think we could make it. I know you cannot swim but I'll tie you to me in case, by some slim chance, we tip over."

He tilted her face up and smiled into it. Gently, he wiped her tears away with a calloused finger.

"Do you really think I would gamble your life if I thought the stakes too high? After all, Catkin, I've my revenge to think on, if aught else."

Caitrin's body stiffened and she stepped back from him. Her features were suddenly hard with anger and a hurt he did not understand.

"Do not," she ordered, "call me Catkin!"

Her back ramrod straight, she walked to the canoe. Her hand out, she waited for his help into a craft that only seemed all the more frail when she sat in it. Though Roarke had folded a blanket for her to sit on, she could still feel the torrent of water rushing beneath it, its numbing chill. When he tied a thick rawhide thong to her wrist and then around his, her heart only beat faster, threatening to leap up her throat. Yet she held her face averted from his, not realizing that her white-knuckled hands, clutching the sides of the canoe, betrayed her terror.

Caitrin remembered little of the journey downriver. It was a nightmare of cataracts, whirlpools, and rocks that seemed to leap up in front of the frail craft, of eddies that suddenly became stomach-wrenching torrents whose drop threatened to break the spine of the fragile craft. Caitrin found that to close her eyes against the terror only made it worse. She could only stare, mesmerized, at each rapidly approaching obstacle, at the white torrent of water ahead. She could only whimper her fear as sheets of water poured over her, soaking her. She was aware of Roarke behind her, of his skill that was the only hope she had of escaping drowning, of being battered to death on the rocks that reared up all around them.

Even in the smooth stretches of water she shook with fear and cold. She could only hold her breath, waiting for the next maelstrom, could only stare ahead, her hands still gripping the sides of the canoe. Her legs were cramped into spasms of pain from kneeling but she was too afraid of upsetting the canoe's delicate balance to move. She could only sob in terror.

Lunchtime passed but Roarke did not stop. The river required his total concentration. To be distracted for a flicker of a second could be death for both of them. And he dreaded the coming night. He did not know how Caitrin would behave, what he would have to cope with. More, though, he dreaded the next morning. Nor could he tell her the worse was over, that the journey would be easier the following day. It would not. After these waters, the raging flues of the Cedars, the Buisson, and the Cascades, came the sweet, gentle waters of Lake St. Louis. But then, just before Montreal, came the tumultuous rapids of La Chine.

Dusk fell with a soft rain when Roarke at last pulled into a small inlet. He dragged the canoe into shore, then looked at Caitrin. She sat shivering, soaked, and bedraggled. Her lips were blue and bitten raw. Her hands still gripped the sides of the canoe, their tendons white. Her eyes stared straight ahead unfocused, and Roarke could hardly believe she was the same proud, beautiful woman he had seen in Albany.

But she could not be his first concern. He found firewood and pulled several packs wrapped in protective oil-soaked hides from the canoe. From one of them, he took kindling and built a fire. Whatever Indians might be about would be burrowed into their own shelters. They wanted to be out in this weather no more than he did and had less purpose.

At last he went to Caitrin, gently loosened her cramped fingers, and carried her to the fire. Stripping her wet clothes from her, he dried her, then wrapped her in a blanket. Shaking, she was scarcely able to hold the mug of hot stew he handed her. He rubbed circulation back into her cold feet and she roused herself enough to feed herself. Still, she shook from chills and shock. Laying out some blankets, he carried her to them and lay down with her, cradling her. His rough hands moved over her, caressing her, and her skin gradually warmed again. Her shaking eased and she clung to him, gasping as he rubbed life back into her cramped muscles, into her legs and arms, into her knotted hands. Then he held her close, cuddling her, mingling their warmth for a long moment before his mouth pressed against the pulse beneath her ear and felt it leap under his touch. His lips traced along her jaw, then sought her lips. She quivered as his warm breath grazed them, as the soft tip of his tongue brushed their corners, their outline. His tongue delved deeper, exploring the sensitive flesh behind her lips, then he drew the softly swelling lower one into his mouth, sucking at its fullness.

He kissed her a long moment, his mouth telling her of his need, his desire, his love, before he drew back to look at her in the dying fire's dim glow. Its taint flickering cast lights of red and bronze into her hair. It touched her eyelashes with tips of gold and sculpted with warmth the pure contours of the face he held between his hands. But she gazed over his shoulder, her eyes unconcerned, as though a part of her was not there, as though his body did not cover the slim, rounded length of hers, as though his nearness could never touch her. Gently, he traced the arch of her eyebrow, the tip tilted length of her nose with his lips.

"Catkin!" he whispered, his throat thick with thwarted desire.

Slowly, as though she had not realized he was there, that he held her so, her eyes focused on his. Her head tilted slightly to the side.

"I've asked you not to call me that," she stated, her voice hard.

Roarke stared into her cold eyes, then gently kissed them closed, shutting away her apathy. Then he dropped his face into the warm juncture of his neck and shoulders. Gulping down the hard lump of his despair, he rolled over to his side, taking her with him. He held her, his hands slowly moving up and down the curve of her back and buttocks as he fought to control the shudders of need and hurt that gripped him. And he wondered if it was himself or Caitrin whom he soothed.

Long after he fell asleep, Caitrin stared over his

broad shoulder at the dying embers of the fire, her chest tight with desolation. She longed to wake him, to kiss passion back into his eyes, to feel him over her again, within her again, possessing her, giving to her, taking from her. And after their passion was spent, she longed to take his hand and place it on her belly, to tell him of the child she held cradled deep within. Using his words of revenge, she drove the need from her, but tears still glistened on her lashes when her eyes at last closed in sleep.

Waking Caitrin, Roarke held out a cup of stew to her. He watched as she blinked away her sleep, as she realized where she was. For a brief moment, panic leaped into her eyes, then she focused on his concerned features. She took the mug he offered and began to eat. Still, Roarke watched her from the corner of his eye as he broke camp. She was too calm, too relaxed, and that worried him more than any hysterics might have done.

She finished her breakfast and Roarke began to pack the canoe, his back to her as she dressed in clothes still damp from the night before, from the drizzle that still fell. Stowing their blankets in the canoe, he turned to her.

"'Tis time, Caitrin."

Caitrin's eyes flicked from his face, to the canoe, to the raging waters of the St. Lawrence, and back to him. Carefully, as though not certain earth would be beneath her foot, she stepped back one step. Her chin came up and her jaw hardened.

"I'm not going in that," she stated, nodding toward the canoe. "I'll walk."

"Caitrin, there is but one more rough spot ahead, after Lake St. Louis, then we will be in Montreal.

264

'Twould be far more dangerous to walk. 'Twould be longer, more difficult.''

"I'll walk," she repeated, backing away. Then she turned on her heel, heading into the forest.

In two long strides, Roarke was on her. She started to run and he grabbed her, swinging her around. It was like catching a wildcat and he held her at the end of a long arm. Taking careful aim, he clipped her sharply on the chin. Her mouth closed with an audible click and she dropped in a crumpled heap. Tenderly, he picked up her unconscious form and carried her to the canoe.

Twenty

A wave of cold water woke Caitrin. Confused, she blinked it away and a second wave drenched her. She blinked again but could only see a blur of brown and a moccasin-clad foot. The surface under her bucked and heaved. It leaped, then lurched in a sliding, sickening fall that soaked her once again. Bewildered, she blinked yet again and tried to move, but her arms and legs were strangely immobilized. Turning her head, curious and not yet frightened, she looked up, seeing only a grey, drizzling sky. Then a leafless tree limb went spinning overhead and realization hit her.

Panicked, she flopped over like a hooked eel, trying to get to her knees, and felt the canoe tip under her. Grabbing for the side, she discovered too late that her arms were lashed to her sides. She pitched headlong over the side of the canoe and the frigid, rushing river closed over her. Water poured into her lungs as she gasped at the shock and she swallowed more. Terror clamped her throat closed as dark water swirled her around, bounced her off a huge rock, then sent her tumbling on again. Her foot touched something hard and slick and she kicked away reflexively, only to find her legs were tied together. But the kick sent her spinning upward toward light and air. She gulped at the precious oxygen, instinctively trying to tread water, her bound legs hampering her. Then a whirlpool caught her, swirling her under again just as steel fingers gripped her long, streaming hair. Suddenly, she was yanked upward to land belly down and athwart the canoe, gasping and coughing.

A boulder whirled by just under her nose and she jerked back, her body bucking. A paddle slammed down on her upturned bottom and a hoarse voice ordered her to lie still.

With two swift, powerful strokes of the paddle, Roarke guided the canoe into a small cove and leaped out, dragging it up on a small beach, Caitrin still across it. Picking her up by the middle, he threw her over his shoulder like a bag of potatoes as she spewed water down his back, carrying her up the shore. There, he tossed her down. His features were white with fear and rage as he severed her bonds with his hunting knife.

He stared down at her, impotent in his raging terror. He thought he had lost her. One moment she had been in the canoe, safe, then she was gone, flipping over the side like an otter down a mud bank. Immediately, the river's spume had closed over her and she was lost. Time stopped. His arms and back seemed weak and leaden against the swift, plunging water as he backpaddled, desperately searching the river before him. He was strangely calm yet his heart seemed to be grasped in a fist of steel, no longer able to feed his lungs and brain. Frantically, he had scanned the torrent as a small part of him pleaded for aid from every saint he could lay thought to, summoning prayers and litanies long since put away with childhood. He thought he saw her, a small, slim form spiraling down in a whirlpool. In one swift stroke of the paddle he was there, only to find the spot empty. He stared ahead again, his eyes searching for the slightest deviation of the river's wild surface. No matter how he backpaddled, he could not hold the canoe stationary against the rampaging current, yet still he fought it, refusing to believe she could be gone. Then she was there, almost under the canoe, face upturned, bubbles spouting from her mouth, her hair floating about her like seaweed, and he grabbed for her.

Now, he could only jerk her to her feet. She stood before him, the object of all his fear, and his fear turned to rage. His fury demanded that he strike out and the only target he could find was Caitrin.

"You stupid little bitch!" he hissed from between gritted teeth. "You could have died!"

He slapped her, lifting her from her stumbling feet and turning her around to fall face first in the mud and debris of the forest floor. He stared at her as she pushed herself up to rest on her arms and shook her head to clear it. Realizing that his fists were still clenched in rage, that his jaw was knotted with it, that his fury was still a threat to her, he went back to the canoe.

Caitrin would need to be dried off and cleaned up. God knows, he thought, he could not take her into Montreal soaked with water and slimed with mud, not if he hoped to get her there unnoticed. She would be difficult enough to hide as it was.

Still furious, Roarke indiscriminately began to haul baggage out of the canoe. He knew Caitrin sat passively watching as he threw waterproofed object after object to the shore. He had hoped to enter Montreal just before sunset, when the river traffic would be at its heaviest, but now they would be lucky to arrive with moonrise. The only other way was to wait until morning. Either way, he had to calm her down, dry her off, and try to get her into the canoe again, something he wondered if possible. At last, the canoe empty, he looked at Caitrin, eyes narrowed.

She faced him back, angry and defiant. Her jaw was set, her chin firm.

"You should not have tied me," she stated.

Her hair streamed down her back in wet tendrils and framed her features. Damp wisps of curls clung to her forehead and cheeks. The water-soaked buckskin shirt held to her every curve, outlining her high, round breasts, her hips and pelvic mound, emphasizing the body he had held in his arms, had taken in such passion. Suddenly, he wanted her with a need that struck like a physical blow.

"You spoiled little brat!" he rasped. "And how else was I to get you in the canoe?"

For a brief second, he thought he saw a glint of laughter in eyes amber with anger. Then her chin lifted higher.

"I would think the blow to my chin was sufficient coercion! As to being spoiled, aye, I am that—but I wasn't, not until your rape of me!" she taunted. "And not even in passion, as would a decent man, but as an act of cold, calculated revenge!"

Roarke, shaking with rage, stared at her. He thought to mention that no decent man ever raped in passion or otherwise, and wondered what that made him. At last, he turned away.

"Take off your clothes," he ordered.

"And why should I do that?" Caitrin demanded.

Roarke looked back at her, his eyes coldly, deliberately moving over every inch of her. His mocking gaze made her aware for the first time of how the buckskin shirt exposed her body. It brought a sudden rush of unwanted sensations and memories, and she shivered under his eyes.

"Not for rape," he answered sardonically. "And you've more value to me alive than dead of lung rot! And you'll catch it, sure, if you stand there forever, wet and bedraggled as you are."

Anger and hurt rose in her at his mention of revenge, then, perversely, his last words struck her. For the first time, she was aware not only of her body beneath the clinging shirt but of her soaked hair, of the mud and debris that bespattered her clothes and body. She could not remember ever having felt so bedraggled or so ugly before. Absently, she watched Roarke start a fire as she rubbed her hands together, feeling the grit on her palms. Without taking her eyes off him, she wiped her hands clean on the buckskin shirt. Then she wiped the mud off her bare knees. Finished with the fire, Roarke glanced at her, scowling.

"I told you to get out of those wet clothes!"

"Where?" she asked, looking around.

"Holy Mother!" he grated out. "You can't be thinking of modesty, can you? Here? Now?"

Angrily, he went to a bundle and pulled out a blanket. He tossed it at her.

"Undress, dry off, and wrap that around you—or I'll do it for you!"

Caitrin tried to take off the shirt while holding the blanket in front of her but finally gave up the awkward struggle. Turning her back to Roarke, she pulled the shirt off, then wrapped the blanket around her, but not before he caught a glimpse of a slender back and a high, round bottom. Then she tried to hold the blanket up while drying her long, thick hair. Finally, exasperated, he went to her in two long

271

strides and jerked the blanket away. She clung to a corner of it, holding it up against her breasts, eyes defiant.

"You are spoiled, aren't you?" he taunted. "And helpless without your lady's maid."

Caitrin stared at him over the blanket, her chin jutted. Then she released it and turned her back to him as she stepped closer to the warm fire.

The blanket was rough in his hands as he dried her hair, but it soon gentled. He separated it strand by strand, rubbing each dry. At last, satisfied, he folded her hair over her shoulder to fall over her breasts. He wrapped the blanket back around her, but his arms held her encircled with it.

Roarke felt her sudden shiver as his breath grazed the sensitive flesh beneath her ear and along her neck. She stiffened, waiting for his lips to follow, but he drew back.

"Will I do as a lady's maid?" he asked, his exhalation soft again on her skin. Suddenly, her thoughts were in a tumult. Her knees felt weak and her heart seemed about to leap from her chest. A sudden swollen ache deep in her belly throbbed with a life and need of its own. The unexpected, treacherous sensation caught her off balance. All thoughts of his acknowledged using of her were swept away by the need she felt vibrating from him, that she felt coursing through herself. And it doesn't matter now, she told herself as her body relaxed again within his arms. 'Tis not as though I can be got with another child. And after the fall in the river, after almost drowning, she needed so much his comfort and warmth, if only for the moment. Sighing, Caitrin moved her head to the side to expose more of her shoulder to his mouth.

"You'll do," she whispered past the lump in her

throat, "until I get Bridget back."

Her skin quivered again as his mouth traced down the line of her throat, and the ache low in her belly grew to an almost painful need. He turned her around to take her face between his hands. He gazed into it until she lifted her eyes to his. With the balls of his thumbs, he traced the flare of her eyebrows, the length of her cheekbones, the line of her jaw. Gently, he touched the faint imprint of his hand on her cheek.

"'Tis sorry I am, Catkin," he whispered, "for the blow."

Then he lowered his mouth to hers, soft as a baby's breath. He held her so for a long moment, her face cradled between his hands, her mass of hair woven between his fingers. At last his mouth moved, caressing her lips, his tongue seeking hers, demanding hers. He felt her soft moan and his kiss deepened as her mouth opened for him, as her tongue rose to twine with his. Her body lifted on tiptoe to arch against him, pressing against his male hardness, and he groaned in answer. His hands left her face, her hair, to move over her shoulders and down the line of her back to her buttocks, cupping her. He pressed her closer as her arms creeped around his neck, her fingers curling into the long hair at the nape, touching his face, drawing him closer as he kissed her. At last, he took his mouth from hers with a reluctant groan and looked around.

Rain still slanted through the trees. It dripped from naked boughs and puddled the forest floor. But the fire still blazed, a bed of pine needles beneath a huge tree was deep and dry, and Caitrin stood acquiescent within his arms.

He held her so a moment longer, then drew the blanket closer about her, pulling it up to frame her

273

face like a cowl. His lips sought hers once more, kissing her gently, telling her of his need and desire before he lifted and carried her to the bed of pine needles. He set her on her feet and his eyes never left her as he stripped down to his loincloth. She stood before him, her face averted, her fingers white and tense as she clutched the blanket close, her teeth chattering with cold and apprehension.

His thumb under her chin, he forced her eyes up to meet his. Tenderly, he loosened her clenched fingers from the blanket and stepped within the circle of it with her. Then he lay her down, the length of his body covering hers, warming hers, keeping from her any stray raindrops that filtered through the boughs over them.

He kissed her gently, his mouth pleading with hers, teasing, loving, telling her of his need. His hands caressed her face, stroked her hair, her shoulders, twined her fingers with his. He felt her lips part under his, felt her tongue rise to meet his as she whimpered her response. Then she gasped as his hands encircled her breasts, his thumbs grazing her nipples to an urgent erection. Her sob swelled in her throat as his mouth followed where his hands had been, tugging the need that swelled deep within her into an importunate demand. The sudden all-consuming desire terrified her and her hands grasped his hair, jerking his mouth from her breast.

"No!" she sobbed. "No!"

Roarke stared down into her distraught features as he disentangled her fingers from his hair, his gentle hands belying his body's tenseness. Pressing his face into the fragrant juncture of her neck and shoulder, he uttered her name in a groan of apology as he thrust into the deep, wet core of her. Caitrin lay quiet beneath him, held immobile by her conflicting emotions. How, a small part of her wondered, could she allow a man she could never trust to so invade her body? How could she respond to him so, need him so? Then Roarke whispered softly in her ear as his hands stroked her hair, caressed her face, as his lips pleaded with hers.

"Catkin!" he implored. "Catkin!"

Slowly, she turned her head to look at him. She pulled a hand from his to trace the outline of his eyebrow, his cheekbone, his jawline, to graze her fingertips over his lips. Then she drew his mouth down to lightly touch hers. Her breath was soft on his lips. The tip of her tongue lightly teased them before she moaned and accepted his mouth more fully, before her body parted further to him, drawing him in, lifting to take him. She heard herself gasp his name, heard herself plead with him as she had sworn she never would, but her pride, her fear, no longer mattered. The only thing in the universe was the need that shook her, that drove her. Nothing was important but the man over her, within her, the man claiming her, taking her, driving her to a complete, all-enthralling fulfillment.

"Please, oh, please!" she heard herself gasp. "Oh, please, Roarke!"

Then an intense warmth was released deep within her, flowing through her, consuming her. She felt Roarke thrust deep into her once more, felt his release then her own explosion of heat spin her away.

Caitrin was roused by the gentle touch of Roarke's fingertips on her cheek, and she turned to press her face into his hand. She softly bit the flesh in his palm and opened her eyes.

"I wish," she whispered past her languor, "that it was not so good."

Roarke smiled into eyes green with contentment.

"And why would you be wishing such a thing," he asked, "when all the rest of the world is seeking it?"

"Because then I would not have to be afraid of it, of you. Then you would be no threat to me."

"Ah," Roarke said, his eyes laughing at her, "and if 'tis good now, think how threatened you'll feel when I lay you in a bed!"

Caitrin stared at him, disconcerted by the sudden rush of sorrow that assailed her. He would never lay her in a bed, a deep feather bed with soft pillows and silk curtains to shut out the world. That she could never allow, and her throat swelled with grief. Turning, she pressed her face into the male-scented warmth of his shoulder. Roarke felt the damp of tears she could not restrain and drew her closer, caressing her back, comforting her.

"We'll wait out the rest of the night here and be in Montreal tomorrow," he said at last, "if 'tis all right with you."

Late in the night, Roarke made love to Caitrin once more. As he took her, as he felt her give back to him, he wondered if he would ever hold her so again, and his cry of release was as much of anguish as of joy. Nor could he find anything but rage in the realization that so much of their future was in the hands of Lord Cartland, wherever he might be.

The morning meal was eaten. The passion of the night before was put behind them as but a memory that was, perhaps, all they would have. Caitrin sat on a log, her chin propped in her hands as she watched Roarke pack the canoe. Grief over the loss of a dream she had never allowed herself swelled her throat and she stared at the canoe, then at the mist-shrouded river, as panic throbbed her heart.

Then Roarke blocked her view of the canoe and of the river. He squatted in front of her and took her face between his hands. His eyes were beseeching as he nodded toward the frail craft.

"Catkin," he said, "I am asking you to trust me in this, just to Montreal. Please trust me."

Caitrin looked into his eyes, reading his determination and strength, his concern. Then she nodded and put her hand in his as he led her to the canoe. In this she would trust him.

Twenty-One

Drizzle merging with a low autumn mist fell over the city of Montreal as they approached. Yet Caitrin could see, through the haze, a long, narrow assemblage of buildings surrounded by a shallow moat and a palisade of rough stone the height of three men. Trees and the spires of churches rose above the houses, many two stories high, and behind the city reared the bulk of Mont Royal. Ships, eager to escape the St. Lawrence before the ice of winter trapped them, waited for the last of their cargoes, their lights a warm glow in the fog of dusk. The shorefront was a jumble of warehouses, hip to knee, blacksmiths, silversmiths, taverns, and dressmakers. There, too, were the king's storehouses and the Place d'Arms.

Sailors, their hair tucked into tarred pigtails, swaggered in pairs or groups or with whores, most of the prostitutes Indian or half-breed. Coureurs de bois staggered under the influence of brandy, their cowering women, fearful of straying too far, of clinging too close, a half step behind. Merchants, important in wig and silk, directed the transporting and loading of furs, the wealth, the very life blood of New France. Soldiers, both French regulars in blue and white and

Canadians in grey and blue, wove their way through the masses, muskets on their shoulders. Indians, bold in painted arrogance, strutted, their allegiance too valuable to be lost over a war hatchet brandished in play and a woman's scream. Everywhere underfoot were hogs and hounds and the filth of the streets.

Her unusual hair concealed beneath a strip of blanket, a pack on her back, Caitrin followed Roarke, no more than another coureur de bois's woman. She needed total anonymity, at least until they knew where Lord Cartland was, knew that he was not in Montreal or Quebec. Her freedom, perhaps her life and Roarke's, might depend on it.

He had a friend he could trust, Roarke had told her, a friend who would give her shelter until he located her uncle. When they knew where Cartland was, then they could make plans. Even then, they had to be careful. The papers Caitrin had seen in Cartland's trunk proved that he had influential contacts within the government of Montreal and Quebec, Bigot, Intendant of New France, among others. They, too, might be on the alert for her. The English, also, would have a reward offered for her through channels with the French. To respond to that, too, could put her back into her guardian's clutches.

But there was no one who would recognize her by sight, not if Cartland was not there. Even if he was in Montreal, she doubted he would be found rubbing elbows with merchants, Indians, sailors, soldiers, and whores, and certainly not on an evening as damp and as cold as this one was.

Nor would Cartland know her if he did see her, Caitrin told herself wryly, not with a scrap of blanket over her head, a pack on her back, travel-worn moccasins on her feet, and Roarke's hunting shirt covering her from neck to knee. She stayed the required distance behind Roarke but her head was lifted, her eyes roving over the colorful scene. Her fatigue and bedraggled clothing could not disguise her pride and grace, Roarke knew. He only hoped to slip her through the confusion of the waterfront, to find her a haven, to keep her safe until they could fight back. Given Caitrin's temperament, he doubted it would be easy. Nor was there anything of the subservient coureur de bois's woman as she reached out to touch Roarke and ask him a question.

It was the gesture that caught the attention of a ferret-faced woods loper as he swaggered drunkenly out of a tavern. Shrugging off a whore, he scowled in recognition, then laughed as he lifted the jug dangling from his finger and waved it erratically.

"'Eey!" he yelled, "'Eey, Roarke O'Conner! 'Eey, Irishman! *Mon ami!*"

Roarke paused and his jaw clenched in frustration as he spotted the small Canadian.

"Keep behind me," he ordered Caitrin as the coureur de bois approached. "This man's a weasel and deadly for it!"

"'Eey, *mon ami!*" Jacques Leverett grinned, his eyes yellow as a wolf's as they tried to see beyond Roarke to Caitrin. "I had thought you dead! The only thing I thought ever to see of you again was your hair on a war hoop, *non?* Did I not tell Pierre Sorel so? Were you not, *mon ami,* a fool to be rushing off after that English *putain,* and you with your head knocked in? But men do strange things for love, *n'est-ce pas?* And who would have thought you would find her? Not me, Irishman! And I certainly did not expect to see you here, in Montreal, not with her. *Non,* I did not expect so! And others will be surprised to hear of it, will they not? And so late, Irishman! All the other English"—he paused to spit his disdain into the filth of the road—"pigs and sows taken at William Henry were brought in long ago. But you . . . you are so laggard—and you enter Montreal so skulkingly, as though you do not wish to be seen! Do you not wish to be seen, *mon ami?*"

Jacques Leverett paused, his eyes twitching as he tried to see through Roarke's shadow and the shuddering lamplight to Caitrin. He stood, hands on hips, grin greeful. Never before had he had a chance to watch Roarke squirm, but he could not see the woman.

"So," he said at last into his adversary's impermeable silence, nodding toward the tavern he had just vacated, "let me buy you a pint of brandy and you can tell me of your adventures since I last saw you. I buy for your English whore, also," he added magnanimously.

"I thank you for your unaccustomed generosity, Jacques Leverett," Roarke answered sarcastically, "but the woman is tired and so am I. We need an inn, not a pothouse. Another time, perhaps."

He started to push past, keeping himself between the coureur de bois and Caitrin, but Leverett moved, too. Stepping in front of Roarke, he bounced up and down on moccasined feet, a banty challenging a cockerel, and grinned again. But his eyes were cunning and malignant.

"An inn, is it, *mon ami*," he demanded, "and not the authorities?"

Roarke shrugged, looking down at Jacques as he would a loathsome insect.

"And why would I go to the authorities?" he asked, one eyebrow cocked in warning.

For a brief second, Leverett's eyes were baffled, then the consternation was gone and his grin confident again. If the lust-befooled Irishman did not know of the reward offered for the English whore, he, Jacques Leverett, most certainly did. And he would be most happy to collect it, maybe knocking Roarke O'Conner down a peg or two while doing so, maybe even seeing him charged with treason! Montreal was a small city, with few places to hide, and he was a tracker, was he not? He would know the Irish bastard's bolt hole by morning, and he would be wealthy by noon! Shrugging his shoulders, he spread his hands in feigned confusion.

"That one is not the English whore you went after?" he asked, nodding toward Caitrin. "I thought she was! Forgive me!" He shook his head and laughed at his own stupidity. "But if she was, you would have heard about the reward and would have long since collected it, *n'est-ce pas?* And it would be you asking to buy me a pint of brandy, would it not?"

But Roarke did not leap at the proffered lie, the baited hook, as Leverett expected him to do. Instead, he grasped the Canadian by the shoulders and shook him. His eyes were frenzied, frightening the ferret-faced man who could so easily expose Caitrin, who could separate them, perhaps destroy them.

"That Irish bitch!" he demanded. "What happened to her, Leverett? Do you know? Have you heard? I would give my soul to get my hands on her again!"

The coureur de bois, suddenly totally confused, wiggled his shoulders, trying to step out from under Roarke's frantic grasp. If this was not the English slut who Bigot was so eager to get his hands on—and he was beginning to think she was not, why else would O'Conner demand to know where she was—then who was she? He tried to shrug his ignorance under Roarke's grip but the hands were too heavy on his shoulders.

"I don't know," he said at last, his eyes vainly seeking escape to the left and the right. "No one knows. But the government . . . haven't they been asking everyone who comes in from the woods for word of her? They've such a reward never offered for a woman before, and still no one knows where she is, what happened to her. Me"—he tried shrugging again—"I think she is dead. And you, if you did not find her, she must be dead, *n'est-ce pas?*"

Roarke suddenly released Leverett, half shoving him away.

"Aye," he agreed, disgust in his voice at admitting anything in common with Jacques Leverett, "I think she must be dead. The Most Holy Virgin knows I looked for her."

His grip on Caitrin's elbow so tight she gasped, Roarke started to move on, but Leverett was again in front of him.

"At least you were not lonely while you searched," he smirked, a fragment of doubt still remaining. "Nor cold, *n'est-ce pas?* And there must be a reward for this one, too, though not so large."

Roarke turned back to Leverett, his eyes as cold as steel.

"And how much would be offered for the widow of an English sergeant . . . a sergeant killed by you and your kind while lying helpless with the smallpox?"

The coureur de bois ignored the insult, his eyes lecherous on Caitrin's dim shape.

"A widow of an English sergeant?" he snorted. "More likely a whore to half the English army, *n'est-*

ce pas? When you are done with her, remember me, would you? It has been a while since I've had a white woman and I'll pay you well, considering the use on her."

Roarke stepped closer to Leverett as the Canadian, suddenly nervous, backed up. But the Irishman only smiled, animosity strangely gone.

"I'll think on it," he said agreeably. "Perhaps in the spring, if I should tire of her, if the British don't demand her. But 'twill be a long, cold winter, I'm thinking, and not one to bed alone through."

Keeping Caitrin behind him, Roarke stepped around Leverett. His hand clenched on her elbow, he guided her on down the crowded, dimly lighted street. Half running to match his stride, Caitrin stared at him. His jaw was clenched and his eyes were narrowed, but she did not know with what emotion. She had heard him tell the ferret-faced Canadian so many lies that she could only wonder what falsehoods he had told her, could only question the truths she knew. Suddenly, she could no longer even believe in his need for revenge, in his use of her for that revenge, nor could she trust him even in the passion they shared. And if she could not trust him in that, she could not trust him at all. Perhaps he did intend to use her and then sell her to the highest bidder.

Cold, wet, confused, hungry, and stumbling in exhaustion, Caitrin realized that for the first time she was afraid of Roarke. For the first time, she looked back at the security of Lord Cartland's guardianship with longing.

Caitrin was not the only one confused. Jacques Leverett stood staring after Roarke and Caitrin. The jug hung forgotten from his finger as he scratched his greasy, louse-infested hair. He was certain of only one thing: Roarke O'Conner had lied. The Irishman was trying to make a fool of him, and the Irishman had made a fool of Jacques Leverett once too often. How Roarke lied, he did not know. But he would find out. Lifting the jug, Leverett studied it with squinted eyes.

"The Irish bastard's behavior," he addressed it, "is very suspicious, *n'est-ce pas?* But me, Jacques Leverett, will watch and wait, *oui?* And I'll be ready when he slips!"

Nor would it be a problem to keep an eye on Roarke O'Conner. Montreal was a large city of eighty five hundred souls, true, but the Irishman would not be an easy man to hide, nor, from what he had seen of the woman with him, would she.

The streets down which Roarke guided Caitrin rapidly became less well lit. The larger buildings of commerce, government, and God in the lower town gave way to smaller private residences. Pavement quickly yielded to slick mud, potholes, and pig wallows. Caitrin tripped several times in the dark, fear making her clumsy as she realized there was no one she could trust or turn to, not in this alien, enemy city. Each time, Roarke jerked her back to her feet. His features were set, his mouth a grim line. And he did not even glance at her. Finally, he turned down a pathway into a deep doorway and knocked. After a long moment, a shaft of light leaped out into the dark and drizzle. A woman stood silhouetted behind it, her blond hair a nimbus in the glow.

"Roarke! Roarke O'Conner!" she laughed, throwing her plump arms around his neck. "This is such a happy surprise! I thought not to see you this year, it is so late, *n'est-ce pas?* So close to the snows! I thought you would winter with the savages!"

She drew him into the light and warmth, her blue eyes glowing, and did not see Caitrin in the shadow of the deep passage until she moved to close the door. Her eyes grew rounder in surprise and her face went flat. Releasing Roarke's arm as though it burned her, she stepped back, holding her skirts with both hands to keep them away from him. But it was Caitrin her gaze never left.

And Caitrin returned the woman's stare as her own shoulders straightened, her own head lifted high against exhaustion and despair. Suddenly, her fatigue was gone as her eyes swept disdainfully over her adversary's short, plump form. Caitrin had seen the other's proprietary gesture, had heard the pleasure in her voice, her comment on wintering with the Indians, and she knew Roarke had also wintered with this woman. Whatever Caitrin's distrust of him, he had held her in love, in joy, had given her a child, no matter that he would never know of it. The knowledge that he had also held this woman, had taken her into a deep feather bed, something she would never share with him, lifted her chin in fury, clenching her fists with a grief she dared not acknowledge. Roarke had said she would be safe here, but men, Caitrin decided, were fools. And Roarke was more a fool to trust a woman like the buxom little blonde. The woman's eyes were rapacious as they flicked to Roarke, bright with hate as they returned to Caitrin. Nor could she, herself, ever be safe, not here with this woman. Yet Caitrin did not know of any other place to go.

Roarke was forgotten as the two women studied each other from eyes narrowed like a cat's. The blonde's nose pinched tight with scorn as she eyed Caitrin's dirty, travel-worn costume. Unconsciously, she smoothed her satin skirts, fluffed the lace on her sleeves, and patted her carefully coiffed hair. But Roarke had brought the bedraggled slut, and she decided it would serve her better to know why before she drove her away . . . and perhaps Roarke with her.

Clasping Roarke's arm, almost purring, she crushed herself to it. Her smile was bright with faith and adoration as she turned her face up to his.

"You brought me another guest, *n'est-ce pas?*" she asked. "One who needs shelter? One you found in the streets, perhaps, or among the Indians? You have such a good heart, *mon coeur!* You cannot refuse aid to someone in trouble, a stray in the alley. That is why I am so fond of you!"

Caitrin shuddered at the honeyed, lisping tone. She wanted to leap at the bland face, to leave fingernail furrows down those fat, pink cheeks. But she dared not. There was too much at stake to allow emotion to control her, to control Roarke.

Caitrin gripped his other arm in fingers that held no passion, no promise. All she wanted was his attention. Her head was held high with pride, but there was anxiety in her eyes.

"Roarke," she whispered, "I want to get out of here! I don't trust her! She'll turn me in, if not for the reward, then because she wants you! And she'll destroy you, too, if she thinks she can't have you!"

Gently removing the blonde's clinging fingers, Roarke drew Caitrin aside. Tenderly, he took her face in his hands and turned it up to his.

"I've no other place to take you," he told her, "certainly none that is safe. And this is safe, Catkin. If you're thinking I've stayed here before, aye, I have, and in her bed. But Yvette often takes in guests, and other men have shared her affections. 'Twas for the

288

warmth and sport of it, naught else, surely, and 'twas before I met you. I'll not go crawling under her blankets again, not with you in the house, aye, or in the New World itself. There's no cause for fear, little one, and certainly none for jealousy!"

Caitrin stared at Roarke, then furiously jerked away. Yanking the scrap of blanket from her head, she tossed it to the floor before clenching her fists at her sides. How dare he accuse her of jealousy!

"You fool!" she hissed. "You stupid, blind fool! You really think I give a damn whose bed you creep into? You've hardly been welcome in mine, and then 'tis with rape you take me! But that fat little bitch, with her little mouth that butter would not melt in," she gasped, her chin jerking toward Yvette, "that one would have you spread on a platter if she could and her knife in hand! She would turn her own mother in for a sou! I don't trust her and you are a fool if you do!"

"You," he told her angrily, his eyes narrowed on her face, "are the fool! Yvette took me in when I had naught, while she, herself, was still grieving over the death of her husband. Always, she has been here for me and for others who have needed her, and has asked for naught in return but what any boarding house would demand, naught more than that! And you would have me doubt her for your unwarranted suspicions, your jealousy? You insult her, and I would have thought you better bred than that! Nor will I have such behavior, or I'll turn you over to the authorities myself!"

The last he said with a smile mocking his ridiculous threat. But Caitrin did not return his grin.

"You'll not need to," she stated. "She'll do so for you. And if you're concerned about manners, perhaps you should exhibit them and introduce me to my hostess!"

Roarke studied Caitrin's angry, upturned face a long moment, then turned her around to face the blonde.

"Yvette Dumont," he said, his jaw clenched in fury at Caitrin's stubbornness, "I would like you to meet Caitrin FitzGerald. Caitrin, Yvette."

The two women swept into curtsies, their stiff backs, their narrowed eyes, eloquent. Her torn tunic, together with the knowledge that the trunks stored in New York held clothes that put to shame anything the blonde could ever hope to don, only lifted Caitrin's chin higher. But Yvette had been watching their conversation with avid eyes and she stepped forward once more to place a proprietary hand on Roarke's arm. Her eyes were greedy as they searched his face.

"She is English, *non?*" Yvette demanded. "Perhaps it is dangerous to harbor her in my house? And there might be a reward offered for her, *n'est-ce pas?*"

"Aye," Roarke agreed, "there is a reward, but she's not English. She's Irish, and from County Leitrim, as I am. And I knew her when she was a child. She is not wanted by the government but by her guardian, a man she ran away from. If the reward is so important to you, if you are in such need, I'll match it to keep her out of his hands. Or she will; she has money enough herself."

"And does she," Yvette wondered with sudden uncharacteristic insight, "have anything to do with the scars on your back?"

"Her guardian has," Roarke admitted, his eyes shuttered against further questions.

"It is her guardian who also has her money, *n'est-*

ce pas?" Yvette bubbled as she clung to Roarke's arm and gazed coquettishly up at him from hard eyes. "I don't suppose she speaks French?"

Roarke looked at Caitrin, one eyebrow cocked in query. She only gazed back at him, a question in her own eyes, and Roarke shrugged a denial.

Giggling, Yvette snuggled closer still.

"And her guardian is not in Montreal? I would have heard of a rich man from Ireland, so poor is the gossip of New France! There is nothing to talk of but war and the greedy, lascivious Bigot and his comrades. It is so boring, n'est-ce pas? But I am remiss in my duties!"

She swung away from Roarke, leaning out on his arm to look back at Caitrin. Her gaze swept derisively over her and one eyebrow lifted in disdain.

"I have not asked you to supper and you both look as though you are starving! Especially that one! She looks like something the cat dragged in! Either you have had poor luck hunting, or she is a terrible cook. And you . . . you are so excellent at all that you do, so it must be her cooking! I could teach her while she is here, could I not?"

"That is kind of you, but I doubt she would be interested," he told her, remembering Caitrin's scorn. "There would be the language problem, too. But we are hungry, 'tis true, and Caitrin needs a bath after, if 'twould be no trouble."

"Of course," Yvette agreed as she led Roarke to the large living and dining room. "But I have to apologize for the table I now set. It is Bigot and his greed again. It is said he dines like a king while the poor people like me are lucky to get horsemeat, and there is almost no flour. Still, for a price, a favor . . ."

Caitrin followed after, closing her thoughts to

Yvette's babbling. Her mind was a turmoil of rage and fear. Then her mouth turned up into a cat's smile of satisfaction that would have worried Roarke had he seen it. Let them think she spoke no French. They would speak all the more freely in front of her for it! And if Roarke had been something more than an Irish croppie, she told herself spitefully, he would know all well-bred Englishwomen and Irishwomen spoke French. Knowing the slur unworthy of her, she scowled. But there was still gratification, she told herself as a servant seated her, in their ignorance, in her eavesdropping.

Yet the blonde prattled little of interest. She spoke avidly of the rivalry between the Marquis Pierre de Vaudreuil, Governor General of New France, and Louis Joseph, Marquis de Montcalm, Commander in Chief of the French forces in America, of Vaudreuil's desire to command the armies, of his jealousy of Montcalm, his backbiting and gossiping. He even, she claimed, took credit with Louis XV for victories that were clearly Montcalm's. She spoke of food shortages certain to become worse as winter settled in, of wheat rationing, of horseflesh in place of beef or pork, of the threat of rioting, even of starvation. But what could be expected, she wondered with a sidelong glance at Caitrin, when all the able-bodied men were dragged from the fields to fight the execrable English just at harvest? Only those with much money, she declared, her tiny dimpled hand resting on Roarke's sleeve briefly, or with much influence would escape hunger that winter.

Fighting the urge to scratch her eyes out, Caitrin noted that the widow Dumont's table hardly seemed to suffer. The blonde's influence was no doubt more effective when directed at a man's lower parts than at his brain.

But Yvette Dumont was lamenting again the greed of Francois Bigot, Intendant of New France. She went into gleeful detail concerning his many nefarious dealings and those of his henchmen, Joseph Cadet and Michel Péan, her eyes bright with envy of their unprincipled skills, of the social and political positions allowing them opportunity to employ those talents. Though those same dishonest dealings, she admitted with a rueful simper, had much to do, too, with the shortage of food. After all, one could not buy goods from Louis XV for next to nothing, pass them through several hands, each gaining a profit, then sell the selfsame goods back to the king at double or even triple the original cost without someone paying along the line. Yet everyone knew of the dealings, even Vaudreuil, and tolerated them. Sometimes it seemed as though the only person in the whole world who did not know of the systematic bilking of the king was the king himself. But Bigot was greedy in other ways, was he not? she tittered. Had Roarke, just out of the wilderness, heard the scandal concerning Bigot and Péan's wife? Everyone knew she had become Bigot's mistress; it was openly flaunted, and not only did Péan tolerate the affair, but he abetted it, profited from it! Péan had earned much money through Bigot, she added wistfully, and his wife had, too!

And wouldn't the mincing fat little bitch, Caitrin thought, like to do the same? Caitrin's jaw clenched in anger. It seemed as though Yvette never for a moment stopped pressing her overblown breasts against Roarke, had never ceased to simper up at him. Caitrin's hands tightened into fists under the table as she fought the urge to scratch the widow

Dumont's eyes out.

But she could not submit to her rage, to the hurt that felt like a fist in her belly. Nor could she even acknowledge that pain to herself. To do so would be to admit to other, more threatening emotions. She would do best to turn her mind to what lay ahead of her, to what she had to do to protect herself. Obviously, she could not stay in the widow Dumont's home. A frown creased her forehead as Caitrin lowered her eyes to her food, blocking out the blonde's high little voice, and put her mind to her problem.

Caitrin woke in a small, unfamiliar bedchamber with sharply steep ceilings and small, deeply set windows. Sunshine poured through them, a harbinger of a beautiful day. And wouldn't the sun be shining, Caitrin thought, now that she and Roarke had reached Montreal?

Sitting up in bed, she hugged her knees and scowled; she had more to think of than the weather. Judging by the light, she had slept late. Just as she wondered why no one had awakened her, the door opened and a servant entered. In her hands was a cup of chocolate, the typical light breakfast of Canadian women.

But Caitrin was not looking at the hot beverage. Her eyes were on the narrow, tight features of the servant. The face beneath the mobcap pulled over thin, mouse-colored hair was querulous. The small, cunning eyes touched Caitrin, then flicked away, but not before she had seen the rancor in them. The maid did not look up again as she pettily placed the chocolate far enough away on the table that Caitrin would have to crawl to reach it. Then she turned and shuffled her way back to the door, not seeing Caitrin reach under her pillow to extract something.

"Bonne!" Caitrin addressed her.

The servant turned back peevishly, her mouth resentful. She was to have brought the beverage up, nothing more. Then all impatience was driven away by the louis d'or Caitrin held up, turning it to flash golden in the light. Caitrin smiled, congratulating herself on her foresight of taking seven of the gold coins from the hem of Roarke's hunting shirt as he lay ill with smallpox.

"There are two more of these for you if you will but run an errand for me—and keep quiet about it."

The maidservant's eyes flicked back to Caitrin, suspicious. Her thin lips twitched with greed.

"What kind of errand?" she asked, her eyes compulsively flipping back to the coin.

"I want you to take a note to Bigot, telling him I am here, nothing more."

"And the widow Dumont will kill me, *n'est-ce pas?*" she sneered, snorting her disdain through her nose.

"Will she? And how will she know if you do not tell her? If I don't? She will simply think that someone else saw me and followed me here, then reported me. Or even that Monsieur O'Conner did so, not wanting to share a reward with her. She will think that. She is greedy, is she not? And he will think that she told, will he not? Or that a certain coureur de bois who bears him enmity did so. He'll not know for sure. Nor will Bigot tell. To find me could earn him millions. To lose me again will cost him more; of that I will assure him. And I will that way assure myself—and you—of his silence. And I'll not talk.

295

I've cause to dislike your mistress. Roarke O'Conner was my lover—until we came here."

Caitrin paused to study the maid. She could almost read the thoughts speeding over her features.

"But Bigot would not give a reward to a mere coureur de bois, would he?" Caitrin continued. "Nor to a servant. Don't think that he would. He would find a way to trick you out of it, would he not? To try for it would get you nothing at all, I'll wager. Do you care to chance it?"

The coin disappeared into Caitrin's palm as though it had never been visible, and the servant blinked, dismayed. Then her eyes refocused on Caitrin.

"And why, if I'm not good enough for a reward, would Bigot see me at all?" she sneered.

"Because you will give the guard at his door one of these to deliver it to him and you will keep one for yourself," Caitrin smiled, the coin flickering again in her fingertips, drawing the servant's eyes back to it. "And when you come home and after his troops have taken me, you will come to this room and find two more under the pillow."

"How do I know you will leave them for me? How do I know you even have them?"

"You don't, do you? But you'll have one, regardless, and a bird in the hand is better than no bird at all, *n'est-ce pas?*"

The louis d'or glimmered through the air as Caitrin flicked it. The servant's hand twitched out and snatched it faster than Caitrin's eye could follow, then a second one went after. She stood there, indecisive, as the coins grew warm in her clenched fist. Then she nodded and slammed out the door.

Smiling, Caitrin sipped her lukewarm chocolate

and waited for Bigot's men. The maid would not talk. Her mistress would beat her black and blue if she discovered she had been cheated out of a reward . . . and by a servant. However Roarke might suspect she was found, he would never think she had turned herself in. It was but an added satisfaction that he might think the widow Dumont had done so. Nor would he ever believe her denials.

Twenty-Two

He looks like a toad, Caitrin thought, studying
Francois Bigot across his desk in Quebec. The
Intendant of New France was short and squat, with
wide, fleshy jowls, an oily florid complexion marred
by crimson pustules, and acne scars. The large, wide-
set eyes bulging out beneath hairless eyebrows were
greedy, true, but there was a deeper craving in them.
The man was avaricious, Caitrin knew, but for more
than the wealth he systematically drained from New
France and her mother country. He needed approval,
assurance of his own value, friends. And the bribes,
the embezzlements, the misappropriations of funds,
the grafts and frauds, all of the spoils that came from
them, filtering up and down the line, brought him
that. Yet he would always doubt his friends, unable
to separate them from the sycophants. It was that
doubt, that craving, that made him a corrupt,
debauched man all the more pitiful, all the more evil.

For a moment Caitrin pitied him, then reminded
herself that she dared not. In all the gossip she had
heard of Bigot, she had not heard of his intelligence,
but it was there and that she had to respect and fear.
Nor had she known what to expect when Bigot's men

299

came to escort her from the widow Dumont's, and the three-day voyage by sloop to Quebec had only fed her apprehension. The whereabouts of her uncle was her largest concern, but Bigot said nothing of his presence in New France. He would have if Lord Cartland was there.

Remembering the sudden appearance of Bigot's men, Caitrin's mouth quirked. They had set the house in a turmoil, just as she had hoped. Only the maid had not been confused, dashing up the narrow stairs to collect her wage. Then Caitrin had been whisked away, leaving Roarke no opportunity to speak to her. And he may never do so again, a small voice whispered to her, a voice she quickly suppressed. But the fury, frustration, and bewilderment on his features had given her a queer twist of gratification. Such was the social structure of New France that they might never come face to face again. Thieves and crooked government officials might be welcome in the highest circles, but a coureur de bois, no matter how wealthy, might not. The thought caught in Caitrin's throat and she swallowed it down, using the bovine features of the widow Dumont to keep it there. But Bigot, elbows leaning on his huge, ornately carved and filigreed desk, was addressing her.

"Your uncle and your fiancé have been very concerned about you," he told her, his eyes sincere. "We thought you dead. The savages had brought in all the others taken at Fort William Henry, those still alive." He shuddered in sincere horror. "Some terrible things happened to those poor people!"

Caitrin's eyes hardened in rage and her chin lifted.

"I know," she stated grimly. "I was there. I am glad to know, though, that my uncle and cousin escaped unharmed."

So Lord Cartland had not told Bigot of the disaffection between them. And if Bigot thought she was to marry Ashley, all the better. At the very least, it would buy her time. With winter so close, no more ships would come up the St. Lawrence, and she could not envision Lord Cartland braving the blizzards to travel overland from New York. She was safe until spring. But Bigot was clearing his throat, calling her attention back to him.

"Two daughters of Monsieur and Madame Decoteau recently married," he told her. "They have three left at home, but I know they would welcome you. They are wellborn and from Paris itself, and very suitable chaperons for you—or so Madame Péan assures me. It has already been arranged. Also, you will receive a generous allowance—against your uncle's credit, of course."

His gaze dropped over her, taking in the shabby leather tunic and her travel-thin moccasins, the unusual hair pulled hastily back into braids. His eyes caught on her high, round breasts, then regretfully returned to her face.

"You'll need a wardrobe, of course. I'm certain Madame Péan would be happy to share her dressmaker and to accompany you, should you wish."

For a moment, Caitrin wondered at the audacity, the insensitivity of the man, suggesting that his married mistress become her companion. Then she saw the crafty challenge in his eyes.

"Ah, no, monsieur! It would not be proper, would it," she replied, "to beg shelter from Madame and Monsieur Decoteau, then not involve their daughters in my wardrobe? And women are jealous of such trivialities, *n'est-ce pas?* Surely the charming Madame Péan will understand, and I wish you to convey to her my gratitude and my regards."

Bigot's eyes narrowed as Caitrin adroitly avoided insulting his mistress, then he put his suspicions aside. She was, after all, beneath her shabby apparel, a very beautiful woman, and Bigot liked beautiful women. Scrambling from around his huge desk as Caitrin stood, he grasped her hand, lifting it to his lips.

"You do understand," he asked regretfully, "that you are nominally a prisoner of war? But it is a pretense only, of course, your uncle being who he is. . . ."

For an instant his eyes shuddered away from hers, the complicity he shared with Lord Cartland evident in his sudden nervousness. While he did not know of the estrangement between her and her uncle, Caitrin realized, he also did not know of how much she was aware. It reminded her again of her perilous position. Nor could she trust the man she smiled at.

"Of course, I understand," she laughed. Then she lifted one eyebrow coquettishly. "And am I to have an armed guard?"

"Mademoiselle, why? Your uncle and fiancé will be here in the spring and you must be eager to see them, especially after your ordeal. I can assure you, too, that while Quebec is not London or Dublin, we do have our entertainments. You will not be bored, I promise you. Unless the coureur de bois who rescued you impressed you with more than his gallantry? He is not, as I understand it, an unhandsome man and from Ireland, also."

Caitrin's face closed. For a moment Roarke's features taunted her with the desire to run to him, to find shelter in his arms. But it was a false shelter, she reminded herself.

"He was," she stated, the lie smooth on her tongue,

302

"perfectly correct at all times. Believe me, he was always much more interested in a possible reward than in my person."

"Then," Bigot responded, "the man is blind or a fool or both."

She shrugged, dismissing his flattery.

"I only hope he finds the reward worth his effort."

Bigot lifted his hands in a Gallic gesture of dismissal.

"Your uncle offered an excessively generous sum for your return. I fear to set a precedent on the exchange of other captives. You could hardly know the coureurs de bois. This Roarke O'Conner is, perhaps, not typical, but coureurs de bois, most of them, are greedy. I feel that a quarter of the sum offered would be more than sufficient. The rest, of course, will go to your care and needs."

No, Caitrin thought, not to my needs, but to your purse. And Bigot is not a toad. He is a spider, a fat, ugly spider squatting behind that desk, weaving a web that draws to him all of New France, not a sou escaping, while the people starved, while the people of the American colonies slowly gathered strength and will enough to destroy him and his. And in that desk, she knew, were papers, deeds of sale similar to those she had found in Lord Cartland's trunk. One day she might need to find them. In the meantime, he was a man to watch and fear.

"You are right, of course," she smiled. "I know so little of New France and even less of the workings of government! I hope to learn more. In the meanwhile, I thank you for your concern and hospitality."

"Mademoiselle," he murmured, bowing and kissing her hand, "if there is anything I can do to entertain you or make your stay easier or more pleasant,

303

please let me know. I am certain we will see more of each other soon. Quebec is, after all, a small town."

Suppressing a shudder, Caitrin inclined her head graciously and moved to the doorway. Just before she entered it, she turned back.

"One more thing," she said, unable to resist, and Bigot smiled his frog's smile. "The massacre at Fort William Henry . . . how many people were killed?"

Bigot's face reddened at her poor manners. For a moment, he could not speak.

"The reports vary," he said, affronted. "Some say as few as fifty, some say several hundred. But all of them were heretics."

"As is my uncle," she reminded him. "Nor do you hesitate to deal with him. But I understand," she smiled with a disarming shrug, "that business is different." Then her face grew hard again. "And is that combatants only, or does it include the women and children I saw killed or carried off? Does that include the men too wounded or ill too be moved and left behind in the fort, who were slaughtered with their wives and children? Or the seventeen men too ill to join the march who were left in charge of your regimental surgeon? They, too, were killed before the massacre on the road to Fort Edward had even begun. Monsieur, no matter the entertainment Quebec offers me, I'll not soon forget those sights or that 'twas Frenchmen who allowed it to happen."

Bigot drew himself up to the limit of his squat height. His features assumed the guise of insulted dignity.

"I assure you, mademoiselle, that had Governor Vaudreuil been in charge instead of Montcalm, the whole incident would never have occurred."

"Aye," Caitrin thought bitterly, "had Vaudreuil

been in command—as ineffective as he is said to be—
the French and Indians would never had made it to
Fort William Henry."

But she dared not go so far as to tell Bigot so.
Instead, her chin lifted higher still.

"Nor would I have been sentenced to death," she
answered. Roarke's face as she had first seen it in the
longhouse returned to her. Somehow she had
known, then, that he would, whatever his purpose,
save her. He had, and he had taken her, used her,
given her passion—and a child. And she might never
know that passion again. An unexpected grief
assaulted her and she closed her eyes, swaying with it
for a moment. Then she blinked and shook it from
her. There would be time enough for sorrow, to
wonder if she had done the right thing in leaving
Roarke, time enough for regret.

"Did you know I had been sentenced to death?" she
asked Bigot. "The Indians paint the victim's face
black when they sentence him to death. If he is
foolish enough to have hoped before, he will lose it
then. Have you ever watched someone die at the
torture stake?"

Bigot, his features wary, shook his head.

"I thought not, or you would not be so eager to loose
your Indians. It was Roarke O'Conner who saved me,
and I would have you release all of the reward to
him."

She smiled and placed her hand on his arm.

"You'll do that for me, won't you?" she asked
sweetly.

"Mademoiselle," Bigot sputtered, and Caitrin's
smile grew.

"I knew you would," she told him, giving his arm
a pat. Then she swept out of the room with all the

dignity her bedraggled attire allowed.

Bigot stared after her. She was a pretty little kitten, he decided, but one with claws and definitely to be watched, as Lord Cartland had advised. Perhaps that was why, for all the concern Lord Cartland's letter had expressed, he had the feeling that her uncle would have been just as happy if she was never found. Perhaps there were other reasons.

Twenty-Three

Bigot had not lied about the entertainments Quebec extended that winter of 1757, and his vast palace at the head of Palace Hill was their center. Every evening something was offered—banquets, skating parties, dances, gambling, masquerades— but there was a current of frenzy beneath the gaiety.

Huge sums of money were won and lost and won again at the gambling tables, and always Bigot was at the center of the web, the money flowing in and out of his fingers. Nor did he seem to care which way it went or where it stayed. Only the game itself mattered, and there was none of the cold calculation with which Lord Cartland gambled. Yet there was an eager avarice in his eyes as he welcomed General Montcalm's young officers, scions of the great families of France, to his tables. More sheep for the shearing, wealthy sheep, Caitrin cynically thought; the lust for wealth and the need to impress was so tightly ingrained in Bigot that she doubted even he knew which appetite he fed. But the young officers, as much disgusted with the dissipation as their general, made their excuses as often as they could, much to Caitrin's regret. She liked their honesty,

307

their sense of purpose, and shared their distaste for the debauchery in which the leading citizens of Quebec indulged. Their absence, too, only widened the breach between Montcalm and Bigot and Governor Vaudreuil, a breach as dangerous to New France as the English. She shared with them, too, their dislike for the masquerades to which Bigot was addicted. Quebec's society was so small, so select, that there seemed no purpose to them, yet the people sought out more and more outrageous costumes in their futile attempts at disguise.

But the banquets, Caitrin thought, were the worst. Never had she seen tables set with such opulence, always far, far more than even the many guests of Francois Bigot could consume, while the people of Quebec starved. There was no bread for them, she knew, while the tables of Bigot groaned with the finest of pastries. Rations had been reduced to half a pound of horseflesh a day for the populace and Montcalm's men alike, while Bigot's guests dined on pâté de foie gras, quail, and the smallest of suckling pig. Nor was there a lack of cattle, for Bigot bragged of his vast herds. And what, she wondered, would the people eat when the horses were all slaughtered? Already, women and children were behind the shafts of the carts and sleighs where horses had once been.

Yet, for the most part, the populace accepted their circumstances like the oxen for which they were used. Their dumb stoicism created in Caitrin anger rather than pity, and she wondered if William Johnson had been right when he explained the differences between the American colonists and the Canadian.

Americans, he had told her, had left the Old World to escape tyranny, to build a better life. They never looked back, and where they went, they stayed. But it was this same independence that kept them divided among themselves, although they far outnumbered the French. It was their greatest strength, their greatest weakness. If they ever united, little could defeat them. The French had come to trade for furs, to become wealthy, to return home. And they had come to convert the Indian to Christianity. If they created an empire for the glory of France and the king in the process, all the better. But they were a united people, a people who submitted without question to one ultimate authority. It was their strength but now it was a liability, for they did not challenge the authority that robbed and starved them in the name of that same king. And the system promoted greed. The greed corrupted, opening doors to other, greater sins, sins that could only be turned to the advantage of men like Lord Cartland.

Caitrin envied Montcalm's officers their excuses, for the Decoteau daughters would seldom allow her to make her own. She was their own personal triumph, this beautiful daughter of a wealthy Irish family who had been captured by Indians and rescued by a handsome, mysterious coureur de bois. They thrilled at the romance of it. And she was so recently arrived from Europe! She knew all the latest gossip, the latest fashion. She was their great success and they would not allow her to deprive them of it.

At least, she did not have to attend the affairs offered at Beaumanoir, Bigot's less publicized hideaway outside Quebec. There, even greater debaucheries occurred, while Angelique Péan, Bigot's mistress, ruled with her husband's glad approval. Although the happenings there were whispered about among the Decoteau daughters with salacious glee, they, as chaste, unmarried noble women, were not welcomed, nor was Caitrin. Would that change, she wondered, when her pregnancy was discovered?

She could not hide it much longer. The Decoteau daughters had begged and nagged her to order a new dress for the affair she now attended at Bigot's estate on Palace Hill. His teeming warehouses had released a selection of new silks and the smaller, more fashionable hoops, and Caitrin, they cajoled, was slim enough to wear them so well! She had refused, pleading the boredom she truly felt. Hoops, worn progressively higher, would conceal her belly for a while longer, but no matter how tightly she laced, the small bulge that fluttered within her could no longer be hidden while she wore only camisoles and petticoats. The dressmaker had a sharp eye and a gossiping tongue.

Caitrin studied the frenzied men and women as they gambled and gossiped, their exertions bringing hectic color to their faces beneath the powder and paint and beauty patches. Would she become prey, she wondered, to the rapacious men, the decadent women, when her secret was known? There was nothing, she knew, that the licentious enjoyed more than to watch the virtuous humbled. It somehow justified their own behavior.

The child moved within her at the thought and Caitrin's hand automatically touched her abdomen. There was nothing to do but to tell the truth, to claim Roarke O'Conner as the father. That the baby had been conceived in an act of rape would be assumed. Roarke. Twice she thought she had seen his dark, gleaming head in the steep, narrow streets of Quebec. If he was in Quebec, he, too, would hear of the child. What he would do, she did not know, but she sometimes thought the very worst would be if he did nothing. And her uncle. His arrival grew closer with the coming of spring. What would he do when he saw her state? At the very least, he might try to force her into marriage with Ashley, under the guise of giving the child a name. At the very most, he might try to force her into a convent, to protect her, he would claim. However she considered it, the child would give Lord Cartland more control over her. And she could see no way out.

But if she entered a convent of her own volition, if she claimed sanctuary, then he could not touch her. The Ursuline nuns would help birth the child, would protect them both afterwards. And the papers that she was certain were in Bigot's desk would be added insurance, especially if she could find a way to send them to William Johnson. Tonight, somehow, she would find a way to get them.

"Mademoiselle, why so troubled?" asked a deep male voice, and Caitrin blinked. Louis Bougainville, aide to General Montcalm, grinned down at her from his tall, slim height and Caitrin smiled back.

"I was thinking of my uncle's arrival."

"And that does not please you?"

"He is in league with our host."

"And who is the lamb for the shearing this time," Bougainville asked, lifting one dark eyebrow and grinning again, "the French or the English?"

Caitrin shrugged and looked away, suddenly uneasy.

"I don't know," she lied, "but I doubt their relationship is based on aught but larceny."

"And does Bigot have any friends without a sou as cement between them?"

Caitrin laughed and shook her head. "There is Governor Vaudreuil and many women—and I wonder about the women."

"*Oui*, Vaudreuil," Bougainville scowled. "Is he only vain and stubborn, or is he stupid, too? I cannot decide."

They glanced over at the governor and exchanged a grin. Vaudreuil was in animated conversation with two women and a man. As he spoke, he studied himself over their shoulders in a mirror, carefully touching his wig and straightening the flawless lace at his throat. A beauty patch accented his cheekbone.

"He is vain," Caitrin commented, "and Bigot flatters him. In turn, Vaudreuil turns a blind eye to Bigot's larceny."

"And the women? Tell me what charm Bigot has for the women other than his wealth."

Bigot was tossing dice while three women clustered about, touching him, clinging to him, laughing at his every comment. Their hair was dressed and powdered in intricate curls about the face and several ringlets down the back. Their corsets pushed their breasts up into high mounds that threatened to spill out from their low-cut bodices. Black beauty patches in the shapes of hearts, moons, stars and fleurs-de-lis rested on powdered high breasts, shoulders, and faces. But Madame Péan was not among them. The woman who had worked her way up on her back to become mistress of the most powerful man in New France held her own court of hopeful supplicants. However charming they might be, whoever could best aid Bigot or Péan stood the best chance of securing Madame Péan's momentary favors. She was not beautiful but there was a gaiety and wit about her, together with an exuberance that drew men, and she was said to be good in bed. Well, she should be, Caitrin thought, considering how many she had occupied in her social and financial climb.

From her perusal of Bigot's short, squat figure, his toadlike features and angry complexion, Caitrin turned back to Bougainville.

"It is strange," she told him. "He does have charm

beyond his wealth, his power. He is witty, he is intelligent. He is generous and he likes women. He flatters, true, but he likes their company. He even genuinely seems to prefer it to that of men. Not many men do. Women like that."

She gave a Gallic shrug.

"But there is also his dishonesty, his greed, but more, his affiliation with my uncle. If New France is defeated, 'twill not be as much by the English as by Bigot, himself, and Vaudreuil's compliancy."

Bougainville hunched forward, a frown marring his handsome features.

"And there is little we can do, Montcalm, myself, Levis. It is as though there is a rot in the very soul of New France itself."

"But would it be so here," she wondered, "if 'twas not so in France itself?"

Bougainville's jaw tightened and he looked away.

"I was raised," he told her, voice tight, "to believe in the glory of France, even above that of the Church. Now, I have to watch it fade, perhaps die, because of greedy fools like Bigot. It is strange. I can say that to you, an Englishwoman, and you can understand, but a Frenchwoman would only laugh and shrug, not seeing it."

"I am Irish, and we've suffered our own defeats, God knows, most at the hands of the English. France has always provided refuge for my people. It hurts me, too, to watch her magnificence fade. But this opulence—" Caitrin shrugged as her gaze swept the extravagant chamber, "how can someone see this opulence and not think it will go on forever?"

Then she laughed.

"And why, Louis, are you sharing this magnificence tonight?"

"For the menu, of course. Horseflesh, meal after

meal, becomes boring, and you know how a Frenchman appreciates good food. The art of cooking horseflesh has not yet been well developed."

As if in response, his stomach rumbled. Caitrin giggled and he grinned back.

"Your pardon, mademoiselle, but starvation does that."

"And I think you'll have to starve a while longer. Supper was set for nine, but we'll be fortunate to dine by midnight. The gambling tables seem to enthrall our hosts."

"So I must entertain them like a trained puppy until then," he said bitterly, "to earn my supper?"

Caitrin's smile faded.

"I feel it, too . . . the guilt, the responsibility."

"And the rage."

"And that."

"And the gluttony. Have you ever seen sharks in a feeding frenzy?"

Caitrin shook her head.

"I did, in the Mediterranean," he told her. "It is like this."

He waved his hand over the room, then turned to her, his features downcast.

"I regret, Caitrin, but I've lost my appetite, certainly too much to stand on my hind legs and balance a ball on my nose for any meal. I hope to see you soon in a more wholesome atmosphere."

Disappointed, she watched him make his way through the crowded room. But it was better that he was gone. He was attracted to her, that she knew, and even if she was not pregnant, it was impossible. Lord Cartland would do his best to destroy someone like Bougainville; he would be a slap in the face of her uncle's corruption.

Caitrin sighed and turned to the mirror at her back.

314

Perhaps, she thought, if she viewed the room through the reflection of the glass, it would appear cleaner. Leaning her forehead against the ornate frame, she gazed into the mirror—and saw Roarke O'Conner. He was dressed in a pale blue satin suit with frothy lace at the neck and spilling over his hands at the wrists, and his hair was neatly powdered and queued, but it was Roarke O'Conner. She blinked, not believing her eyes, but he still stood across the room, leaning negligently against a door frame, his gaze on her. Then he moved, weaving his way through the crowd. Not turning, she watched him come, her heart suddenly leaping within her chest.

"Mademoiselle," he said, bowing gracefully, correctly, "at your service." His brogue gave the word *service* an intimate suggestion. His blue eyes laughingly mocked her as he lifted her hand, kissing it longer than protocol allowed. Then his tongue flicked lightly over her palm, nor did he release her.

"Does Bougainville," he asked, "desire my lady?"

"The widow Dumont?" Caitrin responded, unsmiling. "I doubt he even knows her."

"I think you are more to his taste . . . and mine."

"And I like him. He is an honest man with no revenge as his motive."

One dark eyebrow lifted as Roarke grinned.

"No, perhaps not, but lust seems to be."

Caitrin's chin lifted.

"Not lust, hunger for something besides horsemeat. The people of Quebec are starving, as you may have noticed, Montcalm's men among them. I doubt hunger brings you; you do not know such honest needs. Nor did I think Bigot would welcome a woods loper to his drawing rooms."

"Bigot would welcome the devil himself if he had a

sou in his pocket."

"Not everyone here has his generous selectivity."

"And you, Catkin? Do you welcome me?" Roarke asked, his eyes suddenly intent on hers.

"I do not," she told him, trying to pull her hand free. "I had hoped never to see you again!"

"Then why," he asked, shifting his fingers to her wrist, "does your pulse leap so at my touch?"

"Because," she stated, her jaw tight, "I wish to be away from you!"

"Just as you did in Montreal?"

"Aye, just as then!"

"And 'twas you who turned yourself in?"

"It was, and glad I am I did so! Now let me go or I shall scream!"

Roarke's eyebrows quirked and he glanced around the large drawing room.

"And do you really think any of these people would come to your rescue? I think them more likely to watch and cheer as I rape you."

Yet he let her go and watched her move gracefully through the crowd, her back straight, her hips swinging disdainfully. Instead of leaving, she squeezed in at a table and joined a game of euchre, never raising her eyes again to seek him out.

Caitrin automatically watched the fall of the cards and placed her bets, but her mind was in turmoil. It seemed as though she could feel Roarke's eyes boring into her back, and she longed to throw down her cards, to go to him, to ask him to take her away from the debauchery around her. She longed to tell him of the child, their child, to ask him to forsake his revenge and take her to the place of soft winters and magnolia trees. But her jaw clenched and her back straightened at the thought that he might, would probably, refuse. Her pride would not let her take that chance. Nor

316

could she leave without the papers she knew were in Bigot's desk. She would, she decided, claim faintness just before supper and ask to lie down. From a bed-chamber it would be easy enough to slip to his office, and there was a wire tucked into her garter that was said to be able to open any lock. It was but a matter of watching until the hunger for food overcame the gambling frenzy.

Twenty-Four

The halls of the palace were empty as Caitrin slipped through them to Bigot's office. Lifting her skirts, she took the wire from her garter and, after looking both ways, tried the door. It opened under her hand, and surprised that it was so easy, she watched it swing soundlessly inward. Stepping in, she glanced apprehensively around. Other than a mammoth desk, several delicate chairs offered for his visitors, and a disproportionately large chaise longue where Bigot was said to nap and to pursue other activities, the chamber was empty.

Lighting a candle from the low fire in the fireplace, Caitrin went to the desk. Its drawers were unlocked, and quickly, methodically, she began to search.

"Is this," a voice drawled, "what you are looking for?"

Caitrin gasped and jumped, her heart leaping to her throat. Roarke O'Conner stood against the door. The white of his hair powder gleamed in the firelight but his face was shadowed. In his hand was a roll of papers. Reaching behind him, he locked the door, trapping her.

"Next time you plan a burglary," he advised, advancing into the room, "look behind the furniture."

Caitrin's chin lifted.

"Those are mine."

"Oh, are they? And I had thought they were Bigot's."

"I need them. You know that. Without them my uncle . . ." She gave a dismissive shrug. "You know all that. I have to have them. Without them, I don't know what he will do to me, with me, and he will be here soon. I have to have them! You know that!"

Roarke stood over her, his eyes sardonic.

"Do I? Perhaps if you beg for them. Or we could work out a trade."

Her chin lifted higher and Roarke chuckled, slapping the papers in his palm.

"I thought not. But I am wondering why you are desperate enough to sneak in here like a thief for them. I need them because their gift to the English would go a long way to keep my neck out of a traitor's noose. But you are now of age and Lord Cartland is no longer your guardian. He no longer has a hold on you, does he? Your estates are your own, are they not? So why do you want these?"

Tucking the papers into the back of his breeches under his satin waistcoat, Roarke took Caitrin's face between his hands. She stared at him unflinchingly, her features a mask.

"What hold does he have over you then, Catkin?" he asked, his eyes becoming concerned. "There has to be something."

She stared back, her jaw set.

"I want to see him brought down. That is all."

"Here? Now? You may no longer be in Cartland's power, but there is Bigot. He would turn the world

320

upside down to get them back, and you would be his first suspect. If I have them, you can honestly say you don't know where they are—and you won't."

"I want them," she stated again stubbornly.

"Why? Just tell me why."

"I can't! But I need them. I have to have them! You have to trust me in that!"

"Trust you?" Roarke scoffed. "Trust the woman who left me without a word in Montreal? Who told me she had hoped to never see me again?"

Grinning into Caitrin's unyielding eyes, he then dropped his gaze to the high twin mounds displayed by her low-cut gown. He lightly traced around the edge of her bodice, then inserted a finger to touch her nipple as she stood, defiantly unmoving.

"You seemed concerned, too, over the hunger of the populace, but you, my love, seem hardly to be starving. I love your breasts. Did I tell you that? But I don't remember them this large. Be careful, sweetheart. You are in danger of becoming overblown."

Caitrin knocked his arm aside and swung at his taunting features. Catching her wrists easily, Roarke grinned as he held her arms behind her back and laughed down at her.

"Does that mean, Catkin, that you'll not lie down with me tonight?"

"I want those papers!" she demanded, furious that he would play with her so.

One dark eyebrow lifted to taunt her.

"And I told you that perhaps we could trade for them. Or you could tell me what hold Cartland has over you."

"Never! It does not concern you!"

The mockery left Roarke's features.

"But you concern me. I would not have you in jeopardy." Then he smiled again. "For all your inex-

321

perience, you were the best bedding I've ever had. You may put my concern down to merely that, if you will. And I would have had you on your back before now if 'twas not for these damned hoops. But there are ways to surmount those, are there not?"

Transferring her wrists to one large hand, he again traced the fullness of her breasts, watching as her gaze held to his, trapped by the sudden onslaught of the feelings that shook her. They drove away all thought of the papers and left her with terror that he might touch her more intimately, might discover her secret.

"No!" she whispered. "No!" But Roarke only laughed as he picked her up, ignoring her struggles, and carried her to the couch. He held her there, her hands caught behind her by his unyielding grip. With his other hand, he forced her bodice down, freeing her breasts. He traced their outline lightly, then drew his fingers over her nipples.

"No?" he mocked her softly. "You tell me no, but see how they tighten into buds for my pleasure?"

"I'll scream," she threatened. "You'll find your neck in a French noose for rape!"

"Will I? And who would hear you? They are all at their play. And all you have to do is tell me why you want the papers and I will let you go, if you find me so odious."

Caitrin stared up at him. Perhaps if she yielded to him, perhaps if her skirts and hoops became a mass of fabric and whalebone bunched over her middle, he would not notice the bulge of her belly.

"Damn you, you bastard! No!" she hissed between clenched teeth. "I'll tell you nothing!"

Roarke lifted one black eyebrow.

"You have my curiosity aroused—and my lust. My curiosity I'll satisfy later."

He bent over her as his lips touched her earlobe and

traced their way over the line of her jaw, to press against the pulse in her throat. It leaped under his caress and she gasped, her head tossing in denial of the warmth she felt course through her. She twisted under him in a vain attempt at escape as his breath drew its way downward, seeking her nipple once more. He touched it lightly with his tongue, moistening it, and smiled as it grew hard beneath his breath. Then he took it into his mouth and heard her reluctant moan as his tongue caressed it into further firmness, as he sucked at it. She shook beneath him with her need, with her denial, as she felt his mouth tug an ache of unwanted desire into being deep within her.

"No," she gasped again. "No!"

He lifted his head to look at her. "You tell me no," he whispered, his voice husky, "but your nipple swells in my mouth like the sweetest of berries."

His eyes never leaving her face, he drew her skirts up, bunching them over her belly as she stiffened beneath him. He watched her close her eyes and draw her lower lip in beneath her teeth as his hand smoothed the roundness of her thigh, then touched the wet softness of her warmth.

"You tell me no, Catkin, but you are cream to my touch, heat to it."

He jerked his breeches down, releasing the hard strength of his manhood, then drew her hands over her head as his body covered hers. His mouth sought hers, pleading with it for a response she refused to give, then he drew back to look at her. Her lips were swollen with passion, her eyes heavy with it, but her gaze was defiant as his body moved over hers, into hers. He took her with a deep, hard thrust to the core of her and she sobbed beneath the onslaught, then gasped as he drew back. His mouth dropped to press into the curve of her neck. When he entered her a second time, it was gently. Moving over her tenderly, he slowly drew her need into her, tugging it into a deep, responding passion. Her hands escaped his grip to twine her fingers through his, as she used his strength to lift her hips, taking him more fully, rocking with him in love.

"No!" she whispered. "No!" Then her whisper became a moan that swelled her throat. He felt the brush of her breath as she whispered her denials, as she moaned her need. Then she drew him in deeper still, opened to him further, and the moan in her throat became a sob as a wave of heat shook her with its release, as it drew his seed from him in a shuddering, relentless drive to possess her fully.

Roarke held his face in the warmth of Caitrin's neck, feeling her pulse leap beneath his lips, then slowly settle into a slower beat. He cradled her against him, wondering if their lovemaking had touched her at all. Always it had seemed as though they had met in a passion he had never known before, a passion in which, at the end, she had given herself fully. Then, when it was over, when they had both found complete fulfillment, she would rise, shake down her skirts, and draw away from him, totally untouched. Would she, he wondered, do so again? Reluctantly, he lifted his head to look at her. She gazed back at him, eyes shuttered, jaw tight.

"May I have my papers now?" she asked.

Roarke's features closed, his eyes narrowing.

"Do you truly feel you have earned them, my love? I seem to remember a certain reluctance on your part. Perhaps I would find you more willing a second time."

He ran his hand up her skirts again, placing his palm over her mound, his fingers spread over her belly. Her eyes widened and she started to jerk away, then settled back, her gaze intent on his.

"So soon?" she taunted. "I thought even you not man enough to rape twice so quickly."

Roarke smiled.

"I've been a while without a woman . . . since you ran away from me in Montreal. There are many more men than women in New France, as I'm certain you've noticed. Nor will I pay for it."

His hand moved higher, caressing her belly, and Caitrin stiffened, trying to draw in her stomach. In response, the child moved within her. Eyes wide, Caitrin stared at Roarke. But he wasn't looking at her. His eyes were puzzled as he stared down at the hand hidden beneath her skirts and he spread his fingers further over her swelling abdomen. Beneath his hand the child moved once more, and Roarke lifted his gaze to Caitrin, his face incredulous.

"Holy Mother of God!" he whispered. He touched her face in wonder and laughed, shaking his head in disbelief before drawing her into his arms, cradling her. He held her so for a long time, whispering her name, touching her face, pressing his hand against the child within her. Once, the baby moved and he chuckled, as though he could not believe the miracle of it. At last, he drew back to look at her, his features once more closed.

"But you would not have told me," he accused. "You did not want me to know."

Caitrin stared back at him, unyielding.

"I did not want you to know. It is my child."

"'Tis mine, too. You haven't the right to deny me that. And 'tis no wonder you wanted the papers, that you fear your uncle. If you say the child is the result of rape, he has but to declare you hysteric, unable to care for yourself. If you say the child is a result of love, he'll declare you immoral, degenerate. Either way, Bigot will then declare him your guardian again."

"But if I have the papers, if they know I have them, they will have to leave me alone!"

"And you don't think they will try to get them back? That they won't turn the earth over to find them? That they would not lock you up with the lunatics until you would gladly tell them anything? And you would. Cartland's tender care would seem like paradise after two weeks in the madhouse. Nor, after you told them, would they let you out. You know that, too. Nor would they allow you to keep the babe . . . if they allowed it to live at all."

Caitrin stared at him, her hands clenched against her belly. He was right, she knew, and she looked away, tears flowing unchecked down her face. Kneeling beside her, Roarke took her hands in his.

"When is the baby due, Catkin?"

"The end of May."

"Then it happened in the village," he said, smiling, male vanity overwhelming his concern for a brief moment. Then he sobered. "And 'tis February. I would take you away from here but you cannot travel, not by snowshoe."

Then his eyes grew graver still on hers.

"There is a way, Catkin, to protect you, aye, and for me to take the papers . . . to condemn Cartland in the English colonies, aye, and in England itself." He squeezed her hands. "Look at me! Catkin, they would not dare touch you, not if you were married! If we go to the bishop, I'm thinking he'll waive the banns with you so pregnant. I'll leave funds enough so you'll need naught, aye, and I'll set you up in a house with a maid and a handyman big enough to

326

guard you where I cannot!"

Caitrin stared at him in disbelief. All she could really hear was his continuing need for revenge. Then she shook herself.

"I'll not marry you or any man for the sake of vengeance!"

"And for the sake of your life, your sanity, the baby?"

Caitrin bit her lip and looked down at her hands. Her fingers were twined around Roarke's as he gently rubbed her white knuckles.

"Consider this, Catkin. Marry me, then when this is over and done, when you and the child are safe, we can get an annulment, nor will I fight you on it."

"On what grounds?"

"On the grounds that you are Protestant . . . that you will not raise the child in the Church."

"But I am Catholic. I was baptized secretly by a hedge priest and instructed by him. No one knew but my parents."

"Aye, and who would they dare tell?" he commented bitterly. Then his brow puckered in thought. "We can tell them the marriage was never consummated . . . that you reject me—as you sometimes do."

Caitrin's brow creased in turn.

"That would name the child a bastard. Nor would I lie."

Roarke's hands gripped hers tighter.

"I would have this marriage, not for the next few months, but for always if you, too, would have it so. But if not, I'll not touch you after we wed; you'll not need to lie. The child was conceived before the marriage, aye, and there can be no denying that."

"You swear?" Caitrin asked, her eyes proud and unyielding on his. "You swear you'll not touch me after and you will give me an annulment should . . .

327

when I ask for one?"

Roarke held her gaze with his, wondering how he could give her up once she was his. That, he decided, was a pain he would deal with when the time came. Now, her safety and the child's was his only concern. He took her face gently between his hands.

"Aye," he whispered, "I so swear."

Seeing no other way, she slowly nodded.

"I'll do it, then."

Roarke closed his eyes in relief, then kissed her lightly. When he drew back, his eyes were laughing.

"But I did not," he told her, "promise not to touch you before we married!"

Caitrin considered him a long moment, then she traced the line of his jaw with one finger.

"Aye, you did not," she whispered as she lifted her mouth to his.

Twenty-Five

Was there, Caitrin wondered, ever a more dismal wedding? The small church was cold and drafty. The frigid stone of its walls glistened with the moisture raised with the breaths of the few guests . . . more guests than she had wanted. The fewer witnesses to the mockery, the better. Bigot was there on his insistence that he give the bride away. So were the Decoteau sisters, giggling and sighing behind fur muffs and within fur-lined hoods. It was so romantic, the tall, handsome coureur de bois and the beautiful heiress, coming through such trials to this. What matter if she was pregnant? It but added to the romance! Nor did they know that soon Roarke would be on his way south. The rest of the guests were the curious and the homeless seeking shelter and warmth.

The small house Roarke took her to was better. Situated on a winding, narrow street, it was small, built in the French Canadian manner with a steep roof to shed the heavy snows and thick walls against the bitter cold. Two bedrooms were up the steep stairs, each backing against the chimney for warmth and with two dormer windows to catch the summer breezes. The first floor was but one large room with a cubicle for the manservant Roarke had hired. The rest was the combination sitting room, dining room, and kitchen so preferred by Canadians for its warmth and companionship. Occupying half of one wall was a large fireplace. In the back was a large vegetable garden shielded by tall hedges. In this house Caitrin was to bear her child and wait for Roarke's return, protected by a harridan housekeeper and a giant of a handyman.

Caitrin quickly learned that Jean, so large and laconic, had a wry humor and skillful hands. He puttered about the house, shoveling snow, chopping wood, fixing old things or creating new ones, yet she sensed he was ever watchful. He ignored the sharp tongue of his wife, Fleur, the housekeeper, and Caitrin wondered if he even heard it, until the day he winked at her behind the harridan's back. When he was not about the house, he toured the taverns, the waterfronts, seeking word of Lord Cartland's arrival. Later, after the child was born, it would be Jean who would sit for hours, the baby supported in his huge, work-roughened hands, as, wordless, they gazed into each other's eyes.

Fleur, Caitrin thought, was an absurd name for such a rasp-tongued, heavy-handed woman. She more resembled a dragon than a flower. Behind the caustic, scalding tongue and the heavy, plodding figure was a woman who had lost eight children in infancy. Only the ninth, Martin, had lived, Fleur told her, her pride concealing her fear; Martin was with General Levis in Montreal. Yet, under Roarke's soft Irish brogue and soft teasing, she was transformed into a blushing, giggling clumsy girl. Then he would tease her about her clumsiness. And after his child was born, she would become a fiercely doting grandmother, competent and clucking. Her devotion

330

would extend, then, to its mother. The funds Roarke had left for her use, Caitrin discovered after he left, were far more than ample even with the inflation that plagued New France. Did it mean, she wondered, that he thought he might be gone far longer than they both hoped?

In November, the French had destroyed German Flats, leaving William Johnson's fort the prime remaining stronghold on the Mohawk River. The English settlers were pushed back farther than they had ever been before. The English, Roarke had told her, would eventually defeat New France. They had to; they outnumbered the French ten to one, and there was their hardheaded sense of purpose when they were finally aroused. But he could not say when. In December, too, the cowed populace of Montreal had rioted for bread.

Considering these things, Caitrin began to carefully watch their spending. Fleur, too, from a lifetime of poverty, was frugal, counting every sou, cutting corners and finding bargains where no bargains were to be had.

On May 9, the official daily ration of bread was reduced to two ounces per person. Yet, incredibly, Fleur kept the table well laid.

On May 13, Lord Cartland arrived in Quebec, but like a cat playing with a mouse, he did not visit Caitrin. Anxiety added to the burden of her pregnancy and to the unseasonably warm weather. Five days later, the child was born, delivered by Fleur. She was no midwife, but after having borne nine of her own, Caitrin thought she understood the process. This was Roarke's child, too, and Caitrin knew Fleur would do her best, that she would be gentle, caring. Nor could she risk a midwife; in a starving, desperate Quebec, everyone had a price. Nor would

Lord Cartland hesitate to kidnap a child to control the mother, even a newborn.

But Caitrin had had no idea how much a hostage of the heart a child could be until she at last held Roarke's son in her arms. Before, the child had been but a concept, a problem with which to deal, a weapon her uncle, Roarke, and society held against her. She had purposely suppressed the wonder she felt when the child had moved within her, the joy when Roarke had held his hand to her belly, the rapture on his features as the child kicked and turned in her womb.

She stared down at the newborn in her arms, studying his tiny, perfect fingernails, the dark fringe of eyelashes, the thin shadow of fine infant hair. He seemed a miracle. She laughed in wonder as he gave a prodigious yawn, his features puckered. His tiny hands opened and closed, and curious, she slipped a finger into his grip and her eyes opened wide.

"He's holding my finger!" she whispered in awe.

"Of course, he is," Fleur snorted. "All babies do that."

"But I've never had a baby before! I've never even held a baby before! I don't know what to do!"

Fleur turned from her tidying of the room and studied the new mother.

"You'll do fine," she said at last. "You are not like some, who want nothing to do with the babe after the birth pains, at least for the first few days."

She returned to her tasks with even more vehemence than usual, and Caitrin waited. She had learned that that meant the housekeeper was upset and that she would soon speak her mind. Nor could anything stop her.

"We've not hired a wet nurse yet," Fleur finally said, giving a quilt such a shake that the feathers flew. "But there are enough out there who would be happy for a job if it meant but a meal a day."

Caitrin stared at her. It was something she had not thought of. Then she looked back at the infant.

"We don't really need a wet nurse, do we?" she asked plaintively. "Can't I feed him myself?"

Fleur turned back to her with a new respect.

"I had not thought you would. Most ladies do not. They say it spoils the bust, but I fed all mine and they"—she weighed her massive breasts in each hand—"did but get bigger. Jean can tell you."

Smiling, Caitrin returned to her study of the infant. Then she looked back up at Fleur, laughing.

"I just noticed! His eyes are blue. They're just like Roarke's! I somehow did not think of them as being any color at all!"

Fleur peered at the baby, snorting, "All babies have blue eyes at first, if they're not Indian! I don't know about those babies from Africa or China."

"But look at the shape of them!"

The housekeeper studied the soft, unfocused eyes a moment more, then looked at Caitrin, her gaze calculating. All babies looked alike at birth, she thought, but a little lie did not matter.

"*Oui*, you may be right. He does look a bit like his father."

Gratified, Caitrin smiled, then her eyes clouded.

"I wish," she whispered, "that Roarke was here . . . that he could see his son."

The words seemed to echo about her ears, and reluctantly, she lifted her stricken gaze to Fleur. The woman was staring back at her, hands on ample hips, resembling, Caitrin thought, a Flemish draft horse, with her long face and heavy build.

"Do you know," Fleur accused, "that you often go for days without even mention of his name? I thought there was no feeling in you for him at all."

"It is the other way. I am no more to him than a tool for his vengeance. The babe, too."

"If you believe that," Fleur grunted, "you are a fool—and blind, too! That man would die for you and the babe! And for revenge he needs nothing but a knife, a gun! Or money! And the saints know he has enough of that! Truth be known, you hinder him!"

Humphing once more, she turned and plodded out of the room, slamming the door behind her. Then the door opened again and she stuck her head in.

"So, what will you name the babe, *mon petite?*"

Caitrin touched the child's round cheek with a gentle forefinger and smiled as he turned, seeking it with his mouth.

"We—Roarke and I—never discussed it. I think perhaps James, after my father. *Oui,* James Roarke O'Conner. If Roarke is not happy," she added, forgetting the annulment for a moment, "then we can change it when he gets back."

Fleur nodded her approval and was gone again, leaving Caitrin to cuddle her child and consider what Fleur had said about Roarke. And it was true, she knew, that she wished he were there with her, with them.

Twenty-Six

The knock Caitrin had so fearfully awaited came suddenly, three days after the child was born. She stared at Fleur and Jean, then drew a deep breath and nodded. With a push of one slim foot, she set in motion again the rocking chair Roarke had designed for her from a model he had seen in New England and Jean had built. Her face was calm as Fleur opened the door to Lord Cartland and two of his henchmen.

"How very bovine," he commented nasally, staring over his thin aristocratic nose at Caitrin as she nursed her infant.

Caitrin stared back.

"I want them out of here," she replied, inclining her head toward his henchmen. Her eyes narrowed in recognition of one as he grinned at her. It was the coureur de bois who had accosted Roarke the night they entered Montreal. Somehow the sight of him frightened her more than Cartland did. Tearing her eyes away from him, she addressed her uncle again.

"I want them out of here now!" she repeated.

"You object to their company?" Cartland asked, lifting one eyebrow. "You prefer that of an Irish bogtrotter? Perhaps they are not the most desirable, but they serve their purpose, as the bogtrotter did his, I see. And your servants . . . I want them gone, too."

"No," she answered. "They stay. They do not understand English, if that is your concern. The rapacity of your companions is mine."

"As you will," Cartland agreed, seeing the set of her jaw. "Your servants do fit into your humble dwelling, but you do not, my dear. If you tire of it—and of your bogtrotter—I am staying with Bigot. He has assured me of your welcome there. Of course, you would have to cease in the disgusting habit of feeding your brat that way. It is not as though there are no wet nurses."

Caitrin smiled down at the nursing infant.

"It offends you? You always did have delicate sensibilities—if only in regard to yourself. I suggest, then, that you leave. . . . And, no, I'll not live with Bigot. I prefer this company. 'Tis more honest."

She looked back up at him, mouth stubborn.

"If you've no more purpose here than to issue me an invitation and to sneer at my husband, my servants, the way I care for my child, then I suggest, again, that you leave."

Cartland glanced over at Fleur, who stood beside the fireplace, a long, heavy poker in her hand, then at Jean standing by the door, armed with a flintlock. He looked back at Caitrin, his frosty smile gone.

"Where is your husband?" he demanded.

"He is a woods loper," Caitrin shrugged. "Where would he be but in the woods with the Indians?"

"He might be in the English colonies."

"Aye," Caitrin agreed, "he might. In the forest, one tree looks like another, one colony like another."

"Or he might be an English spy."

"He might, but he is an Irish bogtrotter, as you

336

pointed out, and he was driven out of Ireland by an English landlord. He has little love for the English."

"People forget much for money, even hate," Cartland commented, smiling in disdain.

"Aye, that they do," she agreed. "Living with you taught me so."

His smile disappeared and he took a step toward her, then halted, brought up short by the flintlock Jean casually aimed at him. His jaw clenched in rage as he turned back to Caitrin.

"You have something I want," he stated from between clenched teeth, "and I want it now!"

"Then the rumors are true?" Caitrin asked, unconcerned. "They say you are in debt, but I doubt you can milk me or mine for aught more than you already have. They say you've left me nothing."

"You stupid little slut!" Cartland hissed before gritting his teeth at a warning grunt from Jean. His face grew crimson beneath the powder before he continued in a calmer tone. "You know what I am talking about—and I'll pay you for them! With cash if you give them to me now, with grief if I have to take them later!"

Caitrin casually covered her breast and lifted her sleeping son to her shoulder. She set the rocking chair in motion again as she gently rubbed his back to raise a burp.

"I assume you are speaking of the papers in your trunk—or Bigot's copies of them. I assume he has copies, and I can see why you would not want them in the wrong hands, but as much as we could use the money, I do not have them. Would God I did!"

Cartland stared. She never could lie well and her gaze was direct, her face calm. Still, he did not believe her. He knew the Irish, how they could turn the truth, twist it, yet never lie. That she said she did not have the papers did not mean she did not know where they were. Or it could mean she did not have them in her hand, yet they could be in the house.

"But you know where they are," he stated, his eyes never leaving hers.

"I do not."

"Who has them?"

"I do not know that, either," Caitrin stated, smiling inwardly. Roarke had been gone several months. The papers could be in anyone's hands by now, but hopefully they were in William Johnson's possession, as she and Roarke had planned.

"Have you ever," she observed, "watched Bigot at his gambling? Have you noticed how he always hedges his bets?" Then she smiled slightly. "How well do you trust Bigot?"

Cartland's thin lips drew taut, then he shrugged contemptuously.

"Do not let me find out that you are lying to me. And do not ever need me, Caitrin," he warned, "or if you do, come to me with the papers in hand."

"That," she observed, "would be difficult, as I do not have them."

Cartland studied her innocent features a moment longer, then turned on his satin and rhinestone-studded heel and was gone. Caitrin stared after him, suddenly shaking in fear.

"That," Fleur stated, "is an evil man."

Caitrin drew in a deep breath and nodded.

"Fleur," she asked at last, "how many people know you have a son in the army in Montreal?"

Fleur met her eyes, a deep frown on her face. Then she shook her head.

"No one. We are from Lachute and know no one here. Nor do I gossip! And Monsieur Roarke . . . didn't he tell me he would have the tongue out of my head if I told anyone anything? Nor is it," she huffed, suddenly indignant, "anyone's business what we do!"

Then they both stared at Jean. He looked from one to the other, suddenly ill at ease. At last, he cleared his throat.

"I have not told you, *mon petite*," he addressed Fleur. "I wanted to spare you, but Martin is no longer with General Levis. As much as he loves Levis and Montcalm, too, he grew sick of this"—his hands spread to encompass all of New France—"and he went with Monsieur Roarke."

Fleur stared at her husband, incredulous, then she collapsed into a chair, her shoulders shuddering with her weeping. Jean patted at her broad shoulder, his eyes helpless. Lying the baby in his cradle, Caitrin kneeled beside her and took her hands.

"Roarke will keep him safe, you know that, much safer than he would be in New France. And there is no shame in it. If more men did so, men big and small, if they ran from the corruption, the evil, then, perhaps, France, the king, would do something about it."

Fleur nodded, her face red-blotched and tear-stained.

"I know! I know!" she sobbed. "But I just remembered that I had told the fishmonger's wife about Martin . . . that my wagging chin could have endangered the petite babe! Now, he is safe again . . . as safe as we can keep him!"

She began sobbing once more and Caitrin leaned back on her heels, grinning at the sight of the harridan in tears. Nor could Martin be used to threaten James Roarke.

*　　　*　　　*

A week later, Jean and Caitrin, the baby in her arms, returned home to find the house ransacked and Fleur once more in tears, this time from indignation. Caitrin stared about at the food, clothing, and household goods scattered over Fleur's immaculate floors, at the batting drifting in the air from Jean's ripped pallet. Then her eyes focused on the secret flagstone of the hearth, which appeared to be set and immovable.

"Did they take anything?" she asked at last.

"No," Fleur hiccuped, "nothing, but the little one, the one with the face of a weasel, he squeezed my!..."

She gestured toward her ample bosom and Jean went white with rage. Grabbing his flintlock, he was gone, slamming the door behind him. Caitrin carefully tossed aside a shard of broken plate.

"Isn't that just like a man, to leave when there is a mess to clean up?" she commented, and Fleur giggled through her tears.

Twenty-Seven

New France settled in for a long summer of rationing and war. On the ninth of July, the English were defeated in their attempt to capture Fort Carillon, calming French fears. Montcalm had held out although Vaudreuil delayed sending aid, leading to speculation that the governor secretly wished to have Montcalm defeated.

But the French sense of relief came too soon. At the end of July, Louisburg surrendered to the English general Amherst, and Fort Frontenac, on Lake Ontario, fell on August 27. In mid September, the English attack on Fort Duquesne failed, but the French were looking toward a long, hard winter. By November, the poor of the populace of New France were existing on a diet of salt cod and horseflesh. That same month, too, the French deserted Fort Duquesne, while Robert Rogers and his men harassed the French, seeming to be everywhere. With spring came the desertions of the Iroquois, tribe by tribe, seduced away by the silver tongue of William Johnson and the smell of defeat they sensed on the French. Starvation, famine, and pestilence threatened. May came again and Montcalm was refused military aid by France. Having suffered reverses everywhere, she could only send four hundred ten men. However, Montcalm and his chief aides received promotions and orders to preserve essential points only, and those most closely connected.

Bigot, too, had cause for alarm. He had become trapped in his own web of greed and deceit, and France was calling him to account. Suddenly, he no longer controlled corruption, it controlled him— and with him, Cartland. Listening to Fleur's gossip, Caitrin felt the cold hand of fear clutch at her heart. Cartland was always dangerous. Cornered by the inevitable fall of New France, he would be doubly so. And she and her child might unwillingly be his last, his only means of self-preservation.

Nor could she do anything but wait for the English to come, for Roarke to come. It seemed as though he had been gone forever, not just over a year. Sometimes she had to fight to remember his features. Other times she had but to glance at her child's dark hair and blue eyes, and memories of Roarke would assault her like a blow. Unwanted memories, she told herself. She dared not remember him with love. Too many things were unsettled between them. No matter how vehemently Fleur promoted her employer, how often she insisted he was in love with her, Caitrin could not suppress her doubts. She had heard too often the cold hate in his voice when he talked of Lord Cartland. She had felt the deep scars on his back too often in their lovemaking not to know his need for revenge was engraved as deep, perhaps far deeper, than any love for her that Fleur so ardently insisted upon. And, sometimes, when she gazed into the eyes of her child, she saw the defiance and hate in the eyes of a boy bent over a whipping block. He had been gone so long! Perhaps he had never intended to come

342

back. Perhaps their marriage, the house, the money, even Jean and Fleur, had been but an elaborate ploy to take the papers Cartland wanted so badly.

Or he could be dead, unfound in the immense forests, scalpless, rotting. Even if he was found, who would tell her? The thought always came like a blow to Caitrin's belly, driving her breath from her, leaving only fear and a grief far exceeding any love to which she dared admit.

On July 26, Fort Niagara fell to William Johnson, but the news only added to the fears in Quebec, for suddenly, on that same day, in full view of the city ramparts were the sails of sixty English warships. In those ships was the army of General James Wolfe. Quebec was under siege. All inhabitants able to bear arms were mustered. Women and children were sent out of the city to safety.

Caitrin, though, chose to stay. The house had become a sanctuary to her. To leave would be to be vulnerable, an easier prey to Cartland, and there was food enough still. Fleur had planned well, nor was there any shortage for those with enough money.

Caitrin rarely left the security of the house and idleness fatigued her, drawing dark circles under her eyes and an ache into her head. But she felt exposed outside its stout walls—and watched. The last time she had left its security, she caught a glimpse of Cartland's weasel-faced henchman in the crowded streets and knew he followed her. There would be wounded to tend, she knew, once the bombardment of Quebec began, just as she had tended those at William Henry, but she dared not go out, dared not leave her sanctuary. And always there was the thought that Roarke might return.

At the end of June, Governor Vaudreuil launched a plan to destroy the English fleet with fireboats.

343

Ships and rafts were loaded with pitch, tar, and explosives and set adrift, but their commander set them afire far too soon and not an enemy ship was damaged. It was a magnificent sight, though, Jean told the two women, all those ships and rafts blazing away against the moonless night, the fires reflecting on the dark river. Caitrin smiled and shook her head, thinking of the starving populace, the expense of the fireboats, the folly of men, and the vainglorious Governor Vaudreuil.

By the end of June, Wolfe had positioned his artillery on Point Levis, across the river from Quebec, and the bombardment began. A pall of smoke from the many fires blanketed the city and people dashed from one cover to another, or huddled in dubious shelters under the blows of shell and noise. The inhabitants gritted their teeth, determined to hold on, but many of the militia, far from their farms and villages, began to desert. Jean, grinning, told the women of Vaudreuil's futilely proclaimed death penalty to all deserters, but Caitrin only frowned. Only if Lord Cartland was among those so fleeing could she rest easy, regardless of the bombs and the fires surrounding them.

Then, on the moonless night of July 18, the English general Wolfe did the impossible, slipping his ships past the Quebec batteries, and the next morning he was above the city, forcing Montcalm to split his forces. Two weeks later, Wolfe attempted an assault and was forced back, losing almost five hundred men. The siege entered its third month, and it didn't seem as though there would ever be an end to it.

Caitrin sometimes thought she had never had a life beyond one filled with the smell of smoke and the deafening sounds of bombardment. It seemed as if she had always lived within the four whitewashed walls of the house and in the enclosed garden that had become her sanctuary. Her only reality was Jean, Fleur, and her son. And fear. Always, she lived with fear. Time was measured by the apple trees within the garden walls. They had burst into blossom with her child's birth, had grown fruit as he had grown, had ripened with the hope through the long summer that the English, that Roarke would come. Then, like that hope, the trees had become bare, seemingly without life through the long, harsh winter, only to burst into flower again. The fruit began once more to grow, like her hope, and one night, while the apples were still small and hard but with seeds within, Roarke returned.

The knock came late in the evening, startling them. They exchanged apprehensive glances before Fleur picked up the poker. Caitrin took a pistol from a shelf and went to her position behind the rocking chair, the gun hidden in the folds of her skirts. Jean picked the primed flintlock up from its corner and went to stand with his back to the side of the door as Fleur flung it open.

Roarke stepped in, Martin behind him, and Caitrin felt her knees go weak. She had waited so long, and sometimes she could no longer believe he would ever return. Suddenly, all her conflicting emotions overwhelmed her. She would have gone to him but she doubted her legs would support her. She could only stare at him, clinging to the back of the chair as the pistol fell to the floor. But he looked so tired! she thought. His clothes were worn and travel-stained. Fatigue scored deep lines in his features, darkening his eyes, and a week-old beard matted his face. And never, Caitrin thought, had he looked so handsome!

Fleur, in tears, rushed to hug him, and he stared at Caitrin over her shoulder. How, a small portion of Caitrin's mind wondered, could such a rough-tongued woman cry so much? Then Fleur turned to encompass her son, but Caitrin still could not move. She wanted Roarke's arms around her more than anything she could think of, but there was something forbidding within his eyes, in the set of his face.

"I would like a bath," he stated at last, rubbing a weary hand over his eyes.

The household leaped into action, Jean and Martin bringing in the tub. Fleur heated water while Caitrin went to her room to find a change of clothes for Roarke. Pausing, she gazed down at her sleeping son. He was so big, so strong for fifteen months! She thought briefly of waking him, of taking him to his father, then dismissed it. Roarke needed his bath and rest. A bubble of happiness swelled in her throat and she gently touched the fat cheek with her finger.

"Your daddy is home," she whispered softly, then she went back downstairs.

Roarke was immersed in the tub, his eyes closed, nor did he open them when Caitrin entered. She studied each of his features, a strange ache of need tightening her throat, swelling deep in her belly. She wanted to hold him, she realized, to cradle him, to watch him sleep in her arms. And she wanted to see him wake, his weariness gone, replaced by passion. She wanted his mouth on hers, on her breasts. She wanted to feel the weight of him over her, to feel the thrust of him deep within her, to answer his every motion with her own until fulfillment consumed them both, drawing them into a deep forever-abiding passion for each other. But what if he rejected her?

The need swelled her nipples, drew a deep demand in the core of her, and she had to look away from him. Nor did she dare look at him again until he had finished his bath and stood in front of a small mirror to shave.

He was turned away from her and she could safely study his reflection in the mirror. Then her eyes dropped to his back. The deep scars stood in ridges, crisscrossing each other from shoulders to waist. Caitrin wanted to touch them, to press her lips to each, drawing away the last remaining trace of pain. Tears welled in her eyes as she remembered the boy bent over the whipping block, his screams ringing again in her ears. Hate for her uncle shook her with its intensity. He had dared hurt someone she loved, and never, she realized, would she forgive him for it.

That she did love Roarke drew her chin high in pride, filling her with fear. But perhaps Fleur was right. Perhaps he did want her for herself alone. Hadn't he come back to her? Nor did he need to; he had all he needed for revenge in the papers that she had traded for her safety, for the child's safety.

Roarke wiped the last speck of soap from his face, then sat down at the table as Fleur placed food before him and her son. Neither of them looked up again until their plates had been wiped clean. Taking a cup of ale from Fleur, Roarke leaned back on the hind legs of his chair and, at last, looked at Caitrin.

"I meant to be back earlier," he told her. "You know that. But bureaucracy held me up."

He shrugged, deciding not to tell her of how he had been captured by the New York Militia, of the time spent in jail, a whim away from being hanged as a traitor, while the governor refused to allow him to send word to the outside world. At last, bribing a gaoler, he had sent word to William Johnson, reminding him of his promise to Caitrin. Only Johnson's intervention had kept him from a hangman's noose and Caitrin from widowhood. But perhaps that was what she wanted. It would be easier than seeking an annulment. Only William Johnson's persistence had forced New York's governor, William Shirley, to examine Bigot's papers. Then came weeks and months of waiting, of worrying about Caitrin and the child, of the driving need to be back, to see them, to protect them. It took forever as the papers were examined and finally declared authentic as he went from one official to another, explaining how he had come by them, how Caitrin had discovered duplicates in Cartland's trunk. Then word had to be sent to England and an investigation begun in Ireland while all the time he cooled his heels, only his word of honor keeping him in New York. Only three weeks before, had word finally come from England and he was free to go. In that time, doubts began to grow. Only his promise had brought him back. Now, he could only wonder why he had even returned to someone who did not want him, who had never wanted him. All he could think of was the way she had just stood, the rocking chair a barrier between them, and looked at him, no joy in her face, when he at last came home.

Caitrin looked down at the twined fingers in her lap. The knuckles were white with tension.

"And Cartland?" she finally asked, looking up again. "What of him?"

Roarke shrugged.

"He is condemned to death as a traitor. Never again can he dare set foot anywhere in the British Empire." He scowled before adding, "Unfortunately, 'twas your estate invested in his mad scheme. Little is left. Enough to make you comfortable, perhaps, but little more.''

"'Tis no more than I expected," she answered. "He would not have brought me with him had it not been so." Then she smiled. "But I never thought you married me for my money."

But Roarke did not smile back and his eyes were dead with more than fatigue as he shrugged again.

"No, your inheritance was not part of our agreement."

Caitrin looked away. Whatever she had expected of his homecoming, it was not that he would be indifferent. Suddenly, she was frightened, with no idea of how to proceed, of what she could expect from him.

"And Cartland," she whispered, "this will make him doubly dangerous. He must know who betrayed him. And the war, 'twill be months, perhaps years, before 'tis over! Bigot, too, will be after us!" Her chin lifted suddenly in her old spirit of defiance. "Can we leave Quebec? Surely 'tis possible to slip through the lines! There are deserters who do it every day!"

"Not when word is out to stop any woman with a child. And it is surely out by now. Nor will the war last much longer—a week, perhaps two, I'm thinking, no more, and Quebec will be taken."

"One or two weeks?" Caitrin repeated in disbelief. "But Quebec is all but impregnable! Even Montcalm thinks 'tis so!"

Roarke shook his head.

"There is a way, and General Wolfe will have it. Now, I'm tired and I have to leave early. I'll sleep before the fire so as not to disturb you."

Caitrin looked down again at her fidgeting fingers. So they had agreed, she thought, nor could she ask him to her bed, not through the wall of cold indifference he had erected between them. The words would not come, not through her pride, and his refusal would be too painful, even more painful than his indifference.

"Would you like to see your son?" she asked at last.

Roarke studied her, then shook his head.

"No, I would rather not. I would rather not love him, only to have him taken from me."

The words were a slap in her face and Caitrin could only stare at him. At last, she rose and stumbled up the stairs to her bed, her legs nerveless, her knees shaking. Roarke watched her go. He had to slip back through the lines early the next morning. There was something he had to do yet in this hellish war, something that might hasten its end. After that, he had but to return home once more, then he could be gone from New France, could seek out a new life, and could try to forget he had once had a wife and son.

Twenty-Eight

Wolfe's aide-de-camp entered the tent, interrupting the general's conference with his senior officers. Twice he cleared his throat before the thin red-haired general looked up from a map, scowling. The aide-de-camp nervously cleared his throat a third time.

"There is a man here, General," he stated nervously, "a woods loper, I think, who says he knows of a way up the cliffs to the Plains of Abraham."

The scowl disappeared from Wolfe's face. A way might yet be found to crack the hard nut that was Quebec . . . and soon. The miracle he had hoped for entered the tent in the form of Roarke O'Conner.

A day and a half later, at two in the morning on September 13, twenty-four volunteers led the way up the cliffs in the rain and dark. They silently pulled themselves up root by root, rock by rock, while below them the major force waited for the signal of success. Musket shots rang out when they discovered enemy forces, which fled, and the cliffs were secure, the battle begun.

Within the walls of Quebec that morning all was

351

chaos. People were screaming and running in the streets. The sound of cannon fire penetrated even the thick walls of Caitrin's house. Suddenly, her shelter, her sanctuary, was a trap. She felt blind as a mole, and as helpless. Fleur and Jean, too, nervously went about their chores. The child became fretful, demanding attention, but Caitrin dared not take him into the garden to play. Out there, the cannon would only be louder, the shouts of the people only more tantalizingly unintelligible. Finally, toward dusk, she sent Jean out for news. Then she and Fleur waited impotently for his return.

The long northern twilight deepened to evening, the noise of the cannon quieting, and still they waited. Putting aside her needlepoint, Caitrin paced, while Fleur, seemingly relaxed, knitted, not noticing the many dropped stitches. Nor had Fleur spoken to her beyond what was necessary. It was obvious she blamed the estrangement with Roarke on her mistress. But Caitrin did not want to think about Roarke's rejection. Nor did she want to talk, and if silence was the result, she welcomed Fleur's censure. She wanted to do nothing but pace and leave Fleur to her knitting.

It seemed hours later before Jean's knock came—three raps, a pause, and two more. Caitrin leaped to the door, swinging the bar up and opening it. Jean stood there, tears streaming down his face, and Caitrin drew him in. He stumbled over the threshold and looked helplessly from Caitrin to Fleur, then back, mute. They stared back, waiting, and at last he gulped and swallowed hard on his grief.

"The English, they came up the Plains of Abraham. No one knows how they found the way. The city is surrounded and everyone talks of surrender, but no one knows. We've lost! All of New

352

France is lost! And Montcalm—" he paused, gulping again, "Montcalm is mortally wounded. Perhaps he is dead already. And the English Wolfe, they say he, too, is dead."

Caitrin could only stare at him. Grief for Montcalm and joy that the English were so close warred within her. And all she could do was wait for the surrender, for Roarke. Turning without a word, she went up the stairs to bed.

Then began more days of waiting. The cannonade from Quebec's batteries deafened the ears. The return shell from the English batteries shook the walls, rattled the windows, and caused Caitrin to leap in sudden terror. How close they came, she did not know, but Jean, back from one of his forays, told her that several houses on their street had been destroyed.

It was Jean, too, who came back with news that the army, with Vaudreuil and Bigot, had deserted the city. Fewer than a thousand men were left for the defense of Quebec. The cathedral had been burned to a shell. The people who had sought refuge from the bombardment before the battle on the Plains of Abraham in Quebec's suburbs had come streaming back, fleeing the English. They wandered about, seeking shelter in the burned-out husks of their homes, plundering and quarreling amongst themselves. There was provision enough for the populace, gossip had it, for less than a week, for six days, five, four. And over all, the rumor of surrender prevailed.

On the morning of September 18, Jean went out again in search of news, leaving Caitrin and Fleur to wait once more. But soon—too soon, they would realize later—the secret knock came at the door and Caitrin opened it to Lord Cartland.

He stood there, smiling triumphantly down at her, and she stared back, stunned with disbelief. Then she tried to slam the door in his face just as one of his henchmen shoved it inward again. The force propelled her stumbling back, and Caitrin watched helplessly as Cartland and his men strolled into the house, Jean, arm twisted behind his back, with them. Her eyes flicked desperately from Cartland and his three lackeys, to her pistol lying so uselessly on its high shelf, to the flintlocks in the hands of her uncle's men. Then her gaze returned to Cartland as he advanced toward her. The smile was gone from his thin lips, and his eyes were as cold and as lifeless as lead.

"You goddamned little bitch!" he snarled. "You and that bitch-born, bogtrotting, meddling husband of yours have destroyed me!"

His hand descended against her face and spun her up against the wall. Her vision went black and her knees threatened to buckle beneath her. She was aware, though, that Jean had leaped forward, an angry growl in his throat, only to take the butt of a rifle in the back of his skull. He dropped beneath it, inert. Fleur sobbed and tried to go to him, only to be brought up short by the weasel-faced henchman's knife at her throat. He chuckled, backing her to the wall, and thrust his skinny body against hers. Giggling through broken teeth, he pressed his unshaven face into her neck. His filthy hand grabbed her breasts, squeezing, pinching, as tears of pain and humiliation flowed down Fleur's cheeks, though her eyes never left Jean's recumbent form.

Caitrin blinked against her blurred vision as Cartland strolled toward her. The lace at his throat, she noticed, was soiled and limp. His blue satin suit was dirty and frayed. Then her chin lifted along with one

354

eyebrow and she smiled.

"Have you lost your laundress, Uncle?" she asked. "And I've no doubt your lackeys do poorly at the washtubs and with the iron."

Cartland's features tightened with fury, then relaxed. His smile chilled Caitrin more than his rage had done. Languidly, he reached out and drew his finger down her cheek, his smile deepening as he saw fear flick in her eyes.

"Aye," he nodded, "that son of a slut husband of yours, and you, bitch, have ruined me. But you, my darling niece, will yet save my skin!"

"Leave the old hag!" he snarled, turning to Jacques Leverett. "You'll have this slut to play with soon enough—when she has served my purpose. And you will serve me," he told Caitrin, his smile cold.

Caitrin's chin went higher.

"I think not, Uncle. I never have before, not willingly, not knowingly."

"You will now."

Turning to a huge, scarred man with slablike hands, Cartland jerked his chin toward the stairs. Mesmerized, Caitrin watched him go, knowing well with what he would return. But she could only wait, not taking her eyes off the stairs. There was the whimpering protest of a child awakened from sleep, then the man descended once more, Caitrin's son in his arms. The ill-visaged man was baring large, square teeth in a grin, the scar that dissected one eyebrow and flattened his nose making his smile hideous. And her son was grinning back at the dull face and hair like rotten straw of the man who held him.

"See," the man chortled, "the petite infant likes old Edouard Clerc! You like old Edouard, don't you, little one?" he asked, and James Roarke chortled.

355

Caitrin realized in horror that the huge, ugly man was simpleminded. She moved to go to her son, to take him, but Cartland stepped between.

"No," he said, smiling down at her. "Edouard will watch the brat for a while. You are coming with me, nor can I guarantee your return. Jacques there fancies you, and Jacques is not gentle, as you may have observed. The brat in Edouard's care, I think, will promise me your wholehearted cooperation. And if you don't give it, the brat dies."

He jerked his head toward Fleur. She sat on the floor, tears still streaming down her face as she cradled Jean in her arms. He was still unconscious.

"Tie them up, and you," he ordered Caitrin, "get your cloak. We are going to Montreal and I have no time to wait on maudlin farewells."

Stumbling backward, her eyes still on her son, Caitrin took her cloak from its peg and wrapped it about herself. The huge man, she knew, could easily kill him, could snap the child's fragile neck with one twist of his giant hand if he should become angry. James Roarke saw his mother don her cloak and knew she was going out—and without him! His smile turned to a shriek of anguish, his baby fists hitting out at the man who held him. Looking back over her shoulder, Caitrin saw the huge man's affability turn instantly to rage. He shook the wailing child once, his face distorted with fury, then tossed him across the room to land in Fleur's soft, ample lap, the child's cry cut short. With a sob of fear, Caitrin turned to go to her son, but Cartland caught her arm, swinging her hard up against the wall. His eyes were reptilian as he stared into hers.

"Understand me!" he hissed, his face inches from hers. "I do not care if you live or die, not once you get me to Montreal! In truth, I doubt very much you will survive Jacque's tender attentions; he has a way with knives. But I can promise you that the brat will die if you do not do as you are told! Now, get on your horse!''

He stared into her eyes, reading her distress and submission, then shoved her out the door and down the stairs.

A heavy haze of smoke hung like a pall over the city of Quebec on this seventeenth day of September, 1759. An occasional cannon from the French batteries growled, to be answered by a desultory shot from the English. People wandered about, their faces vacant. Others searched futilely through the rubble of their homes for anything that could be salvaged. If they lifted their gaze at all to watch the passing of Caitrin, Lord Cartland, and his two henchmen, it was to stare covetously at the horses they rode. Their eyes held only dull hunger and apathy.

The few men of the Canadian Militia guarding the gates were lethargic. They barely glanced at the four horses, at Cartland's tattered finery, and at Caitrin's strained features. They had seen so many of the wealthy and the nobility escape while they could not, and many women wore that strained expression in the last days of Quebec. Then they swung open the gates.

Caitrin hesitated, wondering what Cartland would do if she told the guards she was being abducted, that her uncle held her son hostage. But perhaps James Roarke was no longer even at the house. Perhaps Edouard had taken him away to a place where she would never find him and was waiting there for Cartland's orders. Perhaps she was never meant to find him again. Perhaps Edouard had orders to kill him no matter what she did, or maybe he was dead already. Caitrin's heart contracted at the thought. Or simpleminded Edouard might have already become bored with his role of nursemaid. Perhaps he had already forgotten his responsibilities and left James in the care of Fleur and Jean. Perhaps he could be persuaded to give up the child or maybe her son could be taken by force.

But she could not take that chance and she urged her horse forward through the gates of Quebec. It seemed as though she left her soul behind. And what if she died, she wondered, and was never to know what happened to her child? That, somehow, was the most terrifying thought of all.

Instead of heading east toward Beauport then north to circle the English lines, Cartland led them directly west on the road following the St. Lawrence River, a road blocked by the English. Caitrin's curiosity overcame her reluctance to address her uncle.

"Why," she asked, "are we riding directly into the English lines with a bounty on your head?"

Cartland looked at her with a mouth shaped in scorn at her stupidity.

"I'll not skulk about like a fugitive bogtrotting thief," he answered, looking down his aristocratic nose at her. "I do not need to; I have you."

"But you are a thief—and a traitor," Caitrin answered, smiling her contempt. "You kidnap me and hold my son hostage, giving him over to an idiot. Can there be anyone more corrupt than a man who uses a mother's love to such a purpose?"

Fury flicked in his eye, then he smiled.

"If you are sentimental enough to become attached to a puling, squalling, disgusting little animal that cannot even control its bowels, then you deserve to be used. You always were mawkish and too much like your mother, no matter how I tried to rid you of such weakness. I should have known it was useless to try. One cannot, after all, fight blood, and the Irish always were a foolish, maudlin people given to misplaced loyalties and excessive honor. It is why they will always be a subject people, to be used, sucked dry, discarded. Just as I intend to use—and discard—you," he told her, his mouth self-satisfied. "Had you no attachment to that puling infant, you would be useless to me. As to why I choose to go directly through the English lines, it is also a much shorter distance, and I need to be in Montreal as soon as possible. There is a flotilla leaving there and I intend to be on it. I doubt there will be another."

"And Ashley and Anna?" Caitrin asked.

Cartland shrugged his indifference.

"They are in Montreal, but I doubt they can pay for passage."

Caitrin stared ahead, not seeing anything. Her uncle, she realized, was a much more desperate man than she had thought. And the more dangerous for it. Fear opened a cold pit deep within her, a pit she knew she could be lost in forever. Nor was it the cruel, unbalanced smile and greedy eyes of Jacques Leverett licking her naked that fed it.

Soon, too soon, long before Caitrin was prepared, they were challenged. Two colonial soldiers suddenly materialized out of the underbrush. There was no order to halt. The soldiers simply stood there. Their grim eyes and flinty features belied their ragtag and battle-worn uniforms. Both held flintlocks on the ready. One shifted about a stalk of hay in his narrow mouth, his pale blue eyes taking in every detail of the party.

"Speak English?" he asked at last.

Caitrin eased her horse forward one step.

"I do," she stated, her French accent thick.

"Who are you?"

"My name is Louise Marie Dubruille. This is my uncle, Charles Dubruille, and his retainers. We live in Montreal but were trapped in Quebec after the birth of my sister's child."

She shrugged, smiling beguilingly, but there was no softening in the soldier's eyes.

"Papers?" he asked, holding out his hand.

Fear thudded in Caitrin's heart. She had used the names her uncle gave her but she had no papers. Her hands twisted in the bridle reins to hide their shaking as she turned to Lord Cartland.

"Les documents, Oncle?" she asked.

Cartland languidly dug into his saddlebag and drew out several parchment documents. He handed them to Caitrin and she passed them to the soldier. The colonial officer unrolled them, scowling as though they made sense, then handed them to his companion. The other soldier took them and trotted down the road. After an interminable wait while sweat slicked Caitrin's palms, he reappeared with an officer on horseback. The officer had the same grim jaw as his men and his eyes were just as flinty as they studied the party.

"Mademoiselle Dubruille," he stated, his eyes never leaving Cartland, "we are looking for a man whose description greatly resembles your uncle. He is English and his name is Cartland. We know he was in Quebec and would associate only with the nobility. Perhaps you know him or know where he is."

Caitrin longed to look at Cartland as he nonchalantly gazed about, but to do so, she knew, would be to give the game away. The colonial officer was sharp-eyed and disbelieving. Instead, she puckered her brow in thought, then shook her head.

"I don't think so. We arrived in Montreal in June. My uncle's wife died a year ago and we were in mourning until recently, so we had little social life. Even after, there were few places to go, few people to visit. My uncle would not associate with people like Bigot and Péan, and there were few others in Quebec of our station. He is a proud, honorable man, *n'est-ce pas?*" she stated, her mouth dry on the falsehood. "He would spit on such as they are! I do not know what this man—Carter?—has done, but if it was dishonorable, my uncle would spit on him, too!"

Realizing she was babbling, she shrugged an apology and smiled as the officer's eyes focused on her. He saw the streaked hair beneath her little tricorn hat, and a full mouth bursting red and made for passion. His gaze dropped to her high, round bust, her slim waist and round hips that swayed easily with the slightest motion of her mount. Then he looked into eyes that smiled back, promising him anything. If her jaw was tight with fear, if a vein throbbed at her temple, betraying her, he did not see it.

"You said you live in Montreal, mademoiselle?" he asked at last.

"We do, much to my regret," she smiled back. "It is a dull city, with so little to do, with so few men to come calling."

The officer's eyes raked her once more.

"I expect to be in Montreal next year, when it falls," he informed her as he returned the papers. "Perhaps I will see you there."

"Perhaps. I know we have little left to return to in France."

Caitrin bowed from the waist to them as she urged her horse forward, a bitter, angry taste in her mouth. She rode too fast, she knew, expecting to hear a shout from the soldiers behind her, but she did not care. Fury at her impotence shook her. Tears threatened to burst and she swallowed them back. Never had she let her uncle see her weep nor would she do so now. Then, her emotions under control, she pulled her horse in to allow him to ride next to her.

"Do you," she asked, "remember a croppie boy you once had flogged for stealing apples?"

Cartland glanced at her, disinterested.

"I remember that you pleaded for him, that you created a disgusting display of sentimentality, while my concern was protecting your property."

"Aye," Caitrin answered, lapsing into an Irish brogue, "and you enjoyed it . . . his pain, my compassion, my pleading, my distress. 'Tis true, the Irish are given to sentimentality, if you choose to call it that, and to honor. They are also given to righting wrongs, to revenge."

She leaned forward in the saddle, the better to see Cartland's face.

"'Twas the Irish croppie boy who has destroyed you."

Cartland displayed no emotion as he turned his cold gaze on her. He regarded her as though she were something nasty lodged on his satin pump.

"With your help, I would wager."

"Aye, with my help, as little as it was. We have that in common, my husband and I, our need for revenge. Had you not come to him, he would have gone to you wherever you were. Believe that and consider this," she added, her features hard. "If he has destroyed you for a flogging given so long ago, if he would gamble all his wealth to do so—and he is wealthy—what will he do to you if you harm his wife or child? Sleep well on that thought, for if hurt comes to me or my son, you will never sleep well again."

She had the satisfaction, at last, of seeing fear flick in his eyes. Then his face became a mask again.

"Do you really think I would deign to fear an Irish croppie boy?" he asked.

Caitrin only smiled and settled back in her saddle. An orchard grew in a long, narrow strip up from the St. Lawrence, and it seemed to her she could smell the pungent odor of windfall apples, although she knew the trees had long been stripped of their fruit. There was comfort in the fragrance and she knew what she had told Cartland was true. However Roarke felt about her, never would he rest if she or their child was harmed. If he returned to find her gone, their son held hostage, he would come after them. Nor did it matter to her anymore that only revenge drove him.

Twenty-Nine

Roarke rode through the city of Quebec a day later, Martin behind him. A light drizzle fell as though even the sky mourned the French loss. With the surrender of the city that morning, the red ensign of Britain had replaced the lilies of France. Quebec was a mass of rubble, of smoke, of still-smoldering fires. A third of the buildings had been completely destroyed while others were two- and three-story shells of their former magnificence. Few structures had been left undamaged, although the destruction was much less evident in the upper town. It was this that kept Roarke's fears at bay. Perhaps, on its quiet little street, the house he had bought for Caitrin had been untouched, its inhabitants unharmed. If not, they could be among the thousands wandering dazed through the streets without shelter. How he would then find one woman, a child, and Fleur and Jean he did not know. It could take precious days, even weeks while he searched, this nameless, unwanted anxiety gnawing at his heart. Or he might find only a pile of smashed and splintered masonry and wood. Then how would he know if they had escaped or if they were buried in an unmarked grave, innocent victims of war?

Fear clamped down on his heart and he urged his horse to a faster pace. Then he slowed. After all, he reasoned, what did it matter if they were alive or dead?

His wife and son were lost to him either way. He had put all hope, all love, all desire aside. Caitrin would never be his, that he knew, nor did he want her now. There were other women as beautiful, as desirable and more steadfast, women of warmer hearts, of less confusion. There were even women of warmer passions, women who would surrender to him, open themselves to him as deeply in love as Caitrin had, perhaps even more so. He had long since let her go in his mind. Now, he had but to be rid of her physically.

He had returned to Quebec for that purpose only. He had but to secure passage for her and the child to England and Ireland, to give her money enough to support herself, then he would be done with her and harsh winters, done with Canada and revenge.

Still, Roarke found his throat tight as he rode up the twisting, rubble-strewn street to Caitrin and his son. But the house stood undamaged next to a neighbor with its roof collapsed by a cannonball. The lump in his chest only tightened further at the confrontation he knew was coming and his hands began to shake. He saw relief flood Martin's face and smiled grimly. Martin only had to face a mother clucking and clutching over an arm broken by a musket ball.

Dismounting, Roarke tied his horse and Martin's, then trod wearily up the stairs to his wife. Yet when Fleur opened the door to his knock, fear instead of joy flooded her face. Her gaze, flicking to Martin, did not even seem to register the white sling on his right arm. Then she looked at Roarke again, her eyes wide over the hand she held cupped to her mouth. Retreating as from a specter, she backed away from him until her

366

back was pressed hard against the wall of the kitchen. Jean, too, stared at Roarke, his countenance both challenging and guilt-ridden.

Roarke stared at them, then at the child rolling a ball across the floor. He gazed back, a miniature of Roarke, turning the lump in his chest into a fist of pain.

"Where is Madam O'Conner?" he asked at last, tearing his eyes from his son. Fleur only stared at him, mutely shaking her head while tears flowed down her face. Feeling a tug at his buckskin leggings, Roarke looked down into eyes as blue as his own.

"Mama gone," the child explained solemnly. "Bad man took Mama gone."

Roarke looked back up at Fleur.

"Cartland?" he demanded.

Fleur only nodded.

"When?"

"Yesterday," Fleur managed to gulp out. "He came yesterday. We thought he was Jean returning, or we would never have opened—"

"I need to know other things besides how it happened," Roarke interrupted, cutting her short. "I need to know how many men, where they went, if they had horses."

Two hours later, Roarke rode once more out of the gates of Quebec but without Martin. The young coureur de bois, with his broken arm and dislocated shoulder, would be next to useless. Roarke had to travel hard and alone. And he had to recapture his wife and destroy the man who had taken her. In no other way could he assuage the cold rage and purpose that consumed him. Cartland had a twenty-four hour start and two men with him. Those were odds, Roarke told himself in his fury, he could easily match. But there was also the possibility that Caitrin had gone with Cartland willingly. Perhaps her hate for her uncle, her love for her child, even the passion she had shared with him, were nothing more than pretenses, a means of survival. Perhaps she had learned all too well the lessons Cartland had tried to teach her.

Roarke's jaw clenched at the thought. The gripping pain in his chest clutched tighter, but he could not put aside the possibility, and the more he considered it, the more sense it made. Only the thought of Caitrin captive to Jacques Leverett roused any concern for her in him; it was a fate he would not wish on any woman. But Caitrin, at last, was right. There was no room in Roarke's heart now for anything but revenge.

Thirty

Caitrin sat huddled against a tree. There was no gratitude on her features as she accepted a mug of stew from Jacques Leverett. Her eyes held only enmity and contempt, and her nose wrinkled at his stench. He grinned at her and drew a grimy finger down her cheek, tittering when she jerked away. Then he held up his knife, the blade gleaming in the firelight at his lips twisted to display dirty teeth in a perverted smile.

"See this?" he said. "See how sharp she is?"

He picked up a corner of her cloak and sliced the heavy wool as easily as through water. Then he grinned back up at her.

"Can you imagine," he asked, an insane glee in his eyes, "what this can do to flesh, soft flesh, tender flesh . . . to your face, your breasts, your nipples . . . to other soft, tender places? And Geraud," he told her, nodding toward the short, bearish man who sat like a hulk on the other side of the fire, his boarish eyes never leaving Caitrin, "he will hold you down for me. He likes doing that—holding a woman down for me. He likes to watch—and he likes my leavings. Sometimes, if he has been patient—for I like to take a

369

long, long time—I might let him have her when I'm done. She might even be dead by then, but Geraud doesn't mind. In fact, I think he likes her better that way, as long as she is still warm."

Against her will, Caitrin's eyes flicked to Geraud across the clearing, and he bared his broken teeth at her in a joyless smile. Caitrin stared at him until his gaze fell before hers, then she looked back at Jacques. Gathering moisture into a mouth gone dry with fear, she spit into his face.

"Putain!" he hissed, his fist flying back to aim itself into her face.

"Jacques!" Cartland rapped out. "Leave the bitch alone! You'll have time enough for her later!"

Jacques slowly lowered his arm, his insane gaze never leaving Caitrin's. Then he smiled, the glitter in his eyes frightening her more than his upraised fist ever could.

"Oui," he whispered, "I'll have time enough for you, and sooner than that lying monkey in his satin suit thinks I will! He has gold in his saddlebags, that Geraud and I know, and more than he ever intends to pay us! One night soon, long before we reach Montreal, he'll wake up to a knife in his ribs! Pffft! Like that! And you'll have Jacques! You'll like Jacques," he snickered, running his finger down her face again. *"Oui,* and much more than that bastard Roarke O'Conner! And Jacques will enjoy having Roarke O'Conner's woman!"

His foul breath withdrew from her nostrils and he retreated to the other side of the fire. But his eyes, along with those of Geraud, seemed to remain always on her, stripping her of her clothing, of even her flesh, stripping her down to clean, white bone.

Refusing to look at them, she ate her cold stew, then lifted her face to the drizzle that sifted down

370

through the night. It seemed the only clean thing left in the world. The filth of Jacque's breath, of his touch on her face, made her shudder, and she wondered if she would ever feel unsullied again. Never, even in their most passionate moments, even when they had done things to each other vehemently forbidden by the church, had Roarke ever made her feel soiled, as had Jacques's slightest touch.

Roarke, Caitrin thought, evoking his name like a prayer. He was the only hope she had left. But where he was, if he even knew she was gone, she did not know. Nor could he know that Cartland had added a third man to his string of lackeys, a man who even now was exchanging guard duty with Jacques. And they had been traveling six days. The journey by land from Quebec to Montreal took, at the least, a fortnight. Her uncle, she knew, already considered her little more than an added burden, little more than another mouth to feed, someone who only slowed them down. That she did in every way she could, no matter how small. He would have long since thrown her to Jacques, if he did not still need to dangle her in front of him like a carrot on a stick. How long he could continue to do so, she could only guess, but the worms would turn soon, too soon, perhaps. And Cartland, in his infinite vanity, would not expect it. Never could he imagine an underling conspiring against him. There was no one he considered his equal, either in cunning or intelligence. All she could hope for from him was that when . . . if . . . Jacques slipped a knife between his ribs, he would be awake and aware.

Caitrin smiled to herself, imagining his astonishment, his incredulity. Then her mind slipped to her son and she jerked it away. Not knowing what had become of him or even if he was still alive brought too much pain, weakening her, and she had to be strong. All she had left was a frail, futile hope in Roarke.

Turning, she wiggled around, trying to find a comfortable position between the roots of the tree, and felt a lump strapped to her thigh. She pressed her hand against the hard coolness of the pistol. That she had, too, she comforted herself. Withdrawing her hand, she gazed at the dying fire and at last dozed.

Something woke Caitrin from a light doze sometime later. Freezing like an animal at an unknown danger, she was instantly alert to all sound, all motion. Listening, she realized it was the heavy plash of a man urinating that woke her. A second later the smell of ammonia itched her nostrils, threatening a sneeze.

There was something heavier in the air, though, something more dangerous than a man waking with a full bladder, and she remained motionless, expectant. There was a feeling of anticipation, of suspended time, of something hovering just beyond the fire's glow. Even when the tall, lumbering man Cartland had last hired walked back into the clearing, tugging his leggings up over his wormlike manhood, she did not relax. He tossed more wood on the fire, then scratched himself deep between his buttocks. His hand wandered to the front and he fondled himself as his speculative gaze sought out Caitrin huddled beneath her tree.

He took a step toward her, a simple grin forming, then he halted abruptly. He stood there swaying, his eyes crossed to stare in astonishment at the war hatchet that had suddenly sprouted from his forehead. The thud of the tomahawk reached Caitrin's ears a long moment later and she watched, stunned, as he at last toppled forward like a felled tree.

Geraud and Cartland leaped out of their blankets, Geraud hunkering down to reach for his flintlock with one hand, his tomahawk with the other. His tiny eyes were wild as they reached the dark beyond the fire. He looked, Caitrin thought impassively, more like a bear than ever, with his full, greasy beard, his huge shoulders and short legs, his boarish eyes. Cartland stepped back into the night. He moved gracefully, delicately, from shadow to shadow, his pale apricot satin suit a shimmering glimmer before he eased toward Caitrin. Then all was expectant silence once more.

Carefully, holding her breath, her gaze never leaving Geraud, Caitrin lifted her skirt. Her hand found the pistol and she withdrew it carefully, slowly. The tiny snick as she drew back the hammer sounding as large to her as a thunderclap. Then she waited. They all waited, frozen, for what would happen next.

It was Geraud who broke first. With a growl of rage, he leaped for the forest, astonishing Caitrin. Never would she have expected that such a clumsy, bearlike man could move so fast. And the roar of a flintlock, the crimson flower that suddenly burst into bloom between his shoulders, propelled him faster, until he stumbled to fall face first into a puddle.

At last, Caitrin drew a breath into lungs starved for nourishment. But there was still her uncle, still Jacques somewhere out in the forest. Cartland had left Quebec with two men and perhaps Roarke did not know there was now a third. Nor could she do anything still but wait, paralyzed by fear.

A moccasin-clad foot stood next to her for a long moment before Caitrin became aware of it, its presence felt more than seen. An involuntary sob of fear escaped her. She jerked up to her knees to scramble away and a strong hand gripped her shoulder, pushing her back into her nest. She looked up into familiar eyes but there was no warmth there, only a cold purpose that froze her wordlessly in place. Roarke shook his head, warning her to silence, then melded back into the forest.

"Jacques," she whispered past the lump of terror in her throat, trying to warn Roarke. "Jacques Leverett is out there!"

But she doubted he heard her. Nor did she dare speak louder, not after Roarke's warning. She could only wait.

Then another moccasined foot, another buckskinned leg, replaced the first. A foul odor assaulted her as a filthy hand slipped over her mouth and nose, and Jacques's malodorous breath was in her face. She screamed soundlessly from behind the clamped hand and twisted away, slamming her elbow into his belly, but he only chuckled as the knife he pressed against her neck rendered her motionless.

"Ah, *putain*," he whispered, teasing the razor-sharp blade up and down her arched throat, "this becomes better and better! Now you will come with me and we shall see just what kind of prey Jacques's sweet bait shall bring out of hiding!"

He forced her to her feet and pushed her into the fire's glow. Holding her as a shield in front of him, he turned in a circle, peering into the dark forest surrounding them, her arms twisted behind her back, the knife never leaving her throat. For a long moment, the only sounds were Caitrin's soft sobs, Jacques's harsh breathing, and the plopping of drops of moisture from drizzle-laden tree branches. Jacques's breath became more agitated, his steps more erratic, as he circled, always facing the forest, always with his back to the fire, dragging Caitrin with him.

Then he laughed and shouted, "O'Conner! *Mon ami*, this is Jacques Leverett! You remember Jacques Leverett, *n'est-ce pas?* See what I have, *mon ami?* I have something of yours. Something I think you want back!"

He paused and his only answer was more silence, Caitrin's sobs, and his own leaping pulse. The fire popped and he jumped, the knife slipping on Caitrin's throat, leaving a faint trickle of blood.

"Scream, *putain*," he whispered. "Scream! Bring him out to me! Plead with him! Beg him! You know what to say to bring him to me!"

Arching her throat back from the knife, Caitrin carefully turned her head to look at Jacques. Although sobs still shook her, her eyes were defiant.

"No!" she whispered back. "No, and if you kill me, you will have to face him alone. I don't think you want to do that."

Thwarted fury flared in his eyes, then he grinned, displaying rotten teeth.

"I like you," he chuckled. "Jacques always likes the ones who fight! They live longer."

Then he shouted to the forest once more.

"O'Conner, *mon ami!* See this!"

In one swift motion, the knife split the front of Caitrin's bodice, and Jacques ripped it away to display her breasts. She gasped, then grew still, her chin lifting proudly. Her breasts gleamed in the firelight, high and full, the nipples taut with the cold. Roarke stared at them, remembering their warmth and roundness, how they fit his hands. He remembered the sweet taste of her nipples, how they filled his mouth, swelling with her need. Abstractly, he thought that childbearing and breast-feeding had not altered them, having only made them fuller. Then he put the thoughts from his mind and waited, watching.

"O'Conner," Jacques shouted. "See how pretty they are! Are they not pretty? And so white! Would not blood make them seem but all the whiter?"

Jacques's eyes grew avid and they left the forest to gaze at Caitrin's breasts, as he very lightly traced their roundness with the knife. Tiny beads of blood followed the knife's course and he grinned in delight.

Move! Roarke silently willed Caitrin. Move! Just give me a target, a small one. I only need a moment!

But Caitrin stood immobilized, her eyes squeezed shut, her lower lip drawn white between her teeth, her head proud. At last, Jacques looked up again, his eyes searching the forest.

"And her nipples, *mon ami!* See how hard they are, how proud!" He drew the side of the knife over first one then the other. "See how they become harder still at my knife's touch. They like Jacques's knife!" he crooned. "They like Jacques! Have you touched these nipples, *mon ami?* Have you taken them into your mouth like a baby? But they like my knife more. They like Jacques more! Would you like to see how sharp my knife is, *mon ami?* Would you like to see how easily she can cut off a nipple, your *putain*'s nipple?"

He watched the knife with avid eyes as he grazed the side of the blade over each nipple. His excited breath came in pants in Caitrin's ear. His hand slackened on her wrists and beneath one fingertip she could feel his swollen manhood. Turning the knife, Jacques touched the point to the rose-colored areola, and Caitrin's eyes squeezed tighter still. She heard her own involuntary sob and a harsh voice in her

376

head that seemed to tell her, "Move, move now!" Twisting back away from the knife, she reached down with one desperate hand. She had but one chance and she grabbed the ovoid spheres, squeezing, twisting.

Jacques screamed in agony, rearing back, the knife flailing aimlessly in front of Caitrin's terrified eyes as he tried frantically to loosen her grip. A hum, then a thunk sounded in her ear and she felt Jacques's hold on her wrists slacken. His knees buckled and he fell, pulling her down with him, Roarke's knife embedded to the hilt in his chest. She lay there under the weight of his arm, staring at the knife dangling from his nerveless hand. Then Roarke reached down and drew her to her knees. But there was no welcome or relief in Caitrin's features. Instead, her eyes were focused past him and they held, finally, acceptance of the inevitable.

"I assume, Caitrin," a cultured voice drawled as Roarke felt a pistol pressed to the back of his head, "that this is your croppie boy husband."

Roarke stiffened and the voice became amused.

"Don't move, bogtrotter. I don't want to blow your head off until I have had a chance to truly savor this moment. Now, turn around. Let me look at you. No, stay on your knees. I want to see you kneeling before me, but turn around."

Cartland stepped back as Roarke turned to face him. A thin smile touched the Irish peer's lips, then he chuckled silently.

"And for this my niece rejected all my tutelage, my care, my concern, my best plans and intentions for her, and a plot that, but for your meddling, might have made me a fortune."

He studied Roarke with a cocked head, smiling disparagingly at the six-day growth of beard that

377

darkened his jaw, at the long hair that had escaped his queue, at the days of accumulated travel grime. Then his smile disappeared. He waved the gun.

"I want your hands behind your back, croppie boy. I want to enjoy this. I want to see you grovel, to hear you beg before I put a bullet in your head."

Caitrin's eyes never left her uncle as Roarke moved his hands behind him. He was, she knew, as dangerous as a cornered rattlesnake, regardless of his slight smile, his indifferent attitude. She dared not move, afraid of antagonizing him. But Roarke, she knew, would never give Cartland the pleasure of seeing him grovel, seeing him beg. Then the pistol jerked once toward her.

"You," Cartland ordered, "saddle two horses. I have use for you still. Perhaps I will use you for years. Perhaps I will send for your squalling brat. Would you like that . . . your brat reared under my tutelage? Perhaps he will not turn out as weak and sentimental as you, and don't worry, I'll allow your croppie boy husband to live until you return with the horses. You need a lesson in the effects of meddling where you do not belong and in the high price of sentimentality."

Her body rigid, her features impassive, Caitrin rose and passed Roarke without even a glance. His gaze followed her, finding no hope in her straight back, her high head. Then he looked back at Cartland, his face hard and proud, telling him he would receive no pleas for mercy from him. Cartland only smiled, luxuriating in his revenge, his power. He glanced up as Caitrin led the horses back, then smiled at Roarke.

"She came back quickly enough, didn't she?" he asked, smiling. "Perhaps she, too, is eager to be rid of this benighted country. Perhaps she is eager to be rid of you, croppie boy."

A muscle leaping in Roarke's jaw was Cartland's

only clue to his rage and frustration, but his smile grew, savoring it. And perhaps Cartland was right, Roarke thought. Perhaps Caitrin only wanted to be gone from the New World and from him. Perhaps she would pay any price for it, including himself, their son. His jaw tightened further at the thought, the muscle twitching white again, and Cartland's smile broadened. A rock pressed into Roarke's knee, numbing his leg. He shifted his weight, the pistol following his slight move, warning him, and he grew motionless again. A sore knee would not matter soon, very soon. There was some satisfaction, though, in knowing that, while he might be dead, Cartland had been destroyed, named traitor, his titles, his honors, all stripped from him.

Caitrin moved toward her uncle, her arms stiff at her sides, and Roarke thought to tell her that their son was safe. But perhaps it was not important to her. Then she moved, her arm extending, pointing at Cartland's head. In her hand she held a pistol.

"Never, ever," she whispered, "will you ever harm me or someone I love again!"

Cartland turned, his eyes widening as he stared into the pistol barrel. Then he smiled.

"You would never use that," he stated. "You are too weak, too sentimental."

"Am I?" she asked, shaking her head. "You have always made that mistake, haven't you? But never again."

Never, Roarke knew, would he have another chance—and he made a dive for the gun in Cartland's hand. Cartland jerked back and pulled the trigger, the ball flying harmlessly over Roarke's shoulder. But Caitrin could see only Roarke's death and her own fear. A second pistol's retort sounded over and above the first, and Cartland, an expression of aston-

379

ishment in his eyes, crumbled slowly to the ground. A bruised, slowly seeping hole, dusted with powder stains, marred his temple.

Caitrin stood motionless, studying him, her arm still extended, the gun aimed where Cartland's head had been. Then she dropped her arm, the weight of the pistol pulling it down, and she looked at Roarke. Her features were calm, controlled, and tears streamed down her face.

"I'm sorry," she told him. "I'm so sorry. All your life you've lived for but one thing—vengeance, and I took it from you. I had no right. Nothing else in the world ever mattered to you but as a tool for your revenge, not me, not your son. And I took that one thing from you. Even he," she said, nudging Cartland's corpse with her toe, "even if he had killed you, you would have died knowing you had destroyed him, but I killed him. I robbed you of the one thing he never could take, the one thing you lived for. I should not have done that and I'm sorry. But he," she whispered, hate making her voice husky as she nudged Cartland again, "he will never, ever harm anyone I love again."

Caitrin turned and moved stiffly back to her blankets under the tree. She covered herself and leaned back, staring up through the drifting clouds to the moon.

Roarke stood and went to her, kneeling down. The tears still flowed down her cheeks, and unaware she wept, Caitrin made no move to wipe them away.

"Caitrin," Roarke said softly and she turned, her gaze focusing on him, "the child is safe. He is with Fleur and Jean, and he is fine."

A faint smile curled her lips and she nodded.

"Thank you," she whispered, then her gaze returned to the moon.

380

"Caitrin," Roarke said, wiping her tears away with one broad thumb. "I'm going to rid the camp of the carrion. They might attract wolves. Then I'll be back. Will you be all right?"

But she did not answer and Roarke doubted she had even heard, not in the place in which her soul had retreated. Nor did she watch as he went to Cartland, picking his heels up to drag him away into the forest. He thought of burying the corpses, then rejected the idea. He was too tired and his mind too heavy. At last, his grisly job complete, he went to the river to wash. The moon made a wide, peaceful swatch of light across the St. Lawrence and he lingered, gazing at it, too tired to move. Caitrin, he thought. What could he say or do to bring her back from where her mind had gone? Finally, he shook himself, standing up to go to the clearing. Unsaddling his horse, he spread his blankets beyond the fire's glow, then went to his wife.

She had not moved from where he had left her, although her tears had stopped. Nor was she aware of Roarke's return until he kneeled before her, gently turning her face toward him, and spoke her name. She blinked and her eyes focused on him, as apathetic as when she had gazed at the moon. Dark bruises of fatigue were smudged beneath her eyes and her cheekbones seemed to press out beneath her skin.

"Caitrin," Roarke asked, "have you slept like this, sitting up, each night since you left Quebec?"

She blinked, considering the question.

"I dared not sleep," she stated at last.

Roarke studied her, wondering at her incredible strength, her will, her capacity to survive. If being reared by Cartland, if battling him for her survival, her soul's survival, had given her that, then he had cause to be grateful to him.

"You're safe now. Tonight you can sleep."

He drew her to her feet and led her to the bed he had laid out. She moved with him like an automaton and did not object when he undressed her. Brushing her hair from her face, he gently kissed her, her face between his hands, before stripping away his own clothes. Then he laid her down on their bed and held her for a long moment, breathing in the odor of green, of living things, of wood smoke, and beneath it, the fragrance that was so much hers, that always drew a skein of desire deep within him. At last, he lifted himself up to look at her. Caitrin's eyes were still open, staring sightlessly up.

"Catkin," he whispered. "Catkin! Don't leave me, not now, not this way! Listen to me!"

Slowly, her look focused on him, detached and incurious, politely attentive—but partway back. Roarke swallowed hard against his hope.

"Catkin," he told her urgently, "had you ever asked me to let it go, the hate, the need for vengeance, I would have done so for you! From the first moment I saw you in Albany, so proud, so vulnerable, I wanted you! And not for vengeance, though I lied to myself then. I wanted you for this!"

His mouth moved to hers, caressing, tasting, trying to tell her of his love. She did not respond and at last he drew back.

"I wanted you in my bed, loving me, giving to me. I wanted you to bear my children and to see in them your pride, your strength, your passion! I knew when I first saw you that never would there be another woman to meet me in love, in need, as you would. And always I thought that you, too, wanted vengeance, that if I could but destroy Cartland for you, as my gift to you, you would turn from your hate to me. Always I thought he was taking you from me through your hate for him, and I could only hate him the more in my loss of you! I thought that, if I could but destroy him, you would be mine! There is a place, Catkin—did I tell you of it?—where the air is soft with the smell of pine trees, of magnolias, where a man is not judged by his religion, his birth, but by his own merit. Did I tell you of it? Catkin," he whispered, his voice naked in his plea, "I want you to go with me there, with our son. I want you with me there, or 'twill be but another cold, harsh, empty place for me always."

Still, Caitrin's gaze was empty and Roarke dropped his head to press his face into her fragrant hair, his body shuddering with his grief. Then he felt Caitrin touch his face, softly, tentatively. He drew back to look at her and she smiled slightly, reaching up to gently smooth away his tears.

"You cry for me?" she asked in wonder. Then she drew him down again, her mouth meeting his, answering his hope, giving to him in a sweetness he had only hoped to know.

"Take me there!" she whispered. "Oh, please, take me there!" And Roarke knew she was not speaking of soft winters, of magnolia trees.

His mouth left hers to trace an urgent pattern along her jaw, her throat, to her breasts. Gently, the tip of his tongue touched each slight wound made by Jacques's knife, soothing them, teasing the hurt away. He drew their coral tips into his mouth, feeling them engorge beneath his tongue, and heard her moan her need, felt her hands demanding on his back. Her body lifted to him, parting to him in the heat of her desire, and he entered her, watching as need and passion chased each other across her face. He moved deep within her, his body telling her of his love, his desire, feeling her open further to him, answering him. His need, his love, overwhelmed him, driving him to possess her, driving her passion before his. He took her to a place they had never been before, then they fell together, borne down by waves of heat and joy and promise.

They lay, still joined, in the afterglow of their love-making. Roarke gently brushed back the tendrils of hair clinging to Caitrin's damp forehead and felt her hand idly touching, tracing the ridges and furrows of the scars that marred his back. Was she thinking of them, of how he had come by them? he wondered, kissing her brow. Then he reached back and took her hand to still it, to clasp it between them.

"Sleep," he told her. "You can sleep now."

"I know."

Then she shook her head, rejecting his command.

"Do they," she asked, answering his unspoken question, "have apple trees in this place where you are taking me?"

"They do."

"Good," she whispered against the warm skin of his chest. "Good. I want you always to have apples."